# Death on the Adriatic

# *Death on the Adriatic*

## Georgina Stewart

CONSTABLE

CONSTABLE

First published in Great Britain in 2025 by Constable

1 3 5 7 9 10 8 6 4 2

Copyright © Georgina Stewart, 2025
Map © Shutterstock, 2025

The moral right of the author has been asserted.

*All characters and events in this publication, other than
those clearly in the public domain, are fictitious
and any resemblance to real persons,
living or dead, is purely coincidental.*

A CIP catalogue record for this book
is available from the British Library.

ISBN: 978-1-40871-979-4

Typeset in Caslon by Initial Typesetting Services, Edinburgh
Printed and bound in Great Britain by Clays Ltd, Elcograf S.p.A.

Papers used by Constable are from well-managed forests
and other responsible sources.

Constable
An imprint of
Little, Brown Book Group
Carmelite House
50 Victoria Embankment
London EC4Y 0DZ

The authorised representative
in the EEA is
Hachette Ireland
8 Castlecourt Centre
Dublin 15, D15 XTP3, Ireland
(email: info@hbgi.ie)

An Hachette UK Company
www.hachette.co.uk

www.littlebrown.co.uk

*For Janet and Ian*

*Thank you for everything.*

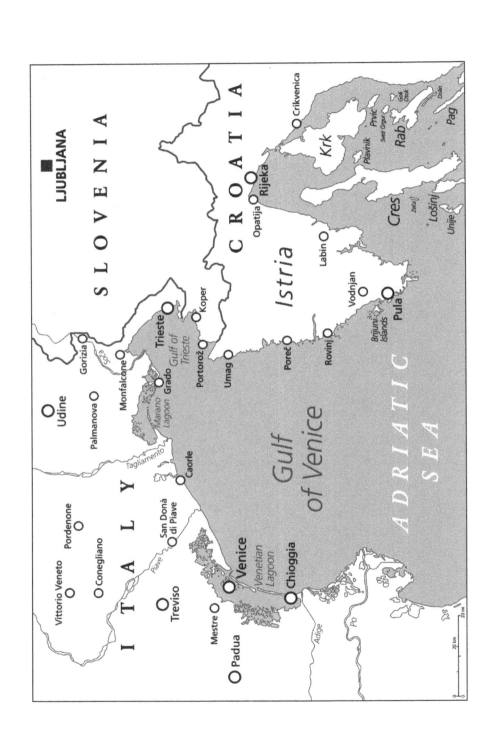

# Prologue

At this time of year it was not rare to find scores of dead jelly-fish littered along the rocky beach that stretched from Koper to Izola, and today was no different. Their plump, translucent bodies quickly turned pink and slack on the pebbles, sitting in haphazard piles wherever the slight tide had pushed them. In the shallows where the waves broke across the shore yet more of them were tossed around, thrown up before crashing back into the water, soon to join those already beached. As Andrej walked along the concrete coastal path just a couple of feet above the jellyfish graveyard, he shuddered to remember the summer when his brother had found a particularly large specimen stranded in a tiny tidal pool and triumphantly launched it at him. When it had collided with Andrej's face he could have sworn he felt it wriggling, although his grandmother had told him that they were barely alive to start with, let alone after Matej had had his grubby hands all over it. Even at six years old Andrej had concluded that the swarms of jellyfish were best avoided, alive or dead, although this had put a significant dampener on his adolescent socialising.

It turned out that most people weren't interested in hanging out with the boy who refused to go swimming after school as soon as it was warm enough, just because he wasn't keen on the *meduze*. The ones they got on the Slovene coast didn't even sting.

The arrival of the jellyfish was, he mused, an indication that spring truly had its foot in the door, edging out the admittedly mild winter of the northern Adriatic coast. Soon Andrej could enjoy the blissful but desperately short period in which he didn't have to spend half his income on heating or air conditioning his small apartment. He would be able actually to enjoy his dizzying proximity to the sea, and justify the small fortune he spent on the privilege. No matter the weather, Andrej made a point of marching from Koper to Izola and back again every morning, following in the footsteps of his grandfather who had made the same trip every morning from when he could walk until the day he died, or so he claimed. From November to February these trips were made hastily, so as to avoid the freezing winds sweeping in off the water. From May until mid-September they were even swifter in an attempt to reduce distressing sightings of naked tourists attempting to make themselves even redder than they had managed last summer. Not that Andrej disliked the tourists, of course. A not insignificant portion of the town relied on them, at least partially, for their incomes, but that didn't mean that he had to enjoy zigzagging through their beach towels and plastic buckets every day for months on end; especially when those were the months he'd have most liked to be down by the water himself. Crucially, the jellyfish didn't tend to make an appearance in summer.

Andrej had almost reached Izola now, the skinny church spire rising up strikingly against the hills behind. Around it sat the lower, redder roofs of the hotels and cafés in Veliki *Trg*, the main square, their colourful façades and wooden shutters visible even from this distance. He stopped for a minute to take in the scene, admiring the way the water glittered and danced with the morning light. On the steep bank that rose up on the other side of the coastal path he could hear birds chirping merrily in the trees, accompanied by the rustling of leaves and the occasional disturbance as a lizard made a mad dash into the undergrowth when it saw him approaching. It was a fine Sunday, the air a little warmer than it had been up until now, and he started to deliberate over whether he should treat himself to a drink and a rest at one of the little bars that lined the shorefront in Izola. He had just decided on his order, a white coffee with a cottage cheese *zavitek*, and started to resume his walk when he noticed something else lying below him among the rocks a little way ahead. From where he was standing, it looked like someone had left their jumper and jeans on the beach, the legs of the trousers half-submerged by the sea. He continued to peer down from his slight vantage point as he walked along the path, assuming it was simply a bundle of clothes abandoned by a tourist or a drunken local, although it seemed a little seasonally premature for either to be this far along the coastal path and happy to be unclothed. As he got closer to the pile, Andrej started moving faster. What had previously been obscured by rocks and jellyfish was now starting to look more like a hand sticking haphazardly out of the sleeve, the skin pallid. When he was a few metres away, Andrej scrambled down off the path and onto the slick rocks, praying as he went that he was wrong and that the clothes were unoccupied, and that this could all be an amusing story he would tell his grandmother next time he visited her in the nursing home. When the neckline of the jumper was fully and undeniably in view, Andrej stopped. He pulled his phone from the pocket of his coat, and quickly dialled the police.

He was aware that he gabbled when the call handler picked up, but he hoped he'd still got the salient points across: dead man on the beach, coastal path about fifteen minutes' walk from the outskirts of Izola, *hurry*. After all, while it was common to find jellyfish corpses along this stretch of shoreline, the same could not be said of human ones.

# Chapter 1

As *Inšpektorica* Petra Vidmar sat in what must have been the third traffic jam of her journey so far, she found herself re-evaluating her childhood jealousy of friends who were taken to the coast every summer. As soon as temperatures had reached twenty degrees there had been a great rush on a Saturday from Ljubljana down to the sea, everyone throwing themselves into their cars and joining the legions of foreign-plated campervans and saloons already choking the ring road around the capital. Their desperate goal, her friends had informed her, had been to make it onto the Koper-bound A1 in time for a late-morning *malica*, the habitual mid-morning snack, on the beach. How a slice of bread topped with *pršut*, Slovenia's answer to prosciutto, was any better by the coast than in the city, Petra had never quite understood. Asking, however, admitted ignorance that, as a teenager, she'd been unwilling to demonstrate. As soon as they had drained their cappuccinos, the more adventurous apparently then piled back into their cars, continuing along the winding road to the Croatian border before sitting grumpily in a gridlocked queue at the checkpoint, bemoaning the mere existence of everyone else doing exactly the same thing and rudely delaying their first sip of *rakija* in Umag. Come Sunday, they would make the return journey, probably crammed at the border crossing next to the same people who had impeded their outbound trip. Petra had heard this story dozens of times from various friends over the years, always told with a strange mixture of loathing and desperation to do the same thing again next weekend. Since she had never done it, she had always been jealous that she didn't get to join in the swapping of stories about grumpy Croatian border guards poking through beach bags to check for unspecified contraband or share recommendations for the best fried calamari to grab from a roadside *gostilna* before continuing onwards. Her own family had been stoically capital city folk, and any vacation time had been saved for a trip to her mother's family in Prekmurje, the region as far from the Adriatic as it is possible to get and still be in Slovenia. She had had more than one row with her parents about how it would be nice to make just one weekend trip to the seaside, if only to see what all the fuss was about.

Now, sitting in a conga line of oversized family SUVs and caravans that stretched as far as the eye could see, she made a mental note to compliment her father on his foresight and good sense next time she visited. Quite how this many of her fellow Ljubljanans had decided that a Thursday morning in mid-April was the perfect time to explore the wonders of Istria was unfathomable to Petra, let alone why countless Germans and Austrians saw fit to join in. Surely there were nicer beaches nearer them? She'd seen enough sponsored adverts online about holidays on the Baltic coast that she'd vaguely considered it herself. Even if they had to come south, weren't Trieste, Venice and the Italian Adriatic just as accessible, and boasted fewer Communist-era concrete hotels clustered on the coastline; eerie in their sameness? Did they really enjoy the wonders of formerly Yugoslavian road networks to the extent that they wouldn't rather fly? With Croatia set to join the Schengen area soon, she supposed the era of sweaty border queues would soon come to an end.

As the traffic crawled imperceptibly forward, she reflected on her mental list of people to blame for putting her in this situation. Campervan owners of Teutonic origin, certainly. *Inšpektor* Jakob Mlakar, for insisting that the impending birth of his second child should prevent him from being sent on an assignment away from the capital, despite him being the one who had worked in Koper as a young officer. And then, of course, the police officers of Koper themselves, whose apparent incompetence and insistence that they could handle everything internally, without an interloper from the big city, meant that Petra's presence hadn't been requested until late on a Wednesday evening, condemning her to the Thursday morning migration of the long weekenders. Even then it had been anonymous. Could they really not have put their pride aside and accepted that they needed help earlier, or never asked at all?

Petra pulled her phone down from where it had been cradled in its holder to act as a GPS, angrily stabbing at the

screen to close her map app. It wasn't as though she needed
help with directions, the A1 by this point was simply the road
to the coast, and she and the majority of her fellow travellers
would be on it until it petered out at Koper. Swiping through
her emails, she read the bullet-pointed list that her commanding officer had sent her once it was established that Mlakar
was going to be appeased, despite Petra's pleas and seniority.

The case was, Petra had to admit, more exciting than most
that came up in Slovenia. On Sunday morning, a young man
walking along the coastal path from Koper to nearby Izola had
discovered a corpse. Despite being found at the water's edge,
the body had not apparently spent any time at sea. The cause
of death had been a gunshot, with the head bearing a significant wound that Petra would have appreciated not seeing
a photo of while she was trying to eat her canteen breakfast
that morning, already disgruntled at the impending journey
and workload. All of this made the case one of the more tan-
talising to have crossed the desks of any police station in the
country in recent memory, and if it had been six months earlier
and in Ljubljana, then Petra would have relished the chance
to add it to her career highlights. However, it was happening
now, when, with luck, she no longer needed to plump up her
CV, and was over an hour away from her home even without
the tourists. It was also sure to be far more aggravation than it
was worth due to the identity of the victim.

The walker who had found the body hadn't recognised it,
which was perhaps unsurprising. Andrej Kos was an elementary school teacher whose main hobbies included birdwatching

and playing the accordion for events at his grandmother's retirement home, thus he had predictably never experienced any run-ins with the law. When the emergency services had arrived, however, they had recognised the deceased immediately. It would have been hard not to, considering it was one of their own. *Inšpektor* Ivan Furlan was coastal born and bred, and had served his entire career in Koper. By all reports he was well-liked, a family man, but always willing to work an extra hour in the evening to help junior officers learn and gain experience. His commanding officer had described him as uninterested in promotion, just in keeping the city safe, which might have explained how he was the same rank as Petra despite being old enough to be her father. It also raised Petra's eyebrows a little. The police were known to be laughably underpaid, and it could be a thankless career even if it was much safer than police work was in most countries. Everyone Petra had ever met in the force had been focused on promotion, simply because going up a rank was the difference between being able to buy your mother a nice birthday present versus spending your entire salary on rent and food. Petra chose to put aside her initial incredulity and assume that the rather saccharine sentiment was simply the result of a commanding officer who had no experience in eulogising his colleagues, especially not to other police officers.

Watching a small and particularly ancient Yugo triumphantly zoom off at the motorway exit she was about to inch past, she wondered how *Svetnik* Golob, her own superintendent, might memorialise Petra herself. Hard-working, she

hoped, perhaps even relentless. Definitely considerate, ideally
kind. She'd have to be, considering how often she had been
nominated to do the bad news door-knock when a body was
fished out of the Ljubljanica river, or there was a fatal car crash
after a particularly heavy St Martin's Day celebration. She
could have throttled whoever had suggested that kind of interaction was best handled by a woman, particularly as women
of any seniority were rare beasts in a male-dominated force.
Observing her reflection in the rear-view mirror, she hoped
that her decision not to wear her uniform for this first meeting
with the superintendent in Koper had been the correct one. In
the mirror her face seemed thin and pale, dominated by her
large sunglasses. The ponytail she had carefully styled in the
harsh lighting of Ljubljana station's bathroom now looked a
little scruffy, her brown wavy hair fighting against the slim,
black hair tie. She felt again the familiar stab of imposter syn-
drome, and prayed that she was up to the task ahead. She gave
the hair tie she always kept around her wrist a sharp twang,
the shock momentarily clearing her head, and returned her
attention to the stationary traffic ahead of her.

There was no reference in the email to the exact circumstances that saw Petra on her way to Koper, although that
was not entirely unexpected. It was shaming enough for the
superintendent that a whistle-blower had written to the capital accusing their colleagues of mismanagement of the case
at best, and deliberate covering-up of a murder of one of their
own at worst. Petra supposed there wasn't much the superintendent could say, all things considered. He could hardly

demand that he'd rather the capital keep their nose out, not when Ljubljana had decided it was worth looking into and had told the Koper directorate that they would be sending someone to answer the informant's call. Even if there was no corruption or incompetence to answer for, resistance would make the superintendent look either petulant, or complicit. It was probably better for everyone's pride and working relationships that no one engaged with the original circumstances of Petra's involvement, although she doubted that the men on the ground in Koper would share the same belief. It was not going to be a pleasant case.

Furlan had left behind a wife and two adult sons, both of whom now lived in Ljubljana, and after immediate visits to their widowed mother, were back there again. Although Petra had attempted to use this fact as a way to delay her drive, the traitorous Mlakar had quickly offered to do any necessary interviews with the sons. He had phrased it in a way that suggested he honestly thought he was doing Petra a favour, which had rankled, but then so had his suggestion that it might be nice to have a quick coastal assignment and get a bit of a tan before she headed off to 'bigger and better things' in Lyon. Never one to tempt fate, Petra had simply asked him to pass on her best wishes to *Gospa* Mlakar on the upcoming birth and beaten a hasty retreat out to the Skoda, which had now been her prison for almost two hours. The traffic surged forward a few metres before grinding to a halt again, but Petra was now wise to the juddering pattern of the coastal rush and didn't bother to pull forward. Instead, she looked out of the window and gazed longingly at the empty carriageway going in the opposite direction. It couldn't be too long before she was cruising back to her apartment in Ljubljana, surely. She would count the days.

By the time she reached her guesthouse it had taken her nearly twice the time she had initially anticipated, and she was ready to murder either Mlakar or a large cappuccino. Deciding that the second was both easier to carry out and less damaging to her career, she eased herself out of the car and stretched dramatically in the late morning sun drenching the car park. She was already woefully overdue for her original arrival time at the station in Koper, so she decided that she could afford to be a few minutes later if it meant she could gather her thoughts. The budget for her lodgings had been small, and with the tourist season apparently already beginning to warm up, the poor soul who had been in charge of making her booking had found only slim pickings. Indeed, although she'd been assured that she'd be staying somewhere close to the police station, she had long since passed every exit signposted 'Koper/Capodistria', the Italian name for the town, and had climbed a not insignificant way up the next hill by the time she eventually pulled into the dusty car park.

The guesthouse was a medium-sized, concrete affair, which seemed to have been haphazardly extended and refurbished over the years to create a building that had as many doors and corners as it did windows. The original structure might have been the ground-floor restaurant with rooms above, but there were now terraces and glass-roofed extensions from various eras sprawling out in all directions. From the car park and the largest of its extensions, the guesthouse boasted a view straight over the straggling two-lane road, offering excellent observational opportunities for anyone interested in the variety expressed in European numberplates. As Petra pulled her shoulder-bag out from the passenger seat and started to make her way around the back of the building, she was surprised to be met with a gorgeous view of a vineyard running down the hill, green leaves glistening in the sunshine. Halfway down the field she could see an old man and a young boy walking through the neat rows of vines, the boy skipping ahead as the man stopped to peer at the occasional plant. Near where Petra was standing, and in perfect view of the next roundabout along the road, someone had erected a homemade sign that read in clear, black capital letters 'VINO IN OLIVNO OLJE', wine and olive oil, followed by a large green euro symbol. An enterprising individual had then translated the same sales pitch into German, Italian and English on an A-board, which was propped up next to it. Petra smiled at the signs and stood for a minute longer taking in her surroundings before heading through what appeared to be the main door of the establishment.

After checking in with what she assumed was the owner's unenthusiastic teenaged son, Petra wasted no time in setting herself up in the restaurant, bedroom unseen and duffle bag of clothes still sitting in the Skoda. She whipped her laptop out of its neoprene sleeve and opened up the email explaining the case once more, sipping gratefully at the coffee that had been

procured for her. This time, as she read through, she started to
jot down notes on one of the thick reporters' notebooks she'd
snaffled from the stationery cupboard back in Ljubljana. She
hated walking in anywhere without a plan of attack, let alone
into a police station where she knew most of them didn't want
her, and which would require her commandeering a case that
must have been incredibly personal to them. After a moment's
hesitation she opened another email sent by *Svetnik* Golob,
which contained the text of the whistle-blower's cry for help.

> *To whom it may concern,*
>
> *I write regarding the death of Inšpektor Ivan Furlan of
> Koper Police. The man we have arrested is not guilty,
> and there is little evidence to suggest his involvement. It
> would be a gross miscarriage of justice to allow him to
> pay the price of someone else's crime. Requests to Svetnik
> Horvat that he bring in another police directorate for an
> impartial view have been ignored, so I have had to resort
> to this.*

Reading through it, she was reminded why she had been sent
to the coast and felt momentarily guilty about her reluctance
to answer the author's call. The note was brief and had been
sent from an email address apparently created specifically for
the purpose, although the author had made no attempt to hide
that they were evidently an officer of the Koper Police themselves. Petra knew that the Powers-That-Be in Ljubljana had

seriously considered ignoring it but had decided it couldn't hurt to send someone down to poke around, even if only to ensure that both the investigation and the national police grievance procedures were above reproach. She snapped her laptop decisively shut and stood up from the table, heading back out to the car park as she stabbed at her phone for directions to the police station. It was time to get started.

# Chapter 2

Finding the police station was not as easy as Petra had originally assumed. She had been warned before she left Ljubljana that Koper was a warren of increasingly difficult to predict roundabouts, and discovered as soon as she pulled back off the A1 that this was not an overstatement. Vague assertions from Google about which lane might be most appropriate had also proved unhelpful. She crawled along in the right lane as much as possible, peering hopefully through the windscreen for a signpost indicating *Policija*, switching lanes as soon as she caught sight of the familiar pictogram of a behatted figure wearing a sash. It was one of her favourite things about Slovenian towns, the sort of thing that you didn't appreciate until you'd found yourself lost in one too many foreign holiday destinations: they were always well-equipped with large white signs clearly showing the way to the nearest public services. As a teen she and some friends had occasionally prowled down Dunajska Cesta, one of the main streets through Ljubljana, furtively scribbling moustaches on the police pictogram and arrows on the bullseye used to signify the town centre.

Shockingly, this hobby had never made it on to her CV. She smiled at the bilingualism of the signs here, with the Italian translation written out under the Slovene no matter how closely related the words were. Spotting that *Policija/Polizia* required a left at the next roundabout she quickly shifted across, glad of the lighter traffic now she wasn't fighting her way through the holidaymakers.

Petra had been to Koper once before that she remembered, for an ill-fated New Year's Eve party when she was a teenager. A friend's family had acquired a holiday apartment following the death of an elderly relative, and her memories of the town were a mixture of grappa-induced haze and the oppressive atmosphere created by years of excessive usage of vanilla-scented talcum powder. The flat had been in one of the large concrete blocks built in the 1960s that appeared in crops of three or four in the area just outside of Koper old town. She remembered from school geography lessons that Koper had once been an island, and that the buildings on the belt of land reclaimed to join it to the mainland dated from centuries after the medieval centre. Naively, she had assumed that Koper Police would occupy one of the stunning sixteenth-century buildings hailing from when the town had been a jewel of the Venetian Republic. As a teenager, she and some friends had once spent New Year's Day stumbling around the winding streets of central Koper, following a tourist guide who led them from various *palazzos* to historic churches to memorials, all hidden in the rabbit-warren of medieval streets. Instead, and perhaps a little disappointingly, it seemed that the police had been relegated to a Yugoslavian-era industrial park, several roundabouts away from anything that could be even vaguely described as Venetian. The signage led her to a squat, grey building bordered by a large car park on one side and a post office on the other. Most of the parking spaces were empty, save for a few police cars in the slots directly in front of the building. Manoeuvring the Skoda into the shadiest slot remaining, she sat for a second watching as two uniformed officers juggling greasy white takeaway bags and disposable coffee cups jostled up the three shallow stairs leading into the station, guffawing with laughter as they threw open the glass front doors. Petra took a deep breath as she grabbed her bag, slid her sunglasses off her face and got out of the car.

The plastic frame of the main door was warm to the touch as Petra opened it, reminding her of quite how much later in the day it was than she'd initially planned. Although it had been bitter when she'd woken up in Ljubljana this morning, it would seem that proximity to the Adriatic and a few hours of the sun shining had created a pleasant spring day in Koper. Petra immediately realised the downsides of the climate, however, as the door swung closed behind her, leaving her in a sparsely-furnished, square entrance hall that was already starting to get overly warm and stuffy. She could smell kebab meat and fresh coffee, and quickly noticed that one of the paper bags carried in by the officers earlier was now sitting next to the desk sergeant's computer, cheap white napkins balled up and strewn around her keyboard. Petra smiled at the female officer as she approached the desk, and was met with a grin in return.

'*Dober dan, Inšpektorica* Vidmar! I am so glad you made it here safely.'

Petra blinked in confusion, stopping slightly short of the desk. Was this town so small that she was so obviously a stranger? Did they have so few visitors that the only woman who walked in who wasn't immediately recognisable had to be the inspector from the capital?

'*Dober dan, Policistka. . .*' Petra paused to take in the name badge pinned to her front, desperate to return the woman's personalised friendliness, 'Medved. I am sorry if you have been waiting for me. I know I am running late for my meeting with *Svetnik* Horvat.'

Medved shrugged, wiping her fingers off on one of the crumpled napkins before standing up and offering Petra her hand to shake. She smiled again as she shook, her poker-straight ponytail dancing with the movement. 'Not at all. I'd have been sitting here either way. The delay just gave me the chance to check you were who I thought you were. I thought I recognised your name. I remember people talking about the youngest inspector in the history of the Slovenian Police. I've emailed the female cadets about it and they're very excited. So am I.' Medved blushed a little at her own admission. 'The superintendent is still available, if you want to head up to see him. He's having his lunch, but I'm sure he won't mind.'

Petra swallowed, embarrassed at Medved's praise. She didn't think anyone had ever been excited about her presence, other than her mother when she made the occasional sur-prise visit home, or perhaps her best friend's dog. She silently cursed her lateness again, worried that she'd already disappointed Medved and the cadets. The thought jolted her back to the matter at hand. Petra's eyes flickered to the clock, and she briefly worried how amenable the superintendent would realistically be to an interrupted lunch. In her experience, the canteen lunches of senior policemen were a hallowed and private affair, carried out at a specific table between specific hours every day with no room for the impositions of subordinates unless it was to give a recommendation on which soup was best. She had felt the hunger-induced ire of *Svetnik* Golob only once and was not keen for a similar encounter to be her first meeting with Horvat, especially when she knew for a fact that the man hadn't wanted her here in the first place.

'Are you sure it wouldn't be better to wait? I am sorry to have missed my appointment. I don't want to put him out.' She was displeased to hear slight distress in her own voice. It was her own fault for being late. She should never have stopped for coffee, even if she would otherwise have been stumbling into Horvat's presence half-blind without her little revision session at the hotel. She quickly put a stop to this train of thought and tried to channel the easy self-assuredness of Mlakar and her other male colleagues, their unwavering expectation that people would change plans to suit them. All of them would doubtless have done the same, and without apologies, so why was Petra second-guessing herself and her own decision-making?

Medved shrugged, apparently unconcerned by the potential professional faux pas she had suggested. 'I really doubt he'd mind. He's in his office, you can just go in.'

Petra tried to hide her surprise at this statement, blinking at the young officer. She had assumed that, if the top dogs in Ljubljana could make time for a daily leisurely lunch, the regional police chiefs would do the same. Mlakar himself had told her months previously that all the Koper force did was catch criminals who the Italians or Croatians had let slip across their borders, dutifully ferrying them back to other jurisdictions before getting back to the station in time for an afternoon nap. She had rather been under the impression that the slower pace of life on the coast would be built around a three-course lunch in the canteen, topped off with a coffee and an Amaretti biscuit. Medved saw right through her and laughed, spinning as she sat back down in her office chair. '*Gospa* Horvat has her husband on a strict diet, which means the fried cheese they do in the canteen is banned. Head up the stairs, first door on the left. He's expecting you, obviously.'

For a split second, Petra wondered whether she should take Medved at her word, conscious that getting off to a bad start with Horvat might be in the interests of the local force. Yet, there was something about her wide grin and conspiratorial chatter about cheese that made Petra trust her. She flashed a smile of her own and turned in the direction indicated.

Although she hadn't noticed it when she first came in, there was indeed a narrow staircase just to the left of the main doors. It was covered in the mottled grey linoleum she asso-ciated with Communist-built municipal offices, the banister and handrail made of white-painted metal that was starting to chip slightly at the joints. She started towards the stairs, holding her bag tightly as she shimmied past a uniformed officer halfway up the flight. As Medved had suggested, the stairs opened out on to another linoleum-covered hallway, the wall punctuated by slim white doors, each featuring a name badge. The door for *Policijski Svetnik* Franc Horvat had two uncomfortable plastic chairs outside, and Petra placed her bag on one as she readied herself to knock, straightening her collar and jerking at the loose cuffs of her blouse before rapping precisely on the centre of the door.

The superintendent responded immediately, summoning Petra inside with a brief '*vstopite*', which sounded as though it might have been spoken through a mouthful of his lunch. Grabbing her bag and pushing open the door, she entered a low-ceilinged room lined with overstuffed bookcases that looked suspiciously like the Ikea model she had in her own flat. Petra noted with interest that they were not filled with books as hers were, but instead large brown box files, each carefully labelled with a date and what she assumed was a case number. The office had only one window, another plastic-framed number with an oversized twist-and-turn handle currently angled to let in some fresh air. Directly in front of this window, at a wooden desk facing the door through which Petra had just entered, sat *Svetnik* Horvat. As Petra had suspected, Horvat had been mid-mouthful when he had called her in, although it did not seem to be his lunch. Discarded on the top of his in-tray lay a round plastic container half filled with what appeared to be chicken salad, a hunk of bread balancing unappetisingly on top. Directly in front of the superintendent, however, was a pale green cardboard box, its lid thrown open to reveal several perfectly golden doughnuts nestled among greaseproof paper and napkins.

Despite the presence of the doughnuts and his apparently enforced diet, the superintendent was not a particularly large man. His blue uniform jacket was perhaps stretched slightly tighter across his front than was ideal, but Petra was certain it was not even the largest size the force offered, having seen far larger men striding around her own station. Other than the slight button straining, his uniform was immaculate, the gold buttons that held his rank insignia in place on his shoulders gleaming in the light shining in from the window behind. His salt-and-pepper hair was cut short, the only hair out of place being his incredibly bushy eyebrows. As Petra entered he rose to his feet, offering his hand. '*Inšpektorica* Vidmar, I assume?'

'Yes, *Svetnik* Horvat. I am sorry for my lateness, there was traffic on the A1.'

Horvat smiled without humour, gesturing for Petra to take one of the plastic seats opposite him.

'Please don't worry. We knew you'd be late.' The superintendent's tone was not as kind and conciliatory as his words sounded, instead sounding rather unimpressed.

Petra bridled. 'How so?'

'Tourists,' replied Horvat, eyebrows raised. Petra suspected he intended to suggest both the road-choking holidaymakers, and Petra herself. She waited a second for the man to continue, but it quickly became apparent that he did not intend to do so. They maintained eye contact as Petra mentally scrambled for the best place to start the conversation. She had rather been hoping he'd have a speech prepared, his side of the story as a tonic to what she'd heard from the whistle-blower. Even in her snatched conversation with Golob over how to approach this delicate matter, they had not predicted that he would be so reticent.

'I am grateful that you were able to see me so quickly,' she responded eventually, deciding that it was in no one's interest for her to start the investigation at odds with the superintendent, or at least any more at odds than they were by virtue of the situation they found themselves in. She stamped down the ever-present urge to apologise or ramble, carefully keeping her tone neutral.

Horvat inclined his head, apparently lost in thought, closing the lid of the doughnut box as he pondered. Across the top Petra could see stencilled the words *Slaščičarna Koren*, identifying the patisserie from which the superintendent had sourced his treats. The font was ornate, delicate and expensive-looking, although the telephone number and address printed below were in a functional, clear script. 'I couldn't exactly avoid it,' he admitted eventually. 'I won't pretend I am happy to have you here, *Inšpektorica*. It is going to cause all kinds of grief, and not just for me. I want to release Ivan's body for burial, hold the memorial, give his wife some closure. Performative box-ticking exercises are only prolonging a highly unpleasant situation. I've spoken to my other inspectors, and they've agreed to help, but they obviously aren't pleased. I trust my officers, and I have no time for some anonymous troublemaker. This isn't some PR stunt for Ljubljana, saviours of small-town imbeciles. This is the cold-blooded murder of our long-time friend and colleague.'

'I am aware my presence puts you in a difficult position,' Petra responded, on more comfortable ground now he'd shown his hand. 'All I ask of your team is that they answer my questions and leave me to my work, and I promise that I will do my best to get out of Koper as soon as possible.' She had practiced this answer in the car and was pleased with how natural it sounded when spoken aloud.

Horvat considered this, eyes narrowed. 'I suppose that time will tell.' He scrutinised Petra's expression for a moment longer, then shook his head once and turned his attention to the box of doughnuts on his desk. He deftly plucked out a particularly round specimen, placing it on a napkin and dusting the resulting cascade of icing sugar into the bin before spinning the entire box around to face Petra.

'Would you like one?' His tone displayed a lack of interest, his question obviously entirely rooted in good manners rather than a desire for camaraderie. 'They are from the best bakery in town.'

Petra demurred, the memory of Medved's indiscreet comment on the superintendent's diet rushing to the forefront of her mind. 'I won't, thank you. If I could just get the case notes, I will be on my way.'

Horvat took a large bite out of his doughnut, sending a puff of sugar into the air and a globule of violently purple jam down his chin. He dabbed at it impatiently with a spare

napkin before answering her. *'Policist* Koren has them. He'll
be working with you on the case.'

It was Petra's turn to narrow her eyes at Horvat. 'I wasn't
informed I would be working with a junior officer.' Although
that was true, Petra couldn't pretend she was surprised at this
turn of events. She had suspected that the senior officers in
Koper would want to attach one of their own to her enquiry,
ostensibly to support her, but more likely to keep them abreast
of her progress.

Horvat scoffed. 'The junior officer in question insisted. He's
been working with Ivan for the last year or so, and is struggling
to come to terms with his death. I doubt we'd have been able
to keep him away from you even if we'd tried.' His gaze shot
up to meet Petra's as he cleaned his fingers off with a napkin.
'And I wouldn't want anyone thinking I had anything to hide
by distancing him from you.' There it was, the hostility Petra
had been expecting, the distaste for her presence distinct from
the impact it would have on the inspector's widow. Even so,
it was milder than she might have predicted, a snide jab from
a place of discomfort rather than a deep-seated resentment.

Petra gave him a look, which she hoped displayed that she
was entirely aware of the subtext of what he was saying, then
decided to go further. There was little point in being tactful in
such an obviously undiplomatic set of circumstances. 'Just for
my own understanding, *Svetnik* Horvat, will *Policist* Koren be
assisting me, or will I be babysitting him?' She almost regretted it as soon as it came out of her mouth, but she held firm,
maintaining eye contact. Expecting some form of blustering

or indignation, she was surprised when her question made
him smile slightly.

'Honestly, *Inšpektorica*, I would like to see anyone try
and babysit him. Aleš Koren is a good officer, he won't be
a hindrance to your investigation. If you would rather have
someone else, I can assign them to you, but I do think he is best
suited.'

Petra raised her eyebrows. 'I suppose that time will tell.'

Horvat shook his head, the thin smile still haunting his
face. 'I don't want any sort of animosity, *Inšpektorica*, truly. All
I want is my friend laid to rest, so that the rest of us can grieve.
I want this put behind us.'

'And as I said earlier, I intend to complete my investigation
as quickly as possible. Even so, I'll need space to conduct it
properly. If you leave me to do my work, I can promise you
that I will make my time here as brief and painless as possible.'

He sighed, leaned back in his office chair, but didn't
respond. Petra sensed that she was sitting opposite a man who
was both completely out of his comfort zone, and exhausted
from trying to hide this fact. She felt mildly sorry for him,
being put through an embarrassing audit of his force's conduct
and practices over a case that must have been personally pain-
ful. Likewise, however, she made a mental note of how keen
he was to get it squared away, or perhaps even swept under the
rug. 'Where might I find *Policist* Koren?'

'Ask Medved at the desk, she'll be able to help you,' he
replied, face now impassive as he gazed sightlessly at the corner
of Petra's blouse collar. 'Let me know if I can be of assistance.'

Petra nodded curtly, glad that the uncomfortable audience was over. They rose to their feet simultaneously, sharing a brisk handshake before Petra headed for the door. After she'd closed it softly behind her, she stood in the empty corridor for a moment, tapping out a text to *Svetnik* Golob back in Ljubljana to let him know about her conversation with Horvat. She struggled to summarise its tone, even though it had ended only moments earlier. Her instincts suggested that any of Horvat's rudeness or reluctance to engage with her came from a place of mixed embarrassment and grief, rather than any form of guilty conscience. His preoccupation with laying his deceased colleague to rest could easily be completely innocent in nature. Yet, the whistle-blower's note damned him by name as party to the miscarriage of justice. Petra couldn't quite shake the feeling that it wasn't just Ivan Furlan's body that the superintendent wanted to bury, but the entire matter. And that, she reasoned, would include missteps made by his officers, and potentially even Horvat himself.

# Chapter 3

*Policistka* Medved directed Petra out through the back of the police station, where she found a roughly-paved courtyard populated with wooden picnic tables. There was only one person there, a young man sitting at the table furthest from the building and apparently totally engrossed in the few pieces of paper lying in front of him. Aleš Koren was tall and slim, bent almost in half as he poured over what looked to be an A4-sized photograph. His dark hair was a little longer than Petra expected of a policeman, his fringe flopping forward slightly and concealing part of his face. The short sleeves of his uniform blue t-shirt, pulled taut by muscles, revealed his tanned arms, his fist propping up his chin as he rapidly clicked a retractable pen open and closed. His blue uniform hat sat facing him, acting as a paperweight, the brim a little greyed and scuffed with use. As Petra started to make her way over she stopped to allow a small green lizard to scurry in front of her, apparently alarmed by the opening of the patio door. It turned to glare at her once more before taking refuge behind a huge terracotta plant pot.

'*Policist* Koren?' Petra called as she got close to him, politely ignoring the surprised flinch she got in response. Koren spun around quickly, throwing his legs over the bench seat and standing.

'Yes?' his voice was deeper than Petra had been expecting, but his face was painfully young. He looked at Petra with wide, green eyes.

'I am *Inšpektorica* Petra Vidmar, from Ljubljana. *Svetnik* Horvat said you would be assisting me with my enquiries?'

Koren relaxed a little, throwing his hand out with notable speed and hastening towards Petra in one movement. She wondered how she looked to him, standing in her travel-creased blouse, clutching her bag, squinting in the afternoon sun. Was she younger than he expected? Was that why he hadn't guessed it was her? Did she look unprofessional somehow?

'Hello, *Inšpektorica* Vidmar! I am so pleased to meet you, welcome to Koper. I hope your journey wasn't too bad?' His tone immediately put her at ease. It was warm, slightly breathless in his obvious eagerness.

'Probably best not to discuss it,' she replied wryly. She indicated that the younger man should sit and walked around to take the bench opposite. 'The superintendent tells me you have the case notes?'

'I've been working on them all week. Well, only since Sunday, obviously. I think they're as thorough as possible, but I can always go back over them if necessary. Just let me know where you'd like me to elaborate, and I'll do my best.' As he spoke, Koren's speech became faster and faster, the words pouring out in what Petra could only assume was a mixture of passion and nervousness. She recognised the babble, had done it before herself.

'I'm sorry, *Policist*, I don't quite understand. You put them together yourself?' Petra had assumed that one of the other inspectors would have been put on the case, although perhaps they had delegated the grunt work to Koren as the deceased's assistant.

'Yes, but I was careful to do it exactly as *Inšpektor* Furlan showed me. They're good quality, I promise. Or, at least, I think they are.' He blinked at Petra hopefully, gesturing to the papers in front of him. They sat in neat, if very sparse piles, each with a crisp neon sticky note on the top. Although she was reading them upside down, Petra could make out '*Crime scene*' and '*Witness statements*' written on the two closest to her. She caught Koren's eye as she looked up and saw that the man's face was open in a picture of earnestness, apparently desperate for Petra's approval.

'It certainly looks very organised. Which inspector has been working on this with you?'

Koren's face screwed up in response, and he shifted uncomfortably on his bench. 'I have been working alone for the most part, *Inšpektorica*,' he replied, forlornly.

Hopes of a quick return to Ljubljana started to dissipate in front of Petra's eyes. 'Alone? As a junior officer?'

Koren nodded emphatically. 'I've been investigating as much as I can, but no one else has much interest. The whole town thought they knew who did it, and *Inšpektor* Božič arrested him yesterday morning. I begged him not to, but he didn't even want to look at what I had.' He waved his arm across the table, demonstrating his work.

Petra sat for a moment, unpacking what she'd been told. The anonymous author had certainly been preoccupied with, and seemingly motivated by, the arrest of a suspect who they believed was innocent. She had assumed this was after thorough investigation, or at least some digging around. If Koren was to be believed, there'd been nothing of the sort. She was also curious as to what the young man meant by the whole town having an opinion on the identity of the murderer. Even without a proper enquiry, it was interesting that police and public had condemned the same man. Petra looked up at the ugly concrete wall of the station, watching a few officers milling around behind the windows. On the first floor a woman with a severe bun stared out at them, apparently undeterred even when Petra caught her eye. Decided on her next course of action, she stood up.

'Is there anywhere we could talk about this, privately?' she asked Koren, who shot to his feet again and started to gather his papers. Although Petra had no reason to believe that anyone would want to listen in on what she and Koren had to say, she thought it best that she gave him the chance to explain without the possibility of eavesdroppers.

'Yes, of course. My mother runs a *slaščičarna* in town, but she closes early on Thursday afternoons. If you don't mind, we could go there? I can work the coffee machine.' Koren's tone reminded Petra of an eager child relieved to be being taken seriously.

'Perfect. Will you drive, or shall I?' Petra hoped quietly that Koren would offer, as she had no desire to try and navigate an unfamiliar city while in the company of her subordinate. Likewise, however, she was not particularly keen on being ferried around in one of the eye-catching white police cars with their fluorescent yellow and blue stickers.

'Walking would probably be faster,' replied Koren, his case notes now safely stowed in a see-through plastic folder. 'We should be there in fifteen minutes or so.'

Petra looked down at her feet, pleased she'd worn her most comfortable work-appropriate flats for the occasion, even if she had worried they were a little too scuffed when she'd put them on that morning. They were old enough that even a diligent polish didn't seem to get them back to perfection, but had served her well over the years. She smiled at Koren and followed him across the terrace and back into the station, managing to spook the same lizard again as they opened the door.

It only took about ten minutes for them to get out of the industrial area with its many shopping centres and roundabouts, which Petra was grateful to leave behind. It seemed like they had just walked past yet another angular, glass-covered supermarket when Koren led them around a corner, and Petra suddenly found herself in a warren of narrow medieval streets, punctuated occasionally with a slender tree or a well-placed bench. It was far cooler here, with the pavement shielded by neighbouring buildings that stretched a few storeys above their heads; balconies covered in assorted laundry, and chatter from open windows drifted down to them on the street below. As they walked, Koren wittered on good-naturedly about what they passed.

'Koper used to be an island, years ago. You can tell pretty much exactly where the island finishes and the reclamation starts, the architecture changes completely. I wish I could have seen it back then, it must have been amazing.'

Petra nodded as she looked around. The houses here were wide-fronted, with large windows outlined by contrasting stone or paintwork and traditional wooden shutters thrown open to let in what light made it down to street level. Some had obviously been recently refurbished, while others were looking a little down on their luck. They were mostly painted in warm shades of orange and terracotta, although occasionally someone had opted for a vibrant pink or red. Petra noted as they passed a particularly potent ruby red door that many of the recently titivated properties bore placards, written out in various combinations of European languages, advertising their availability as holiday lets. Nearly all of the houses now had callboxes at the door, marking them out as having been divided up into apartments. Petra wasn't surprised: this was one of the most expensive areas in Slovenia, and the houses were sizeable. It must have been an easy decision for someone to split them up and make even more money off people desperate to live within a stone's throw of the Adriatic. There was something a little sad about it, though, when she thought about it. These had once been open, airy houses for one family, but were now parcelled up into single-bedroom apartments for young renters or tourists.

As they continued through the streets Petra tried to get her bearings but found it hard to follow quite where Koren was leading her. Some of the turns they took felt like they were going to lead through someone's front door, but actually veered off at the very last second down an even thinner alley than the one they'd been on before. More than once they crossed a small parking lot for residents of a nearby street, shimmying past bollards to do so. Koren never broke stride, very confident in the best route to his destination. More than once he waved at a passer-by, smiling warmly at them as they continued on.

'You've lived in Koper a while, then?' Petra offered by way of conversation.

'My whole life,' he replied. 'I went away for the police academy, of course, but I came straight back.'

'You don't feel a bit claustrophobic?' Petra asked, gesturing broadly at what she hoped encompassed both the narrow, gently downhill street they were currently marching along, and Koper more generally.

'Why would I? It's home,' he replied simply, and with a small shrug. 'My family are here, so are my friends. I love the sea and the food and the way of life. You don't get that anywhere else.'

Petra considered Koren's response as they turned a corner and emerged onto a square that she recognised from both the ill-fated New Year's Eve trip, and from her Slovene geography textbook in school. In front of her towered the smooth cream front of the Praetorian Palace, one of Koper's main landmarks, its rounded crenelations creating stark lines against the cloudless blue sky. On the main balcony she could see tourists snapping pictures of the square below, turning for selfies with the large state flag that rustled softly in the breeze, and standing on tiptoes to view the coats of arms and memorial tablets carved in relief above the many arch-shaped windows. On the roof, seabirds cooed and cawed, occasionally swooping down to the square when a child dropped a piece of ice cream cone. To the left of the palace stood Koper Cathedral, its spire rising far above anything else nearby. Petra had to fight the childish urge to touch its rough stone wall, certain that it would be pleasantly cool despite the warm day. Koren stopped directly in front of the Palace, peering up at it as he removed the dark sunglasses he'd put on as they left the station.

'I'm assuming your mother doesn't run a business on Titov *Trg*?' Petra queried.

'No, but we're nearly there. I thought you might like to see it.' Koren blushed as he spoke, and it looked oddly out of place on a man so tall. Petra felt slightly guilty for embarrassing him.

'Thank you. I would. I haven't been here since I was a teenager,' her tone was conciliatory, an attempt to make Koren feel at ease again. It seemed to work, as the young man smiled at her and turned to look at the building on the other side of the square from the cathedral, directly opposite the palace. It was pristinely white and dominated by seven smooth Gothic arches, through which she could see a large terrace covered in matching tables, all filled with people enjoying a coffee or a tall, iced drink. The waiting staff were all dressed in smart matching black outfits, white aprons tied around their waists. Watching the scene, Petra started to look forward to the coffee she had been promised at their destination.

Apparently confident that Petra had had her fill of Titov *Trg*, Koren started to walk authoritatively through the archway under the Palace, taking them into a narrow street lined with shops and cafés. They had only got a few metres away from the square when he stopped in front of a small shopfront covered by a pale green awning. The shop had a glass door and a large window, giving Petra a clear view of an L-shaped cake counter. As Koren had said, the shop and counter were currently empty, although a spray-bottle of glass cleaner and a large pink cleaning cloth sat on the end of the top shelf. Above the door there was a wooden sign, sticking out into the street above head-height to tempt customers in. Picked out in white cursive against the brown wood were the words '*Slaščičarna Koren*'. Petra briefly cursed her own stupidity for failing to link *Policist* Aleš Koren with the doughnut box she had seen the superintendent indulging from earlier.

'Horvat tells me this is one of the finest bakeries in town,' she said as Koren pushed the door open, enjoying the smell of baked goods despite the lack of any on display. It must have seeped into the wood panelling on the walls, the upholstered padding on the seats. She had no complaints about starting her investigation here.

'Oh, definitely,' replied Koren guilelessly, making Petra smile. 'My mother has worked very hard.'

At the sound of their voices, a wooden swing door behind the counter flew open. Through it marched a middle-aged woman with greying blonde hair tied up in a knot on top of her head, wearing a pale green chef's tunic. On the left side of her chest the name *Marija* was embroidered in the same curling font as on the doughnut box and the sign outside. She beamed when she saw them, bustling around the counter.

'Hello, officers. What can I get for you? I'm officially closed, but I'll see what I can scrounge up.'

'Thank you, Mama,' replied Koren. Under his mother's gaze he had straightened up, squaring his shoulders and smiling easily. 'This is *Inšpektorica* Vidmar from Ljubljana. She is here to investigate *Inšpektor* Furlan's death, properly this time. *Inšpektorica*, this is my mother, Marija Koren.'

'But you must call me Marija,' she interjected quickly, shaking Petra's hand enthusiastically. 'A coffee, *Inšpektorica*? You must have had a long journey, can I get you something to eat as well?'

'And you must call me Petra. A coffee would be glorious, and I would be thrilled to try anything you have left, but please don't go to any trouble.' Petra realised that she was, in fact, quite hungry.

Marija waved her hand to suggest it was no bother before instructing her son to start on the coffee machine. Petra settled down at the table nearest the counter, pleasantly surprised at how comfortable the little wooden chair with its fabric cushion was. Each table was bedecked in a tablecloth covered in a pattern of jellyfish in various pastel colours, and had a wire caddy covered in seashells filled with cutlery and condiments. She preemptively pulled out two packets of sugar, setting them down next to the plastic wallet Koren had brought with them from the station. The coffee machine began to gurgle merrily as Marija re-emerged from behind the swinging door carrying two square plates, one with a pile of four plump doughnuts and the other with two generous slabs of what looked to be *potica*.

'I can offer you either the last of the doughnuts, or the first of the *potica*,' she said as she laid the plates down on the table. Petra had never thought about it before, but she supposed this time of year must be high season for a patisserie. Pust, the Slovenian answer to Italy's dramatic Carnevale, demanded the nationwide gorging of doughnuts before the start of Lent. As soon as Lent was over, the matrons of the country turned their baking skills to *potica*, a traditional Easter nut roll featuring a loaf of golden pastry wrapped around a tempting spiral of walnut or sesame paste. Although her own grandmothers had always fried and baked their own seasonal offerings, by the time Petra had been aware of it her mother had been too busy at work for homemade goods and had instead relied on local slaščičarne for her festive feasting. Seeing Marija's wares reminded her of the excitement she used to feel going into their local patisserie on her way home from elementary school, when her mother would pick her up in front of the glass counter and let her choose which sort of jam doughnut she wanted.

'These look excellent. Thank you very much, Marija.' As she spoke, Koren rushed over with their coffees, somehow managing not to spill a drop. The effortlessness with which he moved around the café made it easy for Petra to imagine him as a teenager cruising around the tables at the weekend, helping his mother.

'You are very welcome, I hope you enjoy them. I'm just popping home, Aleš, but I'll be back later. Could you lock up after yourself when you go?'

'Of course, Mama. See you this evening,' Koren replied, settling down in the seat next to Petra and starting to rifle through his folder, bringing the little bundles with their sticky notes out and reverently setting them in order across the table.

Marija beamed at them again, touching her son's shoulder affectionately before retrieving her handbag from under the counter and bustling out of the door, walking briskly away down the street in the opposite direction from where Petra and Koren had come. Petra decided it was better not to ask whether Marija had made herself scarce for their benefit, worried she might embarrass Koren again. Instead, she removed her jacket and swung it around the back of her chair, giving the young man her full attention.

'Let's get started.'

# Chapter 4

'Where would you like me to begin?' asked Koren, biting his bottom lip. It occurred to Petra that he'd never had to present a case like this before, and certainly not to someone senior to him who he did not know. His notes looked thorough and detailed, and were certainly carefully assembled, but he seemed to have drawn a blank as to how to actually impart this information.

'Tell me about *Inšpektor* Furlan,' Petra began, trying to get the man on solid ground.

'He was a brilliant inspector, very methodical but also compassionate. He taught me so much, he was always trying to get me involved in different cases so I could get experience. His main concern was always the victim, how he could make things better for them,' Koren smiled sadly. 'That's why I'm so angry that now he's the victim, no one seems to be doing the same for him.'

'Could you tell me more about the circumstances sur-rounding his death?'

'It was late Saturday night, we think. He was walking on

the coastal path between Izola and Koper, although no one is quite sure why. I guess he was coming back this way, as I have no idea why he'd be going to Izola that late, but his wife wasn't sure why he'd have been in Izola earlier in the evening either. He went down to the water, on to the rocks, and while he was down there someone shot him in the head. There's just the one gunshot wound, but there'd have been no need for any others. That one killed him immediately, even I could see that, but the pathologist confirmed it.'

'Seeing that must have been awful,' Petra replied sympathetically, 'I'm very sorry.'

'It was horrible. *Inšpektor* Božič looked like he might be sick, tried to make me look away, but he was too late.'

'You were one of the first officers to be called?'

'Yes, I was at the station waiting for *Inšpektor* Furlan to arrive when we got the call. I spent most of the drive over wondering where he was, since he was never late to work and he was on shift that Sunday. It took me a minute to realise that it was his body I was looking at, to be honest. I couldn't rationalise how he was dead when he should have been with me responding to the call out,' Koren looked down at his notes, curling in on himself. 'Sorry, that makes me sound very stupid.'

'Shock makes us all stupid,' Petra replied with confidence, remembering how Golob had told her the same thing when she'd responded to a particularly nasty car accident early in her career. Koren nodded mutely, apparently lost in thought. 'How quickly was the main suspect established?'

Koren laughed darkly. 'Before *Inšpektor* Furlan was even killed.'

There was no point in Petra trying to hide her surprise, it was a strange statement. She raised her eyebrows to encourage Koren to continue, and was pleased when he did so without further prompting.

'The inspector had a long-running dispute with his brother, Marjan. It had become quite unpleasant recently. From the second *Inšpektor* Furlan was pronounced dead, Marjan was convicted in the eyes of half the town.'

'And it was Marjan who was arrested?' The question seemed pointless, but Petra thought it was worth clarifying.

'Yes, yesterday,' Koren confirmed.

'And what had caused the dispute?'

'The same thing as seems to cause every family disagreement in this country: an inheritance,' he sighed. 'Their mother died a few years ago, naturally without a will, and left her sons with a house in Piran. Marjan has some issues with gambling so could use the money, and suggested to the inspector that they sell it. The inspector didn't want to, and they ended up in a horrible row. Whenever Marjan had money he used it to sue his brother, and then when he didn't he just hounded him personally. I felt awful for *Inšpektor* Furlan, but he always took it in his stride.'

'Why didn't the inspector want to sell?' Petra had seen photos of gorgeous Piran, with its slim, cobbled streets and Venetian city walls. It appeared on every postcard of Slovenia, and with good reason. She also remembered a friend considering buying a holiday property there, before baulking at the incredible prices, especially considering there was no parking or vehicular access to large parts of the town since the streets were too thin and the cobbles too uneven. She imagined that half-owning a property with a sure-fire high price point and being unable to sell must have infuriated the apparently penniless Marjan.

'It was their childhood home,' said Koren, sounding a little suspicious. 'And the inspector didn't want it just being turned into someone's holiday house. It was just as much his as it was Marjan's, he had the right to want to keep it.'

'Of course, I understand,' Petra replied placatingly, not having meant offence. 'Had Marjan ever threatened violence?'

Koren reached for one of his piles of documents, drawing out a page of handwritten notes on flimsy lined paper. 'Yes, but only when he was drunk. I spoke to *Gospa* Furlan, the inspector's widow, about it. She said she never thought he'd actually follow through, she and the inspector both thought it was just bluster.' Koren read through his notes briefly, and continued, 'and it was always about "smashing your knees in" or about keying the car, never about shooting anyone.'

Petra nodded contemplatively. 'So, the widow doesn't blame her brother-in-law?'

The change in Koren's demeanour was slight, but definite. He seemed to bristle, apparently displeased at the direction Petra's questioning had taken. 'She didn't, at first. Marjan doesn't even own a gun, that we know of, and he's adamant he has a rock-solid alibi.'

'That being?'

'He was at a casino in Portorož, playing,' Koren broke off as he scrabbled through another pile of notes, topped with a yellow label reading *'Marjan'*. Finding what he wanted, he continued with a grimace, 'Lucky Lady's Jackpot. He says it is a slot machine.'

'Which I imagine is covered by CCTV?' Petra hedged, becoming uneasy about the situation. Quite how anyone had thought it appropriate to arrest a man with an alibi after no investigation was beyond her, even if he was the most obvious suspect.

'No,' said Koren sullenly.

'No CCTV?'

'Not on Lucky Lady's Jackpot.'

'And nowhere else in the casino caught him on camera?' Petra asked in disbelief.

'No.'

Petra sat back in her seat and folded her arms across her chest, unsure how to word her next question. Although she wanted to be on Koren's side, she was beginning to think Horvat was right and that Koren was just unable to accept the ignominious circumstances of his mentor's death. The rapidity of her changing opinion was giving her whiplash. She reached out and picked up a doughnut to buy herself time and was gratified to find it filled with a perfectly balanced apricot jam, neither too tart nor too sweet. After her brother had been old enough to cast a vote her family had become a solidly blueberry household, much to her displeasure. She mopped up some of the fallen icing sugar with a finger, sticking it in her mouth contemplatively.

'He's banned,' Koren volunteered eventually, apparently aware he couldn't skirt around the issue with monosyllabic answers for ever.

'From the casino?'

'Yes, he did some time in jail a few years ago after a violent assault at their sister casino in Lipica, and when he got out they banned him.'

'He's done jail-time for violent assault?' Petra tried to keep the judgement out of her tone, but was aware she'd failed. She could see why Marjan Furlan was behind bars so quickly, she'd have joined the arresting party herself.

'Only six months! He threw a bottle, he claims he didn't mean for it to hit a croupier.'

'Koren, please don't take this badly, but are you intending to defend a violent gambling addict for his conduct?'

The young man deflated, pulling a slice of *potica* towards himself and biting into it morosely. 'No, Marjan is a terrible person. He's gambled his family out of house and home, he threatened his brother and he almost cost a croupier his eye. But I really don't think he killed the inspector. When we brought him in he didn't even realise his brother was dead!'

'Even though he can't substantiate his alibi?' Petra dismissed the supposed ignorance of the inspector's death. It was easily feigned, she'd seen it before.

'He says he deliberately avoided the cameras at the casino,

because of the ban,' Koren explained, pulling at his pastry so that the spiral unwound, leaving him with a long snake of walnut paste-covered dough on his plate. 'He remembers that it was Lucky Lady's Jackpot, as that's the only one out of view of the camera in the slot machine hall. He didn't move from it all night.'

'Which makes sense, I agree. I would avoid anything that could prove I was in a place I had been banned from, especially when I imagine casino CCTV is high quality.'

'Very,' Koren agreed, nodding rapidly. 'The manager I spoke to also said they watch it live, as they're always having to throw out people who've been banned. They're addicts largely, the people on the blacklist. They're desperate to get back in. One of the security team is monitoring it at all times, looking for their faces.'

'And no one saw Marjan Furlan on the night in question?'

Koren shook his head, tearing off a piece of *potica* and chewing it as he flicked through his notes again. 'No, although one of the cocktail waitresses said she's definitely seen him in there a few times since the ban. She'd mentioned it to management, her boss confirmed it, but security never caught him. She couldn't confirm whether that included the night the inspector was killed, though. "The nights all blend into one", that's a direct quote.'

Petra took a long draw from her mug of coffee, humming slightly in appreciation. It was really very good, she would have happily come back had she visited as a tourist. 'What makes you think he didn't do it?' she enquired, honestly interested.

Koren hardly seemed irrational, and although she hardly knew him, she had the superintendent's testimony earlier to support her opinion.

'Because the inspector always said his brother wasn't actually a bad person,' said Koren simply. 'He was always on his side. He visited him in jail, he signed him up for a rehabilitation course in Ljubljana and paid for the first session. And Marjan went! He was really trying, *Inšpektor* Furlan was so proud.'

'You said earlier that the dispute had got nasty recently, though?' Petra reminded him, confused.

'Oh, yes. There was an incident at the station. They'd agreed that the house would stay vacant, although they both had keys. Marjan went in recently and saw that the inspector had been spending time there, and he was furious. It seemed to be lost on him that if he had seen it, he'd obviously gone in too.'

Petra chose not to comment on the insanity of leaving a plum coastal property vacant over a brotherly argument, aware that most of the madness in Slovenia was caused by similar disputes. She had answered more than one call in Ljubljana where family members had ended up in tense stand-offs over some asset left by a relative who died without a will, and which was now nominally divided between family members with different objectives. Her favourite had been an octogenarian woman threatening her nonagenarian sister with a rolling pin over a Hapsburg-era side table, which someone had spilled cigarette ash on and in so doing damaged its starting price at auction. 'This escalation wasn't enough to change your mind over Marjan's guilt, though?'

'No! It was a flash in the pan, the inspector said so himself. He sent Marjan a few hundred euro to placate him, and it was over. It was the talk of the town for days afterwards, though, that Marjan had come to scream at his brother in the police station of all places over some stupid papers he'd found in the house in Piran. My mother had heard about it before I'd even got home, two customers had given her hugely different accounts of what happened.' Koren looked up at Petra, seemingly exasperated. 'Neither of them was even true. I was there!'

'Okay,' said Petra slowly, assessing her options. 'Okay. Let's say Marjan didn't kill his brother. Who else is there?'

Koren's head shot up, his eyes fixed on Petra. 'You don't think Marjan is guilty?'

'I didn't say that. I'm interested in who was overlooked, who you and the person who wrote to Ljubljana thought should actually be investigated.'

'I don't know,' said Koren breathlessly, and although his words were disappointing, his voice sounded hopeful. He stuffed some more *potica* in his mouth and slurped some coffee, fingers shifting his case notes around the table in a frenzy. 'I'm hoping you'll help me find out?'

'We'll see,' Petra replied, ensuring her tone was non-committal. She didn't want to disappoint Koren, whose heart seemed to be in exactly the right place and whose loyalty to his mentor was undeniable and admirable. Likewise, she didn't want to give the man false hope. The investigation may have been rushed, but from what she had been told it sounded like they had the right man, they just hadn't followed the right procedure.

# Chapter 5

By the time they'd ploughed through the details of the case and finished off their baked goods it was drawing close to the end of the working day, but Petra still had one final thing she wanted to see before she returned to her hotel. Koren locked up the *slaščičarna* behind them, and they started the leisurely walk back to the station in a companionable silence. As they neared the car park, Petra made a beeline for her Skoda. She offered Koren the chance of an early finish but was quickly rebuffed. Instead they both piled into the car, Petra's duffle bag of clothes tossed into the boot, before they headed off in the direction of the coastal path and the scene of the crime.

Although until recently a major road on the way to Croatia, the coastal path had now been pedestrianised for all except residents and emergency service vehicles. As soon as they arrived at the end of what was still road, Petra saw what a good decision this had been. What had once been the tarmacked road for cars was now marked up to ensure safe routes for pedestrians and cyclists, while a thinner path ran alongside looking down onto the rocky beach. It was busy even in the early evening, families strolling along as toddlers darted around their feet, Lycra-clad cyclists zooming towards Izola shouting jokes to one another. Although Koren was insistent that even in a private car Petra could get away with driving down the pedestrianised area she was not keen to try and fight her way through the various groups already using it, and so they parked at the furthest extent of the beach car park and began the journey to the crime scene on foot.

'How far is the walk to Izola?' asked Petra, slipping her sunglasses on and tucking the car keys into her jacket pocket, her bag left safely in the car.

'About an hour on foot,' Koren replied. As he spoke, a young girl wearing violently purple roller-skates shot past them, hotly pursued by her father. 'Obviously faster if you have wheels,' he added with a laugh.

They continued along the path in the same companionable silence as they'd shared earlier in the day, which Petra was grateful for. Early in her time as an inspector she'd had the misfortune to be paired with an officer who had never stopped talking, and about nothing in particular. Memorably, she had once had to tell him to shut up so she could hear what a witness had to say, so confident was he that his own story about a nearby bar was more pressing.

A kilometre or so down the path, the landscape changed slightly. To the left of them, opposite the water, the roadside had initially been dominated by impressive beach-front houses, as many balconies as architecturally possible crammed onto their fronts to maximise the sea view. Now, further along the path, the terrain climbed uphill, leaving them walking alongside a waist-height concrete wall. Where the wall stopped, thickets of trees with thin trunks and other scrubby plants clustered precariously on the face of the bank, the concrete seemingly holding them back from spilling onto the road and taking over the walkway. The path suddenly felt very quiet, and exposed. They kept walking, Koren pointing out the view back to Koper, and a series of signs memorialising a ship sunk in the bay decades earlier. Petra found herself distracted by the dozens of plump, pink jellyfish bobbing in the water, several of them beached on the shore below her. She wasn't entirely sure she'd ever seen one in the wild before, let alone in this density. She tore her attention away from them, attempting instead to work out whether there were any cameras at this point along the path, if there were bushes or structures a gunman could hide behind. As Izola started to come clearly into view, the distance small enough that Petra could see where individual roofs ended and the neighbouring building began, Koren started to slow down.

'Andrej Kos said he was about here when he spotted the inspector,' he said quietly. 'He didn't realise it was a body at first, he said it didn't even cross his mind.'

Petra nodded, but didn't speak. She noticed that Koren hadn't needed to scramble for his notes, having committed this to memory.

'He carried on a little further,' Koren's movements mimicked his words, and he took five wide, decisive steps forward. 'Then he climbed down onto the rocks, when he realised what it was.' Both Koren and Petra copied Andrej, stepping onto the large boulder butted up against the concrete path before nimbly stepping down onto the smaller stones and pebbles below. Koren was much swifter than Petra, and gallantly turned around to offer her a hand. Her childhood self would have been disappointed at how unskilled at scrambling she'd become in adulthood.

Just a metre or so in front of them was a gravelly area surrounded by knee-height rocks, a small tidal rockpool behind it. In the rockpool Petra could see a jellyfish on the cusp between life and death, stranded in the small pool of water, barely enough to cover it. Nearby were two crushed beer cans and a bleached chocolate bar wrapper, suggesting that it was a popular place to sit and watch the Adriatic glimmer and sway.

Koren stopped again, hands now shoved into his pockets as he gestured with a rough arm motion. 'That's where we found him.'

Petra cleared her throat and turned a slow circle, getting her bearings. In front of her there was nothing but sea, no marinas or peninsulas from which someone could take a shot. Not that that mattered, she thought, when the photo she'd seen just that morning demonstrated that the man had been shot in the back of the head. She continued around, now standing with her back to the Adriatic and facing the coastal path, still humming with evening activity, and the pockmarked rock face on the other side of it. She could still see the purple-skated girl and her father in the distance, the visibility was so good, although she supposed it would have been pitch black by the time Furlan had been here on Saturday night. Whatever was above them on the other side of the path now was shielded in trees and silent, none of the noises of life she'd heard nearer Koper.

'Where do they think Marjan was, when he shot the inspector?'

Koren grimaced. 'Standing directly behind him up on the path, although not point-blank range. It was windy on Saturday night, the sea would have been quite choppy, but the tide still far enough out that standing among the rocks isn't unpleasant. You can be down there by the water in those conditions and not hear a thing. We're assuming the inspector hopped down onto the beach, looked out at the sea, and someone crept up behind him and fired,' he explained. 'You've seen the photo?'

Petra indicated she had, and he gave her a slightly sympathetic look. 'But we found him with his legs out this way,' he pointed towards the sea, 'and his head back here by the rockpool. If he was shot in the back of the head, he must have pitched forwards. The pathologist found sand in his eyelashes and around his mouth, which suggests he did fall on his front, so how did he end up on his back again?'

'What do the rest of your team think?' she asked.

'That Marjan climbed down here and flipped him over in a fit of remorse, dragged him around so his head didn't get wet. Maybe he thought he could save him. Or maybe, once Marjan realised what he'd done, he just wanted to give the inspector one last look at the stars,' Koren sighed. 'He was so irrational when he came to threaten the inspector at the station that it is plausible that he'd do something like that in a rage, then maybe he regretted it. Propped his head up on the rockpool, to give his body some sense of dignity.'

They stood quietly, Petra staring at the spot where Ivan Furlan had died, Koren looking out to sea. She wasn't quite sure what to say, so decided it was best to revert to her most professional demeanour. 'We passed a snack vending machine and a set of disabled changing rooms a few minutes ago, do they have CCTV?'

Koren huffed, turning to face her. 'No, they don't.'

'And none of the properties we passed earlier have anything that would show who came this way?'

He shook his head, kicking his toe around in the surf. 'They're mostly holiday lets, so they have cameras right on the front door but don't show the path. Anyway, you could easily come the other way from Izola.'

'And there's nothing at that end which would catch anyone, either.' She didn't phrase it as a question, not wanting to insult Koren's intelligence. He had obviously done his due diligence, and would have found something like that already, even though he'd been having to do the groundwork alone. Not for the first time in her career, she felt a surge of jealousy for the police teams she saw on British and American crime procedurals. Slovenes were private, and would hate to be filmed at all times. As such, as a nation their camera coverage could be described as patchy at best. There was none of the tapping into banks of cameras and watching a street from every conceivable angle, like she saw on TV.

'Give it another month and this place will be crawling with tourists until five a.m., and then the local early morning swimmers will show up by six a.m.,' said Koren, distress clear in his voice. 'But at the moment, it seems to be pretty quiet in the evening. We haven't had any calls yet this season about beach parties, or screaming drunks. This part of the path is pretty far from most people's houses, and anyway, it gets too cold at night for anyone to fancy a swim or a beer. I haven't swum yet this season.'

'So, the case against Marjan is that he has no verifiable alibi and is known to have threatened the deceased recently?' she summarised succinctly.

'Yes, that's about it.'

'How long ago was he arrested? How long do we have to build a case?'

A light seemed to go out in Koren's eyes, and Petra realised that she'd inadvertently made it clear that she was still planning on following the case against Marjan Furlan. If you'd asked her to her face, she would have struggled to decide whether she wanted to continue down that track or look for other options. But, as she spoke, she realised that she couldn't afford to let Marjan slip away when he seemed so clear a culprit. She told herself that her desire to get back to Ljubljana and sit at her desk awaiting the phone call that could change the trajectory of her career, the course of her life, even, was not clouding her judgement.

'He was arrested on other grounds, not murder,' he replied eventually, although didn't disclose exactly what other crime Marjan had committed. 'Substantiated grounds, but everyone knows it's just while they try and find a way to pin the inspector's death on him.'

Petra decided not to press Koren on the exact circumstances of Marjan's arrest, sensing it was a sore subject. She sucked her teeth as she thought, aware of the interested looks they were attracting, Koren's tall frame and eye-catching uniform standing out harshly against his surroundings. She wondered how many of the passers-by knew exactly why the police were there, whether any of them knew more than she did about what had happened. It unnerved her slightly that it was almost definitely the case. A middle-aged man walking with a similarly aged woman and speaking loudly in Hungarian pointed obviously at them as they passed, and Petra rallied.

'I think that's enough for this evening, Aleš.' She could see the toll this little outing had taken on him, how sad his eyes had become and the jitteriness of his general demeanour. He looked very young, blinking out at her from under his fringe, his hat dangling from his hands in what she assumed was a sign of respect for the deceased. It seemed wrong to call him anything but his first name when he looked like this.

He smiled tiredly, deliberately walking a few steps away from the rockpool to climb back up onto the path, apparently unwilling to stand where his mentor had fallen. He offered Petra his hand again and she picked her way over a pair of small jellyfish to take it, patting him on the arm in thanks once she was back on the concrete. They headed back along the path, the crowds noticeably thinner than when they had started out earlier.

'Can I give you a lift home?' Petra asked Koren once they reached the car, jangling her keys at him for effect.

'No, thank you. I'd like to walk, it isn't far.'

Petra nodded in understanding. 'If you're sure. Thank you for your help today, I appreciate the context. I'll see you at the station in the morning?'

Koren agreed and handed Petra his plastic file of notes before moving off across the darkening car park. He turned to wave as Petra pulled out of the exit, her phone set to give her directions back to her hotel. She was grateful he'd already looked away as she tried to negotiate a very ambiguous round-about at the end of the beach road, and grumbled to herself as she accelerated away from the inky sea and towards the hills behind Koper.

# Chapter 6

The car park to her guesthouse was packed when she pulled in, a riot of different nationalities represented in the Tetris of vehicles crammed into the dusty space. She tucked the Skoda in between an enormous Austrian motorbike and a tiny Italian Fiat, grabbed both her work bag and duffle full of clothes, and went back through the door she'd entered earlier. It was dark enough now that the vineyard she'd gazed at before was hidden from view, but in the distance she could see lights twinkling in the windows of what looked to be a farmhouse, the scene no less picturesque than it had been in the daylight.

Deciding she was too hungry to miss dinner, she found a seat at a small corner table of the restaurant downstairs and was gratified to find a remarkably simple menu. Every option seemed to be a regional speciality, written initially in Slovene in bold capital letters before being translated into Italian, German and English below. As the menu went on it seemed that the English translations became shakier and she wondered if the teenager she'd met earlier might be the culprit, the menu becoming a victim of his increasing apathy. She ordered herself a plate of homemade pasta in a black truffle sauce and a small glass of *malvazija,* thrilled to hear from the chatty waitress that the wine came from the small vineyard behind the guesthouse, which she'd admired earlier.

As she waited for the food to arrive, she thought about the case she had been assigned. From what she'd seen, she could sympathise with both the opinion of Koren and the anonymous author, assuming they weren't the same person, and of Horvat and the others who she was yet to meet. If you truly wanted to go by the book, then Marjan Furlan should only be a person of interest in the case, and should certainly not be sitting in a cell on the basis of secondary crimes unknown, waiting to be charged with murder. Likewise, considering he had motive, no alibi, and was apparently a regular offender who had good reason already to be sitting in said cell, Petra could see why Ivan Furlan's colleagues had seen red and put Marjan away. As she looked at the sparse notes she'd scribbled on her pad, she thought about what she'd currently be doing in Ljubljana. Sitting in front of the television, she supposed, eating whatever she'd decided to defrost from her stockpile in the freezer, which was really too big for her small flat, but that she had justified through her devotion to batch cooking. She'd been trying to eat through her frozen hoard recently, in anticipation of the phone call from Lyon. At first she'd worried this might jinx it, that she'd munch through her last serving of lentil bolognese the evening before she received a rejection. Her mother had told her that this was utterly ridiculous, and that if she was going to think that way then she'd be sending her daughter a delivery pizza every night until she heard the outcome of her application to Interpol.

A passing waiter deposited her wine on her table and she took a long sip, enjoying its mild flavour and the cool trail it left down her throat. When she'd first applied for the secondment to Interpol she had felt she was in a rut, having seen everything Ljubljana had to offer. It had seemed an obvious choice, to go and see what interest international policing might hold, even if putting together her application and making her case to the senior policemen in her own station had been incredibly demanding and stressful. She had been ecstatic to be offered an interview, although she had still told only her parents and *Svetnik* Golob. The idea of letting everyone know was too terrifying when she could still fail. She wasn't sure how Mlakar had even found out, come to think of it. His pervasive niceness must have worn Golob down one day, made him loose-lipped.

Moments later, her pasta was delivered to the table with a cheerful *dober tek*. She started to spear the tubes on her fork, thinking about one of the questions the panel had asked her. They'd been interested in hearing her opinion on whether someone with a criminal record, and so a history of breaking the law and lying, could be trusted to give a witness statement or testimony. She'd argued, she hoped persuasively, that if the idea of a prison sentence or criminal punishment was to rehabilitate, then someone who had served their sentence should indeed be given the same benefit of the doubt as any other member of society. She'd come across it in her own career when a young drug dealer had come forward to report domestic violence he'd witnessed on a delivery, which had both amazed her and slightly restored her faith in humanity. Revisiting her answer now, she tried to view Marjan Furlan in another light. Yes, he was a criminal, and not entirely rehabilitated if there was cause to arrest him over something else. Likewise, no one could prove he had been at the scene of the crime, and from what Koren had said, his motive was dampened somewhat by the actions of *Inšpektor* Furlan. If she was going to stand by what she'd told the Interpol interviewing panel, she would be remiss to place the blame at Marjan Furlan's door without any further investigation. However, she thought as she nibbled a piece of grated truffle, she would be a fool to discard him as a suspect. There was still a strong likelihood Marjan Furlan was guilty, the local force just hadn't gone about proving it in the right way. Or at all, really.

Pasta finished and wineglass drained, Petra paid for her meal and climbed up the dark wooden stairs in the direction of her room. She was suddenly exhausted, a long drive and a day of intense concentration catching up with her with the help of the *malvazija*. Her room was easy to find, a tarnished bronze number fixed securely to the door at head height. Like the staircase, the door was made of a heavy, dark wood, lightly embellished with inlaid panels. The key looked as old as this part of the building, with a thick barrel and an ornate head, the tip ending in a chunky square with just one or two prongs. She wondered whether it would be harder or easier to copy than the slim, heavily notched key to her modern apartment. It was certainly a lot harder to lose, she had felt its weight in her pocket all afternoon. Unlocking the door and stepping over the threshold she was met with a strong smell of furniture polish, perhaps explained by the dark wainscot that covered every wall up to waist-height. The walls were otherwise cream, although boasting a contrasting band of burgundy moulding decorated with white painted doves around a foot below the high ceiling. From the ceiling hung an interesting wrought-iron chandelier bearing three round lightbulbs. A double bed made up in pale bedding was pressed up against the wall opposite the window, which was already covered by burgundy shutters. She wondered whether a member of staff had noticed her absence and popped in to close them.

Tossing her duffle bag onto a square-backed wooden chair sitting next to the wardrobe, she made a beeline for the internal door in her room. Behind it was a small but functional bathroom, one corner filled with a white plastic shower tray and semi-obscured by a transparent shower curtain. She washed her hands and splashed water on her face from the tap, and went back out into the bedroom to get changed for bed. The mattress was thankfully comfortable, the bedding the perfect weight for the quickly cooling evening temperatures, and she only just remembered to set an alarm before drifting off to sleep.

# Chapter 7

Petra jolted awake to the sound of her phone blaring the next morning, and was confused to find it wasn't her alarm. Instead, *Svetnik* Golob's name flashed across the screen. Always keen for an early start and an even earlier finish on a Friday, she wasn't entirely surprised he'd decided it was a good time to call. He hadn't responded to the text she sent yesterday, which had struck her as strange but she had quickly forgotten about once she had met Koren.

'*Svetnik* Golob, good morning,' she croaked, well aware that she sounded as though she'd just woken up.

'Petra. Just checking in, how is everything? Still looking like it'll be finished quickly?'

Golob had never been one for chit-chat, which she was grateful for. If they got straight to the point, she could get off the call more quickly and try and gather her thoughts before heading down for breakfast. 'I can't say for certain at the moment, I'm afraid. The suspect does look promising and can't prove his alibi, but likewise we can't prove he was at the scene either.' She noticed the slip up as soon as she said it, the 'we' linking her own beliefs to those who had prematurely arrested Marjan, just as it had slipped out yesterday on the beach.

'I see. Are you getting any trouble from the locals?'

'None, I've been assigned an officer who is very diligent, and haven't met anyone other than *Svetnik* Horvat otherwise.'

Golob hummed in response but didn't say anything.

'If that's all?'

'Yes, yes. Thank you, Petra. Let me know how it progresses,' he trailed off, and she heard clattering on a keyboard at his end. He was notorious for multitasking, okaying reports while simultaneously making appointments with his dentist and emailing the entire station to remind them not to bring fish in at lunchtime. 'I'll be out after lunch today, but I'd like a report on Monday, if you could.'

'Of course. Have a good weekend.'

The line went dead, and Petra flopped back down onto the mattress, stabbing at her phone to turn off the alarm preemptively. It was amusing how predictable people could be, though she was sure she was equally culpable. If Petra was a betting woman she'd have €50 on Golob being ready to tee-off at Royal Bled by 2 p.m.; she imagined the pool had already started in the station over how early he would slink away, clubs safely in the boot of his car. She wondered if she would be able to get a little break in, should the Interpol secondment be approved. Koper seemed nice, but she wasn't keen to stay longer than necessary. Perhaps the Croatian coast? When this was over, she'd ask Medved.

Finally disentangling herself from her cocoon of duvet, Petra busied herself having a hot shower before pulling on a fresh blouse and heading out the door, making sure to grab Koren's file of notes on the way. Downstairs in the restaurant she found a tempting array of breads, condiments and fruit. She grabbed a warm roll, an apple and a small pot of honey before ordering a cappuccino and settling at the same table she'd had her dinner at the previous night. Browsing the titles of the files Koren had given her, she pulled out the slimmest: the report on Ivan Furlan's body, and the crime scene. It was an overly wordy document, filled with jargon, but experience helped her pick out the most important points. The sea, and a light rain shower in the night, had washed away any physical evidence there might have been. He had been shot in the back of the head, and Petra recognised the bullet as the same as she had been issued at the start of her career, to fit the Beretta which always felt oddly heavy on her waist. It was also, the report said, one of the most common bullets in manufacture, although it had only been invented in 1990. The shot had come from far enough away that the murderer's aim was impressive, if Koren's assertion about the wind and the noise was correct. They had traded off certainty with not wanting to be too close to their victim. To Petra, it seemed the shot of either a confident marksman, or an impressive stroke of beginner's luck. Someone had then moved the body, turning it around so that its head was by the path and legs out by the water. Petra assumed that this must have been the murderer, but made a note of it anyway, consigning the fact over to her subconscious to digest while she continued with other details.

She moved on to the section on Marjan Furlan, separating the sheets out around her breakfast. Koren had typed up Marjan's statement about where he was on the night of the murder, and Petra carefully reread the salient points about Lucky Lady's Jackpot and the deliberate avoidance of CCTV. She generously slathered the soft white roll with honey, chewing thoughtfully as she flicked through a headshot of Marjan from when he went to jail for the incident with the croupier in Lipica, as well as documentation regarding the house in Piran. Koren had also slipped in a copy of the paperwork done when Marjan was arrested, and Petra set down her meal to assess it more carefully. The arresting officer's name was *Inšpektor* Denis Božič, which she recognised from Koren's story about the discovery of Ivan Furlan's body. Božič had recorded the reason for the arrest as property damage, specifically the smashing of windows at an address in Piran. Grabbing the property details she'd skimmed past earlier, Petra confirmed that the property Marjan Furlan had been vandalising was the one he shared with his now-deceased brother. The date on the arrest report was Wednesday, the same day as the plea had reached Ljubljana, although the crime was recorded as having taken place a week earlier, before Ivan Furlan had been killed.

Petra's coffee arrived and she sipped at it, almost burning her tongue in her distraction. When Koren had failed to explain what Marjan had been arrested for the previous day, she had assumed it had been because it was a minor crime used as a tool to get him into custody. With the knowledge that he'd been destroying shared property just days before his brother had been killed, Marjan started to look even guiltier. She wondered when exactly he'd made his visit to the police station to threaten his brother, making a note of the question to ensure she wouldn't forget. Her discovery also made her question Koren, she realised with a stab of anger. He had lied by omission. Petra had been so willing to believe him, with his earnest face and wide eyes. She felt a little foolish and decided to channel the negative emotion in the way her mother had taught her, by not letting it happen again.

Gathering together her papers and hastily finishing her breakfast, Petra hurried back up the stairs to her room to brush her teeth and grab her bag before going back out to the now empty car park, her fellow guests having apparently continued on their way to warmer beaches. She was largely confident in her ability to find the station unaided, but still set up her phone in its holder suctioned to the windscreen. It never hurt to be cautious.

# Chapter 8

Several police cars were missing from the shadiest spots outside the station, but Petra hesitated to pinch one despite the forecast that today would be unseasonably warm. Instead, she chose the same slot as yesterday, keen to avoid any station politics. The front desk was once again manned by Medved, who greeted her with a wave.

'*Inšpektorica*, good morning. How can I help?'

'The same to you, Medved. I was wondering if you could direct me to *Inšpektor* Božič?'

Medved snorted, spinning lazily in her office chair. 'Aren't you a lucky one, *Inšpektorica*. The one day this year that Božič arrives before eight a.m., and it's the morning you're looking for him.'

Petra wasn't quite sure what to do with this information and felt her eyebrows furrow. 'When does he normally arrive?'

'He likes to do a quick surveillance down at the market every morning before work, make sure there's no illegal asparagus trade afoot or any shifty strawberry salesmen. That he also manages to do some shopping while he's there is totally coincidental, of course,' she replied with a laugh. Petra was becoming used to her willingness to share information about her colleagues, and wondered what Medved had to say about some of the other people in the station. She considered asking outright about Koren, but the moment passed as Medved continued, 'He's in the back, go through the door behind me and then second one on your right.'

'Thank you, Medved. I appreciate your help.'

Medved grinned at Petra in response, a strangely conspiratorial glint in her eye.

The door behind Medved was propped open and gave Petra a clear view down a long, electrically-lit corridor, every available inch of wall space filled by either an internal window or a noticeboard. As she marched down it, Petra saw A4 sheets advertising everything from a compulsory health and safety seminar to what appeared to be an over-sized birthday card for someone named Leonardo, written entirely in Italian. The door that Medved had described was also thrown wide, a battered rubber doorstop shoved under it to keep it that way. It bore the same signage as *Svetnik* Horvat's upstairs, indicating that this was the office of *Inšpektor* Ivan Furlan and *Inšpektor* Denis Božič. Petra remembered the account of Božič's visceral reaction to the scene of the crime, and she felt a wave of sympathy for the man, especially if he'd tried to protect Koren from seeing the same thing.

Inside were two desks, one covered in clutter and the other almost empty except for a set of three matching picture frames in descending height order. Petra approached the photographs, assuming that the tidier of the two would be Furlan's desk. The smallest of the pictures was of three young girls sitting together on a bench, the Adriatic stretching out blue and still behind them, the outer two holding the youngest down between them to prevent her escape. The middle one was of a woman in a flowery summer dress sitting at a restaurant table, toasting the photographer with a large Aperol Spritz. The largest was of a shining silver vintage car sitting on a tarmac pad, a golden dog lying in front of it and smiling eagerly at the photographer.

'She's a beauty, isn't she?' came a voice from behind her, and Petra spun around to see a man close to her in age sauntering in. This room seemed to be attached to the one next door, joined by an arch cut through the wall, making his entrance silent. He was tall and lightly muscular, already sporting a slight tan. His sandy hair was cut short and had indentations from sunglasses, which were now folded up and dangling from his shirtfront.

'Your wife?' Petra ventured, gesturing to the woman in the middle picture.

'Of course, but I meant the car,' he replied with a conspiratorial grin. 'Citroën 2CV built right here in Koper, at the Tomos factory. My little Spaček.'

'It is a very lovely car,' Petra lied. She had little interest in cars, the highly unsexy Skoda her father had helped her buy was testament to that. If it worked, had enough room for her to take her friends' dogs on walks, and wasn't an obnoxious colour, then she was perfectly happy. She had never quite understood the national fascination with the classic Citroëns, even if they were built locally. Until very recently, owning a Spaček had been a trademark of the elderly, not a status symbol.

'Took me over two years to re-build her, but she's on the road now,' he told her, proudly. 'You must be *Inšpektorica* Vidmar, I'm *Inšpektor* Denis Božič.' He held out a hand for her to shake, and Petra's attention was taken as his large metallic watch caught the light. She spotted the oversized numbers around the bevel, and identified it as a diving watch. 'Do you dive, *Inšpektor*?'

'Please, call me Denis. Yes, mostly off the coast of Izola. There's a whole submerged Roman harbour out there, it's amazing. I'll take you, if you're a fellow frogman? Or woman, I suppose,' he added with a laugh.

'I'm not, I'm afraid,' she replied, wary of his overt friendliness. 'Thank you, though.'

'Don't mention it. If the mood takes you while you're down here, just let me know.' He settled himself behind his desk and took his sunglasses out, polishing them with a bright red bar towel he pulled out of the top drawer of his desk. 'So, are you here for Ivan's things?'

'Sorry?'

'I thought you'd drop in yesterday to have a snoop around Ivan's desk, so I wasn't sure if you're here bright and early to try and get to it before anyone else arrived.' A slow smile unfurled across his face, and he winked. 'Better luck next time.'

Petra looked in slight dismay at the clutter on the other desk in the room, realising that she would indeed have to go through it at some point soon. She doubted anyone had let Koren near it, and he would have had a hard time sneaking in here in his uniform without attracting attention once the inspector was dead.

'No, *Inšpektor* Božič, I was actually hoping to speak with you.'

If it bothered the other inspector that she'd ignored his request to use his first name, he didn't show it. Instead, he shrugged and kicked back in his office chair, crossing his legs. 'Sure, what do you want to know?'

'I'm interested in the arrest of Marjan Furlan,' she began, trailing off to allow him to fill in the gaps. With criminals, she'd found they sometimes incriminated themselves in the space she left, gabbling their innocence while letting slip their guilt in an unrehearsed slew.

Unfortunately, Božič didn't bite. He raised one brow slowly and dramatically, as if to invite her to continue.

'I saw that you're recorded as the arresting officer?' she finished.

'That's correct.'

'And that his crime was smashing the windows at Tartinijeva Ulica 21, in Piran? The house previously belonging to his mother, now shared with *Inšpektor* Furlan?'

'Now shared with the widowed *Gospa* Furlan, I imagine,' Božič replied, failing to answer the question.

'Of course, with his widow,' Petra corrected herself, a shot of irritation coursing through her when she saw how it made Božič smirk. This was it, she supposed. She'd finally encountered a Koper policeman who wanted to make her life difficult. She had been waiting long enough. She decided to change tack, and sat down carefully on the scratchy grey sofa pressed up against the wall behind her, facing Božič.

'*Inšpektor* Božič,' she began, 'I don't want to make this difficult, I am just trying to marshal the facts. I spent most of yesterday afternoon with *Policist* Koren, who gave me the picture of Marjan Furlan as an innocent victim of police misconduct, but failed to tell me about the vandalism. I would appreciate your take.'

She saw immediately that suggesting she'd respect his opinion had the desired effect. He shifted forwards again, elbows propped on his pristine desk and hands clasped together. '*Inšpektorica*, Marjan Furlan is a dog, plain and simple. We all saw him threatening Ivan right there,' he pointed elaborately out the window, indicating the crop of cypress trees that shaded half the station, 'on the Monday before he was murdered, and then days later he smashed up the place in Piran. Ivan refused to see it, but his brother was a lost cause. He can't even come up with an alibi for the murder, and what he does come up with is basically admitting to another crime.' He shrugged, dropping his hands into a pleading position. 'That's all there is to it.'

'I understand. If I could ask one more thing?'

'Of course,' he replied, although she could tell she'd lost his attention. He needlessly reached out to straighten his trio of photographs, wiping his fingerprints off the metal frames carefully with the same bar towel as he'd used on his glasses.

'Why did you wait to arrest Marjan regarding the vandalism in Piran?'

Božič barked out a laugh, the harsh sound making Petra blink. 'Because Ivan asked us not to, said he'd deal with it in the family. I wish we'd ignored him now, obviously. He smashed the place up on Wednesday night. If we'd taken him in immediately then Ivan wouldn't be dead.'

Petra rose to her feet, approaching Božič's desk to shake his hand. He shot up himself, grasping her hand firmly. 'Thank you, *Inšpektor*. This has been very helpful.'

'Don't worry about it,' he said with another grin, his playful mood returning as quickly as it had evaporated. 'And don't let Koren get in your head. Aleš is a good man, honest to a fault, but he's got this one wrong. I went to school with his brother, and I remember him as a kid. He was always getting upset over some injustice or other, normally the inconsistency of chocolate milk serving sizes. Trivial stuff, but it got to him. It used to send his brother crazy, trying to reason with him. Aleš thought Ivan was perfect, so Marjan has to be the lost soul waiting for a second chance that Ivan always described. It isn't true, *Inšpektorica*.'

She smiled noncommittally and walked to the door, heading back out in the direction of the front desk and Medved. At the last second, she turned and was surprised to see Božič staring at her retreating back, looking mildly distressed. He quickly wiped any sign of discomfort from his face, and smiled easily at her.

'Could I speak with Marjan Furlan?' she asked plainly.

Božič squared his shoulders, sitting up straighter. He obviously viewed it as a slight to his skills as a policeman that she'd want to reinterview the suspect, despite the fact that any interviews pertaining to his brother's death must have been carried out while he was ostensibly under arrest for something else. Let him be offended, Petra didn't have time to care.

'If you really want to, I suppose you can.'

'Considering I'm investigating this case, I'd like to do some of the most important interviews myself. Re-do them, if necessary. I'm sure you understand.'

Božič looked like he very much understood, but was also very unhappy about the turn of events. She watched as he vacillated, apparently unused to being put on the spot. 'Yes, fine. Today?'

'Ideally.'

'Speak to Medved, say I've okayed it.'

'Brilliant, thank you,' she beamed at him, turned on her heel, and left the room. She had the unshakable feeling she'd won that interaction, but wasn't able to pin down exactly what she'd won.

# Chapter 9

When Petra got back to the entrance hall, she found Koren waiting for her. He was standing awkwardly a few paces from Medved's desk, which was empty.

'Koren, good morning,' she greeted him. 'I hope you haven't been waiting long?'

'No, no,' he hastily replied, 'Eva asked me to watch the desk while she grabs a coffee.'

Assuming Eva was Medved's first name, Petra nodded in understanding. 'Perfect, I need to speak with her. *Inšpektor* Božič has agreed that I can meet with Marjan today.' As soon as she finished speaking she kicked herself for buying into the delusion that she'd need Božič's permission to speak with the prime suspect in her own investigation. She was demonstrating professional courtesy, not begging a favour.

'You spoke with Božič?' Koren asked, sounding a little put-out. 'Will he be joining us for the interview?'

'No, I doubt that'll be necessary.'

Koren looked relieved but said nothing, instead shuffling from foot to foot as he looked down at the contents of Medved's desk. She had an assortment of scribbled notes laid out in front of her monitor, apparently left by other officers who had tasks for her. As Koren moved his hand, Petra noticed that they were in a mixture of Slovene and Italian. She was about to ask Koren about his own linguistic abilities when Medved returned, steaming cup of coffee in hand, jolting Petra out of her reverie.

They agreed that she'd meet with Marjan shortly before lunch, then Petra led Koren back out of the station. It was starting to warm up already despite the early hour, although the concrete under their feet was still patchy with damp in the areas shrouded in shade. In the tree above Petra's car, a small bird shrieked angrily, although who its ire was aimed at Petra couldn't say. She looked down at her watch, then up at Koren.

'How early does *Gospa* Furlan tend to be available?' she hedged, watching as the first few customers started to make their way into the post office next door. A stream of cars was already queuing to enter the nearest shopping centre, music blasting from its car park entrance.

'Oh, shall I text her?' Koren asked eagerly, pulling his phone out of his front pocket.

'On a personal phone?' Petra tried to keep the horror out of her voice. She remembered it being drummed into them at the academy that the most crucial distinction a police officer needed to draw was between work and real life, that they would be taking unnecessary and unprofessional risks if they let the two mix. She remembered Božič's assessment of Koren's character being based on time spent on the elementary school playground, and of the local prejudices that had informed Marjan's arrest, and dreaded to think what other muddling of business and private lives had influenced the case so far.

'Gospa Furlan has been very kind to me,' Koren replied, coming out fighting. Petra was interested to see the fire in him, having largely seen the moping, wronged Koren the previous day. 'And she and my mother are friends, I've been to barbecues at their house every summer since I can remember. I really don't think it would be appropriate for me to show up without warning her.'

Petra chose to ignore yet another reference to personal relationships, and resolved to start making a list of all the things she'd had to swallow during her time here. 'Of course, Koren. Please ask her when would be appropriate.'

Koren started tapping away at his phone, large thumbs seemingly making no difference to the speed at which he could type. Petra pursed her lips, formulating her next plan. She had half decided that she wanted to go to the house in Piran to try and get some context before her meeting with Marjan, when a movement from the police station changed her mind. She and Koren were standing slightly out of the way of the front doors, on the opposite side of the shallow stairs to the police cars. Suddenly, the doors flew open, startling the angry bird from its tree. She watched as *Inšpektor* Božič blew down the steps and across the car park, marching purposefully down the street and away towards the centre of town. If he noticed them he did not show it, seemingly too distracted by his purpose. Koren had also spotted him, his right thumb arched up in mid-flow. He looked askance at Petra, but she had already turned back to the building and started up the first step.

'*Inšpektorica?*' he called to her, unsure of whether to follow.

'Have you had the chance to look at *Inšpektor* Furlan's things yet, Koren?' she asked, turning around to face him. From a step up she was much closer to him in height, not having to peer above her to meet his eyes for once. She rather liked it.

'No, that's a job for another inspector. It would be rude,' he sputtered. He used the male form of inspector, which made Petra grin as she spun back around. Yes, it was a job for another inspector, and she planned to get started immediately.

'Text *Gospa* Furlan, then meet me inside.'

As she went back through the entrance hall, it seemed Božič's rushed exit had been of less interest to those within. Two middle-aged women wearing lanyards identifying them as civilian staff stood chatting at the corner of Medved's desk, neither of whom seemed to care about either his leaving or Petra's arriving. Medved herself was concentrating on something on her screen, shooting the women the occasional dirty look. Petra hustled past her with an unnoticed wave, returning to the office she'd been in earlier.

The door was still propped open, and she could see no discernible change in either desk, save that Božič hadn't bothered to tuck his office chair in. It sat facing the window, adrift from the desk. She ignored it and headed straight for Furlan's chaotic workstation. As she appraised it from above, she reminded herself that she had every reason to be poking through the deceased's papers, even if she did agree with Koren's assessment of rudeness. Having never met the man, it seemed impertinent to go through his belongings. That being said, perhaps it was better it was her than someone who knew him. She had no idea what she might find.

The multi-layered in-tray was full of paperwork regarding various arrests, along with reports from other officers. She noticed that a lot of what she found had nothing to do with his billed brief of homicide and sexual offences, and wondered how many hats the inspectors here ended up wearing. One of his desk drawers was empty, the second filled with stationery purloined from the stationery cupboard, identical to what Petra herself had stocked up on from the cupboard in Ljubljana the day before. The third contained a half-eaten packet of *Napolitanke* biscuits, a dented metal coffee tin filled with euros issued by various countries, and a Slovene to Italian dictionary. She flicked through the pages, disturbing three small notes. On impulse, she snapped photographs of them where she found them before even looking at them properly. All were in Italian, and so she fished an evidence bag from her stash and stowed them away, to be looked at later. As she closed the drawer she looked sadly at the biscuits, a symbol of Ivan's life being snatched too soon. Petra tried not to make eye contact with the cluster of faces smiling out from the dozen photographs crowding his desk, both framed and simply tacked to his monitor. She made a mental note to chase Mlakar on the sons' interviews, and stood up straight, her back aching from the crouched position she'd been in.

As she straightened, she caught sight of a woman leaning against the archway that Božič had surprised her through earlier. She was petite, long dark hair knotted up elaborately behind her head, and wore a faintly bored expression as she assessed Petra.

'Hello?' Petra offered, turning to face her properly.

'*Ciao*,' the woman returned, maintaining her lounging position. The informal *čao* had entered the lexicon of coastal Slovenians years ago, and had now also become fashionable in Ljubljana, but the way the woman took her time drawling it sounded definitively Italian, not like the staccato Slovenian pronunciation.

'Can I help you?'

'*No*,' she replied with a lazy smile, confirming Petra's suspicions. She spoke slowly and languidly, seemingly confident that anyone she was conversing with would wait to hear what she had to say. It suited Italian, Petra thought. You'd struggle to affect the same insouciance when speaking Slovene. '*È l'ispettrice di Lubiana?*'

That was easy enough to guess, thankfully. 'Yes, I'm *Inšpektorica* Petra Vidmar of Ljubljana Police. I don't speak Italian, do you speak Slovene?' She refused to play this silly game and was pleased that her bluntness seemed to surprise the other woman. Something petty at the back of her brain tempted her to switch into English just to prove that she wasn't some linguistic dunce, but she decided against it.

'Of course,' the woman said, one eyebrow raised. 'If I must. I am *Inšpektorica* Giulia Rossi.' Somehow she managed to make her job title sound beneath her, spat out as though it was an ugly word. Petra had to admit it sounded strange next to her name, the Slavic sound jarring against the Italian.

'It is good to meet you, *Inšpektorica* Rossi.' Petra strode across the room to shake the woman's hand and was surprised at how gentle her grip was. Petra had expected a bone-crusher despite the woman's stature, several inches shorter than Petra herself.

'And you,' Rossi replied, unashamedly giving Petra a once-over. Whether she found her unimpressive Petra was not sure, as Rossi merely gave another unhurried smile that did not reach her eyes. 'You are here to see Ivan's things?'

'Yes.'

'While Božič is away?' she seemed to enjoy this fact, fixing Petra with a look that told her that Rossi knew exactly what she was up to. Petra wondered if Rossi had deliberately used Furlan's first name but Božič's second, perhaps offering an insight into what she thought of them.

'I didn't want to be interrupted,' she replied pointedly, not enjoying the knowing, scrutinising look the other woman was still giving her.

'Of course, I understand. I won't bother you any longer, I just wanted to introduce myself. I was interested to meet you.'

This brought Petra up short. She cocked her head slightly, going back over her conversation with Rossi so far. She had hardly started their meeting in a way that suggested she had been seeking it out. Petra had rather assumed Rossi wanted her to feel caught out, judged, not welcomed. 'Really?'

'Yes,' she said simply. 'I am the only female inspector in Capodistria, I was glad to hear we'd be getting another. Even if only briefly.'

'Oh,' Petra replied, still taken aback. She clocked the usage of the Italian name for Koper, even in the midst of spoken Slovene. 'Thank you, I suppose.'

'It isn't a compliment. I wanted to ask if you'd like an aperitivo tonight, or dinner. To swap war stories,' she sounded completely unbothered about Petra's reply, her tone suggesting she was mere seconds from checking her nails in boredom.

Petra tried to decide whether saying yes would be unprofessional, if saying no would be worse. She was finding Rossi very hard to read and wasn't sure if she wanted to spend more time in her company than necessary. However, she'd be interested to hear what war stories Rossi had to share. It never hurt to have contacts.

'That would be lovely, thank you.'

'Of course,' Rossi nodded. 'I'll meet you here at five p.m.' It wasn't a question, and Rossi didn't bother waiting for an answer, just turned on her heel and returned to the adjoining office. She sat down behind the desk furthest from where Petra was standing, and didn't look up again, the audience over. Petra busied herself with returning to Furlan's desk and doing one final check, sifting through every pile once more while she waited for Koren to appear. When he eventually did, hurriedly explaining that he'd been waylaid by some of the civilian staff needing his assistance in removing a particularly large scorpion, she hustled him out of the room, eager to make her escape before Božič returned.

# Chapter 10

'Have you worked much with *Inšpektorica* Rossi?' Petra asked Koren, looking across at him from the passenger seat. Koren was driving them to *Gospa* Furlan's house in one of the police cars, his hands carefully placed on the steering wheel in the textbook driving position. Petra thought this was probably for her benefit.

'Rossi? No, barely at all. She's on the drug task-force, so she spends a lot of time with the border force and over in Italy with the *Guardia di Finanza*. You know, their financial police. Around here they're more like smuggling and drug police, that seems to be all they do.'

'That's interesting,' said Petra, turning to gaze out the window. They had breezed through various roundabouts she hadn't encountered before as they left the station and had just crossed a wide concrete bridge across the canal, heading uphill into a residential area. The houses and flats were staggered up the hill, all seeming to peer down on the road below. Petra didn't enjoy the idea of the potentially dozens of eyes watching their progress, guessing at their purpose. 'She tried to speak to me in Italian.'

'She tries to speak to everyone in Italian, it's like she forgets that it's the minority language. She gets away with it down here as so many of us can speak it too.'

Petra considered this, looking out at the pedestrians struggling up the steep footpath next to her. She was familiar with the minority communities, as her mother's family in north-eastern Slovenia came from the area where there was a significant Hungarian population. They generally spoke the minority language as their mother tongue, attending schools that taught in that language and treated Slovene as foreign. Government business could be carried out in the minority language in these areas, and many Slovenes who lived there could converse in it. She remembered the first time she'd heard her grandmother give directions in Hungarian, baffled at how unintelligible it was to her. Koren changed down a gear, and they surged forward.

'She's asked me to drinks,' Petra remarked.

'Really? You should go. Her husband runs a wine bar in Izola, I bet she'll take you there. They specialise in this orange wine, made of the fermented white grape skins. It's an acquired taste, but I bet you'll like it.'

Petra chuckled. 'What makes you think that?'

'You seem sophisticated,' he said simply, as though it was obvious. Petra wriggled slightly in her seat, pleased that this was the impression she gave off. It wasn't often someone was so open about their first impressions of you, and to have it be 'sophistication' made her happier than she could have predicted. She'd have to remember never to tell Koren about her favourite dinner, when she couldn't even be bothered to defrost something: supermarket own brand breaded cheese, shoved straight into her toasted sandwich maker. A meal best eaten standing huddled over the sink with a large glass of water, in case she'd messed up the timings and superheated it.

Koren turned right down a side street and pulled to the side of the road before turning the engine off. The houses on both sides were skinny and multi-levelled, built into the hill to maximise space. Their driveways faced downwards, and slightly below them Petra could see a teenaged boy fixing his bike outside one of the garages. From where they'd parked the front doors of the houses on the right were at street level, as were the garages and basements of those on the left. The houses were painted in various bright colours, some red with white-stencilled windows, others a bright green that reminded Petra of her childhood highlighter pens. Koren led her towards a comparatively sedate pale-yellow house, beautifully maintained, with a pale brown door and large windows covered from the inside with delicate lace curtains, the shutters pinned out against the exterior wall. Next to the doorbell was a small sign reading 'Furlan'.

Koren braced himself before knocking, straightening up and forcing his shoulders back. It was amazing how much he curled in on himself, Petra thought. She thought about Božič's claim that he found injustice everywhere he looked, and thought about how much that might weigh him down. Her mother had told her long ago that she'd age herself prematurely if she got too upset about the great unfairness of the

world, and Petra had tried to follow her advice to let all but the
most important things pass her by, although it was far easier
said than done. She wondered if Koren had learned that trick,
or if years of caring too much had left him a little burned out
and jaded by the time *Inšpektor* Furlan's death hit him.

The door swung open, revealing a small entrance hall on
the corner of a flight of stairs. A narrow unit was pressed
against the wall opposite the door, on which a selection of
slippers was resting. At first Petra struggled to see who had
opened the door, her eyes used to the brightness outside and
surprised by the dim interior. After a second, she noticed the
thin woman standing on the stairs to the left of the door,
blinking out at them.

'Irena, good morning,' said Koren, his voice tight. The
woman pounced immediately, bundling him into a tight hug.
Petra could see that she had neat blonde hair cut into a bob,
and perfectly lacquered fingernails, which matched the knee-
length green dress she was wearing. A pair of glasses perched
on the end of her nose, almost slipping off as she grasped
Koren.

'Hello, Aleš,' she said as she hugged him, her voice clear
and measured, slightly at odds with her behaviour. Petra was
left wondering whether the hug had been for Irena's benefit,
or Koren's. She released him with one last pat on the arm,
and reached out to shake Petra's hand. Petra introduced herself, then followed Irena into the house as she beckoned them
inside.

Once in the hallway, Koren immediately took his shoes

off, putting on instead a huge pair of black leather slippers. Petra followed suit, glad for the umpteenth time in her life that she took a common size of shoe. As a child she had always pitied her large-footed friends when they'd been forced into too-small slippers at a friend's house. Koren seemed confident of which slippers to take, which Petra took to mean he hadn't been joking about how often he'd visited this house before. He was obviously comfortable here.

Irena Furlan led them up the small flight of stairs she'd previously been standing on and into a rectangular sitting room, two large sets of French windows bathing it in a warm light. A pair of tan leather sofas faced each other, a squat wooden table between them. The table held a round white plate of *Napolitanke* biscuits, a painted pattern of vines and flowers peeked out from under the stack of wafers. She had also laid out three matching cups and saucers. As they entered the room, she gestured to Petra and Koren to take the sofa further from the door.

'Please, take a seat. What can I get you to drink? Tea? Coffee?'

'Coffee would be wonderful,' Petra replied, sitting down carefully.

Koren remained standing, and collected the cups from where they sat. 'Please, Irena. I'll make drinks, you speak to the inspector.'

Irena nodded tiredly, absent-mindedly tucking a bit of her carefully coiffed hair behind her ear. She sat gingerly opposite Petra, smoothing her skirt under her and watching as

Koren disappeared through a connecting door into what Petra assumed was the kitchen.

'Thank you for seeing us so quickly, *gospa*. I am very sorry for your loss.'

Irena fluttered a hand at Petra, then let it drop like a stone back into her lap. 'Please, call me Irena. Of course you're welcome here, Aleš said you want to help.'

'Then you must call me Petra. Yes, I hope so. If you're happy to get started straight away?'

Irena nodded, leaning forward to pick up a wafer biscuit and placing it on one of the empty saucers. She then settled the saucer in front of her on the table and left it there, untouched.

'I apologise that you've probably answered all this before,' Petra began, but was stopped with another wave.

'You're the first to interview me, Petra. The others didn't want to cause me any pain, I think. They just want it all over with, so I can bury Ivan and they can move on. Aleš asked me a few questions when he and Denis came to tell me what had happened, but that is the extent of it. They both seemed as horrified as I felt, so I doubt any of us was making much sense. Please, ask what you will.'

Petra was brought up short at this. She gathered herself, waiting for the sound of Koren clattering around to subside a little before she started again. 'Of course, and I am sorry to be the one to cause you distress now. I'll start with the most obvious question. Can you think of anyone who might want to harm your husband?'

Irena paused, her gaze drifting from Petra up to a large

landscape oil painting hanging on the wall above her. 'I assume Aleš has told you about my brother-in-law.'

'Yes, both *Policist* Koren and *Inšpektor* Božič have shared their views on Marjan with me. I am interested to hear your thoughts.'

'I imagine they're rather different views,' she gave a short, humourless laugh. 'My husband told me that his brother wasn't a threat to anyone, and initially I was inclined to agree. I liked him when we were young, he was an excellent uncle to my sons. Then he went to a work event at one of the casinos, and he got hooked. It was like he became a different person. His wife left him, she had to. She took the children with her. But they'd already lost the house, the children knew what their father had become. He was so angry all the time. Ivan was adamant we could get the old Marjan back, and I wanted to believe him, but I was never convinced.'

'Is his ex-wife still in Koper?' Petra asked, scribbling in her notebook.

'No, she moved back to her family in Maribor. I can give you her contact details if you'd like them, we're still in touch. Marjan used to come and shout outside the window some-times, begging me to phone her for him. She has his number blocked.'

'I don't think that's necessary at the moment, thank you. Did you ever think Marjan might actually hurt your husband? Koren mentioned that he was under the impression it was all bluster.'

'I don't know. He used to make all sorts of threats, but he

never actually did anything. We'd grown numb to them, or at least Ivan had.'

'What did Ivan make of the vandalism in Piran?'

'What?' she looked back at Petra suddenly, a piece of fringe falling over her eyes with the movement.

'Tartinijeva Ulica 21, neighbours witnessed Marjan smashing the windows a few days before your husband was murdered. That's what he was arrested for.'

'Oh,' she said mildly, looking down at her superfluous wafer. 'I didn't know. That house hadn't crossed my mind at all.'

'You don't go often?'

'I don't go at all. It is old and dusty and full of my mother-in-law's things, as though she's just out at the shops. She's been dead for almost a decade.'

Petra knew this phenomenon too well, having as a child visited the family farm in Prekmurje where her great-grandfather had built a second farmhouse for his son, her grandfather. This house had become the main house, and when her great-grandparents had died the family had just shut the door on the older building, instead using it for storage, piles of discarded things fitted in around all her great-grandparents' belongings. She'd hated going in every summer to retrieve her bicycle, afraid of the clouds of dust and huge spiders that lurked among her great-grandmother's jackets, still hanging on the coat hooks by the door. It was not uncommon to end up with such a property in a country where wills were scarce and there was no inheritance tax. She should have guessed the house in Piran would be another example.

'The property was important to your husband?' Petra left the question open-ended, interested in a perspective other than Koren's.

'I suppose. He didn't want it being sold off to some Russian to rip all the walls out and fill with tasteless furniture.'

'Which upset Marjan?' As she spoke Koren re-entered the room, holding a cup of coffee in each hand. They were both quite full, but he seemed unperturbed. Petra remembered his ease of movement at his mother's *slaščičarna* and thanked him quietly as he placed a cup on her saucer and the other on Irena's, before scuttling back to the kitchen to fetch his own.

'He'd have sold it for anything. He looked at that house and saw euro signs, he didn't care where they came from.'

Irena had confirmed everything Koren had told her, which was both useful and very much not. There was nothing new to work from in her account, other than that the investigation had been truly shoddy in leaving her out of it. Once Irena had finished speaking, Koren beamed warmly at her, apparently trying to reassure her. Petra nodded at the woman and gave her a small smile of her own before moving on.

'Other than Marjan, you can't think of anyone who might want to harm Ivan?'

Irena twisted her mouth as she thought, still sitting ramrod straight. She seemed very in control, a force to be reckoned with. Petra thought she was holding herself together very well, and found herself hoping that if she was ever in a similar situation she would weather it like Irena Furlan.

'Not a soul. But then, I don't even know where he was

immediately before he was killed. I have no idea why he was on the coastal path at that time,' she admitted eventually. 'He's been heading off to do chores and taking far longer than he should have done. Who can say what else I don't know.'

Koren's face fell suddenly, his brow furrowing. Petra shot him a look to get him to keep quiet, noticing how Irena had shifted awkwardly when she saw his reaction.

'What do you mean?'

'It is probably nothing. I shouldn't have mentioned it.'

'My next question was going to be about why he might have been there,' Petra offered. 'I'd like to hear anything you have to say.'

'Last Thursday,' she said eventually, clutching at her own elbows with her arms crossed. 'The week before Ivan died. I invited a friend to have supper with us unexpectedly. I didn't have enough lettuce, so Ivan said he'd pop out and get some. He came back almost two hours later, with a lettuce from the shop just down the hill. It's a five-minute walk. I didn't really notice at first, as I was showering and getting the house ready for her and laying out the rest of the meal. He ended up only beating her here by a few minutes, I had started to worry something had happened.'

'And this wasn't the first time he'd done this recently?'

'No, it wasn't,' she said sadly. She took a slow sip of her coffee, although she didn't seem to register anything about it, just swallowing listlessly.

'You think his walk along the coast might have been one of these trips?'

'Who knows? They weren't regular, it seemed random. I was trying not to think much of it. But if he was meeting someone, maybe they'd want to hurt him. I don't know.' Irena trailed off, obviously holding back tears. Her strong façade had been cracked by her admission, and she seemed to be struggling to hold it together.

Petra looked away for decency's sake, turning her attention to Koren. He looked stricken, and was doing a bad job of hiding it. Petra nudged him with her knee, and he managed to school his features slightly. Irena was still staring down at her rapidly cooling coffee and untouched wafer, nose and lips moving slightly as she tried to stop herself from crying. Petra rose to her feet.

'Thank you very much, Irena. I am so sorry to have upset you.'

'It isn't your fault,' she replied, her voice quiet. 'I feel so traitorous even saying it, but how can I not mention it in the circumstances? If whatever he was doing killed him, you need to know.'

'You have done the right thing,' Petra reassured her, aware that Koren was looming behind her. 'Can we get you anything? We can show ourselves out.'

'No, no. I'll be fine. Thank you.'

They left the house in single file, walking back up the slight incline to the car in silence. Koren was nibbling the inside of his lips, lost in thought. As they drove back to the station, Petra tried to think of how she might go about seeing what Ivan Furlan had been up to when he hadn't been at home.

'Did anyone get the inspector's bank records? Phone history?' she asked suddenly, as Koren slowed towards a red light.

'Yes, Božič did. To check whether Marjan was telling the truth about the inspector paying for his first rehabilitation appointment in Ljubljana. I put a copy in the case notes I gave you,' he added. Petra felt guilty at the reference to the notes, which she still hadn't gone through in detail. She had been so taken by the detail of Marjan's vandalism that she hadn't gone back to look at the rest. She vowed to go through them carefully after her interview with Marjan later, and before she met with Rossi.

'And?'

'Nothing strange. He'd paid for the appointment as Marjan said, and he took a few hundred euro out in cash the afternoon of the row at the station, presumably the placatory offering he told me about.'

She was far from shocked that there was nothing notable. If he was going to do anything dubious, Petra would put money on Ivan Furlan doing it with cash, and she'd never even met the man. Anyone would do the same. She blew air out through her mouth grumpily and stared out the windscreen, starting to recognise the route back to the station. She would speak to Marjan, then regroup.

# Chapter 11

Medved was glaring at her screen when they arrived back at her desk, typing angrily with two fingers in a technique Petra had never seen used by anyone under the age of sixty-five. She was jolted out of her rage by Koren coughing quietly, her head jerking up at the sound. She smiled broadly when she saw who it was, relaxing back in her chair.

'Time to meet the devil, *Inšpektorica*?' she asked, apparently impervious to the pained look Koren shot her. Petra stifled a laugh, instead nodding sharply.

Medved rose to her feet, gesturing to them to follow her, and led them down a corridor parallel to the one leading to Božič's office. At the end was a small set of cells manned by a broad-set young man slurping busily from what looked to be a protein shake.

'Matteo, this is *Inšpektorica* Petra Vidmar, from Ljubljana,' Medved announced, folding her arms across her chest as she spoke. The man nodded, apparently both unsurprised and uninterested in this information, taking another long draw from his enormous bottle. '*Inšpektorica*, this is *Policist* Matteo Crevatini. I'll leave you in his capable hands.'

She turned on her heel, giving Petra another wicked smile before heading back the way she had come. Petra looked expectantly at Crevatini, whose capable hands remained occupied with his frothy concoction. From next to her, she could feel the irritation radiating off Koren.

'We're here to speak to Marjan Furlan, Matteo. If it isn't too much trouble.'

Again, Petra enjoyed the spark Koren displayed, and was pleased she hadn't had to chivvy the bulky officer into action herself. It seemed beneath her. She also hated letting younger or lazier officers think they'd managed to get a rise out of her, whether that had been their intention or not. She mentally scolded herself for leaping to conclusions about Crevatini, aware that others did the same to her.

'You know where he is,' said Crevatini with a lazy shrug. 'He can hear you from here. Speak up, Furlan.' So, her conclusions had been entirely correct.

'He's right,' came a solitary voice from one of the cells. 'Is that you, Aleš?'

'Yes, Marjan. Good morning.' Koren started to move down the corridor, stopping in front of the final cell. Inside, Petra could see a thin form hunched over on the built-in cot. She knew how old Marjan was, having seen it among Koren's notes, but he looked far older. Huge purpling bags under his eyes dominated his face, seemingly only interrupted by sharp cheekbones. His chin was stubbly, raw red patches showing through the hair demonstrating that it itched. His hair was greying and his hairline receding, seemingly trying to escape the misery so clearly etched in the man's features. Petra thought back to the photos she'd glimpsed on Ivan Furlan's desk, particularly one of him standing with his wife in front of the tourist-magnet red metal heart positioned facing out on Lake Bled. She could see the fraternal resemblance, but if their faces were anything to go by then Ivan's life had been less trying, and far less haunting.

'*Gospod* Furlan,' she began, holding her hand out through the bars so he could shake it. Marjan himself looked confused by this action, and from behind her she finally heard movement from Crevatini as his chair scraped back on the floor.

'I wouldn't do that, *gospa*,' he said hurriedly. 'He's a criminal.'

'*Inšpektorica*,' Koren corrected him before Petra could say anything. 'And he's been arrested, not convicted, Matteo.'

'He's been convicted before,' replied Crevatini, although Petra could hear how little he cared about fighting this point. He was already returning to his seat.

As the men bickered, Marjan stood up and shuffled over to the bars, grasping Petra's hand and shaking it warily. '*Inšpektorica*,' he echoed Koren, nodding at her politely. 'Aleš told me you'd be coming. All the way from Ljubljana? My brother would be proud.'

'That his case is of interest?' she asked.

'That someone in this station was willing to put themselves on the line to prevent an injustice,' Marjan said solemnly. 'He would be very unhappy that it had come to this, though.'

Crevatini snorted behind them, finally pushing Petra over the edge. 'I'd like a moment alone with *Gospod* Furlan, *Policist*,'

Petra informed him, thrilled at the conviction in her tone. 'If you could wait at the end of the corridor?'

Petra was mildly disappointed at the lack of macho posturing this request received. Crevatini stood up, again without a word, grabbing his phone out of a desk drawer and loping off down the corridor and out through the door they had come through earlier. She sent a silent apology to Medved, now the unwilling recipient of his oafish presence.

As they watched him go, Marjan gave her a wry smile. 'He isn't that bad, *Policist* Crevatini. He just sits on his phone all day. One of the other officers they station here sometimes never stops singing.'

Petra laughed, settling down into one of the chairs opposite his cell. Marjan returned to his cot, resting his hands on his knees and waiting patiently. Petra noticed how his eyes darted around the room, never fixing on anything. It made her uneasy, the inability to make sustained eye contact with him. She felt Koren shoot her an anxious look, and remembered how important this interview must be to him. He had staked a lot on Marjan's innocence, whether he had written the plea to Ljubljana or not. She gave him a reassuring smile, before consciously putting on her game face. She punctuated the shift in tone by grabbing her notepad out of her bag, having deliberately left it right on the top earlier that morning. Her father, always one for organising everything to the tiniest degree, would have been proud.

'*Gospod* Furlan, I'm here to talk to you about the house in Piran that you shared with your brother.'

She could see immediately that this surprised him, and was glad of it. That had been part of the point. She also noticed the look of confusion that he gave Koren, which she was less pleased about. She respected Koren for his doggedness over proper procedure and dedication to exhausting all avenues of investigation, but remained troubled that he had apparently deliberately teamed up with a very likely suspect in the murder of a fellow officer.

'What about it?' his tone was less warm than it had been earlier, any trace of humour gone.

'You were seen vandalising it, which is why you were arrested.'

'I smashed the living room window while drunk,' he admitted. 'I was angry.'

'About what?'

Marjan seemed to shrivel in on himself a little, his shoulders caving in almost imperceptibly. Petra refused to feel sorry for him, although the instinct arose.

'Everything,' he replied.

'Could you not be more specific?'

'I thought you were here to investigate Ivan's murder?' Marjan's head shot up, his eyes still darting around. 'Why do you care so much about Piran?'

Petra did not deign to answer, instead neatly crossing one of her legs over the other. She had worn her tailored black trousers today along with her shiniest black flat shoes, the ones with the bright lining that no one other than she herself knew about. She enjoyed how professional they made her feel, in control. She hoped the effect was felt by Marjan. She sat in silence, pinning him with her gaze.

'I was angry that he wasn't respecting our agreement,' Marjan said eventually, dropping his chin back to his chest.

'"He" being Ivan?'

Marjan nodded. 'We'd agreed we wouldn't even go inside the house until the latest legal case was sorted, but he'd been there anyway. He'd left things lying about. He wasn't hiding it. I suppose because he thought I wouldn't be going in, so I'd never see.'

'Forgive me, but I was told that Ivan paid you compensation in light of this? Following a dispute in the station car park?'

Marjan's eyes flashed in annoyance, his jaw tightening from where it lingered in the baggy neckline of his t-shirt, his posture still hunched. 'Yes, the first time. The second time, I smashed the window.'

Koren made a poor show of hiding his surprise, his head half whipping around to face Petra before he caught himself and continued staring blankly forwards. Petra's mind started whirring. There had been two separate disputes over the house in Piran recently, over the same issue? This was the first she'd heard of it, and seemingly Koren too. She wondered why it hadn't come up before, though the possibility that no one had cared enough about the details to ask was all too likely.

'You found that your brother had been back inside the house a second time?'

'Yes! I told you, Aleš,' said Marjan, suddenly desperate.

'That I'd found more papers. That he'd been at it again. When that smug moron arrested me, I told you.'

'You were drunk when *Inšpektor* Božič brought you in, Marjan,' Koren reminded him. 'And once you sobered up, I had to tell you that the inspector had been murdered. You weren't very coherent.' Koren's words were a little cruel, if fair. Petra watched as they stabbed at Marjan, and recognised Koren's attempt to defend his interviewing skills. She couldn't really blame him for misunderstanding, not if Marjan had been raving. She doubted Božič had even been listening.

'I told you,' Marjan rasped again, wringing his hands together. 'I just went in as I was in town and it started to rain, and I could see even more boxes. I left, I smashed the window, and I went straight to a bar.'

'And then?' Petra wrote down everything he said, both for future reference and in the continued hope that it made him anxious, made him say something he otherwise would have kept secret.

'When I ran out of cash I waited for the bus back to Koper, then I went home.'

'What about on Saturday night, when Ivan was murdered? Where were you then?'

Marjan's fiddling became worse, his thumbs folding madly over each other as he thought. 'I've already told Koren that. And Božič.'

'But not me,' she reminded him bluntly.

'I was at the casino, in Portorož. As I'm sure you've been told, I am technically banned, and so I spent the whole night on the only slot machine that isn't covered by CCTV. More fool me.'

'How did you get to Portorož?'

'I got the bus.'

'From Koper?'

'Yes, to Izola. You have to change there, there isn't a direct route.'

'And when were you in Izola?'

Marjan looked panicked, waving his hand at her. 'Lunchtime? Just before. Nowhere near when Ivan was murdered. They do a free lunch offer on a Thursday at the casino, so it is busy then. I try to get there when the rush goes in, so that I can slip past security. Lots of big-spending men and their glittery wives demanding concierge service, no one notices me come through.'

Petra nodded contemplatively. She doubted either bus service had cameras, but there was some hope that something might prove his presence in Izola at lunchtime. Not that his having an alibi twelve hours before his brother was murdered helped much. He could have gone anywhere, done anything, between lunchtime and the time Ivan was shot.

'I understand. When did you leave the casino?'

'Thirty-five minutes before closing time,' he said immediately, apparently having anticipated the question. 'The gaming machine salon closes at four a.m., so the staff start coming around half an hour before that to remind you. I don't want to be seen, so I have to leave a bit before that starts.'

That explained the remarkable specificity. Half past three

in the morning didn't sound like a good time to have been witnessed leaving the casino, even if Marjan hadn't been deliberately avoiding notice. If it was true, though, it put him safely in the clear for his brother's murder. She could feel Koren jiggling his legs beside her, apparently anxious. She was keeping her tone professional, her expression as neutral as the poker players she imagined haunted the sort of places where Marjan liked to spend his Saturday nights. Petra took Koren's nervousness to be a good thing: he was struggling to decipher what she thought about Marjan.

'And after you left the casino?'

'I walked back to Piran. You can get all the way there along the seafront if you go through the sailing club and cut across the plaza near the church at Bernadin.'

'You went to Tartinijeva Ulica 21?' she confirmed.

'Yes, but I didn't go inside. The neighbour doesn't like me, it was her who saw me smashing the window. There were lights on in her house, so I didn't risk it. I just looked at it from down the street, then went to the Albanian bakery just before they closed to buy a *burek* and watch the sun come up.'

'You don't think the neighbour would have seen you?'

'No, I didn't want her to,' he said.

His tone was self-pitying, and Petra continued her struggle not to sympathise with him. Although he was obviously far from being a model citizen, let alone a good brother, she could see why Koren believed his story. It was sad, bordering on pathetic: an addict slipping into a casino unseen and stumbling along a cold coastline late at night as he'd missed the last bus, eating day-old burek alone in one of Slovenia's most beautiful towns. She thought of the symmetry with his brother, who had marched along the same coastline just kilometres from Marjan hours earlier, before his life came to an undignified end. Or had they been on the same stretch of shore, at the same time? Had the brothers met, rowed, and only Marjan walked away from it? Was he lying to her face, along with Koren's and Božič's?

'What was your relationship like with Ivan at the time of his death?' she asked, turning a page in her notebook to start her new line of enquiry.

Marjan worried at his lip, hands now clamped under his thighs to stop them fidgeting. 'You mean before I realised he'd been going into the house? It was good. He's a better brother than I deserve, I know that. He understands that I want to stop, that I just can't do it alone.'

Petra noticed his continued use of the present tense in relation to Ivan, noted it down. It was very television crime procedural, but she had spotted in previous cases that those who had murdered someone or at least seen their death tended to switch straight into the past tense, having come to terms with it. Marjan didn't seem to have gotten that far.

'You want to stop gambling?' Koren interjected, prompting a stern look from Petra. He gave her an apologetic look, eyes widening slightly, and she let it pass.

'Yes, I do. My wife left me. She took my girls, went back to her mother in Maribor. That was years ago, but I'm only just coming to terms with it. I rent a one room apartment in

Markovec, I can see our old house if I squint out the window. I don't want to be like this, I just can't control it. Ivan was trying to help.'

'How so?' she asked, aware of what he was going to say, but interested in his take.

'He paid for me to go to therapy in Ljubljana. He said he'd pay for the first one, and if I went, we could discuss carrying on.'

'And you went?'

'Yes, I went. But then we had the argument here, at the station, and when he gave me the money to shut me up he said I should use it on the therapist, because he wasn't going to pay for another session after how I'd acted.'

'He said that to you, he didn't just imply it?' Petra had encountered addicts before who assumed everyone was against them, and although they hadn't been gamblers, she could see the same behaviour in Marjan as she had in any of the alcoholics who'd stumbled through the cells in Ljubljana. It was fascinating, in a morbid way. When they were addicted to substances it somehow made sense that there would be physical reactions, nervous ticks. She hadn't expected the same when it was an action, a hobby that they were addicted to. She made a mental note to text her brother when she got the chance, remind him not to take his newly acquired cryptocurrency trading too seriously.

'Maybe it was implied.'

Koren shuffled again next to her, his uneasiness starting to get on her nerves. He had apparently been unaware of this fact too, and she wondered uncharitably whether he had avoided difficult questions in order not to upset Marjan, or whether Marjan was simply becoming more lucid the more time he spent in the cells. She briefly considered the possibility that it was her own style and experience bringing out the pertinent information, and sat up a little straighter at the thought.

'Thank you. This has been very helpful.'

He shrugged, the downwards motion dragging him even lower in his stoop. Petra felt yet another pang of pity for the man, but refused to let it show. Instead, she rose promptly to her feet and headed back down the corridor, hearing Koren blunder after her.

'The cells are all yours, Crevatini. Thank you,' she said, indicating the door they'd come through.

'*Inšpektorica,*' he drawled in response, straightening up and collecting his now-empty bottle from the corner of Medved's desk. He displayed no disgruntlement at all that she'd ousted him from his post, which Petra appreciated. She was also pleased that he'd remembered her title this time, and smiled at him as he walked off down the corridor.

# Chapter 12

Although Petra had been intending to risk the canteen for lunch, confident that it would offer the same institutional staples of fried cheese and schnitzel that she had seen in every police station, hospital, hall of residence and municipal office in the country, she was quickly disabused by both Koren and Medved.

'The frying oil is always old, and I don't trust their lettuce,' Medved told her gravely, grabbing her handbag from under the desk. Petra recognised these as the greatest of sins in a country where fried food was a currency, and a well-dressed side salad practically a human right.

Instead, the three of them left the station and walked in the direction of *Slaščičarna Koren.* On arrival, Koren lead them straight past the counter and through the swing-door into the back, throwing a quick wave to his mother as she served customers at the busy counter. He opened the fridge immediately, revealing various commercial-sized tubs of dairy products. As he rummaged, the largest vat of chocolate spread that Petra had ever seen wobbled precariously on a shelf above.

He stretched to the back of the fridge, dragging out a large plastic box filled with various items wrapped in old newspaper.

'*Pršut*, butchered and cured by a family friend,' he explained, starting to unwrap his haul carefully over the sink, so as not to get the kitchen sides dirty. 'And some of the sheep cheese that my uncle makes. There's a jar of olives and some gherkins in the fridge, if you want them. The bread is over there, Eva, could you pass it? Please, *Inšpektorica*, help yourself.'

Once their ingredients were assembled, they sat in companionable silence at a small table at the back of the kitchen. Koren ate like a starved beast, rolling long tubes of *pršut* around chunks of cheese and swallowing them whole. Medved, on the other hand, constructed a well-balanced and sensibly proportioned sandwich on the thick cornflour bread, cutting it carefully in half before taking a bite. Petra chewed on her own sandwich as she thought, enjoying the vibrant bursts of sheep cheese alongside the salty cured meat.

'Can you walk from Piran to Izola?' she asked eventually, probing around with her fork in the gherkin jar.

'Yes, but it takes hours. There isn't a coastal path, the cliffs are too steep and the tide comes in too far,' Medved informed her. 'You have to do it on the road.'

Petra had suspected this, but was glad to have it confirmed.

'If Marjan was where he says he was, there's no way he made it to the inspector in time to kill him,' Koren said, apparently trying to ensure there was no room for confusion.

Petra hummed in response, taking a bite out of the large gherkin she'd successfully retrieved.

'But if not Marjan, Aleš, then who?' Medved waved her own fork at him to punctuate her question. 'You didn't know him, *Inšpektorica*, but *Inšpektor* Furlan was so well-liked. That's why Božič is so certain Marjan killed him, there's no one else any of us can think of. Actually, it would be quite upsetting if it was someone else, as it would have been so unpredictable,' Medved shifted a little, turned both her gaze and her waving fork towards Petra. 'What about a vagrant? Just, wrong place, wrong time?'

'A wandering vagrant with a gun, Eva?'

She shrugged. 'There are guns about, my cousin goes shooting every weekend. Plus, there's all the old ones left over from before independence, the ones no one likes to talk about.'

'It is a pain to get the licence, though. And the inspector was killed with a bullet like the ones we have, remember? This isn't some war relic.'

Medved mopped up some crumbs with her finger while Koren spoke, narrowing her eyes at him. 'Oh come on Aleš, are we really going to pretend guns don't come in over the Croatian border every day?'

'There are border checks,' he said piously, although Petra could hear the lack of conviction. 'We've both done them.'

'Yes, we've both done them, and we've both just started waving anyone with a Slovenian numberplate through in the summer when the queues get too big and we're sick of being called swine by sun-burned Austrians. Božič literally volunteers for shifts at the Sečovlje border crossing, as he can nap in his car all day! Crevatini met his girlfriend there, that

Croatian policewoman. He'd spent the whole shift chatting her up. You can't tell me the border is impermeable. All we do is scan passports.'

'Is that true?' Petra asked in surprise, lack of experience in Croatian adventures looming over her.

'Well, yes,' Koren replied. 'You're only meant to stop someone if they behave suspiciously, or there's a warrant out for them. And as Medved says, sometimes we don't even scan. The queues get so backed up in high season.'

Medved scoffed. Petra thought back to previous summers, vaguely remembering driving up to her family in the northeast, listening to the cheery voices on the radio detailing the waiting time at every major Croatian border crossing. She had been horrified to hear one August morning that there wasn't a shorter queue than three hours to be found anywhere. Her family in Prekmurje had however assured her that the annual occurrence of a Hungarian tourist somehow driving down the wrong side of the motorway near Murska Sobota was far worse, and so she'd largely stopped paying attention.

'Is it a serious possibility, then, that the gun came in illegally over the border, carried by anyone?' She had encountered such very occasionally in Ljubljana, and had been assuming the same could be true here. It was upsetting to hear just how possible it was.

'Yes,' said Medved. 'I'd say it is the most likely option.'

They fell into a brief silence, punctuated only by Koren chomping on what Petra estimated was his third sandwich of the afternoon. Petra chewed at her lip, staring at the industrial fridge. She was inclined to agree with Koren that Marjan's guilt was hardly a foregone conclusion. Circumstance and local legend might have conspired against him, but the more you interrogated them, the less you were left with. Although the vandalism of the house in Piran suggested he was capable of violence, it was a serious jump to murder. Likewise, he had no gun permit. A thought occurred to her.

'Has someone searched the flat in Markovec that Marjan referenced? His home address?'

'Yes, after he was arrested,' said Koren.

'And, I am assuming there was nothing of interest?'

He shook his head, ripping a piece of *pršut* into strips so that he could wrap it around a gherkin. 'No. And he had no residue on his hands when Božič brought him in, but apparently enough time had passed that that wasn't necessarily proof he hadn't fired a gun.' Koren bit into the gherkin with slightly more force than necessary, evidently unhappy that Petra was still sniffing around Marjan.

Petra pushed her plate away from her and sat back in her chair, aware that Medved was looking at her, waiting to hear what Petra had to say. She caught the other woman's eye, prompting a small smile.

'Marjan Furlan can't prove his alibi, but we also can't place him at the scene,' she said, voicing her thoughts aloud. Medved turned fully in her direction, apparently interested. 'He has no gun, unless it was acquired illegally, and in which case we can't find it. He is, however, the only person with a known motive for killing the inspector.'

'So, he lacks means and opportunity,' said Medved, twisting her hair around her finger. 'Potentially lacks, obviously. He could be lying about the casino, and he could have chucked the gun in the sea and gone and washed his hands in grappa to make sure there was no residue.'

'But he could also have been exactly where he says he was, minding his own business while someone murdered his brother!' Koren exclaimed.

'Feeding his addiction in an establishment he knew he was banned from,' Medved shot back. 'Having just destroyed mutual property, and threatened his brother in both of our hearing within the last week? Plus, you know, the fact that everyone in Piran knew about their issues. They aren't exactly new, or secret. My grandmother's been saying it'll come to blows for years.'

'Rumours seem to have this incredibly timeless quality,' came a voice from behind them, prompting Petra to turn. Marija had entered through the swinging door and was leaning against the countertop, staring evenly at the clutch of police officers occupying her kitchen table. 'People hear them and forget about them for years, then pull them out and dust them off whenever they might be useful again. They never lose currency, they don't depreciate. Once it is out there, it is out there, and you can't get it back. Ivan Furlan is murdered, and everyone digs through their memories for anything they know about him, and they all land on how he and his brother fought. It doesn't matter how relevant it is, if it makes one other person gasp and agree with them, then it is fair game.'

'You agree with Aleš, Marija?' asked Medved, gathering herself after the shock of Marija's interjection. 'You don't think Marjan did it?'

Marija shrugged, tying the strap on her apron tighter around her waist. 'I think we can all be blinkered,' she said, her tone measured. 'And I think that in our desperation to see some people as good and others as bad, then we can end up missing a lot in the middle. Aleš, you haven't eaten all the cheese, have you? Your father will be here in a minute. Did you offer your friends soup?'

Their private investigation interrupted, Petra and Medved hastily tidied up while Koren demonstrated to his mother that there was plenty left for his father. They both thanked Marija and went to wait outside, leaving mother and son to bicker.

'Do you have any ideas, Medved?' Petra asked as they stood in the shade of the street outside, Petra pulling her blouse sleeves up to expose her forearms. 'About who else might have wanted to murder the inspector?'

'You can call me Eva,' she replied with a grin. 'And no, I really don't. I wish I did. I keep going over it in my head, thinking of everything Ivan ever told me, everything I saw him do. I didn't know him that well, not really, not like Aleš. But I was thinking that maybe that's a good thing, as I'm less biased?'

Petra sensed the self-doubt in her words and tried to encourage her. 'Yes, I agree. That's why I asked. You seem to have a good eye for people.'

Medved glowed, standing up a little straighter. 'Thank you, *Inšpektorica*. That means a lot.'

Koren burst out of the shop, a huge green cardboard box in his hands. 'For the road,' he explained. 'Mama was annoyed I didn't offer you anything.'

Medved pounced immediately, grabbing a doughnut and waving at Marija in thanks through the window. Petra smiled at the two officers, taking a small biscuit shaped like a peach from Koren's stash before following Medved back in the direction of the station.

# Chapter 13

Petra released Koren and Medved from her service as soon as they were back inside, hopeful that they might be able to get away for the weekend the second their shift ended. She remembered too well the never-ending tide of little tasks that could delay freedom for a junior officer. When Petra had been in their shoes, she'd promised she would never be the cause of a subordinate's unplanned, and often unpaid, overtime. She could only hope that whoever managed Medved's workload was on the same page, feeling a little foolish as she realised she was nothing to the younger woman. Even so, Medved gave her a trademarked smile, booting Crevatini out of her chair and getting back to her work. Koren, meanwhile, was immediately spirited away for speed-gun duty by an officer who had apparently been lurking in the entrance hall seeking a victim. Petra gave him a small wave as he trudged off down the steps, heavy police-issue laptop clutched in his arms.

Standing in the stuffy hall, Petra assessed her options. No one had thought to offer her a desk, and so she had no designated workspace. She immediately discounted using *Inspektor*

Furlan's due to both perceived indelicacy and the presence of Božič. Although Horvat would have to find her one, should she ask, she was unwilling to be shoved in a corner somewhere, surrounded and observed by strangers who could be nosey, noisy or a combination of the two. It would also be slightly embarrassing. It was never nice knowing no one, let alone in a place where everyone else knew each other. Just imagining trailing after Horvat into a room full of officers who'd probably been at school together, their eyes tracking her every movement, filled her with dread. Petra checked her watch, calculating the time it would take her to get back to the guesthouse. With a final glance around the entrance hall to check that no one had spotted her indecision, she returned to her car.

The guesthouse car park was once again busy, three slots now obstructed by a plastic table shaded by a huge red umbrella. She had spotted cheaply printed signs reading '*jagode in šparglji*' tied to trees for the last kilometre or so, faded black letters superimposed over blotchy stock images of the promised strawberries and asparagus. The table featured a carefully arranged display of plastic tubs of fat, red strawberries, bouquets of skinny asparagus spears artistically interspersed between them. On a folding plastic chair behind the array sat a young woman, attention glued to her phone screen. Petra parked in one of the few remaining slots before heading back on foot, buying the best-looking punnet of strawberries she could see before making her way to the guesthouse.

Finding the restaurant busy with tourists and locals alike, Petra headed up the wooden staircase and into the sanctuary of her room. In her haste that morning she had failed to open the shutters and she shivered a little in the dark, cold space, rushing over to the window to correct her earlier mistake. Light now streaming into the room, Petra settled down at the dark wooden desk that was crammed into the space between wardrobe and wall, the window immediately to her right. Tidying the copy of the restaurant menu and reminder about wake-up calls into one of the drawers, she pulled Koren's notes file out of her bag, biting into a plump strawberry as she began her reading. The sections on Marjan and the crime scene she placed face down on the far side of the desk, instead turning to '*Witness statements*', the bright pink neon note that had caught her eye during her first meeting with Koren, but which she had not had the chance to peruse since. She tucked an errant strand of wavy brown hair behind her ear, having always found it hard to concentrate if her hair was tickly and bothersome around her face, chewing at her bottom lip as she started to look through what Koren had put together.

The first two pages featured a statement from a *Gospa* Jožefa Novak, owner of Tartinjeva Ulica 22 in Piran. It offered, in remarkable and perhaps slightly alarming detail, the movements of Marjan Furlan on the evening he had vandalised the house. Petra was impressed to note it even featured exact timings of when the first rock was thrown, and she wondered what issues on the street had caused *Gospa* Novak to become so invested in the neighbourhood watch, or whether it was merely a hobby. In the notes at the bottom of the statement, a strangely boxy hand recorded that the other resident of the house, a lodger who currently attended university nearby, had heard 'smashing and shouting', but that they hadn't bothered to investigate. Koren's other assembled statements were far closer to the lodger's than *Gospa* Novak's thorough account. His interview with a cocktail waitress at the casino had revealed that Marjan could easily have snuck in, and that the corners of the gaming machine salon were generally abandoned by staff if they were short-handed. In an evidently clerically drafted statement, the casino's manager confirmed that there were no cameras in this area, and that the front door cameras were currently being repaired in preparation for high season.

Finally, Petra came to a few accounts from those who had been near the coastal path at the time, although they were perhaps even less elucidatory than those she had read before. An old man with a well-known penchant for moonlit roll-er-blading regretted that he hadn't been out that night, having gone away for the weekend. Two businesses at the far end of Žusterna beach, the furthest extent of Koper proper, admitted that their CCTV was largely for show, the footage grainy and unhelpful unless you stood directly under the camera. From the direction of Izola, there was nothing. No safety-conscious businesses to catch sight of even *Inšpektor* Furlan's journey, let alone anyone who might have followed him. Not a soul who volunteered their presence nearby. The last sighting of Ivan Furlan came from a gang of teenaged boys who had been fishing off one of the stumpy concrete piers in Izola, past the restaurants and cafés that lined the main harbour. They hadn't interacted with him, but one had recognised him from when he had apparently gone into the local school to talk about careers in policing.

Petra flopped back in her chair, gazing at the little white doves painted on the moulding above her. How could a man who was recognised everywhere he went be murdered, and no one have any idea? She knew that Slovenes were private, wary of cameras and surveillance, but she often found that their ties to both neighbours and their local area made up for this. The neighbour in Piran proved that. You couldn't walk down the street without someone noticing you. What had the inspector been doing in Izola? They hadn't yet found evidence of where he'd been, only that a waiter in a restaurant on the marina had seen him pass about an hour before the medical examiner estimated he had been killed. Had Ivan been with the person who'd killed him, had they followed him down the path until the coast was clear? Or had it been by chance, an unlucky meeting in the moonlight? Perhaps simply random violence, as Medved had suggested? Petra sucked her teeth, racking her brains.

The next subsection of Koren's notes was made up of the inspector's bank statements, followed by a series of printed photographs of the crime scene, which she quickly flicked past. She had seen the wounds, and now she had seen the location in real life. She trusted Koren's assertion that there was nothing untoward in the inspector's personal life. There was little point in going over them again. Instead, she moved on to the

final section. It was formed of a single sheet, identified with
a blue note as *'Motives'*. There was something pathetic about
it, which made Petra feel pity for the dead man she had never
known. The chances of this happening to him seemed so slim,
the list of people with grudges to bear was so short. Furlan had
evidently not been a prime candidate for murder. The man had
drawn the shortest of straws. She also felt a pang for Koren,
industriously trying to put together a packet of information
that would bring his mentor some justice. He had obviously
struggled over this sheet, which was largely blank except for
a short list of bullet points. As she looked over it, she remembered how she'd first seen Koren, bent over double at the picnic
table outside the station, single-mindedly scouring his notes for
answers. She could imagine him painstakingly typing this out,
his agitated fidgeting.

The first bullet point was simply Marjan's name, which
she found fitting. Most of the rest of the file was an ode to
Marjan's probable guilt, so it seemed pointless to elaborate
here. Next down was 'purpose in Izola', which Petra agreed
with. When Koren wrote this he hadn't even been aware of the
inspector's strange behaviour, having failed properly to interview the inspector's widow. With Irena's account in mind, and
Marjan's innocence assumed, this seemed like a logical avenue
of investigation. The third bullet point was simply a question
mark, which made Petra laugh, rubbing her hands over her
tired eyes. If it had been any other case, she'd have admon-
ished Koren for unprofessionalism. In this instance it seemed
warranted. She tapped her fingers one after the other across

the table, picking up tempo as her thoughts raced. What next? Proving that Marjan was lying was the obvious option, but how to go about it?

Suddenly, she remembered the papers she had found in the inspector's dictionary. Scrabbling in her bag, she pulled them out, laying them out carefully in front of her. Petra hadn't noticed previously, Rossi's appearance having caused her to rush, but she now realised they were written on the back of old supermarket receipts, ripped into smaller rectangles. In messy handwriting she could make out some scrawled Italian words, recognising *domani* as 'tomorrow' from watching every available episode of *Inspector Montalbano* with her parents after she got into the police academy. There were several words she couldn't make out well enough even to Google, although it appeared to be the same handwriting. Though imperfect, it was a start. She assumed the inspector had spoken Italian, her conversation with Koren about Rossi earlier confirming it. This area was legally bilingual, after all. Petra remembered seeing the speeding ticket *Svetnik* Golob had received as he returned from a golfing trip to Croatia, having been caught by a duo of officers waiting to catch irritated drivers zooming away from the crush they'd escaped at the border. The ticket was twice the length of those she'd seen before, as it was in both Slovenian and Italian. Tickets very like the ones poor Koren was giving out now.

Petra cursed that she couldn't read the words, let alone translate them. She ran through the possible permutations of recipient and sender in her head, noting down that she needed a sample of the inspector's handwriting to be sure. There was one author, but was it someone writing to Ivan Furlan, or was it him sending them out? As for their meaning, she supposed that she could ask someone at the station. There were plenty of Italian speakers there, the posters she'd seen on her way in confirmed it. As soon as the idea popped into her head, she discounted it. She was here to create some distance between the investigation and the officers of Koper Police, not make the investigation even more incestuous.

Drawing her phone out once again, Petra dialled the number Koren had helpfully provided at the front of his dossier. He answered almost immediately, and Petra remembered the boredom of standing on some back road, radar gun in hand.

'Koren speaking,' he said, a car horn blaring somewhere behind him.

'Koren, this is Vidmar. Do you have an approved Italian translator that the force uses? Not one of the officers, a civilian.'

He hummed, pulling the mouthpiece away from his ear to consult with the other officer. After a second, he returned to the call. 'We do, but we have to pay her by the hour. She isn't cheap, and she's always busy.'

'Meaning you need sign-off?' she confirmed.

'Yes, and when half the force is fluent we only really use it for anything that might come up in court.' The other officer reminded him of something, and Koren continued, 'or if we need to send anything to the Italians, obviously. They prefer it to be stamped and formal.'

Petra wondered how she might phrase her next question delicately, not wanting to offend Koren or anyone else unnecessarily. It was implicit in his tone that she should use another officer to save both time and expense, but the more she thought about it the more certain she became that she needed unbiased eyes. The officer on shift with Koren garbled something that she couldn't make out, and she heard Koren's response drift away as he held the phone away from his mouth. Their conversation continued, then Koren returned.

'Sorry, *Inšpektorica*. Nejc was just telling me that if you need something done quickly, the language school in Izola has helped him in the past.'

Petra opened her notebook, clutching her phone between her ear and shoulder as she clicked open her pen and turned to a fresh page.

'With official business?'

'Yes,' Koren began, trailing off as Nejc continued speaking to him. 'Yes, he says that when he needed help with something in Spanish he just went in and they helped. Before the summer schools arrive the teachers are generally pretty quiet, they don't mind.'

'Which school?' she asked, pen poised.

# Chapter 14

As Petra headed down a steep hill towards the sea, Izola old town with its slender church spire filling the view from her windscreen, she wondered again what might have brought *Inšpektor* Furlan here on his last evening. The town was beautiful, a meandering coastline dominated by colourful buildings with terracotta roofs, a stark contrast with the dappled blue sea. All along the seafront were little promenades and piers, and as she drew closer she saw that they were home to every type of small boat she could think of, from sleek pleasure craft to tiny rowing boats equipped with nothing but a flimsy anchor and a beer cooler. To her left she saw a more professional looking marina, larger boats pulled out of the water on metal trailers, the paint on their bottoms obviously pock-marked and patchy even from this distance. The crush of restaurants and cafés started as soon as the boatyard ended, tables bursting out from under awning-covered terraces, huge menus in several languages placed carefully outside for passers-by to peruse. Petra parked in a large car park boxed in by the sea on one side, the road that meandered along the seafront on the other. She continued on foot.

Before leaving the guesthouse she had established that the language school was in the centre of the old town, although until she was here in person she hadn't realised quite what that would mean. As she walked up the street from the sea, the pavements quickly grew narrow and well-shaded by houses and shops. Any noise from the bustling waterfront restaurants faded away, her own brisk footsteps all she could hear. After a few dozen metres it became only just wide enough for a modern car, and she noticed that many of the properties instead had a covered motorcycle pressed up against their front wall. Above her, laundry lines dangled from balconies, the callboxes outside front doors demonstrating that these houses too had been converted into countless flats. Twice she passed tiny bars, no bigger than a converted living room, with old men clustered outside, propped up against stained wooden tables.

Returning to her phone, Petra followed directions up a side street, emerging out onto a sunny square with a large tree at each corner, and another church at the centre. The bare-brick tower stood separately from the main building, which was rendered and painted pale pink with a crisp white border along every edge. As Petra came around the side of the building, she found that its front face was decorated with thick orange stripes, the doors and windows surrounded by detailed white moulding which matched an ornate trim around the roof. The tower did not match it at all, the naked brick structure topped off with a three-tiered roof made of paler stone, a perfect example of Venetian church architecture. There was something charming about the incongruity, and Petra allowed herself a moment to gaze up at the two structures, enjoying the sun on her face.

Various rendered houses faced out onto the square, their wooden shutters thrown open to welcome in the afternoon light. The house in the furthest corner from where Petra stood was a well-maintained pale pink, the door framed by two wooden benches facing out onto the square. Under each window sat a small window-box, greenery spilling out and sprawling down the wall. Under one window the trailing foliage had been cut back, revealing a rectangular glass sign bolted to the wall. As she approached, she made out *Izola Language Centre* etched into the glass, the letters grey and matte against the clean surface. The door was slightly ajar. Petra slipped through, pulling her sunglasses up onto the top of her head as she went in.

Inside was cool, square terracotta tiles lining the floor and complementing the clean cream walls. The room stretched back further than Petra had expected, ending in a wide wooden staircase. An indoor lemon tree sat in a squat, round pot to the right of the door, but otherwise there was little decoration except for a few watercolour paintings of indistinguishable beaches. Halfway down the hall was a folding table covered in a white tablecloth, currently unmanned. Petra walked to the desk nonetheless, peering hopefully through the painted wooden doors on either side of the hallway that she passed. One was closed, but behind the other she could see a few chairs arranged in a loose circle, facing deeper into the room.

'Hello?' she called, hoping that the silence around her meant that she wouldn't be interrupting any classes. Somewhere above her she heard a thump, followed by rapid footsteps.

*'Dober dan.'* Petra could hear the tenseness in the words, and noticed the speaker's foreign accent immediately. The voice came from the top of the stairs, where she caught sight of a pair of tan leather boat shoes and the bottoms of olive-green chinos making their way down. As the man descended further, she could see he was also wearing a crisp white shirt, the sleeves rolled up to the elbows revealing pale, freckled skin. When he was fully in view, Petra was surprised to see he had thick red hair and a matching close-cropped beard. He was carrying a pair of square-framed black glasses, which he put on as he reached the ground floor. In Slovene, he said, 'I'm sorry, but I don't speak Slovene well. Do you speak English?'

That explained the hair. Petra couldn't remember the last time she'd met a naturally red-headed Slovene, and both his question and his stilted accent confirmed that he was not from around here. He blinked at her hopefully, looking slightly nervous.

'I do,' she replied in Slovene, then cursed herself for it. She repeated the same in English, giving him a smile and holding out her hand. She introduced herself, producing her identification as she spoke, and watching as his eyes flicked over it without taking much in except the official shield.

'Oh!' said the man, giving her hand a brisk and enthusiastic shake. 'Is something the matter?'

Petra cocked her head slightly at the phrasing. 'Yes, I would not be here otherwise.'

'Something with the school?' he asked, eyebrows rising. 'Is everyone alright?'

'Nothing with the school, *gospod*. I have been sent to solve a crime relating to the local police force and need some help with translation.' Petra hadn't wanted to use 'solve', it sounded far too confident and over-simplified. She searched desperately for a better word, but it leapt out of her grasp.

'Ah, you're investigating that murder! I heard about it on the radio. Of course, we will help in any way we can. What translation are you looking for?'

'Investigating', that was it. She tucked it away for later, hoping that other useful words didn't skitter away from her. She had passed a standardised English language exam with flying colours as part of her Interpol application, although it hadn't included much about criminal investigation. Perhaps she needed to watch a few more British crime programmes, should she get the offer from Lyon.

'Italian,' she said. 'Into either Slovene or English, please.'

'I can do that,' the man replied, grinning at her. 'Into English, obviously. I'm not much use with Slovene.'

Petra nodded, ignoring his last statement. 'Excellent, thank you. You are a teacher of Italian?'

'English, mostly. But I did Italian at university, so I can take a stab. If you'd rather wait, one of my colleagues will be in tomorrow. She's bilingual.'

'I am sure your stab will be sufficient.' Petra hadn't heard 'stab' used in this way before and wasn't sure if her echoing it was appropriate. Had he been making a joke? Her response sounded unnatural even to her, but the man laughed anyway. There was something warm about it, the corners of his eyes crinkling in mirth.

'In that case, do you want to come through?' As he spoke, he motioned to the open classroom door Petra had noticed earlier, moving in that direction himself.

Petra followed him, settling in the chair next to the one he chose. She had placed the notes on the top of her bag before she left the guesthouse, and pulled them out fluidly to place them on the table in front of her. She also pulled out her pen and opened her notebook to the page where she'd written the details about the school.

'What is your name?'

'Sorry, that was terribly rude of me. I'm Douglas York. My friends call me Doug,' he said, presumably with the suggestion that Petra could do the same. She might have considered it, had she not been tripped up at the first hurdle. Pen poised over a fresh page in her notebook, she found herself deeply confused over how either name he'd given might be spelled. Seeing her consternation, he started to spell it out phonetically. Petra was suddenly grateful for her primary school English teacher, who had forced them to learn the English alphabet by chanting it aloud at the start of every lesson. By senior school, the chanting had progressed to difficult words they might come across in daily life. Even so, Petra still avoided saying words like 'world' if she could help it.

'Thank you, Doug,' Petra replied eventually, once she was confident she had recorded his name correctly. 'And where are you from?'

'England, I've been working here since January. Do you want to see my identification card?'

'No, that won't be necessary. Thank you.' In her notebook, Petra recorded both these things for thoroughness' sake.

'I'm trying to learn Slovene,' he said as she wrote, apparently averse to silence of any kind. 'I can manage in the supermarket, and at the post office. Around here, though, I can get away with Italian and English so easily. You all speak such good English, it gives me an easy excuse.'

Petra nodded, waiting for him to finish. She wasn't sure what the compliment was intended for, so she brushed it aside. Her interest in his linguistic abilities except for Italian was limited, although she was pleased he was still making an effort. She had stood through more than one garbled attempt at Slovene in her time, just out of respect for someone making an honest attempt to learn her admittedly tricky mother-tongue. If there was a time constraint, she'd always rather switch to English.

'I understand. Please do not worry, I am very happy to speak about this in English.' She shuffled the papers in front of her, handing him the one she'd made the most headway with earlier, the one which featured reference to 'tomorrow'. 'Can you read this?'

Doug leaned forward in his chair, moving the paper gingerly so it was directly in front of him. Petra was grateful for his care, although she already had photographs of the notes on her phone. It never hurt to be cautious. He muttered slightly as he read, brows furrowed in concentration.

'This one is pretty simple, once you get past the handwriting. That's atrocious.'

Petra remembered 'atrocious' as one of the words her teacher had made her chant. Slovene tended to clumped consonants, giving her and her classmates a horror of clusters of vowels.

'And it reads?' she asked, pen ready on a blank sheet.

'It says, "*Punta Grossa*, tomorrow at dusk".'

'Punta Grossa?' she repeated, feeling slightly worried that she didn't recognise this even when it had been deciphered for her.

'I think that's Debeli Rtič in Slovene,' he said, making eye contact with her.

Petra wrote both the translation and this explanation down carefully, not bothering to ask what Debeli Rtič might be. A *rtič* was a sandspit or cape, if it was *debel* then it was large or wide. She could guess what sort of place it was: secluded, far from prying eyes. A good place for a meeting arranged with a secret note that you hid in a dictionary as soon as you received it.

Doug moved on to the other two scraps, squinting at them. The handwriting on these was particularly small and cramped. One looked as though it might have been wet at some point, ink running slightly on the flimsy paper. As he read, Petra studied him. He was leaning close to the table, reminding Petra of the intensity displayed by her nephew when he was particularly focused on a picture book. As he read, he mouthed some of the words, checking whether he had decoded them correctly. He shook his head to himself at one point, evidently displeased with what he'd come up with, and started again. After a few minutes, he tapped the less smudged note with his forefinger.

'This one is strange. I am pretty sure it says, "when and where the mermaid sings". Italian has a lot of tenses, and I sometimes get them muddled, but I think that's the gist of it.'

Petra noted this down, writing a little question mark in brackets after it to demonstrate Doug's uncertainty. She had no idea what it might mean, either. 'What is the word for mermaid?' she asked, leaning towards him.

'*Sirena*, and I assumed it was going to mean siren. But the verb is *cantare*, to sing. It would be *suonare* if it was ringing. Maybe they use *cantare* when it's a police siren? It is strangely poetic, I quite like it. There's no location on this one, I'm afraid.'

Petra noted these thoughts down as well, interested in Doug's take. She wondered how she might find out the specificities of Italian when it came to singing or ringing sirens, whether it would help her work out what time of day this note might refer to. If someone in the station was slipping them to the inspector, had they been able to turn on sirens on a police car to summon him? Part of her knew that a fluent speaker would be more helpful with this detail than Doug, but she couldn't find it in herself to be annoyed, or to wish she'd encountered a different member of staff. There was something oddly charming about his desire to help, his offering of insights, even if they were half-formed.

As she wrote down her ideas, Doug continued on with the blotchiest note. She watched in slight amusement as he picked it up and held it to the light, mouth dropping open slightly as he tried to sound out the letters he could read. Petra could see his main issue, had noticed it in her room when she'd studied the notes herself. What appeared to be the end of one word and the beginning of the next was obscured by a fat, round water stain. It was apparently causing Doug serious difficulty in getting any meaning out of the note.

'If this one is too difficult for you, I can ask someone else,' she said, cringing a little when she recognised the exact phrase used by her teacher when she'd been suffering through listening comprehension exercises. It made Doug jolt, and she wondered if it was a less well-meaning turn of phrase than the individual words suggested. She'd never had to use it herself before, only been on the receiving end of it.

'No, I think I can get most of it. This word is *spiaggia*, I think. That means beach. Then the last bit just says "after your shift". I can't make out the name of the beach, though. If you give me your pen, I'll write out what it looks like?'

Petra handed over her notebook and watched as Doug wrote out what he'd told her. In place of the name of the beach, he wrote the few letters he'd been able to make out. Noticing her notation above, he added another small question mark in brackets, then grinned at her as he gathered up the notes and her belongings and handed them back over. She smiled back.

'I'm sorry I couldn't work the whole thing out, my geography around here isn't as good as it could be.'

'Neither is mine,' Petra replied. 'Thank you for your help, it has been very useful.'

Doug's smile widened as he rose to his feet at the same time as Petra. They headed back out into the entrance hall, Petra leading the way. As she walked, she felt around in the front pocket of her bag for her business cards, drawing one out when they reached the desk.

'If anything else occurs to you, please call,' she said, handing it over.

'Oh, of course. I'll see if I can find anything out about the *cantare* note. That one's going to annoy me.'

She nodded. 'Thank you. I would be grateful if you did not speak about the details of what I have shown you. It is currently sensitive evidence.'

Sensitive because she hadn't shared its existence with anyone, but that was deliberate. Petra didn't want this being public knowledge, not yet. She had an uneasy feeling about the translated contents of the notes, hotly aware that they had been deliberately secreted in the inspector's desk drawer.

'I wouldn't dream of it,' Doug said, eyes widening as he shook his head profusely. 'I ask weird language questions all the time, no one will bat an eyelid.'

This quirk made Petra smile again, as did his apparent lack of embarrassment about it. She reached out to shake Doug's hand, bidding him goodbye. She wondered if he realised that he talked just like the stereotypically British character in her school textbook, that several of the phrases he used she'd had on a worksheet of English idioms.

As she left the school and walked slowly back down to her car, she considered what he had shown her. The inspector had been having secret meetings at strange times with an unknown individual, and he had kept these notes at work. Was this all of them? Would she find more at the house? She doubted it, something about her interview with Irena Furlan told her that they would have been found by now, and that Irena would have either destroyed them or shared them with Petra when they met. Glancing at her watch, Petra confirmed that she still had plenty of time before she needed to be back at the station. She walked straight past her car, and settled at the nearest café, ordering a large iced tea when the waiter appeared, and gazed out at the glimmering sea. There were certainly perks to working here.

# Chapter 15

Petra allowed herself a few idle moments to sip the home-made, peach-flavoured tea. Around her, she could hear children clamouring for ice-cream, waiters seamlessly slipping between languages as they took orders from different tables. In front of her, couples walked hand-in-hand along the sea-front, laughing and pointing at the various boats tied up on metal rings. Tiny dogs skittered along keeping close to their owners' ankles, only breaking away when they passed a res-taurant with a bowl of water outside. Occasionally a seagull careened down to the pavement when a passer-by dropped a *girica*, tiny fish deep-fried whole, their unseeing eyes peering out through a thin layer of batter. Out at sea, three huge con-tainer ships made achingly slow progress towards the port of Koper. Petra watched as a perfectly white yacht cruised past one heading in the opposite direction, its course leading to Croatia.

When her glass was half-empty, she went back to work. Flipping open her notebook, she looked over the notes she had made to herself over the last day. She was no closer to

determining a better suspect than Marjan, although she likewise hadn't turned up any evidence to cement his guilt. As
such, she still had no answer as to why the inspector's body
had been moved after he'd been shot or who had shot him.
She had a better idea of Marjan's movements than she had
previously, including a more precise timeline of the recent disputes over the house in Piran, but she still couldn't put him on
or off the coastal path at the time of his brother's murder. She
took another long sip of iced tea, trying to clear her head. She
attempted to think like Koren, to believe Marjan innocent.
She looked again at what Doug had shared with her, mentally
branding this as a new avenue of investigation. It was highly
unlikely that Marjan had anything to do with these notes, his
style was apparently shouting in car parks rather than slipping
cryptic notes to his brother. By pursuing this, she reasoned,
she wasn't letting Marjan off the hook or siding with Koren
and the anonymous letter writer. She was simply doing her job.

The waiter cruised past again, and she ordered another
drink. The best place to start, experience told her, was to
gather her facts. Three notes, evidently all from the same
person, offering a mixture of times and places for meetings.
Were they threats, or invitations? Had they been delivered to
the inspector at work, or had he simply taken them there for
safe-keeping? Reaching for her phone, she searched for Debeli
Rtič. Her suspicions had been correct: it was a large cape near
the Italian border, boasting a protected beach and a large health
resort. It was only a short drive from Koper, definitely reach-
able in the timescale of the inspector's absences as described

by Irena. Unfortunately, Petra's next few searches were far less elucidatory. Since Doug had offered his translation, she had been holding out a slight hope that there was some mermaid-related monument or myth around Koper or Izola, but nothing hopeful appeared. The police sirens remained more likely, although she was still perplexed as to how anyone could describe them as singing. It could be a ruse, or a joke.

Her final and most labour-intensive task was to peer at a map of the coastline, looking for any appropriately named beaches. She started up on the Italian border at Debeli Rtič in the hope that this beach would be close to the other established meeting point, moving along the coast to Ankaran, Koper and then Izola when this theory proved unsound. Nothing jumped out at her. She had another long drink of tea then carried on, down the coast towards towns she was unfamiliar with except from when she'd seen them on maps. Strunjan with its nature reserve and salt pans, then the picture postcard Venetian jewel of Piran, in sharp contrast to Portorož with its concrete tourist-centric seafront to its south. Finally, her search reached the other salt pan-based nature reserve at Sečovlje, and the Drangonja River and so the border with Croatia. Something told her that the beach she was looking for was in Slovenia, but she still had a quick look at the northern Croatian coast and Italy's last few towns on the Gulf of Trieste. Nothing seemed hopeful.

She scratched at her head in irritation, sucking her lips together as she thought. This, she reasoned, was an obvious question for a local. There was a case to be made that she was wasting time browsing on maps like a tourist, when she could get help from any one of dozens of people who knew this coast like the back of their hands back at the station. Still, she was wary of showing the notes to anyone. Koren would be both thrilled that she was chasing a non-Marjan lead and furious that she evidently suspected the inspector of wrong-doing, and Božič would ignore her in favour of continuing his crusade against a perceived fratricidal gambling addict. It would seem rude to ask Rossi about this detail, when it would mean admitting that she hadn't trusted her to do the initial translation. This left her with one option, and it was undoubtedly the best. She called the waiter over, paid her tab, and headed back to her car, hopeful that she'd get the answers she needed, from someone who was obviously very willing to help.

Back at the station, Petra went straight to Medved's desk, gratified that the entrance hall was quiet this late on a Friday. She had noticed the traffic starting to pick up on her drive back from Izola, an unbroken queue filling the carriageway going in the opposite direction as the weekend rush to Croatia reached its climax. She had felt oddly smug going against the flow, away from the border, looking through windscreens to see harassed fathers clutching the steering wheel, their wives turned around from the passenger seat to break up squabbling children in the back. The cafés and restaurants along the seafront in Izola had been getting steadily busier as well, the ratio of wine to coffee ordered skewing more with every customer that walked in. Medved, for her part, looked excited to see Petra. She waved, pushing back in her desk chair to stretch her legs out. Her ponytail jiggled as she reached above her head, easing out her shoulders.

'*Inšpektorica*, good afternoon. I thought you might have finished for the weekend.'

'Not yet. I've just been following up on a few things. Do you have a moment?'

'Of course!' she exclaimed, rolling her chair forward again and setting her elbows on her desk. 'What can I help you with?'

'I'm trying to find a beach,' Petra said, sitting down lightly on the edge of the desk, tucking the ever-errant strand of hair behind her ear as she did so. Medved scooted closer to her, resting her head on her upturned palm as though ready for a gossip.

'I'm assuming you don't mean for swimming.' Medved's tone was deadpan, her eyes twinkling with humour.

'No, I don't,' she replied with a small smile, enjoying the burgeoning friendship between them. 'I have half the name, but don't know the rest. I hoped you'd recognise it.'

'Most beaches around here don't really have names unless some hotel or restaurant has coined it. They tend just to be called after the town. What's the part you know?'

Petra showed her the transcription Doug had made in her notebook. 'I suspect it won't be a big one, probably a bit off the beaten track.'

'Why's that?'

'Just from context.'

Medved raised her eyebrows but refrained from asking a

follow-up question. Petra was impressed at how gamely she was taking the task of beach-guessing, considering Petra had given her no explanation at all. She felt a little guilty and decided to clue Medved in a little. 'I've found some notes relating to the case, but this one is water damaged. Another one references a meeting at Debeli Rtič, so I am assuming it will be somewhere similar.'

Giving Medved more information had been the right decision. She nodded in understanding, turning to tap away at her keyboard. 'I see. So, you're thinking it won't be somewhere with a cocktail bar and a beachside café,' she mused. 'That makes sense. You've only seen it written down? You wouldn't know it from a picture?'

Petra shook her head, leaning forward to see what Medved was doing. Like Petra, her first instinct seemed to have been to go to an online map and start poking around, although she had already zoned in on a potential area.

'Could this be it?' Medved asked, pointing at a small strip of yellow signifying a beach wrapping around a headland to the west of Izola. 'It would be on the route from Piran to Izola, if you could safely walk along the coast. It is at the bottom of a cliff. You have to go down a pretty steep path to get down to it, or else walk across the rocks from Izola. No car access. It is absolutely gorgeous though, my mother always says it looks like the Côte d'Azur from above.'

'What's it called?' said Petra, crowding forward to look at the little taster images Google provided when Medved clicked around.

'It doesn't really have a name, but the town above it on the cliffs is called Dobrava.'

'That'll be it!' Petra exclaimed triumphantly, flipping open her notebook and writing it down.

Medved clapped her hands together, sharing in Petra's glee. 'Are you going to go?'

She didn't see much point in rushing over there, the likelihood of there being any evidence as to why the inspector had been summoned seemed very small. Moreover, her encounter with *Inšpektorica* Rossi earlier had given her the distinct impression that being late would not be a good idea. Petra considered her other options, where else the investigation might take her. She was starting to feel somewhat guilty for carrying on a line of enquiry totally without Koren's input, the image of his crestfallen face rushing to the front of her mind. She opened her mouth to respond, still unsure of what her answer would be.

The rhythmic tapping of approaching heels rescued Petra from her indecision, the noise heralding the appearance of Rossi through the double doors leading towards her office. She was wearing an incredibly well-tailored blazer, her hair still as perfectly in place and glossy as it had been that morning. She carried a large red alligator-skin handbag in one hand, flicking at the screen of an oversized smartphone with the other. When she finally looked up and caught sight of Petra, she tossed her head back and changed course to approach her.

'Petra Vidmar, just the lady I was hoping to see. You're finished for the weekend? Shall we go off early?' Now Petra was aware of it, she could hear a heaviness to Rossi's Slovene. Grammatically, it was perfect. Yet, some word choices were strange, stresses placed on unusual syllables.

Petra flashed a look at her own watch, aware that she could hardly say no when Rossi was evidently eager to get away, despite it being slightly too early for Petra to be comfortable clocking off. She tried to rationalise to herself that networking was an essential part of a case like this, both to gather information and to provide herself with contacts for her future career. Likewise, Golob would be halfway around the golf course by now, and Božič was nowhere to be seen. She was hardly the first to leave. She needed time to regroup, to think through what she'd learned, and to see what Rossi had to say about station politics and the general culture of the Koper Police. She marshalled her courage, trying to convince herself that she wasn't somehow shirking work, that she didn't have to be the last one in the station just to prove that she was working hard.

'Yes, *Inšpektorica* Rossi. I was just getting some help from Eva, and she has excelled herself. I'm finished for the day.'

Medved grinned at Petra with an eye-crinkling intensity that made Petra return her smile, wide and open. She waited a moment to see if Rossi would bother asking what she was talking about, but her attention was once again on the phone in her hand. Rossi looked up only when Petra approached her, offering Medved no more attention than a quick incline of her head before she strode briskly out of the station, evidently expecting that Petra would follow her. With a hasty wave at Medved, Petra went.

The heels of Rossi's court shoes rapped against the tarmac of the car park, and Petra found herself slightly transfixed by how well the short, sharp sounds summed the woman up. Her charcoal trousers were perfectly fitted, a pale pink blouse with a dramatic bow at the neck complimenting her dark hair. From behind, Petra could see that a series of neat pearlescent hair grips were maintaining her elegant up-do. Petra was just considering how long it must take to attain such a hairstyle every morning when Rossi spun around, giving her an expectant look.

'You are happy to drive?' It was a pointless question, as they were already standing next to Petra's car. Rossi was poised next to the passenger-side door, hand halfway to the handle.

'If you give me directions,' Petra said, pleased that she had come up with some form of sensible response considering that she hadn't even noticed they were heading for her car until Rossi stopped. Petra smiled and got a raised eyebrow in return.

'Naturally.'

Rossi slipped into the unlocked car, smoothing her trousers out as she did so. Removing her blazer with a smooth movement which made the shell-shaped silver buttons glint, she laid it out across her knees, getting rid of any creases. As Petra climbed into the driver's seat she attempted some half-hearted fabric-smoothing of her own. Gratifyingly, she found that there was enough elastane in her own high-street-brand trousers that it was unnecessary. Rossi caught her in the act, and gave her a knowing smile.

'Where are we headed?' Petra asked, keen to put the mildly embarrassing moment behind her.

'Isola,' said Rossi, slipping huge tortoise-shell sunglasses onto her face as she fiddled with the air conditioning. She pronounced it differently to Koren, the 's' sound soft and beautifully Italian. Petra refrained from her normal gripe against passengers taking control of the atmospheric controls, deciding that it was not a hill she particularly wanted to die on. Remembering what Koren had told her earlier that day about Rossi's husband's wine bar, Petra pulled out of the car park, privately thrilled that she could demonstrate that she knew the way to Izola without directions. Even if she had only learned it earlier that day, it was truly the small things that mattered.

# Chapter 16

'He didn't!' exclaimed Petra, for what felt like the hundredth time that evening. She was propped up at the reclaimed-wood bar of *La Medusa*, the achingly chic wine bar that Domenico Rossi had opened four years ago, and apparently poured every drop of his soul into since. Not that Rossi herself, or Giulia as she had insisted Petra call her, seemed to mind. Pride oozed off her as she swirled her last few mouthfuls of their famous orange wine around her elegantly thin-stemmed wine glass. Petra could understand why. A truly exhaustive array of regional wines crowded both the tiers of shelving behind the bar and filled an interesting custom-made wine rack that dominated the far wall. Round, black tables surrounded by delicate silver chairs were arranged artfully so that there was no obviously best seat in the house, although the room itself was small. Even the wood on the bar itself was silvered and understated. Petra had worried she'd got the evening off to a terrible start when she asked if it was painted, with Rossi instead informing her with undisguised irritation that it was in fact driftwood, and so got its colour naturally. Petra had nodded dumbly, afraid to comment on any other element of design and showcase her general ignorance of anything that might be described as 'the pinnacle of Istrian elegance'. She had regretted speed-reading that particular TripAdvisor review almost immediately, as it only served to increase her nervousness.

Not that she had needed to worry. Initial faux pas left in the past, she and Rossi had quickly identified a shared love of television crime dramas and going out for ice cream in the winter, and perhaps a more fulfilling mutual dislike of two very successful celebrity chefs. They also both had a deep well of stories relating to being often the first reasonably senior woman in policing many people had encountered. Although Petra had never really thought of them as the 'war stories' Rossi presented them as, she had to admit the other woman had a point.

'He did,' confirmed Rossi, dunking one of the perfectly crisp calamari her husband had brought out for them in a rich homemade dip and shaking it at Petra for emphasis. 'He told me to wait outside while he called the police. He kept quoting these ridiculous made-up laws at me, saying that a section of some statute meant that impersonating a police officer was an automatic ten-year sentence. I think he'd been watching too much American television. It was wonderful when the other car showed up to arrest me, a sight to behold.' Her tone turned wistful, and Petra laughed.

'I've never had anything as bad as that,' she admitted. 'I'm not sure how I'd have coped.'

'You can get as angry as you like, but there's no point to it,' Rossi said sagely. 'Just laugh.' It was a sentiment that Petra would never have predicted from her initial impression of Rossi, but which she had discovered over the course of the evening was very in-character. Remaining unbothered by issues that she had decided were unimportant seemed to be a cornerstone of the other woman's approach to life.

Petra nodded at her, thinking over all the various little things that she'd put up with, all adding up to make a big thing that had partially led to her wanting to go to Interpol. She was sure it was no different there, perhaps it was even worse. At least it would be a change. She didn't mention this to Rossi, instead taking a long drink from her own glass. The orange wine was very good, and slightly dangerous. It was fruity enough that it was incredibly drinkable, and she reasoned with herself that this third glass was more than enough. She set it down, and picked up one of the tiny, square-cut *pršut* sandwiches that Domenico had sent out with their most recent order, chewing at it as she enjoyed the atmosphere and friendly silence that had descended.

'Have you lived here all your life?'

Rossi shrugged. 'Here and there. I was born in Isola, and my family still have a little house up in the hills that Domenico and I go to when town gets too crowded in summer, and the mosquitos get too bad. But I went to school in Trieste, and a lot of my family live there.'

'A summer house around here must be gorgeous,' enthused Petra, imagining a sun-dappled terrace and wrought-iron chairs, a table topped with a gingham tablecloth bearing dishes of thick-sliced bread and thin-necked bottles of olive oil and balsamic vinegar.

'It isn't much.' Rossi's response was taut, sharp, and Petra wondered what she'd said wrong. She hurriedly changed the topic.

'What made you come back?' Petra asked, honestly interested in the answer. Her mother had fled the flat farmland of north-eastern Slovenia as soon as she could, and never returned. She and her father were both staunchly Ljubljanan, and the desire to stretch her wings that Petra was currently indulging also included being far from home, not just a few miles across a national border.

'The driving in Trieste is awful, they're like madmen. Have you ever seen anyone triple-parked? It happens there every day.' Rossi's wry smile as she spoke made it obvious it was not her real answer, but Petra didn't push. They were obviously back on comfortable ground.

'I'm surprised you would have wanted to join the Slovenian police over the Italian.'

'Eh, a lot of people say Trieste isn't Italy, that Triestinos aren't Italian. I'm sure you've come across the Slovene sentiment that "*Trst je naš*", that it belongs to Slovenia. Then you have all the business about its status as a free territory, the post-war agreement.' Rossi sighed, running her fingers up and down the slim stem of her wineglass, lost in thought. 'There's something special about this area, Petra. I can't really say more than that. I work with the Italian forces a lot, on the drug routes. I think half my time is spent arguing with the *Guardia di Finanza*, truly.'

'Arguing about what?' she asked, barely noticing the calamari she was eating in her focus on what Rossi had to say.

'Oh, everything. They find drugs that came in from Serbia, they phone me to shout. They tell me to go harder on the Croatians, make sure they understand the penalties. And what penalties would those be, hmm? How can a border guard at Sicciole control what another one at Bajakovo does?'

'Sicciole?' Petra repeated, stumbling over the unfamiliar sounds. The Italian pronunciation stood out against the rest of Rossi's speech; the effect was jarring.

Rossi pulled a face like she was going to sneeze, spitting out, 'Sečovlje, in Slovene. Don't make me say it, I can't.' They both laughed, her attempt at saying it truly abysmal. Rossi took another sip of her wine, and acted washing out her mouth.

'And Bajakovo is in Serbia?' This sort of information seemed prudent to collect, if Rossi was offering it. Who knew where Interpol might send her, should she be accepted. If they were anything like most western Europeans she'd met, they'd expect her to know everything about the former Yugoslavia, even if she had only set foot in two of the successor republics including Slovenia.

Rossi shook her head, chewing faster on the olive she had popped in her mouth to help forget the horrors of a Slovenian place-name. 'Croatian side of the border, the furthest south border crossing into Serbia on a major road. It is just one of many, though. The Bosnian-Croatian border is on the *Guardia*'s radar too, every checkpoint. They seem to miss the fact that they could call up the Croatians instead of me, cut out the middleman.' She fell silent for a moment, wiping her fingers off on a napkin. 'I suppose you can't blame them, their reason for being nowadays is suppressing the drug trade and patrolling borders. Every time something gets through, they've failed on two counts. Still, they could be nicer to me about it.'

'You haven't considered changing directorates?' Petra asked, leaning forward. 'Coming over to homicide?'

'You mean, now there's a vacancy?' Rossi's tone was wicked, and Petra laughed in shock at the reference to the recently deceased *Inšpektor* Furlan. 'No, I like what I do. I like a bigger picture.' She waved her arm as if she was pitching a luxury housing development, gesturing widely.

Petra's confusion must have shown on her face, as Rossi shrugged and speared another olive on her toothpick. 'I like feeling like there is a goal, that we're fighting a war with an end. It doesn't matter how achievable it is, or that we might not win. Homicide is too random, too piecemeal. You start from scratch every time, there's no known players and established context.'

'Unless you have a serial killer,' Petra pointed out, aware that she was dragging their conversation into the theoretical but enjoying it enough that she didn't stop herself.

'Well, yes. But if you want one of those, Petra, I'm afraid you'll have to leave Slovenia.' Rossi gave her that same dissecting look that Petra had experienced previously, as if she knew everything that Petra was and had chosen to assess each part. Petra wasn't sure if it was the intended reaction, but she felt herself clam up, unsure of what to say next. They lapsed into silence again, the hum of other patrons' conversations ebbing and flowing around them. Petra finished her wine, downing the small glass of water that had come to the table with it. Rossi did not appear to notice her discomfort, instead re-arranging her cutlery with a contemplative look on her face.

'Is anyone investigating who might have sent the request for help to Ljubljana?' she asked.

'No,' said Petra, keeping her voice neutral. 'My superintendent viewed that as inappropriate, their anonymity needs to be respected. *Svetnik* Horvat said he feels similarly. I am not sure it would be a good look for the police, if we started poking around looking for them.'

'Of course. I'm just fascinated by it. Who sent it? Why are they so convinced of Marjan's innocence? What do they know that we don't?'

'Have you seen the email?' Petra asked, confused. She was under the impression that Ljubljana had shared it only with Horvat. It seemed unlikely that he would let anyone else read it. The contents were, after all, rather insulting to him personally.

'No, but you wouldn't come all the way here if it was just a complaint about our processes, would you?' Rossi surveyed her fingernails as she spoke, buffing one with her napkin. 'I just can't think who would put themselves out for Marjan Furlan. He is the only one who benefits in all this. Božič and Horvat look incompetent, and you have your time wasted.'

'I don't think they're putting themselves out for Marjan. They're trying to right a wrong, ensure the inspector gets justice.' Petra did not mention that Rossi had left Koren off her list, not convinced it was relevant. From how she floated through the station, it was not impossible that Rossi had failed to notice that Koren even existed. If she did suspect him, Petra didn't want to give her ammunition, even if it was just for gossiping purposes. That being said, Rossi didn't seem the type to gossip. Her questions seemed to relate to honest personal interest, not a desire to be the fount of all knowledge at the coffee machine come Monday morning.

'Misguided,' said Rossi with finality. 'Ivan would never have accepted it, but a Capodistria without Marjan Furlan will be better for a lot of people than one with him. Honour Ivan's memory by putting away the scourges of society, I say. And Marjan is, unfortunately, one of them.'

Petra was surprised at the simplicity and binary nature of Rossi's form of justice. She could see where the other woman was coming from, however. Although she had felt some pity for Marjan when she'd met him that morning, it was undeniable that he had made a lot of people's lives worse: his wife and children, his brother, the croupier whom he'd injured. But, that did not mean that he should be used as a scapegoat for murder.

Rossi evidently saw Petra turning her words over in her head, and so continued. 'I've surprised you, but I hope I haven't upset you. I should say that the sort of people I run into in my line of work, the drug bosses and the people traffickers and the unreachable addicts, might have hardened me a little to humanity. I suppose that's the problem with my big picture. You can see one murderer, put them away, and know that it is over. I can put one big dealer behind bars, but I know that three are already scrapping to take his place. You can believe that most people are good, only a few are rotten. I tend to believe that we all have ample capacity to be truly awful, if given the right motivation.'

'Doesn't that go against what you said earlier? That your single narrative has a beginning and an end?' asked Petra, intrigued by the misanthropy Rossi was describing.

'Oh, it still has an end. I'll put the three scrappy successors in jail too, or at least however many survive the brawl. And I'll die one day, and the fight will still be going on. But it isn't random, Petra. It is all linked. There is order in its barbarity.'

There wasn't much that could be said to that. Petra picked up one of the last two calamari rings, pushing the remaining one towards Rossi, who smothered it in more dip. Sensing the evening was coming to an end, Petra moved for her bag, but was quickly waved away by Rossi.

'I'm going to pretend you aren't trying to pay. This is my treat, obviously.'

'Thank you,' Petra replied, feeling a little guilty at having agreed to a third glass now she wasn't going to pay for it. 'Next time, though, I am paying.'

'I'd like that,' said Rossi, with a sincere smile. Petra smiled back, showing her agreement. She was extremely glad she had accepted Rossi's offer of drinks and regretted any misgivings she'd had earlier in the day. Rossi gave off an aura of being judgemental and cold, but from her conversation with Petra this evening she could hardly blame her. She had suffered more than her fair share of embarrassments and workplace unpleasantness when she was a junior officer. It was no wonder she had grown a shell of poise, elegance and ruthlessness.

'Would you like Domenico to call you a taxi?' asked Rossi as they rose to their feet, tidying phones and sunglasses into their bags. As Rossi dropped her smartphone into her bag, Petra noticed that the case was decorated with a picture of Domenico and Giulia on a beach, a chink in her aloof armour. She wondered why she hadn't noticed it in the police station.

'I think I'll walk, but thank you.' When Rossi had gone to the bathroom after ordering their second glass of the evening, Petra had quickly looked into her options for getting home with driving herself in the Skoda no longer viable. She was both amused and gratified when she realised that her guesthouse was within half an hour's easy walk of Izola, up a meandering back road with views across the Adriatic to Trieste.

'If you're sure,' replied Rossi with mild concern, but Petra waved her off. Daringly, she stepped forward to give the other woman a hug, which was returned with gusto. As they pulled apart, Rossi smiled at her again. 'Be careful. See you on Monday?'

'Thank you again for a lovely evening. Have a wonderful weekend.' Petra waved as she slipped out the frosted glass door, her hand speeding up when Domenico shouted a *'buona serata'* at her from behind the bar. With a quick helping hand from her maps app she started off across the small square *La Medusa* sat on, heading in the direction of the gently sloping road that swept out of town and towards the rolling hills further inland.

# Chapter 17

Petra awoke the next morning to her phone ringing, and nearly screamed. To be woken this way two mornings in a row seemed like an unpleasant pattern. She racked her brains for what she might have done to be so persecuted, but failed to come up with anything compelling before she had to answer the call.

'Petra Vidmar speaking.' Her voice sounded raspy and well-used. She blamed the orange wine.

'Petra, good morning! How are you? Sorry for the early call, but I know you're itching to get back home, so I thought you'd want information as soon as it comes in.' *Inšpektor* Jakob Mlakar's voice rang through her head, his cheeriness disconcerting and largely unwelcome. She glanced at the clock, saw that it was nearly 7 a.m. Normally, she would indeed be at work by now, but today was a Saturday. There was little point in going into the station. She pressed the heel of her hand into her forehead, reminding herself that he was trying to be nice. She did want to get back to the capital, to be sitting at her desk when any call from Interpol came through, good or bad.

'Hello, Jakob. Thank you for calling. How is *Gospa* Mlakar?'
Her mother had brought her up well enough to know that she
had to ask, even if she had only met Mlakar's wife once and
couldn't remember the name of their firstborn. Relationships
weren't something she liked to talk about at work, not when
people took it as an invitation to ask if she was seeing anyone,
and when she might have a baby of her own.

'She's well! Thank you for asking. Little Timotej could
come any day now.'

'I'll look forward to seeing photos,' she replied, not entirely
untruthfully. Although their names escaped her, the photos
of *Gospa* Mlakar and her daughter gambolling around that
adorned every available space on Mlakar's desk were very
sweet. There was also something comforting in the birth of
Timotej Mlakar so close after the death of *Inšpektor* Furlan.
Her aunt, who was very invested in the spiritual healing
powers of various natural phenomena, would probably have
described it as 'restorative'. It was certainly a little bolt of happiness, when the case before her seemed so dark.

'I'll make sure to send some!' Her comment had evidently
been well-received, she could hear the pride in Mlakar's
voice.

'I'm assuming you've spoken with Ivan Furlan's sons?' Petra
staggered out of bed and across to the small desk, pulling out
her notebook and pen before settling down on the chair.

'Yes, I met with them yesterday. I'm afraid they didn't have
much to say. The older one mentioned that his father was
starting to look forward to retirement, was trying to train up

one of the younger officers to fill his boots. I imagine you'll have come across him?'

Petra thought about Koren, how he'd painstakingly made notes exactly how Furlan had taught him. 'Yes, I think so.'

'Good. He also mentioned some acrimony with an uncle they don't speak to anymore, the one who the local force arrested. The son seemed surprised that the bad blood had flared up again, he thought it had mostly died down.'

Again, Petra was unsurprised. If Ivan was keen to play down his difficult relationship with Marjan to people in Koper who witnessed its fallout, it was no surprise that he was less than forthcoming with his sons when they were both away with their own families in Ljubljana. She was also unsurprised that Irena Furlan hadn't kept them in the loop. She had seemed a restrained woman, only sharing details of her husband's recent wanderings when pushed.

'It seems to have been on a low boil until recently, but came to a head again in the days before the inspector died.'

'Do you think he did it? The sons both say they think he's capable, but they seemed conflicted. He was like a childhood monster for them, he came knocking on doors and shouting through windows at all hours after he'd driven his wife and children away.'

'He's the best suspect we've got at the moment,' she admitted, careful not to let too much slip.

'That's awful. Imagine murdering your own brother.'

'There's a lot of history between them.' An understatement, perhaps, but she didn't see the point in getting into specifics.

'Well, they couldn't tell me anything specific that happened recently. They both mentioned one other thing that didn't seem relevant to me, but might mean something to you.' Petra had always liked that about Mlakar, his attention to detail. His interview notes were thorough, his questions carefully phrased. He was also rarely embarrassed to admit when he didn't know something or needed help. It was a quality she envied, having always felt as though she had to show no weaknesses when at work, lest she be cast aside and viewed as a second-class officer. She once again felt guilty for having been so angry with him when he'd requested not to be sent to Koper. If anyone was going to get titbits of information out of the sons, it would be Mlakar.

'What was that?'

'The last time they saw their father. There was a vintage car show up at *Grad* Strmol two weeks ago, and the inspector invited both boys. Their mother was away with friends, so he told them he fancied some company. He collected them on his way past Ljubljana, they apparently had a good time. Neither of the sons had put too much thought into it, but both said that on reflection it was a strange thing for their father to drive all that way for. He didn't really care about cars, especially not vintage ones.'

'That is very interesting, Jakob. Thank you.' Petra scribbled madly as she spoke, trying to get all her thoughts down at once. Jakob wished her a good weekend, once again promising photos of Timotej before hanging up. Petra pushed her phone out of the way, looking down at her notebook.

Once again, interviews with members of the Furlan family stretched her in two directions. The sons thought their uncle capable of such a crime, although they had no recent knowledge of their father's relationship with him, and were perhaps unduly swayed by Marjan's role as a childhood bogeyman. Like everyone else who suspected Marjan, they could offer nothing solid to condemn him, only rehashed accounts of his previous unsavoury behaviour. The car show detail was interesting, although strangely nebulous. Like the notes and the disappearances, it seemed to suggest a large part of the inspector's life that Petra was somehow missing. Whether it was linked to his death, or just a distraction from Marjan's guilt, she could not say.

As Petra showered, leisurely washing her hair as a Saturday morning treat, she couldn't get the picture of Božič's vintage car out of her mind. If the inspector was going to start indulging a long-buried interest in classic vehicles, surely he would have sought out the expertise of his friend and colleague, rather than going on a long journey to a car show hours away? If he was looking for company at such an event, wouldn't Božič have been his first call? She supposed that maybe they hadn't been as friendly as she'd been led to believe, or that Božič could have been busy on the day in question, but something continued to niggle at her. As she towelled herself dry, she heard her phone ping cheerily from the bedroom. Wrapping her hair up in a towel turban, she went through to check it. She was surprised to see a text from an unknown number, and in English.

Hello, this is Doug York from the Izola Language Centre. I have been thinking about what you showed me. Do you have time to chat? Best, DY

Petra smiled at his sign-off, despite having already put his name in the body of the message. It was strangely formal, considering the way she knew him to speak. She hesitated for a minute, then phoned the number the text had come from.

Doug answered immediately, sounding oddly breathless. 'Good morning, *Inšpektorica*!'

'To you too, Doug. Please, call me Petra. Thank you for your message.'

'You're more than welcome. I was just making my breakfast this morning, and it came to me! I wasn't sure if it was important, so I thought I'd better let you know.'

'It?' she asked simply, concerned something implicit had been lost in translation.

'Sorry, of course. The note you showed me, the one with the mermaid singing. Only, it isn't a mermaid. Or, at least, it isn't only a mermaid.'

'It isn't?' she said wryly, returning to her desk chair.

'No, I think it is a siren after all,' he replied, eagerness unwavering even in the face of her amusement. 'The siren they ring on the first Saturday of every month.'

Petra nodded in realisation, then made a noise of agreement when she remembered that Doug could not see her. It would make sense. In every town and city in Slovenia, a siren rang for thirty seconds at noon on the first Saturday of the month. It was mostly rung to check the system was still working, as the same infrastructure would be relied on to sound various warnings and all-clear signals to the population in case of attack or national disaster. Having lived in Slovenia her whole life, Petra had learned to tune them out long ago, barely giving them a second's attention, unless they happened to interrupt what she was doing by making it hard to hear.

'Would that make sense with the use of *cantare*?'

'I think it's a joke,' he said, having evidently anticipated this very question. 'I've seen people pretend to sing along to it, and there are videos online of people who have made up a dance for the whole thirty seconds.'

'Really?'

Doug laughed. 'I know, people have far too much time on their hands.'

'And the last siren would have been on the first of April, so very recently,' she thought out loud, adding this to her notes.

'Yes, regular as clockwork. It terrified me the first time I heard it. I thought the end was nigh.'

'Nigh?'

'Coming,' he offered in explanation, the smile evident in his voice. 'I was ready to call my mum and say my goodbyes.'

'You don't have them in England?' she asked, surprised.

'No, nothing like it! If you hear a siren like that in London, it means the Germans are coming.'

Petra snorted, closing her notebook. 'They should have one here for the beginning of tourist season, then.'

Doug chuckled in response, slightly more enthusiastically

than her little joke necessitated. When he was finished, he asked, 'I hope that's helpful?'

'Oh, yes,' she replied. There was no point in telling him the notes hadn't given her much more than sites for a scavenger hunt, that she didn't even know if they were relevant to the case. 'Very helpful. I appreciate your insight. Thank you, Doug.'

'You're welcome! Have a wonderful weekend. Don't hesitate to contact me if I can help with anything else, you have my number now.'

Petra said her goodbyes and hung up, vacillating for a moment before adding Doug to her phone's contacts. It did no harm having someone in her address book who could do a bit of light Italian translation, especially someone who had nothing to do with the case or the force. She plugged her hairdryer in, glad she'd brought her own from home rather than relying on the low-powered hotel offering, and tried to organise her day in her mind. She would see Koren at the station, could organise a trip out to see Debeli Rtič and the beach at Dobrava. If Medved was there, she might be able to come along too. It would be interesting to hear what they made of *Inšpektor* Furlan's jaunt to Strmol to see the vintage cars. She could only hope that Horvat would not be too annoyed that she'd commandeered two of his officers. First, though, she had to trek back to Izola, and apologise to the Skoda for abandoning it in a car park overnight. She hoped the parking charges wouldn't be extortionate.

# Chapter 18

Petra's phone kept lighting up as she drove to the station, momentarily distracting her each time. After the third missed call notification, she pulled into an electronics store car park on the outskirts of Koper to see what the fuss was about. Each call had come from Koren, and she huffed in annoyance as she phoned him back. If he could only have waited a few more minutes, she'd have been there in person.

'*Inšpektorica!*' he exclaimed as she answered, loud enough that she assumed it was not only for her benefit, but also for someone else on his end. Her suspicions were confirmed when she heard the scraping of chair legs somewhere behind him.

'Koren. I will be at the station in a moment, can it wait?'

It wasn't clear whether Koren hadn't heard her, or simply didn't care. He ploughed on, ignoring her statement. 'I've got Marjan's alibi!'

'What?' she asked, feeling herself go very still. Her hand muscles tightened instinctively, on edge.

'Marjan's alibi, I found proof of it.' His tone was triumphant, bordering on crowing. Petra knew it wasn't aimed at her, but rather at those who had called him mad for ever believing Marjan's story: Božič, Horvat, the gossips of Koper.

'Are you at the station?'

'No, I'm at my mother's. I'll head over there now?'

Petra held in a hiss at the unprofessionalism of making important phone calls in front of his mother, instead agreeing that she'd see him at the station as soon as they could both get there. Pulling back out onto the road, she had to pay careful attention to the speed limit, her foot itching on the accelerator as her mind whirred. Marjan's alibi panning out was not something she could have foreseen. She wondered where Koren had found it, how much time he had spent chasing it without her realising. It was good police work, she had to say. Assuming, of course, that it was as cut-and-dried as he was suggesting.

She pulled into the station car park, striding up the stairs as she locked her car behind her. Through the glass panes in the door she could see Koren, fidgeting from foot to foot, a large padded envelope in his hands. When he spotted her, he rushed forward.

'I have it here,' he said, greetings and niceties forgotten in favour of the prize he held.

'Is it a video?'

'Yes, security footage.'

'Where can we watch it?' she asked, but he was one step ahead of her, already striding up the stairs past Horvat's office and up onto the second floor. She scurried to keep up, his long strides pulling him further ahead with every step. She made a noise of irritation, and he slowed down.

'It is security camera footage,' he told her as he opened a door at the far end of the corridor, its name label long since lost. Inside was a graveyard of technology, ranging from type-writers and old overhead projectors to fat black televisions on wheeled trolleys. Koren approached the closest one, turning it on and ejecting a tape.

'Security camera footage recorded on a tape?' Petra was incredulous, watching as Koren discarded the previous long-forgotten occupant of the tape slot and replaced it with another he drew out of his envelope.

'Something Marjan said when you spoke to him yester-day bothered me,' he explained. 'When he was talking about walking from Portorož to Piran. It is a lovely walk, all along the sea, but there are restaurants and nightclubs and shops all along the Portorož coast, and then hotels and cafés when you get closer to Piran. I was hopeful something must have caught him. Anywhere else in Slovenia, we wouldn't have a chance. But that stretch of coastline has so many tourists; every year there's pickpocketing or drunks fighting. Petty stuff, but when it involves foreigners and insurance companies then businesses tend to be that bit more careful.'

The television crackled into life, small white numbers appearing at the top left-hand corner of the screen as Koren stabbed at buttons. Petra didn't bother offering to help, no more confident in the use of an integrated VCR than Koren seemed to be. She stifled a laugh at the thought that this was the sort of technology problem that her father would be able to solve, and would relish doing so.

'And you found one?' she prompted.

'You'd be surprised at the number of fake cameras, cameras that are turned off out of season, and stickers warning you about a camera that doesn't actually exist. People obviously accept that cameras are useful to protect their businesses, but don't actually want to invest in one.'

Petra was not, in fact, surprised by this. She allowed Koren his moment anyway.

'The only business with a working camera along that whole path uses tapes?' she said with a grin, enjoying the strangeness of it. 'Whose footage is it?'

'The sailing club. The commodore told me that they can't afford a newer system, and even if they could then he wouldn't be able to work it. They really seem to like the tapes. I've watched it already, just once, to make sure I wasn't going to waste your time. I rewound the tape, it is all ready for you.' He looked mildly sheepish at this, and Petra couldn't help but smile at him.

On the screen, a picture flickered into existence. Petra could make out a wide concrete slipway, a long pontoon stretching off into the sea tethered to one corner. Halfway up the slipway was a jumble of dinghy trollies surrounding various powerboats that had been pulled up onto land. Two children were frozen on film, paddling in the water and splashing at a strange white blob in front of them.

'Shall I play it?' Koren asked her. Petra held up a finger to show he should wait, dragging two moth-eaten desk chairs out from a herd of them stashed in the far corner. Once they were both seated and she had her notebook in her lap, she nodded.

The children jittered into life, the blob in front of them sloshing around their feet. Petra realised it was a jellyfish as one child tried to waft it towards the other, making them scream and skitter up the concrete towards a waiting parent. At least, Petra assumed it was a scream. The video had no sound, and the picture was a fuzzy black and white, making detail hard to ascertain. Occasionally a ribbon of static would pass from bottom to top of the screen, distorting anything in its wake. Koren saw her eyeing up the quality.

'The image isn't perfect, but if you're looking for someone specific then you know it is them. We also have Marjan's description of his clothing that night to go on.'

Petra nodded, willing to be persuaded until it was clear he was wrong. Koren sped up the video, two little arrows appearing in the top right corner of the screen as hours' worth of walkers and sailing club members careered around the slipway. Dogs sprinted past, old ladies stopped and cupped their hands over their eyes to watch what was going on at sea. A piece of driftwood, trapped in the corner created by the pontoon, ceaselessly crashed from side to side. Darkness fell, and then quickly started to lift again. Koren stopped the dizzying rush as the timestamp hit 4 a.m., changing the speed so that it was only double time.

'How long is the walk from the casino?' she asked, the minutes ticking by with no one to be seen.

'It takes him about an hour,' Koren said, eyes focused on

the clock on the screen. 'Which I'd say is actually at the faster end of what I'd expect. There, do you see?'

As Koren spoke, he hit pause. From the left of the screen, Petra saw a slim figure stagger into view. His coat was wrapped tightly around his shoulders, his head hunched down. She leaned forward, nose centimetres from the screen, catching sight of what looked like poorly fitted trousers and a flat cap.

'Marjan says he was wearing his funeral suit with his father's old hat,' Koren supplied. 'The casino has a dress code, and that's all he has that meets it.'

Petra took in the hunch of the man's shoulders, his apparent desire to make himself smaller. She could believe it was the man she'd met in the cells the previous morning, remembering how he'd twisted and wriggled when he'd been sitting on the bed.

'Keep playing,' she said softly, and watched as the video continued in real time. The figure stumbled halfway across the slipway before stopping, staring out to sea. He then headed out onto the pontoon, standing perilously close to the edge as he peered down at something in the water. He stayed there for a few minutes, hands braced on his knees, far too small on the image for any form of identification. When he stood up, he ambled back to the middle of the slipway, turning towards the camera as he cupped his hands around his face and lit a cigarette. Before she had the chance to say anything, Koren paused the footage.

They both leaned even further forward, Petra in determined interest and Koren in apparent glee. The image was still grainy, but no worse than many other security systems Petra had encountered. She could see his dark eyes, skinny face, grey pixels highlighting drawn cheekbones. Bony hands clutched at his cigarette and an oversized lighter of some kind. If Petra were a betting woman, she would have put money on the figure being Marjan Furlan. In this one frame, she could see whispers of everything she had been told about him: the loner, the addict, the shadow to his brother's light.

'I didn't put the inventory of Marjan's belongings in the notes, as it didn't seem relevant,' said Koren in a rush, scrabbling in his pockets to reveal a folded piece of paper. 'But among his personal possessions at the time of his arrest, he had a cigarette lighter in the shape of Italy. He was wearing the hat at the time, too. It's a brown flat cap, with his father's name written on the inside lining.'

This information in mind, Petra strained even further towards the screen. It was impossible to make out what the lighter was shaped as, though she conceded that it looked far too big in the figure's thin hand. The hat she couldn't comment on, except that she didn't see them worn often outside of men working on their fields during the daytime. She was willing to believe that there were not two men ambling down the path from Portorož to Piran in the small hours of a Sunday morning wearing such a garment. Koren continued playing the video, but Marjan had evidently grown bored of the sailing club, striding away out of shot as soon as his cigarette was lit. The time was 5 a.m.

'You found his alibi,' she said. She turned to face Koren,

saddened to see that he suddenly looked a little nervous. She gave him a smile, reaching out to touch his arm. 'Well done, Aleš. Excellent work.'

Koren beamed at her, nodding his thanks. They stood for a moment, both gazing at the still television screen, digesting the information it held. After a moment, Koren's good humour dissipated suddenly, his body language becoming tense and his shoulders hunching in on themselves. 'I was so excited to find it that I didn't really consider what it means, until now. We have to start from scratch, don't we?'

'Almost,' she conceded. 'But even if we are straight back to where we started, we're doing so in the knowledge that we didn't let an innocent man go to jail. That means something.'

Koren nodded once, the movement sharp and definitive. 'How will you tell *Svetnik* Horvat? And *Inšpektor* Božič? They won't be pleased.'

'I don't have to care about that, thankfully,' she replied. 'They can be as unhappy as they like, it isn't my problem.' She was glad she sounded more confident than she felt, she had to admit that her stomach twisted at the thought of the uncomfortable conversation that awaited her.

Koren picked up the remote control to eject the video and replace it in his padded envelope. He seemed to be collecting his thoughts, lips pursed tight. 'Will we need them to confirm that this is Marjan before we start making other enquiries? Can we let him go?'

Petra sighed. 'I admit that I don't know *Svetnik* Horvat personally, but my own superintendent back in Ljubljana would be horrified to be bothered on a Saturday. I suspect it will serve us better to make some headway with a new theory, and then show him both Marjan's alibi and any progress we've made on Monday. And, since this doesn't absolve him of the vandalism, I think it is best he stays in the cells for now.' She refused to engage with Božič's probable anger. At the end of the day, he was the same rank as her. Even though part of her cringed at the thought of Božič's reaction, she would not let it get to her. It was hardly her fault he'd allowed himself to be so single-minded in his pursuit of Marjan Furlan that he'd allowed the real killer to go free for a week unnecessarily. He should be the one cringing and embarrassed, not her. Her internal bravado did little to calm her, and she fought off the desire to twang her hairband. Not in front of Koren.

'That's sensible,' agreed Koren. 'So, where do we start?'

'There's another line of enquiry that I've been working on.' Petra stood up as she spoke, shaking her shoulders out before returning her chair to the jumble in the corner and moving towards the door. She hadn't noticed that they had failed to put the lights on in the television room, and as she threw the door open she was stunned by the harshness of the artificial glow from the corridor. 'Something I found in the inspector's desk, which I think might be related to the disappearances his wife referenced.'

'What kind of something?' Koren asked eagerly, apparently unfazed that Petra had been keeping him in the dark. She wondered how long the boost of finding Marjan's alibi would carry him and hoped that he wouldn't slump again when it became apparent how little they actually had to work from.

'Notes, which I believe were inviting the inspector to secret meetings.' She pulled her phone from her pocket, stopping at the top of the stairs. It was quiet up here, the majority of the action was on the floors beneath them. She was not going to let the opportunity for some privacy pass her by. 'I've been assuming this isn't the inspector's handwriting?'

'No, definitely not,' murmured Koren, zooming in on the first note about Debeli Rtič. 'And I never saw him write in Italian, he only used it when absolutely necessary.'

Petra smiled, pleased that her assumption had been correct. She motioned that Koren could scroll to the next photo, and watched him read the note about the mermaid.

'I have spoken to a translator, and they suggested that this one might be about the monthly siren test.'

'That's why you wanted to know about the language centre,' said Koren, giving her a quick grin before returning to the phone. 'I was wondering about that one. Do you really trust the rest of the force so little?'

It wasn't an accusation, merely an expression of surprise. Still, Petra felt a little defensive. 'I'm here because someone within the force said they couldn't be trusted,' she reminded him. 'If, as you say, it is common knowledge that Portorož has better CCTV coverage than average, then what you've shown me this morning demonstrates that some of the team are lazy at best, malignant at worst.'

Koren blinked at her, his attention dragged from the notes.

'I hadn't thought about it that way,' he said after a second's hesitation, 'but you're right.' He wilted a little, scrolling to the final note listlessly.

Petra raked her hand through her hair in confusion. 'You hadn't thought that someone might be trying to cover something up in their hasty arrest of Marjan?'

'No!' he exclaimed. 'Never. Everyone was just convinced they had the right man. They aren't hiding anything.'

Petra scrutinised Koren, his open expression of shock. His eyes were wide and pleading, his eyebrows drawn together. He had straightened up from his normal slight stoop, surprise pulling him up to his full height. Petra crossed her arms over her chest.

'Whoever sent the note to Ljubljana was pretty damning in their account of what happened here. They refer to Marjan not being guilty, they suggest that it is a deliberate miscarriage of justice. Koren, please don't take this the wrong way, but I had been rather assuming you sent the note to Ljubljana asking for help.'

'No,' he breathed, shaking his head adamantly. 'It wasn't me. I know everyone thinks it was, but I was still hoping *Svetnik* Horvat would come around.'

Petra retrieved her phone from Koren's slack hands, replacing it in her pocket. He continued to blink at her, seemingly hoping that a doe-eyed expression would convince her. To a great extent, it did. It also made her more interested in the real identity of the author. Something at the back of her mind had been telling her it must be Koren, even Rossi's ignoring of him as a candidate hadn't swayed her. It seemed a given. Now, she was curious as to who else in the station had never believed in the case against Marjan Furlan, and whether they had any evidence of their own. If Koren had been the author, the note would have been written on gut instinct. If it was someone else, then there was at least a chance that they had some concrete evidence.

'Do you have any idea who might have written it?' She leant back against the cold wall behind her as she spoke, dropping her head back to stare at the square ceiling tiles. One was missing its corner, revealing a tangle of wires behind it.

'No, and I've been thinking about it a lot,' he admitted. 'I know I should respect their anonymity, my mother kept saying that, but knowing there was someone out there who agreed with me was just too much to ignore. I am certain on who didn't do it, but that doesn't help much.'

'Horvat,' Petra said, focus still above her.

'Obviously. Božič, Medved.'

'You've discounted Medved?'

'It isn't her style,' he said quickly. 'And to be honest, she wasn't really that invested in the case until you arrived. Plus, she said it wasn't her when I asked. I believe her.'

'I only know about five people in this station. You're much better placed than me to do this thought experiment, I'm sure you've been thorough.' Petra sighed and straightened up, mentally readying herself to plough on. Although she'd talked a big game about removing Marjan from her enquiries being a positive thing when Koren had wavered earlier, she had to admit she wasn't looking forward to it. The investigation's focus up until now had obviously been a push and pull between proving Marjan had killed his brother, and finding him an alibi. Other than her own scrappy investigation into the notes and the testimony of Irena Furlan, there wasn't much else to work from.

'You were hoping they could help us.' It wasn't a question, merely an expression of mutual disappointment. She gave Koren a small smile.

'Yes, but you're right. They chose to be anonymous for a reason. If they know something specific, maybe they'll help us if we get close.'

'What now, then?'

'Let's speak to Irena about the notes, then head out to Debeli Rtič and the beach at Dobrava. I doubt there'll be anything there, but it can't hurt to check.'

Buoyed by the new direction, Koren started off down the stairs, clattering away faster than Petra could keep up.

# Chapter 19

Irena Furlan had no clue as to why her husband might have been invited to either of the places referenced in the notes, and did not recognise their handwriting. She had, however, been able to confirm that although 1st April had been a day off for the inspector, he had still disappeared on one of his mysterious jaunts shortly before the siren was tested. He had come back with a gift for Irena, a large bar of the salted dark chocolate made at the Piranian salt pans, but this was easy to buy at any supermarket in the region. Petra wasn't surprised by any of these things, and so left the woman to spend the rest of her Saturday in peace. Instead, she and Koren crowded back into the marked police car he had taken from the station, heading in the direction of Debeli Rtič.

It wasn't a long drive, mostly along a quiet road with views down to the sea. Petra gazed out at the container ships inching along, their progress imperceptible if you watched it continuously. As they passed the sign marking the end of the town of Ankaran, Petra was surprised to find herself surrounded by vines, fields of them stretching as far as the eye could see. As they continued, another vineyard started on their other side so that they were surrounded by hundreds of perfectly spaced, neatly planted vines. Petra allowed her eyes to fuzz, not bothering to concentrate on individual plants, letting them merge into one green blur.

'Koper's biggest wine producer grows a lot of their grapes here,' Koren said, noticing her preoccupation with the scenery.

Petra nodded vacantly, her attention still on the vines. She thought about the little vineyard behind her guesthouse, wondering if they ever felt threatened by the presence of such a behemoth so close by. She doubted it, somehow. There was something so welcoming about the little handwritten sign she'd seen and the sight of a boy and an old man checking their crop. She resolved to buy a bottle from them to take back to Ljubljana, when this was all over. Maybe a couple, so she could give them as gifts. She was sure her mother would love one, 'my daughter solved a murder on the coast and all I got was a bottle of wine'. Petra mentally scolded herself. She was now without suspects, without motive, relying on three notes that could have been in the inspector's dictionary for any amount of time. It was a bit presumptuous to assume she would solve the murder, let alone be returning to Ljubljana in glory. She slumped a little in her seat, aware that Koren was slowing down to a stop.

'This is the difficult bit,' he began, undoing his seatbelt so that he could turn to face her properly. 'This whole area is technically Debeli Rtič. The note could be referring to anywhere.'

Petra scanned her surroundings, growing less confident

with every passing second. She hadn't thought there would be much to see out here, but the chances of them even searching the area thoroughly enough to be satisfied were dwindling. She took a deep, steadying breath and surged out of the car, walking around it and coming to a stop in front of its bonnet. Koren opened his door, throwing his legs out and pushing on his knees to straighten up.

'Did the inspector ever mention coming here?' she asked, slipping her sunglasses down over her eyes.

'I've been thinking about that. Not directly, but he and his wife walked the last few legs of the Slovenian Mountain Trail to celebrate their thirtieth wedding anniversary a few years ago. The last stop on that is here, you finish right by the sea.' His speech slowed near the end, his eyes widening with realisation. A pang of hope tore through Petra, and she pursed her lips together.

Koren started to move away from her, striding briskly away from the car. After only a hundred metres or so, the road turned from rough-edged concrete into a dusty track. Little puffs of grey rose up with every step Koren took. A little way ahead, sitting back from the road on a small patch of grass carved out among the vines, was a decrepit concrete structure. It was square in shape, the area around it strangely lush and manicured in comparison with its grey shabbiness. The roof had partially caved in, although the walls beneath it looked sturdy enough. It was crowned by a small, sheltered platform, barely big enough for one person to stand in. The whole exterior of the building was strangely devoid of graffiti, except for a fading windmill painted on one side, a stick figure as tall as Petra standing in its doorway. Above the stick figure, just under the decaying roof, was a large window.

'What is it?' she asked as they approached, her attention divided between the structure and the gorgeous view out across the Gulf of Trieste. She stopped briefly, taking it all in. A light wind blew in off the water, cooling her skin, slightly overheated from the pace Koren had set. She could imagine it would be glorious, reaching this point after a long walk across Slovenia. The sea, the breeze, the slight rustle of the vines. Maybe she would do the Mountain Trail herself, if Interpol didn't work out.

'An old observation tower,' said Koren. 'It dates from the Second World War; my grandpa could tell you all about it. The whole peninsula around Ankaran was occupied by the Fascists, they built all sorts of defences and observation points in case the Allies tried to land around here.'

Petra nodded excitedly, starting to walk a slow circle around the building. She could see why such a structure would be built here, it offered excellent views of the water all around. No one would have been able to launch an invasion without the man up on the little platform above knowing, and on a day like today he'd have seen the ships out in the gulf from miles away. Even from ground level and without binoculars Petra could clearly spot a few little yachts out on the water, pricks of white against the dazzling blue.

Her slow perambulation around the tower revealed another window at ground level, big enough for a human to scramble through. The wooden window frame was half rotted, bleached the same silvery colour as the bar at *La Medusa*. She leaned through, slightly surprised at the lack of rubbish on the floor inside. Large shards of plaster, sloughed off the walls by age and lack of care, were strewn across the concrete pad. People definitely visited the tower, the network of graffiti covering the interior walls was testament to that: hammers and sickles, declarations of love, and the image of the Izola football team mascot were all daubed across the bare concrete. She sensed someone behind her, and wriggled a little to the left to give Koren a view past her.

'What made you think of this place?' she asked, eyes still scanning the graffiti. Could there be a note among it, a clue?

'It's one of the final waypoints on the Mountain Trail, the last monument before you finish. I remember the inspector mentioning it. He was a bit of a war buff, this sort of thing fascinated him. We talked about doing some of the trail together one day, maybe after he retired. I was looking forward to it,' Koren trailed off, wrinkling his nose as he tried to regain his composure.

Petra gave him a reassuring smile and nod. There was an atmosphere here, she had to agree. Something about the whispering wind from the sea through the vines, the clicking of insects and the view for miles around. For somewhere so close to a bustling health resort, filled with recuperating patients and rambunctious school groups, it was incredibly peaceful.

Petra stayed still for a moment, allowing Koren to grieve for his mentor, and then turned back to the window. Shrugging off her light linen jacket and handing it to Koren, she hoisted herself up onto the ledge, kicking her legs through.

'*Inšpektorica*? Would you rather I do that?' Koren sounded concerned, her jacket dangling limply in his hands as he moved towards the opening.

She waved him off, dusting herself down. It was dimmer in here than she'd expected from the outside, and she pushed her sunglasses up on top of her head, the movement pulling her errant curl out of her eyes again. Although the roof looked at first glance to have fallen in, she could now see that this first storey remained intact. It was parts of the observational structure above that had tumbled down.

Petra ran her hands along the walls, dislodging another few small shards of plaster as she did so. A lizard darted out from under a pile by her foot, streaking up the wall and behind one of the ageing beams on the roof. Koren continued to loom through the window, his broad shoulders blocking out much of the light. Loath to tell him to back off, Petra spun around. 'Do you have a torch?'

Koren nodded enthusiastically, hands scrabbling for the black utility belt around his waist. He took off his hat, placing it on the ground and carefully tucking her jacket up inside it, before wedging himself in the window again, passing his standard issue torch through to her. She realised as he squished himself into the window that the ceiling would be almost too low for him, that getting through the opening she had clambered through would be difficult for someone with his long legs and wide shoulders. Sadness rocked her a little, as she realised she knew very little about what *Inšpektor* Furlan had looked like in life. Would he have fit through the window easily? What was his eye-height, what would he have seen first when he got in? Could he have got in at all? Crime scene photos robbed the viewer of proper context, just offering macabre flashes of how you died. They did little to elucidate how you'd lived.

Koren seemed to sense her train of thought, or else had arrived at it himself. 'The inspector would have done just what you're doing. He was always touching things, fiddling with things. That's why his desk is so cluttered, he was a collector of bits and bobs. He said policemen nowadays were too reliant on seeing and being told things, they didn't do enough touching and smelling and listening.'

'Is being told things not listening?' asked Petra, poking at the beam the lizard had run behind. As her torch beam passed it stuck its little head out at her, retracting it again when it realised how close her face was to its hiding hole.

'Have you met *Inšpektor* Božič? You can tell him anything you like, it doesn't mean he's listening.' Koren tapped his fingers rhythmically against the decaying wood of the window frame. 'And the inspector didn't just mean listening to witnesses, or suspects. He meant actually hearing what was going on around you. We used to stand in Titov *Trg* and just listen. The people around you can tell you a lot without even speaking to you, if you let them.'

Petra wondered briefly whether *Svetnik* Horvat had been aware of the shift time spent idly standing in Titov *Trg*, but decided not to make a joke about it. Not for the first time in the investigation, she felt the loss of a man she never knew. It was a worthwhile skill to teach the next generation, that relying on technology and modern discoveries was not the way to be a good police officer. Some old techniques may have been superseded, but that didn't mean they were obsolete. She was grateful that *Svetnik* Golob had taught her this, was glad that *Inšpektor* Furlan had been flying the same flag.

She continued to move the torch methodically around the walls and ceiling, stopping to prod at anything that seemed untoward. She shrieked and recoiled when a particularly large spider staggered out from behind a rusting metal sconce, prompting a giggle from Koren that she squashed with a glare. As she staggered backward, her heel hit something buried under the cracked plaster and dead leaves that littered the floor. It was small, pressed up against the corner nearest Koren's window, well-concealed by dimness and mess. Petra crouched, brushing the detritus away to reveal a metal box bolted to the wall. It looked like the ones she'd seen on hikes, used to protect logbooks and the collectible metal stamps positioned at the top of every hill in Slovenia from the elements. It was covered in stickers bearing the names of various hiking clubs from all across Europe, marking out their successful discovery, along with a thin film of dust. She pulled the lid off, finding inside a pair of binoculars affixed to the box by a long chain.

Petra moved out of the way to allow Koren to see, slightly amused at how far he was now leaning through the opening.

His whole torso dangled into the small space, turned at a strange angle to get a good look at what she was doing.

'Binoculars?' he said, confusion evident in his tone. 'Anything else in there?'

She shone her torch in, poking around. 'A pen, nothing else.'

'Where's it from?'

Petra pulled it out, Koren's evident hope that it would be a shining clue becoming a little infectious. 'Just a biro. Sorry.'

Koren let out a noise of displeasure, extricating himself slightly from the window. 'I suppose we can't have everything,' he said mildly, and Petra laughed at the maturity of the statement. She wondered how often Marija Koren had told him that during his childhood.

'Well said,' she replied, taking photos of the binoculars. Confident she had documented them well enough, she pulled them out of the metal box and motioned for Koren to get out the way. Standing in front of the opening, she put the binoculars to her eyes, surprised that the length of the chain limited her motion. If the local hiking club had left them here to take in a particularly good view, then it must have been within the scope of the chain.

'What can you see?'

They were surprisingly powerful for such small lenses, presumably so that any walker who made it to them was rewarded with good views of the ships out in the gulf, and the mountains beyond. Petra ignored this, instead looking down to the coast, the steep cliff at the end of the track giving way to the beach below. A few taller shrubs on the cliff itself slightly obscured her view, their green spikes framing the pebbles, but not enough to concern her. If she turned a little either way, she got a similarly uninterrupted view of the coastline on either side. Down on the beach, a small bird skittered around in the surf, and she followed its progress easily.

'The coast, all along the beach,' she replied. 'I think I can see most of Debeli Rtič.'

# Chapter 20

After Koren had forced his way into the tower and done a thorough perusal of his own, they hurried back to the car and started out towards Dobrava. There was no proof that *Inšpektor* Furlan had been in the tower, but both Petra and Koren were unable to shake the feeling that they'd found something important.

'Do you think someone was having an affair?' asked Koren, tapping his thumbs on the steering wheel as he waited at a traffic light. 'The notes were to draw the inspector out so he could see proof?'

'You think Irena Furlan might be unfaithful?'

'No!' Koren was scandalised. 'Not *Gospa* Furlan. But maybe someone important, someone with enemies. The mayor?'

'Why would an anonymous source inform a homicide detective that the mayor was having a sordid affair on a beach?' asked Petra, although her tone wasn't unkind. Her own brain was also postulating madly, suggesting every possibility under the sun.

'Because he wasn't just a homicide detective, he was *Inšpektor* Ivan Furlan,' said Koren, and Petra was starting to understand what that meant. He was decent, he was honest, he was well-known. Maybe someone would have tipped him off to something, even if it wasn't entirely relevant to his professional brief.

'Having an affair isn't a crime, though. He was either being tipped off about something criminal, or about something personal. I agree an affair is a good call if it was related to his private life, but why would you deliver secret notes in Italian if you wanted to expose something personal?'

'You're right.' Koren didn't seem disheartened by the implausibility of his theory, instead moving on to a new one. 'Blackmail, then. Either someone was blackmailing the inspector, which I find unlikely, or they wanted him to witness a hand-off. Maybe the mayor is in someone's pocket.'

'You have really taken against the mayor this morning,' Petra commented, raising her eyebrows and smiling at Koren from where she lounged against the passenger-side window. 'Is there something I should know?'

Koren laughed, the sound welcome. Petra hadn't realised quite how tense the young man had been up until now, how desperately he had been straining in his quest to get justice for his mentor. With Marjan off the hook and a new lead to follow, he was able to calm down. She also quietly hoped that he was starting to feel more comfortable with her, that they were becoming a team. Petra was beginning to feel that way, and she cringed at the idea that it wasn't mutual.

'He's just an example. Although my father is convinced he took bribes to build all those roundabouts in Koper, so I might be on to something.'

'Big Roundabout, at it again?' she teased, and they both dissolved into laughter.

They lapsed into a natural silence as the giggles subsided. Koren focused on the traffic around them, and Petra on the scenery slipping past. They had already passed through Koper, and were now following her route back to the guesthouse, the last remnants of the weekend rush to the coast crowding around them. Passing her lodgings, Koren turned right at the roundabout she'd spotted on her first night here, then took a sudden left that led them through a strange village that seemed to be entirely composed of hotels.

'Belvedere,' Koren said by way of explanation. 'You should see it in off season, it's like a ghost town. Dobrava is just beyond.'

Petra nodded, tensing as she saw the thinness of the road ahead and quite how many other cars and tourists were milling around, children staggering in front of them as though it was nothing. She had been unimpressed when all the police cars in Slovenia had been revamped to include large fluorescent yellow stickers on the bodywork, but had had to admit that they certainly made them more noticeable. This didn't seem to apply to the tourists of Belvedere, who treated the police car as though it was just another of the vehicles crawling down the street. Two shirtless men shouting in Russian embraced right next to Petra's window, and she shifted her weight so that she was leaning in towards the central console.

Slowly, the vehicles ahead of them started to peter out, slipping into the already-crowded car parks that were squashed in among the resort hotels and camping site. Koren drove past them, teeth gnashing as he was held up again by the queue into a large turning circle at the far end of Belvedere, a harassed looking young man indicating to Austrian saloons and Dutch caravans that they could go no further. When Koren reached the front of the queue, the young man jumped out of the way and waved them on, allowing them to continue onto the unpaved track behind him. Koren gave him a grateful wave, receiving a weary nod in return.

The track was bumpy and uneven, and Petra was quickly grateful both for the impressive suspension on the police car, and that the powers that be in Belvedere had had the foresight not to allow less appropriate vehicles to strand themselves down here. As they drew further away from the resort, the banks on either side of the track quickly became crowded with olive trees interspersed with even narrower drives leading down to white-washed houses beyond. From a shady spot under a particularly leafy tree, a large orange cat assessed the passing police car, maintaining eye contact with Petra as they drove on. After another few minutes, Koren pulled into a lay-by at the side of the road.

'We'll have to walk down to the beach from here, you can't drive to it,' Koren explained once they were both out of the car, sun beating down on them.

Petra looked around herself, at the waist-high coastal scrub and the tall trees growing at various points on the cliffs below. Her view was nowhere near as good here as it was at the tower in Debeli Rtič, and she suspected that if the other note was leading the inspector to a similar observation point then she'd have to go lower. Petra threw her jacket into the back seat, rolling her sleeves up in preparation for a sweaty walk.

The cliff path was hard to find at first, and Petra and Koren spent half an hour or so stumbling along various field tracks leading between olive trees trying to locate where it might start. They sent a pleading text to Medved, both openly thrilled when she replied with vague directions grounded in hazy childhood memories. Eventually, they stumbled onto the top of the path, leading steeply down against the cliff face. Koren strode out ahead, jumping nimbly down any larger steps and offering Petra a hand, which she took with a grateful nod.

When they were halfway down, Petra saw exactly what Medved's mother meant when she said it was like the Côte d'Azur. Although it was the same sea as she had seen from Debeli Rtič, something about the small cove and quality of light here made it far more magical. The beach seemed to have three distinct zones, larger rocks under the cliff face blending into a pebbled section, before giving way to a rim of sand. The water was multi-coloured too, greens and blues shifting under sparkling light, a contrast to the jagged cliffs above. A lone swimmer cut through the still water, their red beach towel clearly visible on the rocks even from this distance. Petra pressed herself up against the cliff behind her and pulled her phone out, unashamedly snapping a picture of the scene. Whether it was for her mother, or to inspire some slight jealousy among her colleagues back in Ljubljana on the team group chat, she could not say.

She was about to continue when she realised that Koren had disappeared in front of her. The turn in the path was steep enough that he was rendered invisible by height difference and foliage. She hurried after him as fast as she could, mindful not to slip as she went. She found him leaning into a slight indentation in the cliff below, concealed both from above and below by the natural shape of the rock, gazing out to sea.

'You don't need binoculars here,' she said, his nod confirming that they were in agreement. 'You could just watch from here, and no one down on the beach would know.'

'You'd have to be confident that no one was coming behind you, as you'd be stuck if they did. But if they just looked down from where we started, they wouldn't know you were even here.'

'He was being tipped off to watch something,' Petra concluded, staring out at the swimmer as they made slow progress towards a large buoy. 'Someone wanted him to see what was going on out here, and at Debeli Rtič.'

'Whatever it is, it is obviously a moving target,' said Koren. 'There can't be much of a schedule to it, if it moves randomly along the coast.'

'That's probably deliberate. Makes it harder for someone to see, unless they get advance notice.'

Koren hummed in agreement, eyes fixed somewhere in the distance. 'There's something illegal going on, and someone with inside knowledge was tipping *Inšpektor* Furlan off to it, so he could see it with his own eyes. Why would they do that? Why just him?'

'They must have thought they could trust him,' Petra suggested. 'They must disagree with what is going on, and hoped he could stop it.'

'I wonder if that got him killed,' Koren said in response, so quietly that Petra had to focus to make sure she heard him. It was the same assumption she was working with. Had the note-writer set Furlan up, ambushed him somewhere to stop him from talking? Or had they been found out by whoever they were betraying, and was there another body lurking somewhere, yet to be discovered?

'I think we have to assume that whatever this is, it relates to the inspector's death.' Her tone was clear, decisive. She could sense Koren wavering next to her, his proximity to the case weakening him temporarily as he came to terms with both his being left out of the inspector's secret investigation, and the murkiness of the web they had started to uncover. If these notes, these viewpoints, had indeed contributed to the inspector's death, then it was fair to say that the job he loved had killed him. It was a sobering thought. While Koren battled with this, she could be strong. They both needed it.

'I think we need to speak to someone who specialises in cases like these,' she suggested when Koren didn't speak. 'Neither of us knows enough about this side of things to know where we should go from here.'

'This side of things?'

'Local corruption,' she began, hoping to lighten the tone by referencing Koren's earlier suggestion. 'Or, more likely, organised crime.'

Koren let out a huge breath, Petra's statement obviously confirming what he had been suspecting but not wanting to voice. 'Drugs?'

'I don't know, but it seems a possibility that secret meetings on the coast this close to both Croatia and Italy could have something to do with the drug routes. I think we should certainly speak to *Inšpektorica* Rossi, get her view on things. Organised crime is her remit, isn't it?'

Koren nodded slowly, briefly looking back out to sea again. Petra started heading back up the path, leaving him to his moment.

# Chapter 21

Petra texted Rossi on their way back to Koper, glad to have something to do rather than dwell on the silence that filled the car. She hadn't had a response yet, but kept the app open, touching the screen whenever it threatened to darken to keep her hands busy. Koren was staring straight ahead, although she doubted his attention was on the cars around him. She could only guess what he was thinking.

'How about we grab a coffee at the *slaščičarna*?' she suggested. 'This time, I'll definitely pay.' She didn't want him thinking she was some sort of free hot beverage and pastry leech, although she knew Marija would hiss as soon as her hand went to her purse.

Between the hospitality of Marija Koren and Domenico Rossi, she had yet to pay for anything in Koper, and it was making her a little anxious. Was this how you became part of the coastal web, unable to be impartial, gossiping about a respected policeman's death and deciding his brother should be put away for it while you waited in the queue at the market? She tried not to be so cynical, reminding herself of the well-known hospitality of people from this region. Since leaving Dobrava, she'd been mulling on how well everyone seemed to know the geography of the area, how confident they were in finding strange, tucked-away places through decades of familiarity. Ivan Furlan might have needed clues to get here to see a specific event, but Koren had been able to guess with enough context. How was she ever to find a killer who potentially knew every stone, every cove, every abandoned building? She could be here for a year and never be able to compete with them when it came to piecing together the puzzle. She was utterly reliant on having her own locals to protect and help her, and it was that feeling of helpless vulnerability that both terrified and enraged her. Petra had found the notes, and since then she'd needed her hand held to translate them, to locate the places they referenced. She felt impotent. A nasty little voice at the back of her head told her that Interpol would be just like this, but worse. She refused to let regret creep in, to let doubt cloud her judgement. Petra twanged her hair tie against the soft flesh of her inner arm, her brain clearing with the shock. Even though she didn't have the local knowledge, she reminded herself, it obviously wasn't the only key to cracking this case, or one of the Koper officers would have worked it out by now. Sometimes a fresh pair of eyes was exactly what was needed.

Koren nodded, mind evidently on other things. What would she want to hear, were their roles reversed?

'You couldn't have known.' She regretted the phrase as soon as it left her mouth, the triteness of it filling the car, making her wish she hadn't spoken at all.

'I know,' Koren responded, hands tightening in their text-book-perfect positions on the steering wheel. 'I couldn't have known without him telling me, but he never said a thing.'

Petra worried at her bottom lip, squinting slightly as she stared at Koren, half hoping that she would be able to read the right thing to say from his posture, his body language. He remained stoically silent, position stiff and eyes trained on the road.

'I imagine it was to protect you,' she ventured. 'Or that he didn't yet know whether it was worth involving you.'

'I'd have involved him,' Koren replied with the same simple certainty as she'd seen him display before. For Aleš Koren, it seemed, there were very few shades of grey. Black and white were all that was available to him, honesty versus deceit.

'He didn't even tell Irena.'

'She's his wife, she'd only have worried. I might have been able to help.'

There was nothing she could say to derail this logic, Petra knew that from experience. She'd never be able to persuade him that there was precious little one plucky *policist* could do in the face of corruption, or organised crime, or whatever *Inšpektor* Furlan had become embroiled in in the weeks leading up to his death. Pointing out that whatever they were dealing with might have been the root of a more experienced officer's demise, and so would probably have ended similarly poorly for Koren, seemed cruel. Instead, Petra fell silent again as they entered the long tunnel carved through the hillside between Izola and Koper, the dimness surrounding them oddly fitting for the mood inside the car.

Although he hadn't confirmed it with Petra, Koren ignored the exit for the station, carrying on towards central Koper and pulling into a small roadside car park near Titov *Trg*. He turned the engine off, but made no move to leave the car. Petra followed suit, sitting quietly in the passenger seat, twisting her phone around in her hands.

'How much can we tell my mother?' Koren asked eventually, making Petra start. Her first instinct was irritation, Koren's reliance on his mother and willingness to ignore professional boundaries rearing their ugly head again. She chose to remain calm.

'What do you mean?'

'That's why we're here, isn't it? You think my mother might know something.'

Petra shook her head quickly, distressed both that Koren thought she'd so willingly get involved in local gossip and that she would be so grasping and callous as to use his mother as a source of it. 'It hadn't even crossed my mind. I just thought you'd like a break before heading back to the station. We haven't heard from Rossi, I think we've earned a pause.'

Koren looked concerned, his eyebrows furrowing as he pursed his lips together. 'We're just here for coffee?'

'If that's alright with you,' Petra said, reaching out to touch Koren on the arm. He relaxed into her light touch, turning to give her a small and rather sad smile.

'We can get takeaway, walk along the seafront and do some more brainstorming?'

Petra decided against insisting that they take the time to

regroup properly, realising that Koren was in no mood to do anything other than plough on. He suddenly seemed very young in his blind determination, lacking the experience to know he would either burn out or slip up if he didn't give himself time to calm down and act rationally. She supposed that was what she was for, in some sense, to guide the passion and try and make sure he didn't get himself or anyone else hurt. For the first time, Petra spared a thought for the working relationship between Furlan and Koren. How had their partnership functioned? Had Koren always trailed after Furlan, learning by watching, or had he been given some agency? It was hard to say, looking at the righteously furious young man sitting next to her, his face strangely neutral in comparison with his body language and desperation to keep working.

They walked to the *slaščičarna* in silence, Koren politely holding the door open for Petra when they arrived. Inside was heaving, a long line of customers waiting patiently for their chance to order something from the impressive array of multi-layered cakes proudly displayed inside the glass counter. Petra told Koren to go and greet his mother, joining the queue behind a young Serbian couple arguing quietly about which flavour mousse cake to share. By the time he returned, Marija marching through the swing door behind him, Petra had successfully obtained and paid for both coffees.

Marija caught sight of the two pale green takeaway cups in Petra's hands and raised her eyebrows, a silent rebuke which Petra took on the chin. Instead, she nodded at Marija, not wanting to spill any of her illicit purchases.

'Good morning, Marija. How are you?'

'Fine, thank you,' she replied. 'You are looking very well, Petra. The coast agrees with you. Aleš tells me you can't stay?'

'Not this morning, I'm afraid.' Petra was tempted to throw Koren to the wolves, pretend that they had all the time in the world and settle in for a long morning of coffee and cake while they waited for Rossi to get back to them. Koren was right, though. For as long as Petra could remain level-headed and calm, there were things to be done. The best time to take a break would be when neither of them was thinking clearly anymore.

'A shame. Would you like a *rogljiček* to take away with you? Apricot, plain or chocolate?'

Petra and Koren finally left the shop a few minutes later, waving madly behind them as they tried to juggle both their coffees and a paper bag filled with day-old *potica* and a *rogljiček* each. Petra had felt forced to put her foot down when Marija attempted to add more goodies from the display case. Day-old goods that would otherwise have been scoffed by Koren and his brother as an after-work snack, she could justify. The *rogljiček* smelled simply too good to be rejected, and as they headed back through Titov *Trg* her first apricot jam-filled bite confirmed that she'd made the right decision.

They walked briskly down the street towards the seafront, dodging out of the way of a group of old women queueing at the theatre's box office and neatly sidestepping a crowd of tourists trekking in the opposite direction, their eyes fixed on the Praetorian Palace. Petra's gaze was trained firmly ahead of her, staring at the cruise ship that was partially blocking her view of the water, hundreds of small windows dominating her field of vision. When they reached the end of the street, Koren led her out onto a stretch of pavement built like a balcony, with wide-spaced, waist-high rails offering some semblance of protection and allowing a view onto the port below. A set of stone stairs and a sleek modern lift were built into the side of the balcony, allowing access to the waterfront. At this end, so close to the town itself, the port was reasonably small and quiet. Further to the right, Petra could see the start of the industrial area, huge container ships being denuded of their cargo by enormous, creaking cranes.

Koren kept moving, heading down the stairs to bring them out onto sea-level. The cruise ship continued to loom, its life-boats seeming to dangle ominously above them, even though Petra was still a significant distance away. Koren seemed unfazed, marching off to the left and leaving the port in his wake. Petra scurried after him, taking another bite of her pastry as she went. She smiled as they passed the area into which passengers evidently disembarked, where an enterprising city planner had placed a trio of expensive-looking vending machines offering everything from cans of chilled beer to tubes of sun cream. They passed a sailing club and a rowing club, both heaving with young children carrying oars and buoyancy aids and water bottles, before coming level with a small beach. A large grey dog stretched himself out at the water's edge, apparently unbothered by the sign on the gate clearly banning his presence, his owners sunning themselves on beach towels.

'My grandparents used to bring me here all the time,' said Koren, gesturing to the beach with his takeaway cup. 'When I was too young to help at the café, they'd look after me in the summer. We'd come here early, so we'd get a good spot, and then I'd rush about all day while Nonna read and Nonno napped. They'd bring all sorts of snacks, biscuits, chocolate and sugary soft drinks. Things that should have made me manic by the end of the day, but I was running around and swimming so much that I'd always fall asleep the minute I got home.'

Koren had stopped walking while he talked, and Petra stood with him as he gazed through the wire fence onto the beach. It seemed to have calmed him a little, the memory of summer days spent with his grandparents, and she was happy to give him a moment of peace. There was something bitter-sweet about watching other children doing exactly what he described, while he stood in a stuffy uniform gazing in from the outside, his heart aching with what had happened to his mentor. It seemed like a loss of innocence of some kind, the cruel realities of adulthood imposing themselves on a happy childhood memory. She hoped he hadn't noticed.

'We used to go to see my mother's family in Prekmurje every summer,' she offered in response, not wanting the calm moment to end. 'I'd have killed to be at the beach, but I just tramped around my grandfather's fields, poking at stones with sticks. Sometimes we'd go to the thermal spa nearby, or play in the river, but it was nothing like this.'

Koren turned to her in surprise, taking a bite from his

chocolate *rogljiček* and leaving a smear across his lip in the process. 'I didn't realise you came from there.'

'My mother's family are from there. I've never lived anywhere but Ljubljana,' she explained. 'I'd be of no more use solving a crime in Murska Sobota than I am in Koper.' Petra meant to sound light-hearted, but she couldn't keep the weight out of her intonation. She winced at the open statement of her internal self-doubt.

Koren shrugged, seemingly unaware of her inner turmoil. 'I'd say you're doing a pretty good job in Koper, *Inšpektorica*. Without you, Marjan would be going to jail for a murder he didn't commit.'

'That was you, Koren. You found his alibi.'

'Because I had time to. If you hadn't supported me then I'd have been pulled onto traffic duty and forced to give up on searching. You found the notes, you got us to Debeli Rtič and the beach at Dobrava.' His tone wasn't obsequious or pitying. He sounded like he was stating the obvious, just telling it how it was. It calmed Petra, his obvious confidence in both her abilities and her record to date. He evidently believed in her. It was embarrassing that she couldn't say the same about herself.

'That's good of you to say,' she said, never one to take a compliment lying down.

'It's true.' His simple, monochromatic thinking appeared again, and Petra smiled at him.

The moment was broken by her phone pinging twice in quick succession, then starting to trill merrily. She thrust her baked goods at Koren, pulling her phone out with seconds to spare before the call failed, swiping desperately at the screen when she saw the identity of the caller.

'Giulia, thank you so much for returning my message,' she gabbled, aware of Koren's wide eyes fixed on her. He mouthed 'Giulia' at her, evidently amazed that Petra had permission for such familiarities. She made a mental note to make Koren aware of the difficulties a woman might face in the police, even nowadays, to suggest that he be a little more aware that Rossi's brusqueness was not because she was cold-hearted.

'Petra, good morning. How can I help?'

'We've come across something in the case that I'd like your thoughts on. Would you be free for a quick chat? I'm sorry to bother you when you aren't on shift, especially at the weekend.'

'Weekends don't feel like weekends when you run a bar,' Rossi replied, her tone playful, if a little strained. Petra thought about the rush back at *Slaščičarna Koren*, imagining a similar scene at *La Medusa*. 'Domenico is short-staffed today, so I'm needed here. Could you come to me?'

'Of course, of course.' Petra started walking briskly back the way they had come, Koren stumbling after her with arms full of pastries and coffee. 'Is now all right?'

'The sooner the better. I've already served my first *Pelinkovec* shot of the day. I can tell that it is going to be a long weekend.'

# Chapter 22

Rossi came bustling out of *La Medusa* as soon as she saw Petra and Koren approaching through the large window. She was dressed entirely in black, a silvery grey apron tied tightly around her waist. The uniform made her look younger, softer somehow. Petra put a large part of this down to the shoes: instead of the chic pair she had worn yesterday, she was now wearing a pair of black leather trainers.

'If I was to murder Domenico, could you look the other way?' she asked as she approached them, ignoring Koren to give Petra a kiss on either cheek. 'As a favour to a friend?'

'This isn't how you planned on spending your weekend?' Petra guessed with a laugh.

'As we speak, I should be at a music and aperitivo event at La Fenice. You should see the dress I bought for the occasion, the beading is exquisite.'

'The opera house in Venice?' asked Koren, forcing Rossi finally to recognise his presence. She gave him an assessing look, unashamedly inspecting him from head to toe.

'Where else?' Her inspection had evidently found him

wanting, and she made no secret of it.

'I am sorry you have missed that,' Petra interjected, trying to draw attention away from Koren's rapidly reddening face. 'I suppose your loss is our gain. We'll try and be as quick as we can.'

Rossi threw her hands up in the air, tutting as she did so. 'Oh, take your time. If I'm going to be stuck in Isola it may as well be interesting. I suppose it could be worse, the opera was *Rigoletto*. I loathe a pathetic female lead.' She flounced over to the furthest two-seater table from the door into *La Medusa*, settling herself in the sun and stretching out. Her tortoise-shell sunglasses appeared from one of the pockets in her apron, and she slipped them over her eyes as she lounged.

Petra settled opposite her, Koren dragging a chair over from the next table and sitting overly close to her, his height even when seated making her feel a little claustrophobic. Rossi either didn't care about his avoidance of proximity, or didn't notice it, continuing to sun herself.

'Firstly, you should know that we have established Marjan Furlan's alibi. With that in mind: if I told you that *Inšpektor* Furlan had been receiving secret notes advising him to surveil various beaches around Koper, what would you say?' She tried to keep her question as open as possible while also catching Rossi's interest.

Her tactic worked, as Rossi sat up in her seat slowly, sucking her teeth. 'At what sort of times?'

'Dusk, midday, at the end of his shift. It varies.'

'And which beaches?'

'Debeli Rtič, and the beach at Dobrava, near Belvedere.'

Rossi hummed to herself, folding her hands together and settling them in her lap. Even though her eyes were obscured by dark lenses, Petra could feel the weight of her gaze. 'Do the notes say anything else?'

'They're in Italian,' volunteered Koren. Rossi tipped her head to indicate that she'd heard him, but made no move to look at him.

'And you suspect what? Organised crime?'

'We were brainstorming everything from an affair to blackmail to the mob,' Petra admitted. 'Which is why we came to you. We suspect that someone was tipping the inspector off, making him aware of something that was happening on the beaches. If that's the case, then it seems likely that whatever it was contributed to his death.'

Rossi remained silent, finally taking her eyes off Petra. She turned her head a little from side to side, apparently people-watching as tourists and locals moved around the square. Koren gave Petra a worried look, which she ignored, allowing Rossi time to gather and edit her thoughts. Finally, she licked her lips. 'Contributed to, if not caused Ivan's death,' Rossi echoed, her tone melancholy.

'Yes.'

'*Policist* Koren, Ivan never spoke to you about this?'

Petra flinched, knowing that Rossi had just touched a nerve. Rossi's gaze was now fixed on Koren, her head cocked to the side in interest.

'No, he never mentioned it,' Koren replied evenly. Petra was impressed at how impassive he kept his voice, his control over his emotions.

Rossi nodded at that, apparently unsurprised. 'And you are completely dedicated to solving his murder?'

'Of course.' This was less neutral. Koren sounded surprised that anyone might think otherwise, perhaps even a little offended.

'Good. Me too.'

Silence fell across the table again, and Petra started to wonder whether this had been a good idea. The Giulia who she'd spent yesterday evening with seemed far removed from the *Inšpektorica* Rossi now sitting opposite her. She felt foolish for assuming that she knew Rossi after one bonding session, was starting to recognise that the harsh exterior Rossi had adopted to protect herself at work extended to any interaction with *Inšpektorica* Vidmar, even if Petra and Giulia were fast becoming friends.

'I can tell you two things, one fact and one supposition,' Rossi said, licking her lips as she finished in a way that suggested she was choosing her words very carefully. 'From what you've told me, I suspect my recent investigations are about to overlap with yours, so I feel comfortable sharing both with you. That being said, I would appreciate it if you didn't mention my name in relation to my suspicions.'

'I understand,' said Petra emphatically, feeling strangely thrilled that she was being let into Rossi's investigation. It wasn't as though it was a favour, this was both of their jobs.

Even so, she suspected that Rossi didn't let people into her confidence regularly, even if they were her colleagues.

Rossi glanced around again, ensuring that there was no one sitting close to them. They were fortunate that it was still early enough in the day that it was the cafés and ice cream shops getting the majority of the business, only a few couples sitting at the sunniest tables and nursing a glass of wine outside *La Medusa*. Inside, at the driftwood bar, Petra could see an elderly man knocking back a shot of something.

'I have had my suspicions about both Punta Grossa and the coastline under Dobrava and Belvedere being used for drug deliveries for some time,' she began. 'Out of season, they are both so quiet. You could get a boat into the shallows easily, someone could even swim out to it, and no one would see. If they did, it would be a hiker or a dog walker and they wouldn't know what they were looking at. Say you launch from Salvore with your haul, on the northern tip of Croatia. You can't land at Portorose, or Pirano. There are too many people, it would look suspicious. Sicciole is a write-off, as a nature reserve it gets patrolled. The same is true of Strugnano. You need these out of the way places, where they're empty until the resorts fill up. Lots of infrastructure, places to park, routes down onto the beach. But no one there.'

Petra blinked at her, trying to work out what she'd been told. In theory, she could understand what Rossi was saying, but she was struggling to get the geography straight in her mind when Rossi was using Italian-language place names. She imagined a map, assuming that Salvore must be the northern Croatian town of Savudrija, and placed the homophone Slovenian towns up the coast along from it: Sečovlje, Portorož, Piran, Strunjan. It made sense, that the quieter stretches between these busier areas would be prime targets for dropping off drugs by boat.

'You think that the inspector was being tipped off to some of these sites?'

'That would be my guess.'

'Do you have any idea why they'd alert him, and not you?'

Rossi smiled, although there was no humour in it. 'People don't tend to like me, Petra. I don't read too much into it.'

Koren shifted next to Petra, wriggling forward in his seat. 'You mentioned that you had both facts and theories. Which was that?'

Petra gave him an admonishing look but didn't say anything. She was wondering the same thing herself.

Rossi folded her arms across her chest, sucking her teeth again. A pair of children with huge ice creams sprinted past them, screaming as they went. 'Fact, I suppose.'

'What's your theory?' pressed Koren, leaning even further forward.

Petra was surprised that Rossi continued immediately, not allowing another silence to fall. There was something in the set of her face that made Petra suspect that she was still in two minds about sharing this with them, that she had to get it out or else she would decide against it. 'Before I tell you this, I'd like to say that if I had any proof, I would have done something by now. I have looked, but I can't find anything concrete.'

'Done something about what?' Koren asked, and this time Petra tapped him on the leg in reprimand. It was obvious Rossi was struggling with what she felt she had to say, her feet were tapping on the paving stones and her fingers were grasped together tightly, held stiffly in her lap. Koren gave her an apologetic look, and sat back a little in his chair.

'How does a police inspector afford a collection of vintage cars?' Rossi's voice was quiet, but not tentative. There was weight to her words, conviction. 'It has bothered me for months, maybe years at this point. That was where it started. Domenico fancied buying a Spaček, whatever they call those ridiculous Citroën 2CVs, and I saw the prices. Astronomical.'

Koren's face twisted in confusion, although he thankfully didn't interrupt. Petra felt herself going cold, something unpleasant writhing in her stomach.

'I transferred from the Isola station to Capodistria to find a mole, did you know that? The *Guardia di Finanza* was adamant there was a mole somewhere, that the drug task-force was being undermined at some point between the Croatian border and Italy. Somehow the gangs always knew when there'd be an increased police presence, when we'd be doing more car searches. I came here, and I met *Inšpektor* Denis Božič with his expensive cars and his ostentatious watch, and I saw that he volunteered for every shift at the Croatian border he could justify, and I knew he was one to watch. You can ask Domenico, I came home and I told him I thought I'd met the source of half my problems. A Capodistrian policeman. In their pockets. But I couldn't prove it, and I wasn't going to start openly investigating a colleague. Not when, as I said, people don't tend to like me. I could see the end of my career, and it was shaped like Denis Božič, if I played my cards wrong.'

Her voice had regained some of its strength, more forceful than the whisper it had been when she started speaking. Petra was so focused on her that she couldn't drag her eyes away, aware of Koren's stiff body language beside her. She felt a little sick, could only imagine what the other two people at the table with her must be feeling, when this was so much closer to home for them.

'I was waiting to strike, I've been waiting for a long time. I followed him once, when he came into *La Medusa* on a quiet night and I knew I could slip out. He had been drinking when some men speaking Serbian came to meet him, and Domenico let me know when they left. I knew some of the men, by reputation if not personally. I followed him down to the coastal path, waiting to see something change hands. I can remember shaking, holding my phone tightly so I could snap a photo. But nothing happened, they all said their goodbyes and he started walking back to Capodistria.'

'You saw him walking on the coastal path late at night, having met with known criminals?' asked Petra, her mind filled with the crime scene image of Ivan Furlan's broken body on the same route.

'Oh yes, I saw him. But I didn't see anything illegal, and I have no proof those men are anything other than tourists.' She looked up at them then, pushing her sunglasses roughly onto the top of her head before clutching her hands together pleadingly on top of the table. 'I thought he was just a pawn, I promise. Just a corrupt policeman who the drug gang had managed to get their claws into. When Ivan was killed on the path, it gave me pause for thought, but I didn't think Božič was capable. Now you've told me what you've found, I have to wonder. Does this have something to do with him? If he didn't mention it to you, Koren, surely it must have been something important. They were friends. If someone told Ivan that Božič was crooked he'd have wanted to be absolutely sure before he did anything about it.'

Out of the corner of her eye, Petra could see Koren was nodding. He obviously agreed with what Rossi was saying, that Furlan would have risked his safety rather than betray a friend without evidence. His face was pale under his tan, his hands dangling limply in his lap. Rossi didn't look much better, her eyes tired and sad. Petra sat up a little straighter, aware that her purpose here was to be an impartial voice, someone who wasn't brought to their knees by the horrifying prospect that one Koper officer had murdered another to avoid their corruption being revealed. She had to view these facts, these characters, dispassionately, no matter how hard it was.

'You're suggesting that *Inšpektor* Furlan was tipped off to *Inšpektor* Božič's involvement in whatever illegal activity was going on at the coast, and that when *Inšpektor* Božič became aware of this he either killed *Inšpektor* Furlan himself, or someone in the gang did it for him?' Saying it out loud made it somehow worse, and she felt guilty when both Koren and

Rossi jolted in response. She fought back the urge to apologise. This was too important to pussyfoot around.

'Yes,' said Rossi, her voice dull. 'I think he's been in their pocket a while, and that he couldn't risk being found out.'

'There's nothing you could have done,' said Koren suddenly, repeating what Petra had told him earlier. She was pleased that he'd picked up on the misery radiating off Rossi, the guilt that must have been eating at her both for her suspicions and for not acting on them. Rossi blinked at him, saying nothing.

'Are there other possibilities which you've considered?' Petra asked, aware that their distress had dragged them down the path of Božič's guilt without looking at alternatives. Rossi's suggestion made sense, but Petra didn't want to investigate a fellow officer unless she was sure. It struck her that this was the same choice as Rossi had been forced to make when she first spotted his erratic behaviour and expensive tastes.

'You've presented me with this information now, and that's all I can think of. It has been troubling me since Ivan died, the location of it. When I saw Božič there with his friends, they seemed so confident. I couldn't get it out of my head, but then when everyone started talking about Marjan I decided to ignore it. Now, I think I was wrong.'

# Chapter 23

Petra and Koren left *La Medusa* shortly afterwards, Rossi waving them off with a blank face as Domenico came out to check on her. Pleased that the poor woman had someone to lean on, Petra hurried Koren away across the square and into the car, forcing him into the passenger seat as she took up position behind the steering wheel.

'We have to consider other options,' she said brusquely, starting the engine. She had no idea where she planned on going, but had come to the decision that moving was the best thing to do. She had briefly considered walking along the coastal path to clear their heads, but quickly discounted that given the circumstances.

'She's right, though. He takes every shift at the border, he's always disappearing from the station. He has some very dubious friends. If there is a leak, it makes sense that it's him.'

'But he isn't on the drug task-force,' she argued, pulling out aggressively at a roundabout to make up for the desperation in her voice. It hardly mattered, at midday on a Saturday the roads were dead, everyone holed up having their lunch. By contrast, the car parks of every *gostilna* and café they passed were heaving. The marked police car moved largely unimpeded up the hill from Izola towards Koper.

'He isn't, but I bet the *Guardia di Finanza* haven't got a clue how much we all know about their operations. The timetable for manning the border is literally behind Medved's desk, anyone can have a look.'

'Seriously?'

'Seriously.' Koren was starting to get angry now, his heartbreak shifting into something darker, more vicious. 'Of course he's in their pockets, how could I have been so stupid? Up until that pay review a few years ago the average policeman could barely afford an out of season weekend away at a thermal spa, even now things are tight. And here he is, swanning around in his Spaček while he's restoring a second one at home?'

'Maybe he's taking bribes,' said Petra, hoping her tone was placatory. She slowed down as they entered the tunnel towards Koper, her mind already set that they weren't going back to the station but needing time to think about where to go instead. She hardly knew the area well. 'But taking bribes doesn't mean he murdered *Inšpektor* Furlan.'

'Even if he didn't do it personally, he could still be to blame. Maybe someone saw the inspector watching, maybe he tried to get Božič to do the right thing and Božič told his bosses.'

'Is there any chance *Inšpektor* Božič wrote the notes?' she asked desperately, breezing out the other side of the tunnel and continuing on past the exit that would take them to the station.

'He doesn't speak Italian,' Koren replied, rage colouring his tone. 'No chance it was him, I doubt he could write a word. Where are we going? Shouldn't we be going to the station?'

Petra ignored him, continuing through town and past the final exit marked 'Koper/Capodistria'. Next to them, a large lake opened up and widened, separating the road from the edges of the city and dominating her left field of vision. 'We need to establish who did write the notes, then. That will give us some idea as to whether we're on the right lines with Božič.'

'Rossi wouldn't have told us anything unless she was worried. The minute she said it, it rang true! We need to do something about Božič.'

'Need I remind you that until recently everyone was saying the same thing about Marjan Furlan? That it was so obvious, everyone knew it, no point in tying up the loose ends? I'm not getting involved in another trial by public opinion, thank you.' Petra hadn't meant to be so harsh, but it needed to be said. Something sounding plausible and having a few coincidental details in common with the crime had already damaged the case, and the reputation of Koper Police. Petra herself was proof of that, her presence demonstrating that they had to be more careful about throwing around accusations without any backing.

Koren deflated, slumping back in the passenger seat and knocking his head back against the headrest. Petra glanced over at him, opening her mouth to speak, but was interrupted by her phone trilling. Koren picked it up, turning the screen to face her.

'Jože Golob?' he said, question obvious in his inflection. Petra's heart leapt at his words, her brain dragging her straight back to the Interpol secondment application process, the hours of paperwork, the nerve-wracking panel interviews conducted entirely in English, her desperation to hide her aspirations from as many people as possible to avoid embarrassment.

'My superintendent back in Ljubljana. I'll call him back.' Petra reluctantly let the call go to answerphone, pulling off at the next exit. On impulse, she followed the signs towards Škocjanski Zatok Nature Reserve. The road curved around over the motorway she had just been on, spitting her onto a paved track next to the lake. She pulled into a lay-by, allowing Koren to clamber out of the car and wander into the park next to the lake, grateful that she hadn't had to ask him to go. His gaze was fixed on the ends of his shoes, his hands deep in the pockets of his uniform trousers.

Petra took a deep breath, staring at the impassive screen of her phone, now dark and silent. Before she could talk herself out of it, she dialled Golob's number.

'Petra, thank you for calling me back,' the superintendent said by way of greeting, speaking slightly faster than he normally would.

'*Svetnik* Golob, I am sorry I missed your call. I was driving.'

'Driving yourself? I assumed they'd give you someone for that. Their roads are strange, you know. Lots of roundabouts.'

Petra smiled weakly, having forgotten the superintendent's tendency to tell you things you were better placed to know about than he was. It was funny how someone's quirks could escape you when you'd been gone for such a short time. She supposed it wasn't that she'd been away from Ljubljana, it was that she'd been learning so many new people's quirks that she'd not thought about those she already knew. 'Yes, there are a lot of them.'

'Anyway, I'll be quick. I was asked to make sure this was done in person and all that, but I couldn't leave you unawares.'

Petra sucked in a breath, still unsure whether Golob's hurry related to the news he was imparting or that she was impinging on his lunch. 'Yes?'

'Your secondment has been approved, Petra. They'd like you in Lyon at some point in the next month or so. I don't see why you can't go immediately, if that's what you'd like.'

'Immediately?' she breathed, the jolt of seemingly unquenchable joy that had rocked through her fizzling uncertainly. Typical that in the moment of her greatest triumph, she would be racked by uncertainty and guilt. 'Once I've finished up in Koper, surely.'

'I don't see why that would be necessary,' said Golob briskly, and now Petra paid attention she could hear muffled adverts at the other end of the line, presumably a break in a golf championship that would also have delayed the Golob family meal. 'Mlakar can pick up where you left off. It sounded reasonably simple.'

Petra grimaced as she remembered how little she had updated Golob, how behind he was in her investigation. So much had happened in a day. Not only him, but also *Svetnik* Horvat, who would at the moment be enjoying his Saturday completely unaware that the prime suspect in one of his officer's murders now had an alibi. That the new prime suspect in the eyes of a few of their colleagues was one of their own only made it worse. 'Unfortunately, that is no longer the case.'

'Oh? That's a shame. You'll have to send me an update. Even so, Petra, no one could expect you to stay on the coast when Lyon is calling. It goes without saying that I am incredibly proud of you, I hope. I remember you when you were in uniform, chasing justice with everything you had. The speeders of Dunajska Cesta didn't know what hit them! There's no one better placed to head off to Interpol and fly the Slovene flag. Let someone else pick up the pieces of Koper's mistakes, don't let it hold you up. This is a special day, I'm only sorry you aren't here in Ljubljana to celebrate with your friends and family.'

Petra teared up a little at this, the joy back and tinged with a feeling of pride unlike anything she'd known before. She had worked so hard, so doggedly, to get to exactly this point and receive precisely this phone call. She imagined another life, where she'd answered the phone surrounded by her parents or her friends, where her father was popping open a bottle of sparkling wine as her mother wept with pride and her friends screamed in celebration. She would be packing her suitcase, researching the weather in Lyon this time of year, treating herself to a new pair of work shoes to make sure she looked the part. She sighed, and thought of Koren's face if she left, of Medved's and Rossi's disappointment.

'In the next month or so, did you say?' she said weakly.

'Yes, but Petra, please don't worry. If it is too much for Mlakar, we'll find someone else. Or I'll speak to one of the superintendents at the station in Nova Gorica, somewhere nearer but still impartial.'

Petra shoved out of her mind the bitter thought that maybe they should have done that in the first place, focused on what she knew she had to do. 'Thank you, superintendent. Really, I am so excited. I can't tell you how much this means to me. But I have to see this out, I have to stay in Koper until we've got the culprit in custody.'

Golob huffed at the other end, a strange throaty noise which she recognised from years of working with the man. He knew her well enough that he wouldn't try and change her mind. Her strong sense of justice and constant pursuit of fairness had coloured her childhood, had led to her picking the career she now loved. There was little point in attempting to redirect her, not when her mind was set in a situation like this. She could almost hear Golob going through this thought process at the other end of the line, weighing up arguing with her and missing the golf when there was no chance she'd acquiesce anyway.

'I'll tell them you have something that needs finishing. Try and make it quick though, Petra. At the moment they're excited about you, but if you keep them waiting too long you'll make them realise they can do without you.'

His phrasing hit Petra like a punch in the gut, although she doubted it was deliberate. Part of her wanted to take it all back, personal standards and officers of Koper be damned. She could be back in Ljubljana within two hours, easily. Interpol would never need to know she'd vacillated for even a second. But she hadn't vacillated. She knew what the right thing to do was, had known as soon as Golob told her she had the secondment. She couldn't leave Koper, not now. Not when they had one dead inspector already, and another who was almost certainly corrupt, if not a murderer. They couldn't handle a third inspector letting them down.

'I understand, *Svetnik* Golob. Thank you so much for phoning. I appreciate it.'

'You're welcome. You deserve it. Please, Petra, don't throw this away.'

Golob hung up quickly, to the sound of golf commentary gearing up again. Petra held her phone in her hand silently for a second, staring out through the windscreen, before slumping forward so her head hit the steering wheel with a resounding thump. She knew she had done the right thing, but that didn't mean it had been easy. She wanted to scream, to throw things, to hit something. It simply didn't seem fair. Instead, she rallied herself, twanging herself with her hair tie on the wrist for good measure before climbing out of the car and walking over to where Koren stood, overlooking the lake.

'Bad news?' he said once she was standing next to him, his eyes trained on a duck paddling in the shallows.

Petra waved a dismissive hand at him, unwilling to start speaking about her exhilaration mixed with disappointment in case she was unable to stop. Now was not the time to get distracted by what was going on in her life, not when they were at such a crossroads in the case. The sooner they solved the inspector's murder, the faster she could get back to Ljubljana and feel guiltless in her joy. She cleared her throat quietly, tucking her hair behind her ear and tightening her ponytail, joining Koren in staring out at the lake.

He turned. 'I've been thinking about what you said, about not condemning Božič too soon. You're right, I'm sorry. I've just never seen *Inšpektorica* Rossi so rattled, she's always so collected. Something has really upset her, and that convinced me that she must be right.'

'She could be right about a lot, without it making *Inšpektor* Božič a murderer,' Petra replied soothingly, looking up at Koren. He blinked down at her, eyes a little wet at the edges. She wondered whether he'd needed to get out of the car as much as she'd wanted him to go, whether he'd longed for this moment by the lake to collect himself.

'Who would write to the inspector about the beaches?' Koren wondered aloud, returning his focus to the duck. 'Someone who wants to bring the gang down from inside? And then, why not Rossi?'

'Maybe they didn't know who does what in the force,' Petra suggested. 'Or maybe they don't think women make good police officers. It is impossible to say, unless we find out who it was.'

'Do you think those were the only three notes?'

'I've been thinking about that. Is there any chance one was missed on the inspector's body?'

Koren shook his head. 'No, it was searched very carefully.'

'By Božič?' Petra ventured, making Koren blanch.

'Yes,' he admitted, his right hand starting to fiddle aimlessly with the strap holding his gun in its holster.

Petra put a hand on his arm to still it, perturbed by his choice of distractions. 'Okay, so if there was one on him and Božič was involved, then it is gone for good.'

Koren nodded listlessly, hands now shoved deep in his pockets.

'I think we should go to Piran.'

'To Tartinijeva Ulica?'

'Exactly. If the inspector was indeed looking into Božič, then it was at about the time when he started going into the house in Piran and annoying Marjan. Perhaps he left something there.'

Koren's nodding picked up in tempo, his eyes widening as he thought about the implications of Petra's suggestion. 'If he didn't want Irena finding something, that's a good place to leave it.'

'Exactly, and if the notes we found at the station are the most recent, then perhaps the older ones are there.'

'I'll drive,' said Koren, already moving back to the car with long, determined strides. 'Piran's a nightmare with a car.'

'We're in a police car,' replied Petra, rushing around to the passenger side. 'I'm not too worried.'

# Chapter 24

They stopped at Irena Furlan's home on the way to Piran, collecting the keys from one of her sons who had come to Koper for the weekend to keep her company. Petra considered popping in to ask him some questions, but decided to trust that Mlakar had been thorough. As she flopped back into the car, she mentioned the vintage car show to Koren, who seemed just as confused as Ivan Furlan's sons had apparently been as to why he might have wanted to go. It had slipped her mind until now, but with the spotlight now on *Inšpektor* Božič, the strange outing seemed to take on new significance.

'It must have something to do with Božič,' Koren confirmed as they pulled onto the motorway, overtaking a Belgian caravan at an alarming speed. 'Maybe he wanted to look into the Spačeks he owns?'

'Perhaps,' conceded Petra. 'But what could some showmen and car club members hundreds of kilometres away know about two specific cars?'

'How much he paid for them? Whether he was in the market for even more?'

Petra nodded, convinced they were on to something but feeling like they were missing the mark somehow. She put it out of her mind, tsking at Koren as he executed another needlessly speedy overtake around a campervan towing a Smart car on a small trailer. A few moments passed, Koren whipping past the Izola exit and on past her guesthouse, zooming straight ahead at the small roundabout and down the hill towards the sea. 'Have you been to the house in Piran before?'

'No, the dispute has been going on too long. I've walked past it.'

'And the inspector never talked about going there?'

Koren shook his head. 'We all knew their stupid agreement that neither of them was allowed in. I just assumed he was honouring it.'

Petra looked away, pretending she hadn't noticed the look of sadness cross Koren's face. He had obviously viewed Ivan Furlan as a man totally above reproach, a man of his word. Even his entering a property he partially owned when he'd said he wouldn't was a disappointment to Koren. She wished for a second that Horvat had never let him near the case, then reminded herself how much help he had been in his passionate quest to get justice for his sainted mentor. It was tragic that he was having to wade through secrets and incongruities that coloured his opinion of the inspector posthumously, but that was unfortunately part of the task he'd assigned himself.

They drove past Strunjan in silence, heading up another hill road that twisted and turned so much that the caravan ahead of them dropped to an aggravatingly low speed. Eventually they reached the top, the caravan trundling straight ahead towards Croatia while Koren turned right, down towards Portorož and Piran. As they drove along the Portorož seafront, Petra was struck by how different it felt to both Izola and Koper. The two carriageways were divided by a central reservation covered in lush green turf, tall lamp posts sitting at regular distances as far as the eye could see. Occasionally an advert dangled from one of them, drumming up trade for a nearby shop or casino. To their left, on the other side of the road, was the sea, although Petra only caught snatched glimpses of it. Her view was blocked by an unending run of restaurants, bars and cafés, all boasting the same offerings for only slightly varying prices. A-boards littered the pavement, the occasional security guard ambling around outside a club between groups of tourists in bikinis and novelty t-shirts. On her right was hotel after hotel, several of them completely identical except for the colour of their façades. She spotted the casinos well before they reached them, huge external TV screens flashing madly to try and entice custom. Everything appeared in handfuls of languages, primary coloured text and cartoon images enticing potential customers with promises of a free lunch in the bar or €10 for unlimited wine in writing so large and vibrant as to be visible from anywhere on the long, narrow beach. Looking out of the window became slightly overwhelming, and so she focused on the crawling traffic ahead of her.

Leaving Portorož behind, they started to head uphill again, now far below the road they had been on earlier. The wall to her right was covered in yet more adverts, taller than Petra and wider than a car. They flashed by as Koren was able to pick up speed, most of the traffic having disappeared into Portorož's many car parks. Koren drove on a little further, concrete walls finally giving way to houses and gardens again, the sea no longer hidden from view by concrete businesses. They passed the sign showing they had entered Piran, although she still couldn't see the famous view plastered on so many postcards and travel brochures. She noticed that the road signs all started directing them to various parking garages, although Koren kept going straight ahead. Finally, they came to another enormous car park, their way blocked by entrance barriers spitting out tickets.

'No cars in Piran,' Koren explained, leaning out of the window to grab his ticket. 'You park out here, and you walk.'

Somehow this fact had escaped Petra, and she blinked at him in confusion as he pulled into the busy car park, nabbing the first available slot. 'What if you live here?'

'You learn to shop light,' he said with a laugh, turning off the engine and climbing out. Petra followed him quickly, watching as he stretched.

'The roads that lead to Piran all lead to car parks?'

'Pretty much. Some of the houses right at the top of the hill have car access, but there's no parking. You can't park in town.'

They started walking across the tarmac, Petra hastening over to the water's edge so that she could peer down at the sea. From this angle, she could finally catch a glimpse of the famous view of Piran, the Venetian stone lighthouse with its coronet

of white spikes standing up proudly against the horizon at
the far end of the peninsula, the spire of St George's Church
at the other end like a miniature St Mark's Campanile. The
buildings around were an eclectic mix of bright colours, their
terracotta roofs all at slightly different heights. She could see
the rich ochre walls of the theatre sitting on the corner of the
cove-shaped marina, the positioning of its round windows and
door like a smiling face welcoming visitors to the town. Petra
found herself drawn along the pavement, desperate to get
closer. They passed various restaurants and cafés, their positioning seemingly deliberate to catch tourists getting off the
huge coaches also pulling into the car park, weary travellers
filling outdoor tables and sipping gratefully at cold beers and
tall cocktails as they watched other people walk into town.
She could smell something frying, and watched as a waiter
emerged from a curtain-covered door to serve a large plate of
golden calamari rings to a table of hungry pensioners. Below
the path Petra was walking on there was another walkway,
half claimed by the water. Small children shrieked as they
splashed each other, their parents occasionally berating them
when the water hit their phones or tablets. The atmosphere
was enough to make Petra temporarily forget the nastiness
that had brought her here.

They continued on, Petra's attention flitting between enticing sights as they made their slow progress along the narrow
street. On the hill above perched the remains of the old town
walls, remarkably intact and still oddly comforting despite
their being long out of use. She could just make out figures

walking along them, and considered whether she'd have time to go up there herself and enjoy the view from above. The main street followed the coast and marina exactly from a few metres above sea level, the wall below clustered with mussel shells and mooring points. The boats they held were an eclectic mix of tiny rowing boats and fancy speedboats, dinghies and low fishing boats. Further along the wall, where the water was deeper and the berths more spacious, Petra could see expensive yachts and day cruisers floating serenely.

She was so distracted by the pebbles and rocks she could see through the crystal-clear water, the odd sea cucumber bobbing about beside them, that she didn't notice the open-sided square until she was directly in front of it. Tartinijev *Trg* was paved like a huge grid, darker squares outlined by narrower bands of pale stone. The open side faced straight onto the sea, a perfect view out onto the marina currently being enjoyed by two old men eating ice creams. On the other sides, slim Venetian-era buildings adorned in various colours and patterns lined the perimeter, winged lions of the Republic embellished on every available piece of stone. Petra spotted one on a column now used as a flagpole, the lion's paw resting on an open book, signifying that it had been built in a time of peace. On the façade of a nearby building it brandished the sword of war. The town seemed to rise up the hill behind the square, uneven roofs peeking out at intervals beyond the buildings Petra could see. A few smaller church spires were dotted among them, although they were dwarfed by the most iconic of Piran's towers. The view of St George's was truly impressive from here, the neat tiers of the roof and the detail on the balcony clearly visible from the ground. Petra watched as the wind moved the copper angel atop its spire very slightly, his hand pointing inland.

'That means a storm's coming,' Koren informed her. 'Or at least, that's what my grandpa told me.'

Petra looked out in the opposite direction to the angel's pointing finger, at the calm water and the gaggles of happy tourists milling around on the beaches that lined the sides of the harbour. The weather didn't look or feel particularly unsettled, but she was willing to bow to the superior knowledge of Koren's grandfather.

They walked slowly through the square, Petra taking in the beautiful pale blue of the town hall to her left, every corner and window outlined with a band of thick and perfectly maintained white. Cafés and bars occupied many of the other, thinner houses around the perimeter, their tables spilling out onto the chequerboard paving stones. Directly opposite the town hall, set back from the sea, was a statue of the composer himself, Giuseppe Tartini gazing down at the occupants of the square from a tall plinth, seemingly mid-stride as he brandished a violin bow. The area in his direct field of vision was paved differently, a smoother, paler stone creating an oval like an orchestra pit awaiting his direction. A young man stood directly under the statue strumming a guitar, his case open at his feet in the hope of donations.

'I'm assuming Tartinijeva Ulica is close to Tartinijev *Trg*?' Petra said, following Koren as he moved into the shade created by one of the smarter looking restaurants and up a narrow and steeply inclining street.

'Up here, and on the right,' Koren confirmed. They picked up speed despite the slope, the densely packed buildings providing shade and making the whole street far cooler than the square they left behind them. In places, the structures on either side of the path were joined, and Petra found she was childishly thrilled at the arches that dotted their way. The houses also seemed to absorb any noise, and so they made their way in pleasant quietness towards their destination.

The road got narrower the higher they climbed, the steepness occasionally necessitating a few shallow steps. Smaller streets branched off to both sides, marked with rectangular red signs bearing the names in both Slovene and Italian, a sight Petra was becoming used to from her time so far in both Koper and Izola. They followed the road around a bend, the houses on either side curving with it, Koren picking up speed when he spotted *Tartinijeva Ulica/Via Giuseppe Tartini* a few metres ahead. Turning onto it, Petra found that she had been being unfair about the width of the streets she'd been on so far. Here, she and Koren could barely stand shoulder to shoulder. Well-maintained cream houses rose high above them on either side, brown wooden shutters pegged open despite the lack of light in the alley. Electricity lines zigzagged a few feet above her, entering every house before heading off to another. The alley curved madly at the other end, descending back down towards where they had come from. The last house before the turn was bare brick, with shutters that had once been a vibrant blue but were now peeling and cracked. The red sign above the door marked it out as number 21. Even without it, Petra could have guessed. It was the only house on the street with a broken window, the damage patched up with cardboard and copious amounts of packing tape.

They approached the house, Petra noting that Marjan had been honest when he said that his neighbour who had given the statement about the vandalism could see all the comings and goings. Number 22 had security lights over its front door, and several windows with perfect views of the Furlans' property. She thought she might have seen a lace curtain twitch on the first floor, but fought back the impulse to stare. She wondered what *Gospa* Novak would be thinking, seeing Koren in his uniform staring up at the dead inspector's house. It would probably be the talk of Piran before they'd even left the property.

The key they had been given was a similar vintage to Petra's guesthouse room key, old and heavy and very low-tech. Koren unlocked the door, eyes flicking around as he took in the spiders' webs that covered the lintel, decades' worth of grime caked in every crevice. Petra was grateful that he pushed on the door gently, wary of the troubling glass to wood ratio considering its age.

Once inside, Petra was surprised to be met with a similar sense of neglect. Dust and dead insects coated the floor, a feeling of abandonment hung in the air. Pictures hung sparsely on the walls, many at strange angles, their frames filthy. Painted plaster crumbled from the walls, reminding her of the observation tower at Debeli Rtič. In places on the walls, multiple layers were visible, the top layer of cream picked away to reveal pink wallpaper behind, then green plaster, then finally bare brick. Haphazard scatterings of uneven plaster chips and shards of wooden door frames sat on the tiled floor, left where they'd fallen. The entrance hall had two doors leading off it, one to either side, both originally painted white but now as patchy as the walls around them. Directly in front of Petra was a twisting staircase, a small landing at waist-height with another dilapidated door leading off it just visible before the stairs turned again and led up over her head to the floor above. Next to the first flight of stairs was a set of spindly coat-hooks, affixed to the wall in a wonky line. A padded winter jacket and a purple fleece dangled from them, and Petra felt a moment of sadness for the old lady whose house this had once been. She wondered what the Furlan matriarch would have said, had she seen the state into which her sons had let her house fall.

Koren seemed less interested in his immediate surroundings, instead opening the door to his right. Behind it was a small kitchen, lost in time. A green enamel-covered oven with two gas burners sat in the middle of the units, the cupboard door next to it hanging open to reveal a gas canister inside. It reminded Petra of the oven her great-grandmother had once owned, Yugoslavian-made and dating from before her parents were born. The chairs around the kitchen table were of a similar vintage, their thin padding bursting through worn brown leather. Affixed to the wall above the sink was a water heater, with a statuette of St Francis balanced on top.

As Koren walked around the room, he seemed to make it look even older, more tired. He was significantly taller than the fridge, and the bright blue of his uniform t-shirt made the cracked off-white work surfaces look even more worn.

'It would have needed some refurbishing before they could have used it as a holiday let.' Koren opened a cupboard door and blinked in surprise when he saw quite how much crockery was stored in it, at least twenty identical mugs stacked up neatly. The cupboard next door boasted two entire sets of dinner plates, the one under the sink more chipped enamel pots than anyone could ever want. 'And a good clear-out.'

'I don't know,' replied Petra, eyeing up a phone so old it had come back into fashion as a retro item. 'Perhaps there's a market for authentic tourism. How the locals really live.'

'Authentic if you're a dead nonagenarian,' Koren muttered, closing all the cupboards and heading back out into the entrance hall. He threw open the other door, revealing a wooden-floored sitting room crammed with wardrobes and bookcases, a sagging sofa pushed against the back wall. He opened the nearest wardrobe and was almost knocked over by a teetering pile of bedsheets within, slamming the door to prevent them spilling out onto the floor. He turned to look at Petra, disbelief written all over his face.

'I'm beginning to think that *Inšpektor* Furlan didn't just want to keep the house itself for sentimental reasons. He wanted to avoid having to throw away all of his mother's things.' Petra gestured to a glass display case, crowded with porcelain figurines and tiny framed photographs. Now she was inside, she thought she understood. Ivan Furlan hadn't been preventing the house sale out of spite towards Marjan, or selfishness. This was still very much his mother's home, her glasses still sitting on the sideboard and her oven gloves hanging in the kitchen.

'Or he was just a hoarder. Who knew?' Koren was oddly unsympathetic to the inspector's evident grief. Again, he seemed very young. Petra wondered if she had been so uncompromising in her assessment of others when she had been his age, almost a decade ago. 'There's no way this was all his mother's. They've dumped everything they didn't want in their own houses and walked away. I have no idea how Marjan knew he'd been here, there's so much clutter that it would be hard to be sure.'

Petra tended to agree with the theory that the house was part memorial to their deceased mother, and part dumping ground. She had recognised it the moment she saw multiple dinner services in the kitchen, mismatched numbers of bowls and plates. Crockery too good to be thrown away but that had been superseded in a living, breathing home, now consigned to wallow in dust until finally someone gathered the strength for a decluttering.

'The inspector must have done something too obvious to miss, I agree. Marjan mentioned papers. I don't see anything like that.'

'Upstairs?' suggested Koren. 'Down here smells stale. I don't think there's been much going on for a long time.'

Petra gestured that he should lead the way, hopeful that his superior height would clear any webs and ensure she didn't get leapt on by disgruntled spiders. The elderly linoleum that lined the stairs was tacky under her feet, the material coming away from the floorboards at various points on the stairs. The door on the first landing revealed itself to be a bathroom, Koren sweeping the door briskly shut when they spotted sitting on the edge of the sink a packet of denture cleaning solution in packaging so dated it belonged in a museum. Their investigation was beginning to feel more and more like an intrusion, a violation of someone's privacy, even if that someone was long dead.

The top of the stairs opened out onto another slim landing, doors at either end echoing those on the ground floor. A third door was directly next to the stairs, which Koren revealed to be a box room now filled with even more piles of books, clothes and shoes. The room at the far end was the master bedroom, an amateurish portrait of a young couple fixed above the bed, the wife's eyes boring into Petra as Koren hurriedly shut the door again. Both of these rooms had the same feeling of emptiness as had the kitchen and living room, the air stale and objects lightly covered in dust, still sitting where the Furlans' mother had left them. Instinct carried Petra to the final door as Koren contemplated a large statue of the Virgin on the landing table. As she pushed it open, he crowded up behind her, peering through the widening gap.

'Well,' he said happily, reaching for the light switch by the door to illuminate the room more thoroughly, 'this is more promising.'

# Chapter 25

The final upstairs room was another bedroom. Twin beds were pushed against the back wall, their footboards almost touching each other. Each was flanked by a side table bedecked with a lace doily. Wardrobes lined the wall next to the door, cardboard boxes piled on top of them. At either end of the room was a desk, one facing out the tall window and the other looking at the opposite wall. A worn rug patterned in red and black flowers revealed where years of chairs had scraped back from the desks, and Petra imagined phantom teenaged boys rushing downstairs from their homework when it was time for dinner.

'The boys' bedroom?' Petra guessed, coming to stand in the middle of the room. It was an impersonal room, the beds covered in plastic bags to stop the mattresses getting damaged, and the wardrobe doors improperly closed as they struggled to hold back another wave of clutter. Even so, it felt lived in. One of the doilies had been moved a little, revealing where its pattern had been scorched into the wooden table below by the sun. The pictures on the walls, framed photographs of groups of young boys posing before a water polo match and outside a mountain hut, were clean of dust. The desk facing the window was stacked with boxes, more fitted in on the floor between its legs. By contrast, the desk on the other side of the room was clear, both on top and below, one of the chairs from the kitchen tucked neatly under it.

'Must have been, although it's mostly a storage room now,' observed Koren. 'I wonder what made the inspector come back.' He nodded at the boxes on top of the window desk as he spoke, drawing her attention to fingerprints in the dust, suggesting that they'd been moved. Seeing how overburdened this desk was compared to the other, it seemed safe to assume that *Inšpektor* Furlan had rearranged them so that he could access the wall-facing desk.

They approached the cleared desk together. Various pieces of paper were scattered across its surface, although none seemed particularly interesting, to Petra's dismay. The topmost sheet was simply a shopping list, written in a blocky hand. Several other sheets were blank, or bore doodles. Unperturbed, Koren pulled the chair out of the way, adding to the scuffs on the rug so he could peer below it. Petra joined him, impressed at his thoroughness and self-restraint in not just ripping open draw-ers, and noticed the dangling plastic surrounding an electric socket that had drawn his eye. It looked like a death trap, wires pulled out of the wall behind and pulled taut by the casing. A phone charger hung precariously from the socket, the most modern thing they'd seen in the house by several decades. Petra and Koren exchanged a look, Petra quickly snapping a photo on her own phone, keen to keep a record of everything they found.

Satisfied that they hadn't missed anything, they moved up the desk. Petra's attention immediately went to the three drawers built into its left side, a few stickers haphazardly dotted around the wooden frame. She recognised the logos of familiar old brands, stickers from apples, even a used stamp partially obscured by franking. She imagined a teenaged Ivan Furlan ripping open a letter, using tape to attach the discarded stamp to his desk. She wondered what the letter had been, thought it must have been important for him to care enough. Casting a glance behind her, she saw that the other desk, the one she assumed had been Marjan's, was bare of any decoration.

Petra tugged the bottom drawer open first, following Koren's example of starting low and moving up. It was so full she struggled to open it, eventually pulling the thin silver handle hard enough that it juddered forward. Inside was a squashed photo album, packed tightly among old glasses cases, a warranty receipt for a mattress dating from the early 1980s, and a dented coffee tin full of old Yugoslavian coins.

'We have one of those,' said Koren, peering over her shoulder.

'A tin of coins?'

'No, a drawer of random clutter we don't need but can't bring ourselves to throw away. Except, ours is actually limited to a drawer.'

Petra frowned at him, leafing through the photo album. She could see why it had been relegated to a drawer of detritus,

it was only half-full and had already been denuded of anything worth keeping. Spidery handwriting next to glue stains
described scenes such as 'Ivan at Lake Bohinj, July 1976', but
the photos themselves were gone. Petra put the album back
where she'd found it, moving up to the next drawer, which
was empty except for a packet of *Napolitanke* biscuits. She felt
a rueful smile spread across her face as she remembered finding the same thing in the inspector's desk at the station and
being offered a plateful at Irena Furlan's house. If this wasn't
proof that Ivan had been here recently, she didn't know what
was. Perhaps it had been the biscuits that tipped Marjan over
the edge. They certainly suggested he planned on spending
prolonged periods of time here.

'He was very particular about his *Napolitanke*.' Koren's voice
was sad, his gaze unmoving from the open packet. 'One of the
last conversations we had was about how unnecessary all the
new flavours are, when chocolate and hazelnut is obviously the
best. He was a traditionalist when it came to biscuits.'

Petra placed the packet back in the drawer, touching Koren
on the elbow in solidarity. She wondered how much of his
grieving Koren had actually been able to do, whether he'd
delayed it all in order to try and investigate the crime alone,
and now with Petra. How long would it take him to recover,
when this was all put to bed? Would delaying his mourning,
setting it aside for so long, mean that it would take longer for
Koren to get over? Or would being instrumental in catching
the killer, as Petra blindly hoped he would be, provide all the
closure he needed?

She closed the middle drawer softly, moving on to the top one, surprised to find that it was somehow jammed shut. She felt around for some kind of locking mechanism, coming up empty. Seeing her difficulty, Koren dropped to his knees and poked at it from the side, although it made no difference. The drawer wouldn't open.

'This has to be deliberate,' he grunted from the floor, now lying on his side and peering at the metal runners with his torch. 'He wouldn't just be coming here to sit and look at a wall and eat wafers. He could do that at home.'

Petra nodded in agreement, her heart racing. She tried not to get ahead of herself, aware that the most likely scenario was that the drawer had become wedged shut decades previously. Koren continued to jab away at the inside of the drawer, pushing up on it from below and wobbling it around in an effort to dislodge whatever was blocking it. He flashed a grin up at her, as he succeeded, hauling himself to his feet and pulling it open.

Inside was a fat padded envelope, the front a patchwork of different addresses and names, each one carefully struck out before another had been added. It reminded Petra of several that her mother had at home, dutifully reusing them until any blank space was a distant memory. It seemed to have been shoved back into the drawer in a hurry, its bulky width crushed up against the front of the drawer.

'Let me take a photograph,' said Petra, waving Koren's hands away as he tried to grab the envelope. He did as she asked, although shuffled from foot to foot with undisguised and slightly childish impatience as he waited for her to be satisfied with her record-keeping. Once she was happy that she had enough photographs to work from, Petra gestured that Koren should pull out the envelope. He did so reverently, the brief delay seemingly having taken some of the urgency out of his movements. He laid it on the desk, opening the long-dried glue seal and pulling the contents out in one smooth motion.

Petra moved forward, helping Koren separate out the various pieces of paper. There were a few more scrappy little Italian notes, which Petra photographed and then pushed to one corner of the desk to prevent them from getting misplaced. There were also some photographs, slightly blurred and printed on basic paper with what looked like a home printer, the ink dark and blotchy. Finally, there were sheets pulled from a notebook, blocky letters scrawled across them as a bullet point list, each with a time stamp written carefully next to it in the margin. Petra could not make out any names in the timeline, just places and times.

'The results of his stakeout?' Koren picked up the photo nearest to him, holding it up above his head like a cashier checking a banknote for authenticity. The extra light did little to help, the image was too dark to glean much detail. Petra could just about make out two figures, both little more than silhouettes, standing in the middle of the frame. The area behind them was thick with black ink, so dense it still looked wet.

'Could that be the sea?' she ventured, cocking her head a little to see if a different angle helped. Koren moved the photo closer to his face, squinting at it. Petra left him to it and continued leafing through the others. Most were just as saturated as the one Koren was scrutinising, pairs and threes of indistinct figures walking or standing against dark backgrounds. The more she looked, the more confident she became that they were all outlined by the sea: the foreground was lighter, with rocks and sand visible in some images around the figures' feet. A few were even framed with tree branches and shrubbery, presumably the result of Furlan taking the photos from a distance, concealed behind undergrowth.

Koren set the first picture aside, watching as Petra laid the others out so they could see them all at once. A few stood out from the pack as being far clearer, perhaps the result of the midday and early evening stake-outs that the notes Petra had found alluded to. Having been there only recently, Petra was vaguely confident that one of them was taken at Debeli Rtič, the view identical to the one she'd seen from the observation tower.

'You can't see this man's face properly,' Koren grumbled, stabbing at another picture. This one also featured two figures, standing close together as they seemingly shook hands. They were in a car park, the sea slightly behind them on the other side of a narrow road. Scrubby grass covered a bank to their left, suggesting they were on its outer edges. The picture was taken from far away, the figures visible from head to toe in the corner of the image. One man wore a baseball cap with a large badge on the front, the shade from the brim obscuring his features. The other was more clearly visible, although he wasn't someone Petra recognised. Both were dressed casually in jeans and light jackets, nothing suspicious in their appearance. If Petra had walked past the scene herself, she would have just assumed it was a greeting between friends. Furlan had thought it was important, however, so she continued staring at the picture, eyes flicking over it as though it was a wordsearch, every section assessed in order.

'Look at that car,' she said suddenly, pointing to a bonnet peeping out from between two larger vehicles. Half of the registration plate was obscured by a flash of light, but the shield marking out which town it was registered in and some of the letters were legible. Not that it mattered, particularly. She was confident she knew exactly who it belonged to. It seemed probable that Furlan had deliberately taken the picture so that it was in shot.

'Božič's Citroën 2CV!' Koren snatched the picture up off the desk, holding it in front of his nose. 'That's definitely it, that's his personalised plate.'

'Is that him?' Petra asked, tentatively tapping on the man in the baseball cap.

'It could be,' Koren said slowly, peering at the other photos and watching as Petra pointed at other times the mystery man had worn the cap. 'I can't be sure. But it seems likely, doesn't it? If his car's there?'

'He could always argue he was just inside the shop.' Petra gestured to a discarded shopping trolley sitting half out of shot.

'We don't have to tell him the photos aren't clear. We can just say we have photographic evidence of him speaking to a known member of a criminal organisation, in a car park.' He picked up speed as he talked, grip tightening on the flimsy paper he was holding. His face screwed up in what looked like a mixture of anger and thought, his passion to bring Božič down evidently reignited.

Petra shook her head, trying to redirect his energy without disappointing him. 'No, he'll see right through us. We have no evidence he knew the inspector had these photos, and we have no idea what they incriminate him in, if anything. We have to identify the other man if these are going to be of any use.'

Thankfully, Koren seemed to see the sense in her suggestion. He nodded once, firmly, before starting to gather up the pages in front of him, giving them each another careful look as he returned them to the envelope, then placed the whole thing in an evidence bag. As he worked, Petra took the opportunity to leaf through the notes, noticing immediately that they were in the same handwriting as those she'd found in the inspector's desk. She snapped photos of them, texting them over to Doug to see what he thought of them. Koren was too fixated on the image of Božič's car to pay much attention to them, let alone translate. He glanced at the small pile, but immediately looked away.

They hurried out of the house and back through the streets of Piran in the direction of Tartinijev *Trg*. Petra was surprised when Koren stopped in the middle of the square, spinning around to face her suddenly, watching as she rushed to catch up.

'What's wrong?' she asked.

Koren blinked at her a few times, then rushed off to his right, in the opposite direction to the car. He waved his arm at her as he went, indicating that she should follow. Petra scurried after him, pulling a few strands of hair off her sweaty neck as she went. He followed the waterfront road around the top of the headland until it finished, then joined a narrow concrete path that skirted between the water's edge and the theatre's large café terrace, heading in the direction of the lighthouse. Petra stared openly at the mixture of brightly coloured and bare bricked houses they passed, their route down to the Adriatic impeded only by the occasional white bench and an attractive sea wall made of small boulders, a metre at its highest. They drew closer to the lighthouse, its white stone tower the highest point at the end of the peninsula. The path widened the closer to it they got, opening out into a generous bend around the circular stone building beneath the lighthouse itself.

Koren stopped suddenly before they reached the turn in the path, skirting past a group of tourists and standing a few steps away from the wall. Petra rushed up next to him, and immediately saw what had drawn him out here.

'A mermaid,' she breathed, taking in the sculpture perched on the rocks. It wasn't a complete body, just a torso and head. The mermaid sat gazing towards the lighthouse, her rough-hewn back towards the sea, her stomach and arms descending into the rock below her. Her tail was formed from another piece of stone, positioned further back on the boulder, giving the impression she was submerged. Her hair and face had been weathered by the elements, giving her an oddly dissatisfied look at odds with the cheerful mermaids of Petra's childhood storybooks.

'It has been bothering me since you showed me the first few notes,' Koren said. He gestured around himself, drawing Petra's attention to other curiosities among the stones that she had not previously noticed. Some of the rocks were not natural shapes, but had been carved to form parts of other sculptures, now dismantled. One was topped with a large shell-like spiral, another decorated in a honeycomb pattern. Further along, Petra could see what looked disarmingly like a huge eye, staring out from the pile, half of a chiselled nose the size of her own head visible beneath it.

'Is she significant?' Petra moved to get a better view, peering down at the rocks below the mermaid.

'Not that I know of. I think it's just a decoration.'

'This is nothing like Debeli Rtič, or Dobrava,' Petra pointed out. 'There are people everywhere.'

Koren conceded this, folding his arms across his chest. 'That's true, it is hardly the place for a secret meeting. I've come here before with my friends.'

Petra frowned, fiddling with the hair tie around her wrist as she tried to fit the pieces together. Consigning the incongruity of this meeting place to her subconscious, she focused instead on what their next steps should be, regaining the momentum she had felt as they left Tartinijeva Ulica 21.

'Good work, Koren. We can head straight back to Izola. Let's see if Rossi can identify the other man.' Petra spoke quietly, suddenly very aware that her investigation was getting mixed up in a world she was unfamiliar with. Rossi had given her the barest of hints as to the extent of the drug trade on the coast, and Petra had no idea who the players were, if any of them could be listening. If Božič was indeed corrupt and had been involved in *Inšpektor* Furlan's death, it didn't seem ridiculous to suggest that someone might be keeping an eye on Petra's investigation. Suddenly, something occurred to her. 'You don't think *Svetnik* Horvat could be involved in this, do you? He hasn't been covering for Božič?' If one policeman was involved in the death of *Inšpektor* Furlan, it didn't seem too far-fetched that another might be too, especially one who was specifically named in the whistleblower's note.

Koren's brow creased, and he shook his head. 'No. Or at least, I don't think so. I hope not.'

Piran suddenly seemed too small, too full of dark corners. Where she'd previously wanted to explore every nook and cranny, she now wanted to get back to the car. A traitorous part of her screamed in fury that Koren had found Marjan's alibi, half wishing that she'd just gone along with the status quo and let him be thrown in jail for his brother's murder. She quickly squashed this thought, felt guilty it had even occurred. Police corruption and the drug trade were not what she had come to Koper expecting, but if this was where the investigation took her then she'd have to roll with the punches. The inspector deserved justice, Koren and the others deserved peace of mind, and the murderer deserved jail time. Likewise, she thought as she threw open the car door and climbed in, if she was going to put Interpol on hold, it may as well be for the case of a lifetime.

# Chapter 26

They found Rossi behind the bar at *La Medusa*, pouring out six complicated cocktails for a table of middle-aged Italian women outside. Her hair was scraped back severely, matching her sharp and robotic movements, her face screwed up in annoyance. Petra recognised a woman ready to garner a poor review from a paying customer and waved at her through the window as she and Koren perched at the same table as they'd sat at earlier that day. Rossi eventually emerged, round black tray balanced on one hand, and distributed the cocktails among the women just as they all dissolved into laughter at a joke Petra could not hear.

'I've spent the morning alternating between wanting to see a friendly face, and hoping no one else comes so I can close early,' said Rossi, collapsing dramatically into the chair next to Petra. She jerked at her hair clip, tightening it even further.

'Where's Domenico?'

'A friend came in, and they've gone off to get pizza.' Her tone was angry, although quiet enough that Petra had to strain slightly to hear.

Petra wasn't quite sure what to say in response, unwilling to be rude about her new friend's husband. She looked around herself, taking in the single empty table inside, the lack of any space outside. It was busy, but hardly over capacity. Most of the tables had full glasses, and seemed in no hurry for more. She wondered what had driven Rossi over the edge, the rising voices of the Italian ladies nearby seeming a likely culprit. Petra hoped that their discussion about Božič wasn't weighing on her too heavily. Several empty glasses already crowded their table, Rossi obviously not willing to pick them up until she'd had a break.

'I'm sorry to barge in on you when you're busy, but we found something at the inspector's house in Piran that we were hoping you could look at for us. It shouldn't take a second.'

Rossi nodded, her focus on a small dog currently crossing the street opposite the square. Petra gestured for Koren to retrieve the photo of Božič's car, placing it in front of Rossi to try and recapture her attention.

'Do you recognise this man?' she asked, pointing to the hatless figure.

Rossi leaned forward and put her elbows on the table, her jaw propped on her upturned hand. She peered down at the photo, smoothing out her eyebrows as she did so. Next to Petra, Koren started to jiggle his knee up and down under the table, impatience at Rossi's slowness rolling off him in waves. A look passed between them as they waited for Rossi to speak, both unsure as to what the etiquette was when she seemed so unforthcoming.

'That's Vuk Jovanović,' she said eventually, speaking strangely slowly.

'Serbian?' Koren interrupted, echoing Petra's immediate assumption.

'Passport-wise, actually Bosnian. He's the younger brother of one of the *Guardia di Finanza*'s most wanted men, Darko Jovanović.'

'What do you mean, passport-wise?' asked Petra, trying to pull her notebook out of her bag without distracting Rossi from her train of thought. She laid it out in front of her, flicking to a new page.

'Their family was heavily involved in the wars in the former Yugoslavia,' she said simply. 'And I don't mean the Ten-Day War. Take from that what you will. I'm assuming that the other man is Denis Božič, or you wouldn't be here. It certainly looks like him. That isn't good.'

Both Petra and Koren blinked at her, Petra's mind spinning as her investigation took yet another potentially dangerous turn. Rossi flopped back in her seat, pushing the picture back towards Koren.

'Don't worry, they aren't Serbian ultra-nationalists. Or at least, that isn't their main motivator. That's their father's gig. They're drug smugglers, in it for the money.'

'You were aware that Vuk was in Slovenia?' asked Petra, trying to piece together what Rossi was suggesting. Evidently, Božič did have some sort of relationship with the drug gangs, or at least whatever organisation Vuk Jovanović was involved in. Whether he could simply pass it off as an old friendship if confronted about it, she did not know.

'It doesn't surprise me. He lives in Salvore, or at least that's his registered address.'

'Savudrija?' said Koren, translating the name into Slovene. 'You can see Portorož from there, Piran too.'

'Exactly. He tends to visit Slovenia by boat. I find it quite amusing, but the Croatian Police think it is insulting that he is so blatant. He probably watches half the drug boats head to Slovenia and Italy from his window. There's a good chance he sees some of them land.'

'Was Vuk Jovanović one of the men you saw with Božič at *La Medusa* the night you followed him?'

'He was.'

'Do you recognise any of these other men?' asked Koren, scrabbling through the envelope to produce some of the darker photos. Rossi wrinkled her nose at them, waving them away.

'I can't even be sure those are men. Is that all Ivan managed to get? What a shame. Not really worth being murdered over, is it?'

Rossi's callousness made Koren flinch, his eyes widening in surprise. Petra couldn't blame him. Although the photos were hardly high quality, they were obviously related to the murder of her colleague, and deserved slightly more attention and respect than they were being shown. Looking down at them, Petra tried to remember how Rossi had been described to her: cold, unfeeling, unhelpful. Was this that side of her personality finally coming through?

'Is there anything else, Giulia? We don't want to keep you.'

Rossi looked up at Petra, her gaze assessing. Petra now knew this once-over well, and maintained eye contact. To her surprise, Rossi looked away first.

'I want to give you a forewarning that I am going to have to take over your case,' she said, eyes still flicking about somewhere over Petra's shoulder.

Petra moved, forcing Rossi to look her in the eyes. Koren's head whipped around, dumb-founded. Petra held out a hand to quiet him before he could interject. 'What?'

'Vuk Jovanović's involvement forces my hand. This is no longer a simple murder case, it is part of my investigation into the Jovanović family. I need to be on top of this, my contacts in the *Guardia di Finanza* will want to be involved. The case will need to be transferred to organised crime, away from homicide.'

Petra supposed she had her answer. The photos, the murder, they were of no independent significance now. They were puzzle pieces in something much larger, with potentially higher stakes, but also a longer deadline. The stuff of Rossi's day job, and Petra had forced them on her on what was already a disappointing day off.

'You didn't have any interest in it when I was begging people for help!' spat Koren, disgust clear enough in his tone that one of the Italian ladies turned around to see what was happening, straw still pursed between her lips.

'Marjan Furlan committing fratricide in a drunken rage had nothing to do with me. Ivan staking out meetings between *Inšpektor* Božič and Vuk Jovanović shortly before he was murdered, however, is directly related to my case.'

'How long can you give us?' Petra interjected, tapping Koren on the arm before he could continue. He gave her a wounded look, but fell silent, hands folded in his lap. She had come up against similar scenarios in Ljubljana, and should really have guessed before she even got in the car in Piran that it might happen. Police corruption and the drug trade were things she hadn't predicted appearing in her case because they weren't things a homicide detective got involved in, they were priorities for other teams with specialised knowledge. She wished she'd had the foresight to warn Koren, and hoped that Rossi would do her a favour and give her a bit more time to contribute.

Rossi raised her eyebrows, folding her arms tightly across her chest. 'Are you hoping to compromise, Petra?'

'No, but I know that you're tied up here all weekend. If you call in the tip, someone else will start working it and you won't get the recognition. You won't be contacting anyone before Monday morning. Give us until then.'

Koren let out a small involuntary noise that both women ignored, attention fixed solely on each other. Petra felt a thrill at the stand-off, and was surprised that Rossi didn't seem to be sharing in it. After a moment, Rossi waved her hand. 'Fine. Monday morning.'

She stood up, shaking her head as though the conversation had fogged up her brain. Dusting her hands down on her apron, she gave Petra one final look, before heading over to the Italians' table to clear up their many empty glasses, pausing to take their order for yet more.

Petra watched her go back inside, aware of Koren fidgeting next to her. As soon as the door swung shut behind Rossi, Petra stood up. Koren scrambled after her as she marched across the square.

'Monday morning?' he said forlornly, following her towards the car.

'Not ideal, I agree. But better than nothing.'

'What will happen when she takes over?'

'We'll make a report of everything we've uncovered, be thanked for our time, and told to go away.' Petra tried to keep the bitterness out of her voice but knew that some had seeped through. She tried to reason with herself, to recognise that this was arguably the best outcome. It had never been her case really, not after Marjan's alibi had been proved. She was a tool to fix an issue, she wasn't meant to get emotionally involved. The inspector's killer would be identified, hopefully brought to justice as part of this larger investigation, an innocent man saved from jail in the process. She could phone Golob back and tell him she'd be back in Ljubljana on Tuesday, having written a thorough report and left any follow-up questions in Koren's capable hands. This was what the Petra of Thursday morning, cursing at tourists and resenting the mere existence of Koper, could only have dreamed of. Yet, she was in equal parts bitter and furious. *Inšpektor* Furlan's murder deserved to be the focus of an investigation, not a side-line.

'Will you go back to Ljubljana?' Koren's voice was quiet, his eyes on his own feet as he walked. She was touched at the emotion in his voice, the obvious hope that she'd say no, that she was staying until the culprit was behind bars. Petra slowed down, ducking to the side of the street so as not to block it.

'I'll have to, once the case is transferred over to Rossi. But that doesn't mean I'm giving up. We have until Monday morning. Let's see how much we can get done before then. I'm not here on holiday.' Petra wasn't going to let Koren down. He'd lost one mentor this week already, he hardly needed to have another rush back to Ljubljana at the first chance. Likewise, this case now felt oddly personal to Petra. One corrupt police officer made them all look bad, made a mockery of the hard work and sacrifices that she and other officers all over the country made every day. Even though she'd never met Ivan Furlan, and barely knew Denis Božič, she was still desperate to see the investigation through to its conclusion.

Unsure of where to go to regroup, and not wanting to return to a station that she would soon be kicked out of, Petra and Koren drove slowly back to Koper. She searched for information on Vuk Jovanović as Koren cruised along the motorway, reading out titles of a few interesting articles published in a mixture of Serbo-Croatian, Slovenian and Italian papers describing minor offences he had been arrested for over the years. No charges ever seemed to stick. One particularly detailed editorial explained that he was one of four brothers, all of whom were now believed to be involved in the drug trade. Petra remembered Rossi mentioning Darko Jovanović as the most notable, and so she searched for information on him too, discovering that he'd been arrested far less often than Vuk but for more serious offences. Like his younger brother, he had never spent any time in a jail cell.

'Have you ever heard the inspector say Vuk's name?' she asked, putting her phone back in her pocket. The heat was still building, and she fiddled with the air conditioning as she spoke.

'Never, I don't think I've heard of any of them before.'

'Who else works on the drug task-force with Rossi? Anyone who might help us?'

Koren shrugged, eyes flicking across to Petra before returning his attention to the road. 'I can't think of anyone. In our station we just have Rossi, I suppose she could grab a junior officer whenever she needed one, but I don't think that happens very often. I think there's someone in the Izola station who works on it, and the other stations near the border, but they probably report to her. Horvat is very interested in looking like he's tough on drugs, so she mostly does whatever she wants.'

Petra had expected this, so refused to let herself be disappointed. 'So, we keep working alone. We've got this far, I don't see why we can't get further. You managed to prove Marjan's alibi all by yourself, with my help we should have this solved by Sunday evening.'

Koren flashed a smile at her, evidently unconvinced by her sentiment but happy to hear it anyway.

'When you don't know what to do next, the best thing to do is isolate the question to which you most want the answer.

That's what *Svetnik* Golob taught me,' Petra continued, look-ing out the window as they entered the tunnel towards Koper, bright daylight replaced with artificial yellow glow.

'Who killed *Inšpektor* Furlan?' said Koren uncertainly, trying to get involved in her thought process but obviously unclear on exactly where she was headed.

'Well, yes. But something smaller, that's the big picture and we're still fumbling with the pieces. I want to establish who wrote those notes to the inspector. Why were they help-ing him? Was it a trap?'

'I don't think it was a trap. There were far too many. Surely if you wanted to trap him, you'd just send one so he saw your information was legitimate and started to trust you. Maybe two, so he was feeling confident. Then you kill him. You don't send half a dozen, that's a waste of everyone's time.'

'And risks him sharing information with someone else,' Petra agreed, pleased that Koren had warmed up to the thought experiment. 'That means they were helping him. Someone inside the drug gang, or a concerned witness?'

'I agree with your translator, they're worded strangely. I don't think that's a concerned citizen, that's someone tipping the inspector off.'

'Tipping him off, but trying to conceal his own identity in case they are found?' Petra had been turning this theory over in her head for a while, preoccupied by the strange turns of phrase and the vagueness in instructions given in the notes. 'If the notes are revealed, either by accident or when the inspec-tor successfully arrests Božič, they can't be linked back to the author.' Not dissimilar to the note that had brought her to Koper, she thought.

'If that's true, it'll be very hard to identify them,' Koren said, although he still sounded invested in their discussion, no sign of the hopelessness that had briefly overcome him previously. 'If they're trying to hide from people they know, then it'll be impossible for people they don't to match the notes back to them.'

A lightbulb went off in her head as they exited the tunnel, the result of her subconscious doggedly scratching away since she'd first come across something that looked important, but which she hadn't made sense of at the time. 'Maybe not,' said Petra, diving into the back seat for her bag and pulling out the notes they had found earlier.

Like the ones she had recovered from the inspector's dictionary, they were scrawled on the back of old receipts. Petra scrutinised each one in turn, ignoring the cryptic Italian in favour of the printed text on the front. They were receipts from a Slovenian supermarket chain, she realised, product names listed in Slovene rather than Italian. Each one was quite short, only a few items per transaction. As she looked them over, it became painfully obvious that the author of the notes was a young man: if you'd told her the receipts belonged to her brother or one of his friends, she wouldn't have batted an eyelid. Energy drinks, packets of cigarettes and enormous bars of chocolate appeared multiple times across the receipts, interspersed with replacement razor cartridges, shaving cream and deodorant. Some of them had legible dates and times, which moved around crazily. One was from almost a year ago, another from three weeks ago. Their age didn't seem to have much to do with their contents. The car swerved suddenly as Koren tried to get a look at what she was doing, and she looked up suddenly as he blushed.

'He's just using whatever paper he can lay his hands on,' she breathed, waving one note at Koren. 'I bet he's just grabbing receipts from his car. He stops at a shop, buys himself an energy drink and a chocolate bar, then dumps the receipt somewhere in the car until he needs paper. He must get the information very last-minute, and hands it over to the inspector immediately.'

Koren turned to look at her, blinking at her hopefully. His eyes were wide, his lips pursed together. Petra could feel a similar look of excitement blooming across her own face, finally feeling like she had a lead. She looked back down at the receipts, irritated that several had been ripped in half to form multiple pieces of paper, the addresses and till identification numbers missing. Finally, she found one with the name of the particular branch it came from.

'Head to the shopping centre in town, Koper Central,' she said, grabbing her door handle for support as Koren followed her instructions immediately and veered off the exit they were passing at the very last second. 'Here's hoping they have CCTV.'

# Chapter 27

Petra could have jumped for joy when the amiable weekend manager of the supermarket on the ground floor of Koper Central informed her that not only did they have cameras outside and inside the store, but that they had recently been updated due to a spike in shoplifting and so were very good quality. She and Koren only had to wait a few minutes before they were welcomed into a harshly lit back room, a young member of staff clicking away on a screen to try and find the exact time stamp indicated on the receipt. Petra watched with bated breath as shoppers piled their goods onto conveyor belts, throwing their goods back into trolleys and bags at the other end as the cashier sped through the scanning.

'There,' said Koren, finger darting up to indicate a dark-haired figure who had just deposited a litre of orange juice, family-sized bag of crisps and a packet of biscuits on the conveyor belt at the far end of the line. Even though his purchases weren't clear from the picture, Petra knew exactly which brands he'd opted for: she had it on the receipt in front of her. His back remained to the camera at first as he

waited, eventually turning to face the lens. Without needing to be asked, the shop assistant helping them snapped a
screenshot and sent it to print. He was young and thin, curly
dark hair framing wide-set eyes. Artfully maintained stub-
ble lined his mouth and jaw, a crucifix just visible around
his neck.

The video kept rolling, and Petra smiled a little as she
watched the cashier hand over the very receipt she clutched
in her hand. They watched the man leave the shop, heading
outside into the car park. Switching to another camera, they
saw him climb into a small Fiat and drive away.

'I've got the number plate,' said Koren, waving a piece of
paper at her. 'It's Italian, so I'll have to call in a favour, but we
can get a name today.'

They thanked the manager and shop assistant profusely
before heading back out to the car park, Petra unable to stop
herself looking up at the cameras that she had just seen the
note-writer through, weeks after he'd made his pitstop here.
She climbed behind the wheel, allowing Koren to settle in the
passenger seat and phone his friend in the Italian police, who
assured him that he'd pass the details of the Fiat's owner along
as soon as he could. Once he'd ended the call, they decided to
head to the *slaščičarna* to await more information, neither of
them willing to run the risk of seeing Božič.

As soon as they entered the café, Petra was met by someone calling her name. She turned in the direction of the noise,
surprised to see Doug York sitting at a table near the door.
A book lay on the table in front of him, a large cup of tea

on a neat porcelain saucer by his right hand. He stood as she approached him, thrusting his hand out to shake.

'Petra, hello!'

'Doug,' she replied, aware that Koren was hovering at her elbow. 'I don't believe you've met Aleš Koren, one of my colleagues.'

'Wonderful to meet you,' enthused Doug, shaking Koren's hand firmly. 'Koren as in Marija Koren, maker of delicious cakes?'

Koren blinked, his brain taking a second to catch up with Doug's quick English. 'Yes,' he said, his accent heavier than Petra had been expecting. 'She is my mother.'

'Excellent. I'm quite jealous, my mother could burn water.'

'You are here to try the pastries?' asked Petra, gesturing around herself. Every table was full, the sound of forks scraping plates and cups being returned to saucers filling the air.

Doug shook his head, smiling widely. 'No, I was actually here to see you. A lovely police officer told me I might find you here for your lunch. I can't say I minded the wait, although if I make a habit of it I'll need some new jeans.'

Petra cocked her head in confusion. 'Waiting for me? You could have phoned.' She was aware that she sounded harsh, but did not know how else to phrase it without seeming overly familiar.

Doug blushed, rubbing the back of his head with one hand. 'I know, it was silly of me. I just thought I'd check if there was anything else you needed help with? The police officer I spoke to said you might have time to spare.'

Petra raised her eyebrows, working out who the lovely police officer might have been, imagining Medved bored at her desk enjoying sending a handsome Englishman off to wait for Petra's next appearance at the *slaščičarna*. Petra was slightly worried she was becoming predictable, but rationalised it to herself that her lunch habits in a new city when accompanied by a café owner's son were bound to be less varied than they might be elsewhere. She chose not to admit to herself that she was, if anything, more predictable in Ljubljana; known throughout the station as someone who always brought their own lunch in a plastic box, never needing to rush out to the shops or a local takeaway. She felt a pang of guilt for Medved, abandoned at the station, hearing updates through texts and the occasional passing visit.

'We do have some time,' she replied. 'May I sit?'

'Of course!' Doug rushed to the chair Petra had indicated, pulling it out so that she could sit down before tucking it back in again. Petra hadn't experienced such chivalry in a while and felt herself blush as Koren slumped into the remaining chair, unaided by Doug.

'You're the translator?' asked Koren, apparently coming to the realisation that Petra wasn't actually going to introduce him. Petra chastised herself, hating her thoughtlessness. One young man seeking her out for a working lunch, and she'd completely forgotten poor Koren.

'Yes, I work at the language centre in Izola,' replied Doug. 'I've been helping Petra with her Italian.'

Koren harrumphed, crossing his arms across his chest.

Petra cringed, remembering that Koren himself would be just as capable, if not more so. Timing and circumstance had led her to Doug, although she was still glad she'd sought an outsider's perspective, even if only because it meant Medved got a bit of excitement on a boring Saturday shift.

'I hope you haven't spent too much time on the new notes,' Petra began as Doug pulled a notebook from his satchel, placing it carefully in front of him as he pushed his novel to the side. 'I suspect they will be very similar to the ones I showed you previously.'

Doug shrugged. 'They are, just more times and places. A few funny turns of phrase, but nothing ground-breaking.'

'Are they all coastal?' asked Petra as Koren summoned a waiter over, ordering their normal coffees. Petra felt strangely pleased that they now had a regular order, partners who knew how each other took their coffee without even having to ask.

'Largely. I thought you might enjoy this one, it is so silly,' he gestured to a page in his notebook where he'd carefully transcribed the text of one of the notes, translating it below. 'It just says "hardware store car park, he says he's at the hairdresser".'

That caught Koren's attention. His head snapped up, his eyes fixed on Doug's notebook. Seeing his interest, Doug spun it around, allowing Koren to see the transcription. He nodded to himself, apparently agreeing with Doug's translation. Petra peered at what he was looking at, recognising the Italian as the note which had led them to the supermarket.

'Something the matter?' asked Doug politely.

'The hairdresser,' said Koren, chewing on his bottom lip.

He paused for a second, eyes fluttering as he thought deeply. When he continued, he spoke slowly, his English good but stilted. 'I remember that day. We were in the office, and *Inšpektor* Božič said he had to go to the hairdresser. When he came back, *Inšpektor* Furlan said that his hair was the same.'

Doug started to laugh, although quickly fell silent when he realised Petra wasn't going to join him. 'Is that important?'

'It could be,' said Petra in English, before returning to Slovene. 'Did the inspector leave while Božič was away?' She was aware that she shouldn't be having this conversation in front of Doug, but it felt rude to leave him now when he had waited to see her and share his work. She hoped that a British language teacher didn't turn out to be working for the Jovanović family, wondering what the state of the world would be if that turned out to be the case. She flashed Doug an apologetic smile, aware that it was rude to speak in front of him in a language he did not understand.

Koren followed suit. 'I don't know. He didn't have any work for me, so he sent me to help Eva. He could have gone anywhere.'

'He was back in the office before you?'

'Yes, I think so. I can't really remember. Rossi would know.'

'Giulia? Why?'

'She was there when Božič got back, she thought it was hilarious. She came through from her office, you know how they connect.'

Petra considered this, already certain that she would not be approaching Rossi again for input before the case had passed hands. She wondered whether there had been other instances like this that had made her suspect Božič, which Koren had missed, all adding up to her confession earlier that day that she thought he was crooked.

A member of staff brought them their coffees, Doug cheerfully ordering a slice of *Sachertorte* while Petra and Koren stewed. He attacked it with gusto, allowing them to continue their thoughtful silence. Petra was desperately searching for a polite question to ask him when Koren's phone flashed, and he shoved it in her direction.

'We have an identification for the owner of the Fiat. Giovanna Bortolotti, aged eighty. Lives in Prosek with her son and her grandson. His name is Luca Bortolotti, aged twenty-three.'

'Prosek?'

'Prosecco, in Italian,' offered Doug, apparently pleased that he could contribute. 'Like the wine.'

'It is in Italy?' she confirmed, switching back to English.

'Yes, just over the border.'

'We cannot go,' said Koren, still in English. 'Not to Prosek. We are not the police there.' He paused for a moment, gave Doug a suspicious look, then switched back to Slovene. 'Luca Bortolotti also has an address in Koper on file with the Italian government. He's a student at the university here, studying Italian.'

Petra gave him a questioning look. 'Italian?'

Koren nodded. 'Definitely strange. Why not an Italian university if he wants to study literature? The university here teaches Italian as a foreign language, mostly to Erasmus students. It isn't intended for native speakers.'

'Do you have the address?'

'I do, it isn't far. Shall we head there now?'

Petra nodded, trying to organise her thoughts.

'Another time for lunch, then?' said Doug, watching Koren stand and head over to the counter.

A pang of guilt went through Petra, as she realised how little of what had just transpired he would have understood. She supposed it wasn't necessarily a bad thing. A member of the public hardly needed to know the details of their investigation, no matter how helpful he was being.

'I would like that. You have my phone number.' Petra switched back to English, and hoped it was clear in her voice that she was being honest, that she would truly like to spend time talking to him about something other than an Italian student's word choice. From the smile he gave her, she thought her message had landed perfectly.

As they hustled out of the shop, Doug waving as they went, Petra heard Marija's voice floating through from the back room, insisting that neither Petra, Koren nor their English friend would be needing to pay.

# Chapter 28

The block of flats which Koren's friend directed them to was further inland than the station, slightly up one of the hills that Petra had come to realise surrounded the city. It was very tall for a complex in Koper, the call box suggesting that each of its eleven floors held three flats. From just outside the main door she had a perfect view down into a garden centre car park, bustling with activity as people took advantage of the sunny Saturday afternoon.

'How do the Italian police know he lives here?' asked Petra, gazing above her. They had hoped another resident would leave, allowing them to slip in and get up to flat 3A without alerting Bortolotti, but his neighbours seemed less inclined to be out and about than did the patrons of the garden centre.

'He registered this address at the last election, I think,' explained Koren. 'That was recent, just in the last few months.'

'Do we know if he lives alone?'

'The Italians don't have anyone else registered here, but that doesn't mean there isn't anyone.'

Petra nodded, steeled herself, and pressed the buzzer.

A little tune rang out as they waited for someone above to answer before a staticky voice crackled a, '*Ciao?*'

Petra indicated that Koren should speak, aware that Bortolotti did not seem to speak Slovene. He spoke in Italian for a moment, Petra picking out the words for 'police' and 'car', before the voice on the other end swore quietly. Petra gave Koren a shocked look, concerned that they were being told to leave, but was quickly corrected when a shrill noise sounded and the magnetic door locks clicked open.

Petra stopped in the entrance hall for a second, indicating that Koren should take the lift while she took the stairs to ensure Bortolotti couldn't get past them. As they waited for the lift to make it down to them, she asked, 'What did you say?'

'That we're the police, and that in the process of investigating a murder we've encountered footage of a car we believe he would have had access to.'

Petra nodded, content with Koren's synopsis. As the lift doors closed behind him she started to make her way up the stairs, expecting to hear Bortolotti's thundering footsteps at any moment. The stairwell remained empty, silent except for the echoed clipping of her own shoes as she headed towards the third floor. Koren beat her there, and was already standing outside 3A by the time she'd straightened her blouse collar and trousers, making herself ready for an interview. She nodded at him and he knocked, the door flying open immediately.

'Police?' Luca Bortolotti sounded tired, and looked worse. Huge bags dominated the skin under his eyes, his dark curls hung lankly around his face. It was undoubtedly the same man as who they'd seen on the supermarket security footage just a few hours ago, but he seemed to have aged in the days since he'd been shopping. Petra couldn't work out whether he was attempting to speak Slovene with a strong Italian accent, or whether he was simply speaking Italian. The words were too close.

'*Sì*,' replied Koren. '*Parla sloveno?*'

Bortolotti shrugged, and held two of his fingers a small distance apart. 'A little,' he replied in Slovene. 'I understand more than I can say.' Petra gave him a supportive smile.

'If I ask my questions in Slovene, you can reply in Italian?' she suggested, following him into the flat when he wandered away from the door, leaving it open behind him.

'Yes.'

Bortolotti settled on a low sofa in the main room of the flat, slouching backwards. He was wearing a white vest and tight blue gym shorts, leading Petra to suspect he hadn't been expecting visitors. The crucifix she'd seen in the CCTV footage hung around his neck, and as Petra watched he started to pull the pendant sluggishly along the chain.

'We will be quick,' she said, getting no response from Bortolotti. Koren interpreted quickly, but Italian got nothing out of him either.

Petra cleared her throat, and tried again. '*Signor* Bortolotti, do you know *Inšpektor* Ivan Furlan of Koper Police?'

'Yes,' said Bortolotti, then switched into rapid-fire Italian that Petra had no hope of understanding. Koren was nodding at him as he spoke, so she hoped it was of use.

'He says *Inšpektor* Furlan came to speak at the university about bike thefts,' Koren summarised. When Petra gave him a confused look, Koren continued, 'he did that for the high school too, gave a demonstration on bike locks. He's telling the truth.'

'And that's the only time you have met him?'

Bortolotti let his head loll backwards, apparently horribly bored. 'Yes.'

'I don't believe you, *Signor* Bortolotti. I think you met the inspector a few more times, and I can prove it. Would you like to change your answer?'

Bortolotti showed no sign of moving from his slump, so Koren translated her question for him. Petra suspected he had understood perfectly well, and was using the language barrier to buy time, but she didn't particularly care. As long as she got the answers she needed, she could put up with it.

'Once again, but that is it.' His Slovene was incredibly heavily accented, spoken with the same intonation as his Italian. The result made some words difficult to understand, stressing the words in the wrong place.

'When was that?'

'Two months ago.'

'And why did you see him again?'

Bortolotti shuffled in his seat, still maintaining eye contact with the ceiling. 'He wanted me.'

'Wanted you? In what way?'

'He asked people where I am.'

'*Signor* Bortolotti, if you would find it easier to speak Italian then please feel free to do so.' Petra punctuated this offer by opening her bag and fishing out her notebook and pen, giving him an assessing look.

Bortolotti sat in silence for a little longer, then straightened up so that he could make eye contact with Koren. He spoke in Italian for a while, his words speeding up as he went. A few times, Koren interrupted him with questions of his own, which he answered frantically and with a lot of hand gestures. As he got to the end of his piece he slowed down again, slumping back into the sofa as he fell into silence. Petra looked at Koren expectantly, unsure of what to make of Bortolotti's erratic behaviour.

'The inspector was asking around for Bortolotti, and eventually someone was able to tell him where to find him. When they met, he told Bortolotti he had received a report of his dealing drugs at the university, but he hadn't yet passed it on to the university authorities as he wanted his help. If he handed it in, Bortolotti would be expelled, probably get a criminal record.' Koren's voice was tight, his eyes fixed on Bortolotti.

Petra furrowed her brow, tucking the errant strand of hair behind her ear. 'The inspector was blackmailing Bortolotti?'

'*Ricatto*,' murmured Bortolotti, repeating a word Petra had vaguely heard in his spiel earlier.

'Yes, blackmail. *Ricatto*. Bortolotti didn't want to get thrown out of the university, because then his father would disown him. I don't think the inspector knew that, he just got lucky.'

'What?'

'He has already been thrown out of two universities in Italy for poor grades.'

'Oh.'

'Exactly. So, when the inspector said he was one phone call away from being asked to leave a third, he agreed to what the inspector asked.'

'Which was?'

'Information,' sighed Bortolotti, staring into the middle distance.

'Dates, times and places relating to drug activity. Not all of it, though. He was only interested in anything that involved *Inšpektor* Božič.'

'Denis Božič,' Bortolotti agreed. 'With his nice car.'

'And so Bortolotti wrote *Inšpektor* Furlan notes to tip him off?'

'I hear information, I write information, I give it to the policeman.'

'And how did you hear this information?'

Bortolotti sucked his teeth, nodding his head from side to side slowly as he thought. Finally, he spoke again. 'People talk. I listen. People say when Božič's friends will arrive. Sometimes, I drive him to meet them, even though he has a nice car.'

Koren looked away from Bortolotti as he spoke, giving his attention to Petra. He shrugged, indicating that Bortolotti's brief statement encompassed anything Koren might have wanted to say. Petra was interested to hear that Bortolotti viewed Božič and men she could only assume were Vuk

Jovanović and his associates, as friends. She scribbled herself a note, for later.

'Did you tell anyone you were doing this?'

Bortolotti shook his head emphatically, eyes widening. 'Policeman take my degree. They take my life.'

'They being the Jovanović brothers?'

Bortolotti switched back into Italian, distress painted across his face as he spoke quickly to Koren, who just nodded. 'He says he'd rather not talk about that.' That confirmed it.

'Okay, we don't need to speak about Vuk Jovanović or his boat trips to Slovenia.' Petra was pleased to see Bortolotti flinch, confirming that she was right about Vuk's involvement and his under the radar trips to Koper. She hoped she was giving the impression that she knew more than she did, aware that if Bortolotti was clever, he could evade her questions and tell her to come back when she had enough to arrest him. He seemed too tired and upset even to try to argue back. She wondered how he survived in the drug business when he had this little fight in him. 'But the men you work for, who you distribute drugs for, they would kill you for what you told the inspector?'

'Yes.'

'And for speaking to me now?'

'Yes.'

'Did they kill the inspector?'

'Maybe.'

'You don't know for sure?'

'No.'

Petra nodded. 'I want you to think carefully, *Signor* Bortolotti. Do you suspect anyone knew about your notes? Not Vuk, I know he'd have killed you. But someone else, someone who might have used it to blackmail you again later?'

'Only the policeman blackmails me.'

'I understand, but I want you to think about possibilities. Might someone have known, but not wanted to reveal your involvement just yet? Because they might want something from you in future? Because they wanted an opportunity to kill the inspector?'

Petra saw the blank look in his eyes, realised he hadn't understood. Koren jumped in, and as he spoke Bortolotti frowned. 'Someone knows, but did not tell?'

'I don't know. Can you think of anyone?'

He sat quietly for a moment, thinking. 'It was strange,' he said suddenly, eyebrows drawn together. 'One information. It was strange.' Aware he'd reached the limits of his Slovene, he started speaking slowly in Italian, Koren paying careful attention to every word. At one point, he turned suddenly to look at Petra, then went back to focusing on Bortolotti. She wished she understood it live, had to prevent herself from wriggling with impatience to discover what had made Koren start. Her pen hovered millimetres above the page, and she distracted herself by quickly rereading what she'd already written. As Koren and Bortolotti continued speaking, she heard the word 'car' a few times, but couldn't make out much more. When Bortolotti finished, he seemed deep in thought, hands clasped in his lap as he stared critically at the floor.

'Bortolotti received word that Božič was going to the vintage car show at *Grad* Strmol to drop something off. He'd never done mule work before, so Bortolotti was surprised, but he handed the tip on to the inspector anyway. It seemed to make sense, with Božič's love of cars and all.'

'But?' she sensed it was coming and pre-empted it.

'He saw Božič at the Croatian border on the day of the car show. Božič didn't go, so he couldn't have been dropping anything off. Either plans changed and Bortolotti wasn't told, or someone was seeing if he was a rat, and who he was tattling to.'

'Who told you about the car show, *Signor* Bortolotti?' Petra spun back to him, noticing that at some point in her conversation he'd looked up and was now staring at her.

'I get texts,' he said simply. 'Texts say when policeman is there to make it easy, at the border. One text was different. It said to leave the package outside Božič's house, so he could take to the buyer at the show.'

'The text gave you that much detail?'

Silence.

'What language do you get texts in? Can I see them?'

Bortolotti shook his head rapidly. 'I talk, I don't show. Italian.'

'Good Italian, or basic?'

'Fine, good, I don't know. They said very little.'

Petra turned back to Koren, who leaned back in his chair. Bortolotti obviously hadn't spotted it at the time, but the car show text sounded like it was out of place compared to the normal information he received. She couldn't imagine that someone as low on the totem pole as him would be told of specificities that didn't involve him, so the detail about *Grad Strmol* should have made him pause, especially when his own life was also apparently on the line. He seemed to realise this at the same time as her, giving her a worried look as his face went pale.

'They know I give information.'

'I suspect so, yes. Someone tested you with the car show, and you as good as confirmed it.'

'They will kill me.'

'I won't let that happen, *Signor* Bortolotti.'

He scoffed, moving his arms so that they were folded across his chest. 'They will kill you too.'

'Because they killed *Inšpektor* Furlan? I thought you said you weren't sure about that.'

'Because they will kill anyone.'

Koren stood up, started pacing behind the second low sofa, which Petra was perched on. She tried not to let his anxious movement distract her, aware of her own rising stress levels. 'Who could it be, behind the texts? Do you know?'

'They text everyone,' he replied sullenly, surprisingly forthcoming for someone who had just realised their impending demise. 'I get texts, policeman gets texts.'

'Policeman in this context being Denis Božič?'

Bortolotti inclined his head in confirmation. 'Everyone gets texts, from different phone numbers. Phone numbers change, all the time.' He opened his mouth to continue, then turned to Koren instead, saying something in Italian.

'He says they have a code so you know it is them contacting you.'

'And the car show message was legitimate?'

'Yes.'

'So, whoever messaged you is important enough that they know the code, but they haven't handed you in to Jovanović?'

'Maybe they're playing with him,' suggested Koren, seemingly uncaring whether Bortolotti understood or not. 'Leaving him to become a wreck before they finish him off.'

'Or they honestly haven't passed the information on.'

'Perhaps they killed the inspector, and they know he's a good candidate to pin it on if Marjan didn't work out.'

Petra blinked at Koren, following through his theory in her head. It worked, in many ways. 'Sacrifice Bortolotti, to protect Božič? They didn't realise Marjan Furlan was such a liability.'

Koren nodded at her, first slowly and then faster. 'Assuming that it isn't Božič sacrificing Bortolotti to protect himself. If Marjan did somehow come up with an alibi, he has another fall guy.'

'I did not kill him,' muttered Bortolotti, having apparently misunderstood their conversation.

'We know,' said Petra impatiently, rising from her seat. 'Thank you for your help, *Signor* Bortolotti.'

'You want to protect me?' he asked quietly as Petra passed him, not bothering to stand to follow them to the door.

'Of course. Would you like a police car to guard the building?' Quite how she would organise this, she did not know. She could hardly leave Koren behind, he was far too useful, and while she wanted to believe Medved had nothing to do with police corruption, she didn't have the authority to dispatch her and a car out here without someone noticing.

He said something to Koren, who replied with a brief comment and a shrug. Bortolotti scoffed and waved a hand at them, indicating that they should leave him alone. They filed out of his apartment, leaving him sitting on his sofa.

'What did you say?' she asked as they stepped into the lift, forced to stand uncomfortably close in the small space.

'He said that would make them suspicious. I said that they already knew he'd done that all on his own.'

'Did he agree to anything?'

'No, he says he'll fend for himself. I left your card on the table, I hope that isn't a problem. He can phone you, if he needs something.'

Petra smiled at Koren, saw the genuineness of it reflected in the mirrored walls of the lift. He towered above her, but still looked down at her hopefully, like a dog seeking confirmation and affirmation from its master. She self-consciously ran a hand through her hair, wiping the shine off her nose where she hadn't used enough powder that morning. 'Good work, Koren. I think we've done all we can for him. At least he has been warned.'

# Chapter 29

Their drive back to the station was quiet, both thinking through their encounter with Luca Bortolotti. Although he had given them a lot to work with, Petra felt she was left with more questions than answers. Establishing the voice behind the notes and the reason for *Inšpektor* Furlan's impromptu trip to the car show had been very useful, but it raised the question of who else knew. Although Furlan had initiated his relationship with Bortolotti, at some point their interaction had been taken over by an unknown individual. That they spoke Italian to Bortolotti was mildly interesting, but hardly noteworthy. He seemed unlikely to be able to cope with written Slovene, and most people in the region could have switched languages for his benefit.

That the inspector was willing to blackmail Bortolotti was perhaps more interesting. All through the investigation so far, Petra had been under the impression that the inspector played everything very much by the book, operating in the same black and white world as Koren. She had somewhat assumed that was where the younger man had picked it up. Now it seemed that he operated in shades of grey, blackmailing and threatening if he saw it as benefitting the greater good. That Koren had so readily believed Bortolotti was surprising to Petra, making her rethink his relationship with his deceased mentor. She had thought that he was incapable of seeing fault in Furlan, that his quest to solve the inspector's murder came from a place of idolisation of his faultless hero. Instead, it seemed that he was willing to find fault with Furlan, but only when it was believable to him.

'Have you heard of the inspector blackmailing anyone before?' she asked quietly as they trundled back to the station, stuck behind a line of traffic evidently unfamiliar with the roundabouts that surrounded them.

'No,' Koren replied immediately. 'But I've known him to give people who didn't deserve it a second chance.'

'What do you mean?'

Koren sighed, then pulled into a car park next to the canal and turned the engine off. He twisted in his seat and pulled off his sunglasses, prompting Petra to do the same. 'My brother stole a motorbike.'

'What? When?'

'Years ago, before the inspector was in homicide. Back when my brother was still at school. He stole a motorbike, but he was acting out as my dad was in hospital and my mum didn't have time for us as she was working in the café. The inspector made it all go away.'

'Before he knew you?'

'Long before. I was a child, I still thought I was going to grow up to be an astronaut.'

'And he's done this before?'

'I assume so. I know he's looked the other way a few times, caught kids with cannabis and never let it get to court, that sort of thing. Nothing huge, no one was hurt. Just giving people a second chance.'

'But you said it was people who didn't deserve it?'

'My brother went on to steal a car.'

'Oh.'

'The inspector believed that people deserved the chance to put things right without being made a spectacle of, to repent privately and be allowed to move on. I assume that's what he was doing with Božič, by not making those pictures public, and with Bortolotti too to an extent. He was making sure he had the facts on Božič's corruption, Bortolotti's dealing, then was offering them the chance to come clean, set things straight.'

'You think he approached Božič?' Petra chewed her bottom lip, thinking of the implications of what Koren had just told her. She had been assuming that the inspector was collecting evidence on his colleague and friend so that he was completely sure of his guilt before he made any move against him, not wanting to risk the man's career and their relationship on hearsay. If he had been planning on confronting Božič, the man's guilt in his murder looked even more probable.

'I think he planned to; I doubt whether he did. Surely if he'd spoken to him, he'd have taken the envelope we found in Piran? If that was still in his desk, I don't think he'd made his move.'

Petra sucked her teeth, agreeing with what Koren said. She thought of how Božič had responded in her own meeting with him the previous day, how he'd evaded questions and given half-answers. If Furlan was going to accuse him of anything, he'd have needed evidence if he wanted to get anywhere. Koren was right, the intervention must not yet have occurred when the inspector was murdered.

'I don't know whether to assume Božič knew Furlan was on to him,' Petra admitted. 'I don't think he texted Bortolotti about the car show, you told me yourself his Italian wouldn't be up to it. That must mean someone else is looking out for him, but I don't know whether that extends to murdering a police officer to protect him, or just to letting him know that he needed to do something about Furlan.'

Koren let out a long breath, sliding down in the driver's seat. 'This is such a mess.'

Petra nodded, looking out of the window at the boats bobbing in their moorings on the canal, their registration numbers painted carefully on their sides in a variety of colours and scripts. A trio of children sat on the back of the boat nearest to their car, being shown how to attach bait to a fishing hook by an older boy.

'Look on the bright side,' she said eventually. 'The police have a mole, but so did the drug gang.'

'Only because *Inšpektor* Furlan was breaking both police protocol and the law by blackmailing him.'

'In your own words, Aleš, we can't have everything.'

Koren chuckled, cleaning his sunglasses absent-mindedly

with the edge of his uniform t-shirt, shoving it back into his waistband when he was done. Petra pulled a face at his lack of care with his gun, watching in displeasure as he adjusted his belt using it as a handhold.

'Very wise, *Inšpektorica*. So, what now?'

'Now, I go into the lair of the beast.' Petra had known this was coming for a while, had been dreading it but knew it had to be done, and that she had to do it alone.

'You, not both of us? What lair?' Koren peppered her with questions like a child, his mouth opening before his brain had engaged. She watched as everything clicked into place, as he realised what she meant. 'No, *Inšpektorica*. I'll come with you. If we're right, he might have killed the inspector. You can't go alone. I know we're short for time before Rossi takes over the case, but this is too risky.'

'You would have to be incredibly stupid to kill one police officer to cover up your murder of another,' Petra pointed out. 'You can't push that under the rug. People would start asking questions.'

'Not if it suited them not to,' replied Koren darkly, sitting up straight again to try and get his point across. 'Please, *Inšpektorica* Vidmar. You can't go alone.'

'He's not going to hurt me, Aleš.' Petra was aware that she'd started calling him by his first name more and more, but it was fitting. Calling him by his surname seemed to enforce an artificial distance between them. Despite having known him for only two days, she felt a kinship with him, having slogged through a lot to get to where they were now.

'I'll sit down the road in the car, and if you aren't back out in half an hour then I'll come in.'

'No. I'm going to leave you at the station, and I'm going to drive over to Božič's house alone. His wife is there, his children. I'll be perfectly safe. I think you appearing mid-conversation would only aggravate him.'

'What do you want me to do while you're gone?' It wasn't an acceptance of Petra's plan, but rather an attempt to point out she'd be wasting resources by leaving him twiddling his thumbs at the station.

Petra was one step ahead of him. 'I want you to contact *Svetnik* Horvat and let him know about Marjan's alibi. I also want you to see if you can get Medved's help in going through some of the security cameras from the station, seeing when and how often Božič was leaving during the day. We saw him rush off ourselves yesterday, I want to know how often he disappears.'

'And if they ask why I want to see internal CCTV?'

'Say you're looking to see who else came to see the inspector in the weeks before his death, who came and went. With Marjan off the table, it would be a good idea.'

Koren narrowed his eyes, evidently still perturbed. 'What am I meant to tell Horvat and Medved about where you are?'

'Say that I'm discussing the case with Božič. It isn't a lie, and Horvat will get the full truth when Rossi approaches him on Monday anyway.'

Koren looked unsure, but started the car back up and drove in the direction of the station. 'You'll call me if anything feels wrong?' he demanded, concern written across his face.

'Of course,' she replied, glad she sounded more confident than she felt. She had a few ideas of how to approach the coming conversation with Božič, but wasn't sure which was the best, whether any would work. She had one shot, she had to give it the best go she could. It was so nerve-wracking to think about that part of her wanted to pack up now, go back to Ljubljana and let Rossi handle it come Monday, but she didn't think she'd be able to look at herself in the mirror. Instead, she gave Koren the bravest smile she could muster and put her sunglasses back on, staring resolutely out the window.

Koren allowed a moment to pass in silence, then sighed. 'Do you even know where he lives?' He sounded defeated, but Petra did not allow herself to feel bad. She was here because she was experienced, knowledgeable. She had to trust her gut, at least some of the time.

Petra turned back to him. 'I was hoping you could tell me.'

With a shake of his head, Koren gave her brief directions to the Božič house, then lapsed into silence again, obviously still troubled. Petra removed her sunglasses. 'I'll have my phone in my pocket at all times, I promise. You're on speed-dial. If he makes even the smallest move, I'll phone for help.'

It was obvious that this did not mollify him, but he gave her a small nod nonetheless, and the car fell back into an uneasy silence.

After Koren dropped her back at the Skoda and marched inside the station, she felt her resolve start to weaken. What she had said to him was true: she was walking into Božič's family home, where his wife and children lived. She was still unclear on whether he had personally killed Furlan, or had just been part of the circumstances leading to his death. Petra was unlikely to be driving to the scene of her own murder, and yet she still felt more uncertain than she was willing to admit to Koren, the hairs on the back of her neck starting to prickle and her skin growing colder the further she drove away from the safety of the station. She tried to tell herself that, arguably, the station was hardly safe either: at least one corrupt police officer operated from it, she had few friends or allies in the force, and had been summoned there unwillingly due to gross incompetence and rug-sweeping. The case was about to be ripped off her and added to a pile on Rossi's desk to be used as fodder for a wider investigation, Irena Furlan left to wait for Rossi's bigger picture to be realised before she got any justice for her husband. She felt a strange mixture of righteous anger at having the inspector's murder shelved, and intense panic that she was about to cause irreparable damage to a long-running multinational drug investigation. Pre-emptively, she twanged her wrist, muting the first tendrils of panic.

She thought of Koren and Medved as she drove, heading south out of town and away from the sea, passing the road she and Koren had turned off earlier to visit Bortolotti and continuing up the hill. While she would have liked their company to quell her own nerves, it would have been unreasonable to ask them. Their presence had the potential to anger Božič, make him feel emasculated when junior officers over whom he had command showed up to interrogate him. Likewise, Petra knew, if this did not go the way she wanted and she had to return to Ljubljana with her tail between her legs and Božič unscathed, it would ruin Koren and Medved's careers and lives in Koper. She couldn't sign them up for that, even if Koren had tried his best to volunteer.

The road continued up the hill, through the blocks of flats and terraced houses that made up Markovec. The houses started to peter out, just one or two larger properties lining the sides of the road. In her rear-view mirror, Petra could see back down into Koper, light dancing on the sea in the distance. She carried on, following a twist in the road around a small crop of olive trees, finally coming to a stop outside a large, tarmacked driveway. An elderly metal gate blocked Petra from entering, a smaller pedestrian entrance left open at the side. Koren had described the house well, informing her that it had been built for multiple generations of the Božič family, and still hosted both Denis Božič's family and his parents, along with an aunt who was known to bring Božič's children to visit him at the station if she collected them from school. The house seemed to suit the purpose, obviously well divided for multiple occupancy: at the front on the ground floor there was a large double door, sheltered from the sun by a wraparound terrace on the floor above which had another entry point, accessible from a wide set of exterior stairs. Skylights dominated the red roof, at odds with the smaller windows dotted around elsewhere on the property. A brick outbuilding sat at right angles to the main structure, left unrendered in contrast to the pale pink walls of the house. The outbuilding seemed to be windowless, its only entrance a brown wooden garage-style door, which was propped open. Despite appearances, it was evidently not used as a garage. Two reasonably new family-sized cars sat on the tarmac, pulled up close to the house.

Petra climbed out of the Skoda, leaving it parked far enough away from the gate that other vehicles could still come and go. The pedestrian gate moved with a squeak as she passed through, which she was strangely glad about. She didn't want anyone to think she was sneaking up on them, she didn't mind having her presence announced. She walked calmly across the tarmac, stopping briefly when a large and well-groomed dog who she recognised from the photograph on Božič's desk came ambling around the side of the house and demanded a belly rub directly outside the front door. It seemed to have little interest in securing the perimeter, tongue lolling happily and eyes closed in contentment as she gave it the attention it wanted.

'*Ljubica*, is that you?' The unmistakable voice of Denis Božič called out from behind her, prompting Petra to straighten up and turn around. The dog at her feet grumbled in displeasure, its long tail swishing around on the floor and colliding with her ankles to try and regain her attention. Petra ignored it, her focus on the man now standing just a few metres from her. He was dressed in paint-speckled khaki shorts, a threadbare white t-shirt and thick black gloves. Oil was smeared across one cheek, mixing with sweat and trickling down towards his jaw. Petra couldn't read his expression. '*Inšpektorica* Vidmar, what a surprise. I thought you were my wife.'

Despite his words, Božič didn't look particularly surprised.

He remained motionless, a dirty rag hanging limply from his hands, his eyes shifting between Petra and the dog. Seeing its master, the dog leapt to its feet and barrelled towards him, headbutting him joyfully. Božič reached down to pat its head, but the motion seemed absent-minded and automatic.

'Sorry, *Inšpektor* Božič. It is just me. I was about to knock, but your dog found me first.'

'Pika loves people,' said Božič. As he continued playing with Pika's ears, he seemed to get a hold of himself. Petra watched as the broad grin he had attempted to dazzle her with on their first meeting spread across his face, slightly strained at the edges. 'So, what brings you up here on a Saturday? You aren't already heading back to Ljubljana?'

'No, not quite yet. Koren uncovered some new information about the case, so I've been working all morning.'

'New information? Anything interesting?'

Petra made a snap decision, opting for the approach she had been least confident about in the car, but which now seemed the right move. 'Nothing that couldn't have waited until Monday.'

She wasn't sure if she was imagining it, her brain making jumps based on context rather than evidence, but she thought Božič might have looked relieved, apparently taking this as a criticism of Koren's methods shared between friends.

'He's really distressed about this case, *Inšpektorica*. Please don't hold it against him. If you'd seen how he was with Ivan, you'd understand.'

Petra balked at the reversal of roles, Božič begging for

clemency on Koren's behalf when just the day before he'd been calling him misguided and overly emotional, telling Petra to ignore him. The urge to announce Marjan's alibi immediately, tell Božič she had him in her sights, was immense. She forced herself to calm down, continue with the tactics she'd decided on. She had found that appealing to Božič's experience, flattering him, making him feel like he was being listened to, had worked in her favour. She could only hope the same would be true again.

'I know, I know. Just a little frustrating to be dragged out of bed on hearsay. Do you have time for a chat? I said I was coming up here to talk about the case, but I think I actually just needed a quick break.'

'Of course! Any time.' Božič turned on his heel, beckoning for Petra to follow. Pika gambolled after him, running a few steps ahead before turning and wagging her tail until he caught up. He patted her on the head each time, muttering encouragement. Petra found herself doubting Božič's guilt for a moment, watching how the dog loved him, how he loved her back. She had always thought animals were good judges of character, and had assumed that would mean they didn't warm to the morally, and in this case actually, corrupt, and certainly not to murderers. She put her disappointment in Pika's character judgement aside and followed Božič through the garage door and into the outbuilding.

# Chapter 30

Petra found herself in a bare-walled room, wooden beams high above her supporting the tiled roof. For an old building it was spotless, no cobwebs or insects in sight. It was also incredibly tidy, several large units seemingly chosen for their impressive number of cupboards and drawers pushed up against the walls. Although there were no windows on the side facing the house, there were two small, square ones on the side facing out onto the fields, light pouring in and illuminating patches on the floor. There were also more skylights in here, supplemented by industrial-sized strip lighting mounted high on the walls. Parked in the centre of the room, surrounded by tools and low tables, was a two-tone vintage car, a white roof contrasting against pale blue bodywork. Its bonnet was open, parts of the engine shining with oil. In front of it, positioned so it could easily get out through the doors, was a large object covered in a white dust sheet.

'Your collection?' asked Petra politely, suddenly aware that she had no intelligent questions to ask. She wished she'd listened more carefully when her father showed her old films, thinking desperately of anything she might have gleaned from a subtitled viewing of *The Italian Job* when she was thirteen.

'My pride and joy.' Božič moved over to the dust sheet, pulling it carefully away and revealing the same silver car as she'd seen in the photo on his desk and the surveillance picture *Inšpektor* Furlan had taken in the hardware store car park. 'Finished restoring this one last year, and swore to my wife I'd never do it again.'

'How long did that last?' Petra asked, playing along with the friendly atmosphere.

'I was on the internet looking at auctions again within the week!' They both laughed, Božič seeming incredibly human. 'My grandfather worked at the factory in Koper which made them. I have no idea if he ever touched either of the ones I've got, but I like to think he did. It feels like I'm bringing them home.'

Božič gave Petra another minute or so to appreciate the silver car before covering it up again, replacing the dust sheet with as much care as you might put a blanket over a new-born baby. Pika kept a polite distance from the car, tail swishing through the air as she watched him work. When Božič was satisfied that it was properly protected, he straightened up and turned back to Petra.

'What did young Koren uncover, then? Anything that might be of use?' Božič was obviously trying to keep his tone neutral, but this time Petra was convinced she heard a nervous edge to it. His voice was tight, his smile slightly frozen on his face.

'Footage of Marjan,' she admitted, crouching down as Pika approached her for more scratches. 'He's still in the cell at the station, though.'

'Nothing concrete?' Božič's words came too fast, blurted out as if his lips weren't strong enough to keep them in. Petra pretended not to have noticed, hopeful that things were going her way. If he was this on-edge, he might slip up. Likewise, if she could reassure him, get him to feel a false sense of security, his overconfidence might lead him to divulge something new.

She shrugged noncommittally, eyes on Pika. 'We'll see. I was interested in hearing more about the cars, but if you want to talk business . . .'

'You're interested in restoration?' Božič sounded relieved, but still unsure. He walked over to one of the benches near the uncovered Spaček, leaning against it and removing his gloves.

'No, not personally. I was speaking to one of my colleagues in Ljubljana earlier, who interviewed *Inšpektor* Furlan's sons.'

Božič blinked, waiting for her to continue.

'They told him that the inspector invited them to a vintage car show at *Grad* Strmol recently, which they thought was a little out of character. Had he mentioned that to you?'

'He was interested in the cars,' said Božič slowly, looking Petra straight in the eye and choosing his words carefully. 'He liked to hear how the restorations were going.'

'But he didn't have one himself, didn't tell you he was going to buy one?'

'No, he never mentioned that to me.'

'And he didn't invite you to the car show?'

Božič laughed, the awkward sound echoing around his workshop. 'Ivan and I were friends at work, we'd go for a beer together occasionally, but we were different generations. I'm not surprised he didn't invite me. Why are you so interested in it?'

Petra pounced. 'His sons mentioned that he looked for you there.' It wasn't true, they had made no such claims, but Petra needed to see his response. What she was looking for, she couldn't quite say. Guilt, that he knew more about the inspector's secret undertakings than he was letting on? Concern that Petra was getting close to knowing something she shouldn't?

'It is the sort of thing I'd go to, definitely,' he replied with a laugh that sounded a lot more authentic than his previous attempt. 'But I'm afraid I wasn't there. He must have just assumed I'd go.'

'He told his sons he knew you were going.'

'Well, he didn't say anything to me about it. I think I was on shift at the Croatian border that day. I was sad to miss it, but there's always next year.'

'For you, yes,' said Petra, pleased that it seemed to stop Božič's growing smile in its tracks. He was obviously warming to his theme, and she couldn't let him get too cocky. 'Not for him.'

'I'm not sure what you want me to tell you, *Inšpektorica*. He was wrong, I never planned on going.'

'Because you had a shift at the border?'

'Yes, I had signed up in advance. I know months ahead when I'll be there.'

'Surely you're too senior to have to do those?' Petra returned her attention to Pika, trying to diffuse the tension a little. She wanted Božič on edge, but not desperate. If she pushed him too far, she'd get nowhere.

'Yes, but I enjoy it. Our kind of police work can be stuffy, you know that. Hours spent inside poring over pieces of paper and computer screens. I enjoy being out in the fresh air, watching the world go by. The overtime pay doesn't hurt, either.'

'Useful for the Spačeks?'

'I need every cent I can pull together!' Božič laughed, running a hand lovingly over the frame of his recent two-tone acquisition. 'They don't come cheap.'

Petra allowed silence to descend, her hands stilling on Pika's soft coat. She was at a crossroads. She could either carry on as they were, politely dancing around the edges of crucial topics and pretending they had no weight, or make a statement she couldn't take back. She risked glancing up at Božič, catching his eye. He suddenly looked very sad, and Petra knew she had to make her move now, or she'd lose her nerve and the moment would get away from her.

'I suppose the money from the Jovanović brothers helps with that, too.'

Božič froze, his hand halfway to the back of his neck. Pika picked up on his sudden change of mood, hauling herself to her feet to rush over and console him, pushing her golden head into his limp other hand. Petra stood up as the dog left her, standing as tall and straight as she could to try and give herself confidence.

'I don't know what you mean.'

'Vuk Jovanović. I've seen photos of the two of you, you seem friendly. I hear you're drinking buddies as well. Or is it the same as your relationship with Ivan Furlan, just work colleagues who share a beer every so often?' Petra kept her tone deliberately light, inquisitive rather than accusatory.

Božič didn't seem to know what to make of this, his eyebrows drawing together as he patted Pika robotically on the head. 'I don't know the name.'

'Come on, *Inšpektor* Božič, you can do better than that. I have witnesses, I have photos. I want your side of the story.'

'Or what?'

Petra folded her arms across her chest, unimpressed. 'This isn't an exercise in bargaining, *Inšpektor* Božič. I have them, I have shown them to colleagues, there is no making this go away. I imagine we'll see some interesting bank records as soon as I get the warrants to look. I don't care about any of that, as far as I'm concerned that's for the Koper force and the *Guardia di Finanza* to sort out. I care about what happened to *Inšpektor* Furlan.'

She watched as he mentally scrambled through his options, whether to deny everything, to run, to ask her to leave. He puffed himself up briefly, standing tall just like Petra was, and she briefly worried she'd been overconfident in coming here alone. Just as she readied herself to take a step back, he deflated, resting back against the bench. Pika made a small noise, nesting her snout between his legs and staring up at him with warm, brown eyes. He dropped his head to the top of hers, taking one of her silky ears in each hand and clutching them.

'*Inšpektor* Božič?'

He looked up, pressing a kiss to Pika's head before sitting up fully, looking straight at Petra. 'You can call me Denis.'

'And you can call me Petra. Can you tell me what happened, Denis?'

'Would you like to come into the house?'

Petra raised her eyebrows at him, a silent question to hide her own indecision. Were there weapons in the house? It seemed unlikely, his little show with Pika just now had her largely convinced that he meant her no harm. Nevertheless, it was a strange suggestion.

Božič seemed to pick up on her concerns, standing up and shaking his head. 'I want to show you something, that's all, and I could use a drink. My parents are both upstairs.'

Petra nodded at him, walking out of the outbuilding first and allowing him to pass her, heading across the tarmac and through the unlocked ground-floor door of the house. She glanced at her Skoda as she closed the door behind her, touching the phone in her pocket for comfort. Inside the house was painfully normal, the clutter of a family life apparent on every surface. A small entrance hall led on to an open plan kitchen, long wooden table surrounded by chairs bearing colourful cushions. A huge fabric dog bed lay next to a traditional ceramic tiled fireplace, the walls around it decorated in family photos. Pika threw herself down on the cold tiled floor, apparently bored by the humans' interactions. Božič headed straight for the fridge, rustling around inside and pulling out an unopened bottle of wine along with two tins of beer.

'Drink?' he asked, showing her his haul.

'Whatever you're having.'

He nodded, eyeing up the options before deciding on the wine. He closed the fridge door behind him, grabbing two glasses from a draining board and leading Petra past the table and through another door into a small sitting room. Petra stepped neatly over the children's toys littering the tiled floor, keeping close to Božič as he turned a corner into a small hall-way, opening the first door on his right. Inside was a room too narrow to be a bedroom, barely the width of the slim desk pushed against its far wall. Božič led her inside, closing the door behind them and revealing an overstuffed armchair in the space behind. He gestured for Petra to sit, settling himself in the office chair under the desk and pulling a corkscrew out of the pen pot on the window ledge next to him.

'My grandfather's retirement project was planting a vine-yard, then learning to make wine,' he explained, keeping his eyes on the bottle as he poured generous helpings into each glass. Petra was glad it was an unopened bottle, feel-ing slightly more confident that there wouldn't be anything untoward. She accepted a glass with a nod, not wanting to interrupt Božič. 'After he died, my father carried on. I suppose I'll inherit it one day.'

Petra waited for him to continue, but he seemed to be lost in thought, staring out the window. Petra glanced out, unsure what about the patch of carefully mown grass outside and the windowless wall of the workshop beyond it was of such great interest.

'You wanted to show me something?' she asked eventually, setting her wine on the floor next to her chair. Božič's was also untouched, clutched in his fist.

Her words seemed to galvanise him into action, and he scrabbled around in the stack of papers shoved against the wall at the corner of his desk, eventually pulling out an envelope similar to the one Petra and Koren had found in Piran. He stood up, passing it to her, before slumping back into his seat and taking a large gulp of wine.

Opening it, Petra was surprised to find photocopies of everything she had seen in the Piran house, with the exception of Bortolotti's notes. Someone had circled points of interest on some of the photos in thick red pen, highlighting the car's numberplate and the reoccurring baseball cap.

'I keep that cap in the car,' said Božič. 'My oldest daughter bought it for me when my in-laws took her to Venice.'

'*Inšpektor* Furlan gave you these?' Petra confirmed, carefully placing the photographs back in their envelope.

'The night he died, yes.'

# Chapter 31

Petra blinked rapidly at Božič, mind racing. Was this a confession? He certainly looked worn-down enough to confess, like something was weighing on him. His hands were shaking very slightly, knuckles turning white as he gripped his wineglass like a lifeline. At close quarters, Petra could see purplish bags under his eyes, reminding her of Bortolotti's haunted look.

'You saw the inspector the night he died?'

'We met in Izola,' Božič confirmed with a sigh, placing his glass on the desk and twisting his chair so that he was looking directly at Petra. 'He invited me for a drink, and I agreed. That's why he was there, why he was walking back to Koper.'

Petra sucked in a breath, growing more concerned. Božič did not seem to be intending her any harm, but she was suddenly very aware of the smallness of the room, the ease with which he could get to her, the slimness of her chances of escape. Even so, she was fascinated to hear what he had to say. She tamped down her growing fear, instead making a show of settling deeper into her chair, demonstrating that he had her full and undivided attention. She hoped she wasn't making a terrible mistake.

'He brought the pictures with him?'

Božič nodded. 'We chatted for a little while, he told me about the holiday he and Irena had just booked, asked about my daughters and the cars. Then he just whipped out the envelope, told me that he knew everything, but that he wanted to give me a chance to make it right.'

'And what did you do?'

Božič laughed darkly, eyes dropping to focus on his hands, which were twisting anxiously in his lap. 'I tried to deny it, then I saw the photos. Then I cried.'

This surprised Petra, wiping her next question from her lips. 'You cried?'

'Just a few tears, nothing dramatic. I thought my life was over, that I'd never see my children again.'

Petra was heartened that he'd mentioned his children, not his cars. 'And then?'

'He told me not to worry, that he wasn't going to share anything with anyone if I promised to stop. I asked what he meant by that, and he just said that if I never took a backhander again, never looked the other way at the border, then we could forget it ever happened.'

'You believed him?'

Božič thought about her question for a second, before finally looking up at her again. 'I did. I'd heard about him doing that sort of thing before, on a smaller scale. What I'd been up to was of another order of magnitude, obviously, but that didn't seem to bother him.'

'You agreed to his terms?'

'I had to. But it wasn't going to be pretty, getting myself out of this situation. I texted my contact immediately then came home in a mess, told my wife I thought we should consider moving house, going as far from here as the car could take us. She thought I was drunk, made me sleep on the sofa. But what else could I do?' He fell silent for a second, chest heaving as he took a sip of wine. 'I wanted to agree, too. I wanted out. I knew what I was doing was wrong, but it was just such easy money. You know what police pay's like, I can't buy my family what I'd like to give them, let alone myself. Half the time, all I had to do was pretend I didn't find anything when the border force flagged a car. It was so easy! Just do that once, and suddenly I can buy my wife that new dress she's been eyeing up, and take her out for a nice dinner in it so she can show it off. Two or three times, and I can take the whole family for a week in Dubrovnik.'

'I can see why that would draw you in.'

'I should have been stronger, but I wasn't. After a while it was easier to say yes than no.'

'Why were you meeting with Vuk Jovanović so regularly?'

Božič laughed, smiling honestly at Petra. 'You know, he's not a bad guy. I know he illegally provides drugs to most of central and eastern Europe, he's probably ordered a few people to have fingers cut off in his time, that sort of thing. But if you set that aside, he's good to have a drink with.'

'You're friends?' Petra was surprised, not having thought her earlier assessment that Božič's relationships with Ivan Furlan and Vuk Jovanović were similar would turn out to be accurate, that Bortolotti could have been so correct in his phrasing.

'Of a kind. He likes classic cars, old-timers. He's actually got a Spaček of his own, I put him on to my contact at the local dealer. We trade tips.'

Petra nodded, then brought her questions back around to the point at hand. 'Did the inspector tell you who was giving him information?'

'No.'

'Did he mention that he'd been sent to *Grad* Strmol on a bad tip?'

'He asked if I'd ever been asked to go there, if I'd had any plans for a drop off. I told him I didn't move product or drop anything off, I just showed up and looked the other way. I'd have loved to go to that show, but Vuk needed me at the border, so I was at the border.'

Petra summarised what she'd discovered that morning, that someone seemed to have tested both Bortolotti and Furlan with bad information. Božič shook his head sadly as she spoke, letting out a long breath when she finished. 'I didn't know anything about that.'

'I have to ask, Denis. Did you let someone know he was on to you? Give them any warning, let them know where he was?'

Petra braced for fury, but instead received a shallow shrug followed by silence. Božič's hands resumed their twisting, his arm muscles flexing with the force of it.

'Denis?'

'I didn't say who it was. I just texted my contact and said that I'd been rumbled and I wanted out.'

'Your contact?'

'The guy that texts me where they want me on the border, which shifts I should take.'

'What did you say to him, exactly?'

Božič patted the various pockets on his shorts, drawing out his phone once he'd located it. He stabbed deftly at the screen a few times, then handed the phone over.

'I'm done, I've been found out. You'll have to find a new pet policeman,' Petra read out. 'Why did you bother going to your contact, when you have Vuk on speed dial?'

'I wasn't thinking clearly,' said Božič defensively. 'I was so panicked, and truth be told, I had had a few beers. I just wanted it over and done with.' He shrugged pathetically, the movement very small compared to his outburst. 'And, as I said, my relationship with Vuk isn't like that. We don't talk about work, either policing or what I do for him. He isn't even in half the photos Ivan took, Vuk doesn't creep around on deserted beaches. That's for his lackeys. Vuk shows up in Piran on the nicest boat in the marina and buys the whole bar a pint, that's his style. I have a text-only relationship with one of his other employees. I have no idea how far up the chain of command they are themselves.'

Petra chose not to comment that, if this was the case, theirs must be the only friendship for hundreds of kilometres of its kind. Instead, she ploughed on with her train of thought. 'If we assume that this person is the same one as tested Bortolotti, then they must have guessed what this meant.'

'That Ivan had approached me? I imagine so.'

They lapsed into silence again, both staring at Božič's phone. The screen went dark, but Petra kept looking at it, trying to get her thoughts straight. Before she could vocalise anything, Božič piped up.

'They killed Ivan, didn't they? Whoever's at the other end of that message. Almost as soon as I sent it. I've suspected it since I saw his body, from the minute I knew he was dead, but I told myself that they'd have killed me rather than him if that was the case. But the demands for my presence at the border are still coming, and I think that must mean that they view the problem as taken care of.'

'By killing him, they remove the threat to your continued involvement, and scare you into line,' Petra said, picking up her wine and taking a restorative gulp. 'I tend to agree. Do you have any idea who it could be, Denis? Any slip-ups, any suspicions?'

Božič held his hand out for his phone, tapping away at it the moment she gave it back. 'I don't know who, but I think I know what.'

'Whether it's a man or a woman?' Petra asked, confused by his phrasing. She placed her wine back on the floor, grabbing her notebook from her bag and laying it out on her lap.

'No, I don't know anything about that. I mean that I think they're a police officer.'

Petra's hand stilled, pen hovering over a new page in her notebook. 'I'm sorry?'

'They know too much!' he exclaimed. 'I never have to tell them when my station is providing officers to a given border crossing, they know that already. They know which vehicles we'll have, which border force agents will be there, everything. The only thing I need to do is make sure I get the slot to be police officer on duty.'

'Maybe someone else is giving them the rest of the information? They themselves might not be a police officer.'

'Perhaps, but who?'

'Koren mentioned the border schedule is just behind Medved's desk for anyone to see.'

'The list of who is taking what shift, and only for our station. I only know anything when our station provides the manpower. They'd need a lot of crooked officers to get a full picture.'

'Who has access to the bigger picture?' As Petra spoke, something twigged in her mind, but she didn't have time to poke at it. Her focus was entirely on Božič's theory.

'Senior officers, from both the police and the border force.'

'No one else?'

'They're the only ones I've been able to confirm,' said Božič. 'I've been looking into it.'

Petra was surprised, and it must have shown on her face. Božič looked embarrassed, turning his gaze back to his phone before twisting it around to show her. 'I know Koren thinks I dropped the ball on Ivan's death and just wanted to pin it on Marjan. I didn't, but I can see why it seemed that way. I just had to do my digging quietly.'

On his phone was a long bullet-pointed list of notes, currently zoomed in so that Petra could see the point about who had access to information on border patrols. She glanced up at him, taking his nod in return as permission to keep scrolling, and saw that he had indeed been undertaking some covert investigations of his own. He had made notes of anything strange other officers had told him, including a note that Crevatini had also asked him about the car show at *Grad* Strmol. Petra jolted at this, but Božič shook his head, seeing what had her attention.

'He was at a spa hotel with his girlfriend that weekend. I've seen pictures and checked with her when she came to the station. He was just asking as he said he'd have liked to go.'

Petra pulled a face, making Božič snort quietly. 'This is thorough work, Denis.'

'It was the least I could do before I was certain Ivan's death had something to do with me, now it is next to nothing.'

'Could I see the rest of your correspondence with your contact? Maybe a fresh pair of eyes will catch something you didn't?'

Božič nodded, waving his hands widely. 'All yours.'

Petra scrolled slowly through his messages with the number he had texted his resignation to, then moved across to the phone number they had used previously. The notes were frustrating in their brevity and formality, simply a time and a date.

'They never specify the location?'

'I was mostly at the same border crossing,' Božič explained.

'For the road crossings, they prefer Dragonja. It is just east of the crossing at Sečovlje, further inland. Lots of holiday traffic as it's the better route from Ljubljana and Austria down to Pula, which means people just get waved through far more often as the queues get so long. It's a quicker journey up to Koper and Italy too, the route through Sečovlje winds around the coast and can get gridlocked if two caravans meet each other going in opposite directions.'

Petra kept scrolling, keeping Božič's explanation in mind. If their correspondence was entirely dates and times, she found it unlikely that she was going to be able to glean anything Božič himself had missed. She changed to yet another phone number used by his contact, scrolling back through the few messages he'd received. 'I suppose Vuk really never let slip who it was?'

'He is unsurprisingly very tight-lipped. When I last saw him, we talked about basketball and our favourite resort hotels on the Dalmatian Coast. We do not talk about business. I am still a police officer, if a corrupt one.' He blushed.

Petra nodded. She was about to hand Božič his phone back when the first text from this number caught her eye, a line longer than the others. She read it once, then again, a knot forming in the pit of her stomach. It was a gnawing feeling, a mixture of nausea and hysteria, growing rapidly. She swallowed, aware that Božič had noticed her discomfort.

'What have you found?' he asked, crossing the room in one stride to peer over at her, his shadow causing the screen to brighten itself.

'Tenth January, four p.m., Sicciole,' she read out, aware that she had massacred the pronunciation of the final word.

Božič nodded, eyes finding where she was reading from but seemingly uncertain why it had caught her attention. 'Sicciole is what the Italians call Sečovlje, you've probably seen it on road signs.'

'But the person texting you speaks Slovene, not Italian. Look, even the date is in Slovene, in the same text message.'

Božič's eyes widened. He straightened up, looking down at Petra with confusion written across his face. 'How did I not spot that?'

'Because it is on all the signs, I imagine. You see the words next to each other all the time.'

'You don't hear people mix Italian place names into Slovene very often, though,' he said. 'My wife is completely bilingual, and she'll say Trst when she's speaking Slovene and then Trieste as soon as she switches into Italian. It sounds wrong, otherwise.'

Petra nodded her agreement, her own attempt at saying Sicciole seconds earlier proving his point. He didn't seem to be taking the next step that Petra had, too caught up in how he'd missed a clue. She waited a second, hoping she wouldn't have to be the one to raise it, not wanting to risk being wrong. The nausea continued, her throat starting to feel dry and uncomfortable. She could identify with horrifying accuracy the only person she had encountered on the coast so far who stubbornly used Italian names even in the middle of a conversation in Slovene, could imagine exactly how the text in front of her would sound if spoken aloud.

'Denis, would *Inšpektorica* Rossi know which station had which crossing on a given day?' Her voice was quiet, slightly desperate. She felt ill for asking it, but somehow even sicker that it might be true. Giving voice to her suspicions somehow made them feel more real, like an uncomfortable cloud had settled over them in the small room. She felt claustrophobic, snapping the band around her wrist to ground herself. Now was not the time to panic.

Božič looked as distressed as she felt. He nodded slowly, dumbly, his jaw falling slightly open. 'I think anyone on the task-force has all that information, and she leads it.'

# Chapter 32

They stood silently for a second, both taking in the gravity of what they were edging around. A small voice at the back of Petra's head took advantage of the quiet, screaming at her for her gullibility, her potential failure. Had she sat opposite a murderer and not noticed it? Gone for drinks with her, and thought they were friends? She had no idea what to say next, crossing her arms protectively across her chest on impulse. As she was trying to pull her thoughts back together, Božič spoke up.

'That *prasica*.'

Petra scowled instinctively at the slur, although Božič didn't seem to notice. He punched his own thighs hard with clenched fists, letting out a growl of anger. Petra noted the difference in how they expressed their emotion, found herself wondering whether this was how Rossi was planning on getting away with it: fury, perceived impotence and blind self-confidence would compel Božič to arrest Marjan, the obvious suspect, another man. Meanwhile, Rossi could sit safely in her bar or at her desk, maintaining her cool façade and avoiding all suspicion.

Petra allowed the silence to fall again as Božič huffed and grimaced, organising her thoughts as best she could.

'You're very quick to believe this of her, Denis.' Petra knew she had to think as rationally as she could, clinically. If Rossi was indeed the culprit, that was how she had approached this. Petra had to mimic her if she wanted to catch her. Likewise, she was painfully aware that two headstrong men had already mentally convicted others for this crime, with Božič condemning Marjan and being condemned himself by Koren. This was not the time to fall down a third rabbit hole.

'I've met her.'

Petra grimaced at him in admonishment. She thought again of the first time she had met Rossi, of the disarming carapace of aloofness and the perfectly coiffed appearance. Then, she remembered the woman who she'd thought might become a friend, an evening spent trading lived experiences like children with marbles. So many similarities, and yet when it came down to it, a crucial difference. Petra thought about how Rossi had described herself and had in turn been described, so Italian and yet also Slovene, a policewoman and a business owner, a cold harpy and a warm friend. It seemed oddly fitting that someone like her could be the perfect double agent, half dedicated policewoman and half ruthless criminal. She thought of the reverence with which Rossi had described the war on drugs, how her fascination with it was unsurprising now it was obvious she waged it on both sides.

Petra shook herself from her reverie, trying to stay impartial, to be as methodical as she could. Romantic notions of dual identity aside, the pieces of Rossi's deceit started to fall into place in her head, titbits of information that had seemed so innocuous or had led her astray now tying together to form the very bigger picture that Rossi had crowed about. Her rank in the task-force would put her in the perfect position to share information with the Jovanović brothers, allowing them to outsmart her colleagues at every turn. Her literal, physical position in the office would have allowed her to see Furlan following Božič on his secret meetings with Jovanović, her suspicions only confirmed when Božič was so stupid as to pretend he was going to the hairdresser and come back looking no different. She could communicate confidently with Bortolotti in Italian, with Božič in Slovene. Her motive was clear: to remove an obstacle to her continued work for Vuk Jovanović. If she was indeed working with him, Petra had to assume it was easy to get the means to murder Ivan Furlan, to lay her hands on an untraceable weapon. The only question that remained was opportunity.

'Where in Izola did you meet with *Inšpektor* Furlan, Denis?'

Božič went very still. '*La Medusa*,' he whispered, voice hoarse with anguish. 'We went somewhere else first, but they closed and we had to leave. Ivan said he wanted some privacy, so we sat at the edge of the terrace at *La Medusa*. Domenico Rossi served us, he gave us both a shot on the house. We weren't there long, only half an hour or so.'

Petra looked down at the phone in her hand, then back up at Božič, who was nodding slowly as he delivered the final death knell for Rossi's innocence. She felt as though she should warn Koren, let him know that he should avoid any contact with Rossi until they'd had a chance to regroup. She was acutely aware that she had no evidence, nothing to prove definitively that Rossi was betraying her team, her force. Nothing to demonstrate without doubt that she had murdered Ivan Furlan, or at least ordered his death.

Božič was thinking on the same lines. 'We need proof,' he said, pacing a narrow circle on the wooden floor. 'Something irrefutable. The gun.'

'That'll be long gone. Why would she keep it?' Petra rose to her feet so quickly that she almost knocked her wineglass over. 'But it doesn't have to be so obvious. Something smaller would do. Anything that proves she's working for the Jovanović brothers. After that, I think we can put a case together that she wanted *Inšpektor* Furlan dead.'

Božič nodded, wringing his hands together. 'She wouldn't keep anything in their flat above *La Medusa*, especially if she thought Ivan was on to her. She isn't stupid.'

Petra agreed, going over her evening with Rossi at the wine bar in her mind. What had she said? That she lived in town, but occasionally went somewhere else when it got too crowded?

'She has a family house, out in the hills somewhere.'

'Really? I didn't know that. But then, I don't think she likes me much.'

Petra smiled at him ruefully. 'She's a backstabbing murderer, Denis. I'm not sure you want her to like you.' Petra chose not to comment on her own keenness to get Rossi to like her, her happiness at their blossoming friendship. It had all presumably been a lie, a deception to trick Petra into sharing things with her, never considering her as a suspect. Petra had been well and truly played, and she knew the shame and self-loathing she was feeling now would haunt her for years to come.

Božič laughed half-heartedly, still pacing. 'Do you have any idea where?'

'No,' Petra admitted. 'I think she regretted mentioning it. She was keen to change the subject. But I think I know someone who can help us.' She reached into her pocket for the phone she had kept close at hand, just as she had promised Koren, then realised she was still holding Božič's own mobile.

'I'm afraid this is evidence, Denis.'

He shrugged. 'Something tells me I won't have use of it for much longer anyway.'

They shared a strangely sad look, before Petra pulled an evidence pouch from inside her bag, depositing the phone inside.

She called Koren as she hurried with Božič out to the Skoda, indicating that Božič should drive so she could talk on the phone. Božič struggled into a hooded jacket as they crossed the tarmac, not bothering to change out of his oily clothes. Koren answered immediately, and she felt both guilty that he'd been sitting worried by the phone, and incredibly grateful that he'd been true to his word and would have come to save her as fast as he could.

'*Inšpektorica*? What's wrong?'

'Aleš, I need you to speak to your mother for me.'

'Mama? Why? Are you alright?'

'I'm fine, don't worry. I have Denis in the car with me. We were wrong, Aleš. He is corrupt, but he didn't hurt the inspector.' Božič had the good grace not even to grumble at her assertion of his bad behaviour, eyes on the road as he headed south-east into the hills that stretched along behind Koper and Izola.

'Are you sure?'

'Yes, I'm sure. It was Rossi, she's been working for Vuk Jovanović this whole time. She was the one texting Bortolotti, she was pulling Božič's strings too. She knew the inspector was on to Božič, and she struck when she had the chance. I assume she planned on using Marjan as a scapegoat, then sacrificed Božič when she realised that wasn't going to work. I don't know if she killed the inspector herself or if one of Jovanović's men acted for her, but I am confident that she's the person we're looking for.'

Koren breathed deeply into the phone. 'Okay. What can Mama do?'

Petra was honoured that he'd believed her so quickly, that he trusted her judgement without question. 'I want you to ask her if she knows Rossi's family, where they used to live. They have a house in the hills behind Izola somewhere, I think that might be where we'll find the evidence we need to bring her down.'

'I'll get back to you as soon as I can,' said Koren, hanging up immediately.

Petra watched the green hillsides pass by, field after field of olive trees and vines, punctuated with the occasional fig or cherry tree. She tried to put a timeline together in her mind. As Božič drove, she realised with growing horror that it was far more likely than not that Rossi had killed *Inšpektor* Furlan herself. The window was too short for her to have gathered Jovanović goons. Even if Domenico had told her immediately when the other officers arrived at *La Medusa*, surely that wasn't enough time to put out a hit. She must have acted on impulse, following the inspector out onto the coastal path as she had claimed to do with Božič and Jovanović. Petra felt sick that she had sat with Rossi, laughing over a shared glass of wine, completely unaware that she was with someone capable of committing a sudden and dispassionate murder of a colleague with no apparent qualms. She had been at interview tables with one or two murderers before, but never a wine bar. She thought about Rossi's rattled state earlier, remembering that it seemed strange when she was hardly run off her feet. Petra could only hope that self-confidence and work at *La Medusa* had prevented her from pre-emptively destroying anything, removing evidence in case Petra realised it wasn't Božič after all, and made the leap to Rossi's own guilt.

Božič came to a stop a few minutes later, pulling into the mouth of a wide track leading into someone's vineyard. He turned off the engine, breathing deeply. Petra recognised his attempts to calm down, was doing the same herself. They sat in silence for a moment, both lost in thought.

'I wrote to Ljubljana,' he said suddenly, making Petra turn to him.

'What?'

'The message to Ljubljana, the one that brought you here. That was me. I knew somewhere inside that Marjan wasn't guilty, and I couldn't just let him go down for it. I left arresting him for as long as I could, hoping I'd turn something up privately, as I couldn't bring myself to investigate openly either. I thought that would be signing my own death warrant. The only way out seemed to be to escalate it anonymously, so I wrote to your bosses. I had one too many glasses of wine that night, sent it off, woke up regretting it. Now, I'm glad I did, though.'

'So am I, Denis.'

'I think I wanted to redeem myself, somehow.'

'You have.'

Božič smiled at her gratefully, tapping his fingers on the steering wheel.

'I have to ask,' Petra began again, unwilling to dispel the companionable atmosphere but aware she had to know the truth of the matter, '*Svetnik* Horvat. He wasn't involved in any of this? You mentioned him specifically in your note.'

Božič snorted, and shook his head ruefully. 'That was one of the bits I regretted, to be honest. He was willing to put Marjan away and throw away the key because he honestly thought he was guilty, and he only believed that because he was so shaken over Ivan's death that he wanted someone to blame quickly, and I offered him that someone on a platter. He trusted me, and I lied to and humiliated him.'

Petra gave him a sympathetic look, and reached out to

touch him lightly on the arm. 'You've done the right thing now.'

Božič shrugged, then cleared his throat. 'What do we do if *Gospa* Koren doesn't know Rossi's family?'

'What people in normal police forces do, we tell Horvat everything and get his go-ahead to look her up on the national database. I'm only asking Marija first as she'll probably be quicker, and won't involve convincing Horvat and getting his signature to snoop on a colleague.'

'You've got the hang of policing around here very quickly,' said Božič. 'You fit in well.'

'Not too well, I hope. An awful lot of you are corrupt.'

Božič guffawed at this, shaking his head as he laughed. Petra's phone lit up with an incoming call, and she hushed him to answer it.

'Her maiden name was Giulia Pascutti, they lived up in Borovnica. Her father did time for witness intimidation in Italy, which is why they moved back here and she goes by her married name. Mama never mentioned it, as she thought it was unfair on Rossi to gossip about the sins of her father. I did a quick check of the land registry and Borovnica 3 is still linked to the same Giuseppe Pascutti, who died four years ago.'

Božič started the car, already heading off in what Petra could only assume was the direction to Borovnica.

'Thank you, and please thank your mother.'

'Do you want me to come out and join you?' Petra could hear him jangling his keys at the other end, could imagine him already halfway out the doors of the station.

'Have you told Horvat what's going on?'

'I told him about Marjan's alibi, that you were going to speak to Božič. He wasn't pleased.'

'Call him again, update him on what we're doing now. Then come out and join me. If you can, bring back up.'

Koren agreed to her demands and Petra hung up, focused on the road ahead of her. Božič drove them quickly along the twists and turns, slowing slightly when they passed the yellow signs indicating they'd entered the village of Borovnica. Petra had been slightly confused at Koren's statement that the Pascutti house was simply 'Borovnica 3', but hadn't questioned it when Božič had seemed content with this level of information. Now she was in the village, she understood. It was one thin, dusty track, a very occasional house studded between vineyards and fields. Some had been refurbished recently, boasting freshly painted fronts and modern windows angled to look out onto the rolling hills surrounding them. Others were much older, small brick houses with windows in only one wall to try and regulate temperatures, their roofs in various stages of disrepair.

Božič pulled in outside one of the nicer houses, the exposed brick on the front wall partially hidden by a metal frame hosting a creeping vine. The plain wooden shutters were all pinned closed, an outdoor table and chairs that sat on the front patio packed away under a plastic cover. A small red sign on the gatepost marked it out as the address Koren had given them. With a start, Petra noticed that there were tyre tracks in the dust in front of the house, a sign that someone else had been here recently. She saw Božič noticing the same thing, and nodded at him as they climbed out of the Skoda.

They approached the front door slowly, despite seeing no signs of life. The area around the house was silent, Petra's breathing seeming loud and distracting even to her own ears. She touched the gun strapped to her right hip, but decided against drawing it. She somehow doubted that Rossi would appear all guns blazing, and was hoping that the visit to the house would be a purely fact-finding mission. She understood Božič's nervousness, however, and was embarrassed at how pleased she was that she had him with her. As they passed the table, her brain flashed back to the scene she had imagined when Rossi mentioned this place, the tablecloth and the rustic meal. Even though there was nothing outwardly wrong with the house, the image still felt implausible, the atmosphere too tense and the situation too twisted for such a lovely picture.

There was no answer when they knocked, and so the two of them hunted around the terracotta flowerpots outside the front door looking for a key. Unsurprisingly, there was nothing to be found. Petra supposed Rossi was too cautious to risk uninvited guests. She considered her options as she watched Božič scrabble around under a tall strawberry planter, then marched decisively back over to the door. Their luck was in; to Petra's surprise, Rossi hadn't bothered replacing the original door or lock when she had titivated the property, instead simply revarnishing it a deep brown. Turning around, Petra combed over the vines on their metal frame with her eyes, rushing over to one of the corner posts when she saw what she was looking for: thick, green gardener's wire. She unwound a tendril from where it was holding a vine in shape, then returned to the door and dropped to one knee.

'You can pick locks?'

Petra continued her efforts, not bothering to turn around. 'Sometimes, if they're simple. Older locks like this are easier.'

Božič let out a low whistle, which Petra took to be a compliment. She continued jiggling and poking at the mechanism, then sat back on her heels with a grin as something clicked. Božič hooted in triumph as she stood up, opening the door with a flourish. She edged in ahead of him, hand still hovering over her gun, but quickly realised there wasn't much point. No one was at home.

'I don't think they come here much,' said Božič, peering around inside. Unlike the house in Piran, this inherited property had been gutted and turned into a holiday bolthole. It was sparsely furnished, wooden dressers empty of ornaments and walls bare of pictures. Dust choked the air, sparkling in the light coming in through the windows on the front door.

'As long as she came here once recently, that's all we need.'

They crept along the corridor and into the first room on their left, both still on high alert. Petra indicated that they should keep moving, not seeing many opportunities for evidence hiding in the small wooden dining table and narrow chairs. The room behind was a kitchen, and while Božič and Petra poked around in the empty fridge and freezing oven, they didn't find anything hopeful. The rooms were strangely impersonal, naked of anything other than the basics. She wondered why Rossi wanted to come here, even when Izola was busy. It had no warmth, no soul.

They crossed under the stairs and into the rooms on the opposite side of the corridor, finding a bathroom and a similarly under-furnished sitting room boasting a television of a similar vintage to the one Koren had found at the station, and a well-stocked bookshelf. Božič hastened across the room and approached the television, inspecting it carefully.

'What are we actually looking for?' he asked, although she suspected it was mostly to himself. He sounded a little put out, presumably having hoped that the answers they sought would be lying out in plain sight.

'Something that ties her to Jovanović,' she replied, moving over to the bookshelf and browsing the titles. 'She's clever, she'll have something. Leverage so they can't throw her to the wolves. Mutually assured destruction.'

Bored of the television, Božič started back towards Petra, his lumbering steps making the floorboards creak. His passing terrified a many-legged insect, sending it scrambling down through the gaps between two of the boards. Watching it disappear below them, Petra had a sudden flashback to the abandoned family house in Prekmurje, how columns of ants would march up through the floorboards from the space below the wooden floor, lizards occasionally poking their heads through any particularly wide holes.

'Check for a loose floorboard,' she said suddenly, pointing where Božič had just been standing.

'Isn't that a bit clichéd?' Nonetheless, he squatted down,

leaning on the ends nearest him to see if could lever any boards up.

'If she does need to keep evidence as an insurance policy, she'll need it to be easy to grab in an emergency.'

With renewed vigour, Božič continued his search, pushing aside a threadbare rug as he scraped around on the floor. Petra resumed her perusal of the bookcase, trying to appease a nagging voice at the back of her mind. When she'd first glanced at it, her brain had clocked something and alerted her to it, but it had slipped away before she'd had the chance to interrogate it properly. Had it been a title? A shape? The books were unsurprising, various classics and modern bestsellers, all in Italian. The top shelf had been given over to CDs, the bottom to videos. Petra smiled at the small collection of plastic boxes, their dogeared paper cover sheets slipping out from behind ageing lamination. All of the films were dated, and she wondered what had been the last Italian language production to be made available on videotape. She crouched down in interest, her eyes skipping across the names of dozens of old westerns, musicals and Hollywood classics. She had gone past one title and moved onto its neighbours before its relevance percolated. She reached forward, snatching it off the shelf and cracking it open, before letting out a little gasp.

'Found it.'

Božič rushed over to her immediately, abandoning his fruitless hunt along the floorboards. He hovered over her shoulder, staring intently down at the plastic box she held in her hands.

'A video cassette box? She keeps her insurance policy in there?' Rather than disdainful, Božič sounded surprised.

'Not just any video, though. *Rigoletto*. An opera she loathes, as she views the female lead as pathetic for dying for an unworthy man.' Now it was laid out so plainly in front of her, Petra could see why Rossi despised Gilda, whose life was completely controlled by her father and then her faithless lover, with little thought for own independence and destiny. Even so, it seemed harsh for Rossi to spurn her. Sixteenth century Mantua and twenty-first century Koper offered rather different opportunities for women. Or maybe, she thought, Rossi wouldn't agree.

Satisfied with her explanation, Božič returned his attention to the contents of the translucent plastic box. Its capacity was small, just big enough for a leather-bound notebook and an oversized smartphone. Petra recognised it instantly. She berated herself for not having noticed it before: Rossi had two phones. In her mind's eye she could clearly see her marching towards her before their trip to *La Medusa*, huge phone in hand. Then, as they left the wine bar, she had admired the personalised case on a far smaller phone, Petra's wine-blurred brain failing to recognise that it was not the same handset as she'd seen earlier.

'She used that at the station,' Petra said in horror, indicating the phone. 'I've seen it before.'

'She never did think much of the rest of us.'

'I suppose she'd been getting away with consorting with the Jovanovićes under your noses for so long she thought she was untouchable.'

Božič shrugged, carefully pulling his sleeve over his hand before moving the phone to the other half of the lid, uncovering the journal. 'I was panicking the entire time that someone was going to catch me out, I don't know how she had the courage to rub it in people's faces.'

'You wear a very expensive watch and drive a vintage car, Denis. You were hardly subtle.'

Božič looked up at her, a slightly shaky but still cheeky smile on his face. 'Good point.'

As he spoke, he fished the journal out of the box. Flipping through it, he revealed pages filled with names and addresses, ship registration numbers and cargo capacities, records of what they could only assume were drops on beaches and car crossings at the border going back months. Interestingly, Petra noted, she hadn't written the names of anyone less important than Vuk himself down next to specific shipments. She saw Darko's name appear a few times, the names of the other two Jovanović brothers once each, but no reference to small fry like Bortolotti and Božič. Most surprisingly, Domenico Rossi's name appeared in one entry, in what Petra could only assume was a pre-emptive detail Rossi could use to demonstrate a willingness to cooperate with the authorities. Petra wondered where in the great scheme of things Rossi saw herself, how significant her role was in the worthy battle she'd described at *La Medusa*. She imagined it was significant, a worthy female lead, a foil to the police and Jovanović alike. At the back of the journal, like a closing flourish, was a list of names, addresses and passport numbers, arranged neatly under headings bearing the names of various members of Jovanović's gang. False identities, Petra could only assume. With this cache in the police's hands, Vuk could neither run nor hide.

'She's got everything she needs to take them down,' Petra agreed. 'It is incredibly thorough. Impressive, even.'

'Thank you, Petra. I knew you'd appreciate it.'

A chill ran down Petra's spine as she recognised the voice, spinning around to face it. Next to her, Božič did the same, positioning himself so that he was slightly in front of her. Rossi stood in the doorway behind them, leaning against the frame exactly as she had the first time Petra had met her, back at the station. It felt like a lifetime ago.

'Business calmed down enough at *La Medusa* that you could take a break?' asked Petra, desperately trying to buy time as she worked out what to do next. Rossi arriving while they had their hands in her stash was the worst possible scenario, and one that she had largely assumed they could avoid. If Rossi had thought to come to the Borovnica house while they were there, Petra had half assumed she'd have run off to get a head start on them, not come in for a confrontation.

'Domenico finally decided to pull his weight.'

'You killed him!' exclaimed Božič, rather ruining Petra's plan to keep Rossi calm until Koren and backup arrived. 'Ivan, our friend. You killed him, in cold blood.'

'I suppose there's no point in denying that I killed him. I won't insult your intelligence again, Petra. I am sorry I had to at all. I can, however, assure you that it wasn't in cold blood.' There was something sad in her tone, a far cry from the smugness Petra had heard in her on their first meeting, the confidence in their second. She sounded tired. As she spoke, her cardigan moved to reveal a holstered gun. She had come ready for a fight.

'You felt guilt over it?'

'Incredible guilt. My conscience will never forgive me. He was a good man.'

'Then why do it?' It was a pitifully obvious attempt to buy time, but Petra wasn't above feints if it prolonged the time before either one of them had to draw a weapon. Her own blocky, black Beretta was in full view of everyone in the room, attached to her right hip in its leather holster. She mentally begged Božič not to make it obvious that he wasn't armed, that he'd come to a gun fight with nothing but illogically righteous anger.

'I don't think we have time to go through that, Petra. I also suspect you know most of it already.'

Petra ignored her reference to being on the clock, not liking what it suggested. 'Furlan was on to Božič, is that it? You were about to lose your tame policeman, so you panicked?'

'Is that all you think his life was worth? His death a reasonable exchange for making sure the Dragonja border crossing was always open? I could have done that myself.' Rossi seemed angry at the insinuation, her face hardening.

'Why, then? If not for that?'

'I suppose you could say for exactly the same reason you're here now,' she replied, straightening up and starting to move into the room with them. Božič flinched, Petra laying a hand on his arm to reassure him that she had everything under control. She was not entirely sure that she did, but she was not about to make anyone else aware of that. Petra needed her hands for this, of that she was sure. She snapped the video box shut, ensuring the phone and journal were safely inside, then handed it over to Božič. He grasped it tightly, his gaze on Rossi as she watched the exchange.

'With Božič's help and the information from Bortolotti, he could track everything back to you?'

Rossi stopped a few feet from them, on the other side of an armchair that now concealed her to the waist. She put her hands on the top of its backrest, rubbing from side to side on the worn fabric. 'And he would have done. He was like a terrier with a rat, that man.'

Uncomfortable with Rossi's closeness, Petra laid a hand over the textured handle of her gun, a warning sign that she was not afraid to pull it. It seemed to have the opposite effect. A smile spread slowly across Rossi's face, her attention flitting from the weapon and up to Petra's expression.

'What's the matter, Petra? Scared?'

'Terrified,' Petra replied, prompting an even bigger smile. 'But don't count that in your favour.'

'I like you, Petra. Honestly. I haven't had as much fun as I did with you last night in a very long time. I kept having to rein myself in, I knew I was showing off, but I couldn't help it. I didn't mean to tell you about this house, but you brought my guard down. Did you like my story about the bigger picture? It is true, you know. Everything I said. Actually, I haven't lied to you once, which is more than *Inšpektor* Božič here can say.'

'I haven't murdered anyone,' he replied, his voice a low growl.

'That isn't strictly relevant to what we were talking about.' Disdain dripped off every word, a look of true disgust shot at him from her position behind the chair. 'You are so very literal, and so very boring. Ivan was worth ten of you.'

Božič went red, striding towards Rossi with a snarl. She snatched her gun from its holster, pointing it straight at his chest, stopping him in his tracks. Petra drew her own gun, aiming for the same place on Rossi as she was aiming at Božič. The room fell silent, the three of them breathing heavily.

'Was it pure chance he was killed that day?' Petra demanded, tension clear in her voice. She'd been taught early on at the police academy that you didn't draw a weapon unless you intended to use it, that it shouldn't be used as an empty threat. She felt adrenaline pumping through her veins, ready to strike.

Rossi laughed. 'You really are thorough, aren't you?'

'I've put my life on hold for this case, Giulia. Forgive me for wanting to see it through.'

Rossi smiled harder, shaking her head. 'An interesting turn of phrase. Yes, I suppose you could say it was chance. I had been thinking about it for a while, how I needed to get him out of the picture. I imagine you've spoken to that weasel Luca Bortolotti? Utterly useless, completely transparent. He helped me establish quite how willing Ivan was to hound Božič though, to his credit. After that it was just a matter of finding the right time. When Domenico told me he was with Božič at

*La Medusa* I could have leapt for joy. Things are rarely handed to you so neatly, you know.'

'You followed him out on to the coastal path?' Petra's arms felt heavy, the weight both of the gun and its potential power dragging them down. She held firm.

'An interesting thing about Ivan that I don't suppose you know, Petra, is that he was a creature of habit. He drank the same coffee every day, went to the same spa hotel every autumn. He never drove if he'd had even a drop of alcohol, and he very much enjoyed bringing Irena to *La Medusa* for a special evening. They'd walk from Capodistria to Isola, have dinner and a drink, and walk back. That orange wine we had last night was his favourite, actually. I suspect Domenico chose it as he thought it was poetic.'

'You knew he'd walk home.'

'I predicted he'd walk home. Experience has taught me that I have accurate instincts for that sort of thing. I am quite a good detective, you know.' Despite the levity in her tone, her stance remained stiff, her gun and body positioned towards Božič.

'Why did you move his body?' It had been the question bothering her since the first time she saw the crime scene photographs back in Ljubljana, before she'd met anyone involved in the case. Even now, when so many of the loose ends had been tied together, she didn't understand it. If Rossi was in a gloating mood, it seemed the best time to ask.

Unfortunately, it had the opposite effect. Rossi's face closed up, her eyes narrowing. She moved her gun a little, seemingly considering aiming for Božič's head. 'You think I would leave my friend to lie face-down in the sand, his head under water?'

Božič made a disparaging noise, taking a step backwards towards Petra. 'That matters to you? You gunned him down from above like some mobster, single bullet wound to the head out of nowhere, and that was where you drew the line?'

'He felt no pain, no fear. He was standing looking out at the water, so peaceful. It was windy that night, so the waves blocked out any sound. I stood behind him, said a prayer, and shot him. If I could pick my end, I would want something similar.'

'Execution style?'

'Here one moment, gone the next.'

Petra had no idea what tipped her off that Rossi was about to fire at Božič. There must have been a change in the atmosphere, a whisper picked up on by her instincts and experience. She fired milliseconds after the other woman, her own bullet tearing through Rossi's shoulder just as Rossi's hit Božič in the left side of his torso. Rossi let out a shriek, swearing in Italian and dropping her gun as she grabbed at the wound with her other hand. Petra barely had a moment to recognise her own successful hit when she was slammed to the ground, Božič falling onto her and trapping her under his bulk. She could feel warm blood oozing into her blouse and wrestled her arms free from under him to try and stem the flow, searching blindly underneath his body for her gun as she put as much pressure down on his wound as she could with her other hand. The videotape box dug into her thigh, wedged between her leg and Božič's back.

She had only glanced down for a second, still desperately hunting for her gun, when another shot rang out. Rossi's laboured breathing and mumbled obscenities stopped immediately as her body dropped to the ground, the room falling into eerie silence. A pool of blood started to form, twin trails from her shoulder and her chest sluggishly joining together and staining the floorboards.

# Chapter 33

Petra only allowed herself to look at Rossi's corpse for a split second before she whipped her head up, attention immediately drawn to the tall figure looming behind it. Standing in the doorway, blocking out the light now blazing through from the open front door, was a man whom Petra recognised immediately. Vuk Jovanović was tall and lean, his face characterised by sharp cheekbones and an angular nose, a small scar bisecting his left eyebrow. His dark hair was cut short, a pair of polarised aviators balancing on top of his head. His eyes were wide-set and pale blue, contrasting with his tanned skin. He was wearing a tight white shirt and dark trousers, his sleeves rolled up to his elbows and his shirt neatly tucked into his belt. Around his neck was a much slimmer chain, a crucifix sitting against the skin revealed by his open collar. He was wearing a pair of dark leather gloves, which he removed slowly as he took in the scene before him, settling his gun back into his holster.

'Stay where you are,' said Petra. Her voice was clear, unwavering, despite her confusion and the weight of Božič on top of her. Later, she would be proud of that. In the moment, she continued to try and recover her gun, looking around herself in a series of quick, jerky movements and spotting that it had spun away from her across the floor. She tried to reach for it, but only succeeded in jostling Božič, making him cry out. She returned a hand to his wound, pressing as hard as she could.

Vuk looked at her, but said nothing. Behind him, another man swaggered into the room. He was burly and tanned, dark hair short and perfectly styled. Petra could see a black tattoo on his arm through his thin white shirt, a thick golden chain around his neck. He was chewing obnoxiously on a toothpick, a gun dangling casually from one hand and a phone from the other.

'I called the ambulance.' He spoke to Vuk in unhurried Serbian, completely ignoring Petra. Instead, he dropped to his knees, patting down Rossi's corpse.

'I said, stay there. I know who you are, Vuk Jovanović. Put your gun down.' Petra was well aware that she was hardly in a position to make such demands, but something about the smug set of Vuk's features infuriated her almost as much as the sight of Rossi's corpse, the justice he had ripped away from everyone who loved Ivan Furlan. She couldn't just sit there and hope for the best. She continued to wriggle, balancing her desperation to get free with a fear that she might hurt Božič.

'You could be a little more grateful, *Inšpektorica* Vidmar. I have just saved the Slovenian taxpayer rather a lot of money. Trials aren't cheap, you know.' Petra was surprised both at his accent, and his tone of voice. He was softly spoken, evidently used to others staying quiet to hear every word he had to say. He sounded conversational, friendly even, and his accent was far milder than his companion's, presumably tempered by years spent away from home. His Slovene was good, grammatical and natural. She didn't bother wondering how he knew her name. It seemed the sort of thing he would make it his business to know.

'You have just murdered a police officer,' she hissed in response, making Vuk's companion snort.

'But she did exactly the same, so perhaps it cancels itself out?' Vuk smiled at his own joke, watching as his companion continued to pat Rossi down. 'In fact, I might argue that I have killed a corrupt, untrustworthy *prasica* who was governed by her emotions, and had loyalties to no one. We have a saying in Serbian, *Inšpektorica. Čovek je čoveku vuk.* Man is man's wolf. It is one of my favourites, I am sure you understand why. Giulia was Ivan Furlan's wolf, but unfortunately for her, I am hers.'

Petra scowled at him, hatred pulsing through her, tinged with slight confusion. She continued attempting to free her rapidly-numbing legs from under Božič, who remained silent, his face pale as he tried to maintain pressure on his wound. Her gun was close enough that if she could just move a few inches, she would be able to grab it. Vuk watched her struggle with unabashed interest.

'You care about her murdering *Inšpektor* Furlan? I thought you'd be more self-serving. The death of a policeman who was on your tail can only benefit you.'

'The blood of Ivan Furlan is not on my hands, and it was

not my tail he was interested in. I never ordered his death, in fact I could have killed her for it. Giulia was governed by her emotions, and she'd have done anything to save her own skin. Furlan's death threatened to bring far more trouble than it was worth, and Giulia vastly overestimated her own abilities if she thought she could control it. Please pass my condolences on to his family.'

Petra couldn't hide her surprise, and raised her eyebrows at Vuk. He cocked his head at her, giving her a dry smile. 'Not quite what you expected?'

'No,' she said simply. 'If that's the case, then what is your goon over there searching for?'

Vuk's smile turned cat-like, smug. His gaze flickered over to Rossi's body again, a self-satisfied gleam in his eye. 'Something that belongs to me, which Giulia stupidly tried to use to buy my cooperation in this foul matter. I don't suppose you've come across anything fitting that description? I know it is here, there's no point in lying. I've had men outside her vile husband's bar watching her for days, and she only ran here after she'd spoken to you and your sidekick. You must have really spooked her, but of course, from what she insinuated, what she has here is worth risking a lot over.'

Petra raised her eyebrows at him, and he laughed.

'My documents are of little use to you, I assure you. Nothing there will help you prove she killed *Inšpektor* Furlan. I doubt she left any evidence that will help you with that.'

'They could be of use to the drug squad,' Petra retorted, trying to keep Vuk's attention on her for as long as possible.

The videotape box pressed into her, she could almost feel it warming up as its importance was discussed, burning her. Vuk knew they had limited time, his bodyguard had called the ambulance for Božič himself. The paramedics would be here soon, the police shortly after. There was a chance they wouldn't get to searching under Božič before they had to leave.

'How are you feeling, Denis?' Vuk changed the subject rapidly, recognising that Petra was not about to be tricked into handing over evidence. She was surprised he seemed unwilling to turn to violence, that he hadn't pressed a gun to her head and demanded answers. She was even more taken aback by the tone he took with Božič. He sounded honestly concerned for his friend, his head cocked to the side to show he was listening.

'I'll survive.' It was the first thing Petra had heard Božič say since he'd been shot, and she was distressed to hear how weak he sounded, the tension in his voice. She pushed down harder with the hand she was using to stem the bleeding, making him hiss in pain. Across the room, she could see Vuk's bodyguard browsing the bookshelf, and hoped he didn't notice the missing video.

'I can't say I'm surprised that she was only a good shot when she could creep up on unsuspecting old men.' Vuk laughed, turning back to Rossi's corpse and giving her wounded arm a nudge with his expertly polished shoe. 'All talk, that woman.'

Božič's body rumbled as he made a noise that was hard to place as either agreement or disagreement, moving minutely as he did so. The weight on her lower body lessened, feeling rushing back into her legs. She made a split-second decision, weighing up recovering her gun versus protecting Rossi's stash, then moved. She hauled herself out, freeing one leg and lunging at her gun, stilling as she felt a foot settle on the back of her neck and force her to the ground. It was all she could do not to scream in frustration.

'*Inšpektorica* Vidmar, can you please just lie still? Giulia is dead, Denis will be fine. All you need to do is wait, your colleagues will be here soon. If you cause me too much trouble, I'll have to put a bullet in you as well, but I'd rather not resort to that.'

Vuk punctuated his threat by kicking her gun away from her again, sending it skittering across the floor and towards the bookshelf. Petra sat bolt upright, rubbing the back of her neck and turning to face him as he crouched in front of Božič. She watched in anguish as he noticed the strange angle his friend was lying at, and reached under him to fish out the videotape box, which he stood up to open. On seeing its contents, he grinned.

'Got it, Lazar,' Vuk called out to his companion, prompting the other man to lumber over and peer down at the bloodied plastic.

Petra took advantage of their brief distraction, edging backwards in the direction of her gun, only turning around when she knew she was in arm's reach of it. She heard Vuk sigh and Božič cry out, and spun back around again to point her gun straight at Vuk.

Lazar and Vuk both had their guns trained on her. She

stared at them unblinkingly. 'I'll shoot him, Lazar,' she said quietly, aware of the perfect silence in the room. 'I know you'll shoot me, but it'll be too late.'

'I thought we could be reasonable about this,' sighed Vuk. 'A trade. You'd never have been able to convict Giulia, so I dealt with your little problem. She'd have got off with a slap on the wrist for being involved with me, at the most. I imagine they'd even have let her get off without that, when she showed them her little arsenal. Instead, I have ensured that she paid for her misdeeds with her life. In return, I get my documents.'

'That isn't justice. Not for Ivan, and not for Giulia.'

'Justice?' snorted Vuk, shaking his head at her as though she were a particularly stupid child. 'This is the best justice you're going to get, *Inšpektorica*. An eye for an eye, and the devil gets paid. Don't die for something so stupid.'

'Are you worried I'm as overly emotional as Giulia?' She could hear the bitterness in her tone, the rage for a woman who she had briefly thought of as a friend, who had felt dismissed and belittled by the police in life, and had been treated exactly the same by Vuk in death. Her finger tightened slightly on the trigger.

Vuk shrugged, his gun rising and falling with the motion. He looked vaguely interested in the turn of events, though his companion still seemed bored. Behind them, Božič grunted as he struggled agonisingly slowly to his feet, taking a deep breath before stumbling past them and towards Petra. Vuk and Lazar let him pass, concern on their faces as they saw the trail of blood dripping down his torso and onto the floor, leaving a trail behind him. He stood in front of Petra, facing his friends, his whole body trembling. Petra had to stop herself from reaching out to support him.

'Don't do this, Vuk.'

'She's the one who pulled a gun on me, Denis. This wasn't my doing. Move aside.'

'Have you got everything you need?' Božič's tone was strangely weighty, as though he was trying to insinuate something without saying it out loud. Petra used him as a shield to rise to her feet, her gun lowered.

'All I wanted were my documents, and to see that Giulia got her comeuppance. I do not want anyone else to die today.'

'Excellent.'

Without warning, Božič launched himself at Petra, knocking her to the ground and holding her there. She shrieked, struggling desperately, hearing the crisp rapping of two sets of shoes hastily leaving the room, the front door slamming behind them. She pushed right on Božič's wound but he refused to budge, howling with pain as she yelled at him.

'Denis, get off me! Let me go.'

'For what, Petra? So Vuk can shoot you? He's already killed one police officer today, let me remind you. The only reason he didn't murder us both is that he has some morals, at least occasionally. I am not letting that happen, not to you. I couldn't save Ivan, but I can stop you from committing suicide by Vuk Jovanović.'

Petra stilled, the sound of their heavy breathing the only thing in the room. He was right, and she knew it, but she didn't have to like it. She wriggled in a mixture of discomfort and rage, pushing at his legs to try and free herself again. The back of her head hurt from where it had collided with the floor, and her ribs were aching from the force with which Božič had hit her. He acquiesced, apparently deciding that Vuk would be long gone, rolling to the side and crying out in pain. Her blouse was now almost entirely shades of red, patches of his blood radiating out into paler and paler pink. She sat there, breathing deeply, pushing her hands onto his wound again in silent apology for having worsened it. Neither of them spoke, sitting in silence for untold minutes until the door flew open.

Petra looked up, locking eyes with Koren as he rushed into the room with his gun outstretched, then stopped dead when he caught sight of Rossi. Behind him, various officers who Petra had never seen before streamed in, all pointing their weapons at invisible assailants. Among them, she spotted Crevatini, who separated from the pack to rush over and put his full weight on Božič's shoulder.

'Took you long enough,' Božič said tiredly.

Petra smiled as she stretched out her fingers, her hand gummy with layers of drying and fresh blood. Freed from her position as Božič's carer, she walked over to Koren, dropping to her knees in front of Rossi's corpse and checking for signs of life. This seemed to jolt Koren into action, and he joined her on the floor.

'Too late, she's gone,' Petra said with a sigh, avoiding looking at Rossi's face as she sat back on her heels. She was struggling conclusively to identify any one of the dozens of emotions flooding through her, unsure whether to laugh or cry, to lie down or run a mile. She blinked, hard, taking a steadying breath. Outside the window, she heard the screech of brakes, and almost cried in relief when a pair of paramedics barrelled past the assorted police officers who were now trying to look busy, making a beeline for Božič and Crevatini on the floor. One stopped to give Rossi a brief look, moving on as soon as he saw that she was beyond saving.

'Who called them?' Koren asked, blinking in confusion as they bandaged Božič's wound and loaded him, complaining, onto a stretcher.

'Vuk Jovanović,' Petra replied, struggling to her feet and following Božič out to the ambulance, feeling Koren hot on her heels.

# Chapter 34

The next afternoon found Petra holed up at a corner table at *Slaščičarna Koren*, a steaming cup of coffee and a slice of chocolate mousse cake the size of her head artfully arranged around her laptop and notebook. Opposite her, Koren sat bold upright, his eyes focused on her while his fork carefully pulled a layer of strawberry jelly away from some thick lime mousse, diligently sorting them into two piles on his plate before eating them separately. Petra grinned at the sacrilege.

'I suspect that your mother works hard to ensure her layers are perfectly balanced, Aleš. I'm not sure you're meant to deconstruct them.'

He shrugged good-humouredly, beginning work on excavating the white chocolate mousse from the layer below. 'You leave me to my work, and I'll leave you to yours.'

She laughed, returning her attention to the laptop in front of her. Through a mixture of adrenaline and excessive caffeine while waiting for a prognosis on Božič the night before, Petra had had very little sleep, and so had managed to get a considerable amount of her report done. She was now proofreading it, adding the finishing touches. For once, she was grateful for the impartiality police reports required. Normally, she struggled not to sympathise with the victim, criticise the perpetrator. In this case, she was glad she could shield her descriptions of Rossi in formal language. She was still deeply conflicted about how to describe the woman, about her feelings towards her. It felt traitorous to pity a fellow police officer who had murdered a colleague, and yet she couldn't shake the feeling that the world had somehow let Rossi down. The way Vuk had described her even as he loomed over her corpse had been the icing on the cake, demonstrating that she had been underestimated from first to last. It did nothing to excuse her behaviour, but perhaps helped to explain it.

Despite all he had done, Petra also found it hard to throw Božič to the dogs. She understood that he had shown himself as unfit to be a police officer, that his corruption had to have consequences, and yet writing it down seemed poor thanks for a man who had arguably saved her life. Even so, her strong sense of justice reminded her that both Rossi and Božič had made their choices, and now they had to live or die with the consequences. She refused to interrogate the other part of her brain which reminded her that Vuk had been correct, that without him Rossi probably would have seen very little punishment for her crimes. That way lay madness, shades of grey that Petra had no interest in becoming embroiled in. For today, she would echo Koren. There was only black and white, good and bad.

She felt Koren's eyes on her again, and looked up.

'Yes, cake-murderer?' She realised as it slipped out that her phrasing could be a little distasteful, but he didn't seem to mind.

'I have another question.'

Koren had spent most of the previous evening peppering her with questions, going so far as to drive her back to her guesthouse and insist on eating takeaway pizza in the closed restaurant so she could explain everything to him. She didn't begrudge him it, had actually found it very useful preparation for the report she'd started on as soon as he'd left. Despite the distress, pain and general tragedy of the days since she'd arrived in Koper, a sentimental part of her thought it was all worth it to see the look of tranquillity and contentment in Koren's eyes when he'd heard the full story, and declared that justice had indeed been done. It was funny, she thought, that he agreed with Vuk Jovanović on that score. She hadn't mentioned that to him.

'Go ahead.'

'Why do you think Rossi followed you into the house? Surely she knew the game was up when she saw your car outside. She could have run then, she'd already threatened Vuk and burned her bridges there. She could have at least given herself a head start.'

Petra had been mulling this over herself since her anger at Božič had subsided, as soon as she knew they were safe. 'I think that's exactly why she needed it, why she had to risk everything to get ahold of it. If she'd let it fall into police hands without a fight, then someone was coming for her, whether it was us or the Jovanovićes who got there first would be anyone's guess. If she had it, then she still had leverage over Vuk. That would protect her both from him, and us. He wasn't going to let her be arrested and tell us everything she knew, not when she had so much on him. And, if the police had caught her, it was something she could barter with. It was her insurance policy, after all. Her days were numbered if she abandoned it. Unfortunately, she underestimated how desperately Vuk would want it. She misjudged him.'

Koren nodded, spooning mousse into his mouth contemplatively. 'She misjudged you, too.'

Petra supposed that was true. Although it was true that Rossi had never overtly lied to her, she had been played for a fool. Had Rossi thought Petra would never actually shoot her, that she was too weak? Had she seen the Skoda outside and thought she was going to find Petra alone, ready to be outsmarted again, tricked by Rossi's superior intellect? Petra hated to admit it, but Vuk's words rang true. Rossi had overestimated her abilities, and had paid the price for it.

They lapsed back into silence, Koren flicking through the notes he'd given to Petra on her arrival in Koper. Marjan's haggard face gazed out at them from his mugshot, and Koren smiled as he flipped it over.

'He says thank you, by the way. For everything. He promised that he'll keep going to those appointments in Ljubljana, in his brother's honour. To try and shake the addiction. Irena Furlan won't be pursuing the vandalism charge, and since the house is half his and half hers, he doesn't have any charges to answer. He can really make a go of turning his life around.'

'Do you believe him?' Petra asked, eyebrows raised. She cut a neat sliver off her cake and popped it in her mouth, enjoying the burst of sour cherry from a thick layer of jelly running through the middle of layers of chocolate.

Koren shrugged. 'No, not really. But I believe he meant it at the time.'

Petra shook her head, taking another bite of cake.

'Similarly, Matteo called me earlier. Domenico Rossi has been demanding to see you since they brought him in last night. Apparently he's a menace in the cells, keeps spitting at people. Matteo told him you were too busy, but he thought you'd want to know.'

Petra grimaced, stabbing her small fork into the top layer of cake and leaving it standing there, held upright like a flag-pole. She had no desire whatsoever to speak to the potentially criminal husband of her murderous almost-friend, but had a horrible feeling that going to see him was the right thing to do. He was a widower, and she had been there to see his wife die. He deserved some closure, if that was what he wanted. 'I'll see.'

'There's no need to rush, it isn't like he's going anywhere. Even if he manages to get himself a deal, he'll be in the cells for a while yet.'

They both jumped in their seats when Petra's phone started ringing, not for the first time that day. She'd let her parents and *Svetnik* Golob know of her victory the night before, and had since had messages of congratulations from her brother, Mlakar and a few friends. The number flashing up on her screen, however, made her smile. Koren saw it too and hauled himself to his feet, trotting back over to the counter to get them both another pastry. Marija had insisted that everything and anything was on-the-house until the report was finished and Petra was free to get some well-deserved rest, apparently unconvinced that her mid-morning power nap would be enough to keep body and soul together. Koren appeared to be taking full advantage of his mother's generosity.

'*Svetnik* Horvat, thank you for getting back to me.'

She heard the superintendent at the other end of the phone clear his throat. '*Inšpektorica* Vidmar. I spoke with Eva Medved a moment ago, and she told me that I was to call you as soon as possible. I assume you have given my offer some thought?'

Late the night before, while they'd been sitting in uncomfortable metal seats outside the operating theatre with *Gospa* Božič waiting for word from the surgeon, Horvat had pulled her aside and offered her a temporary position in Koper. He had obviously assumed she would say no, and had appeared thrilled when she'd agreed to think about it, in light of the circumstances. While Lyon called her name, it was hard to ignore the pleading eyes of those she would have to leave behind on the coast. They were three inspectors down, reeling from revelations of murder and corruption. She could put Interpol on hold a while longer. After all, she'd applied there for a change of scenery, for excitement. She couldn't say that Koper hadn't given her that.

'Yes, and I have spoken with *Svetnik* Golob. He's in agreement. I'll stay.'

Horvat inhaled sharply, and she heard him start to clatter on his keyboard. Medved had added her to the station mailing list just this morning, after Petra had let slip to her and Koren that she intended to stay in Koper, and she had already received two all-station emails from the man. She suspected she was about to be the subject of the third.

'Excellent news. Wonderful. Thank you very much, *Inšpektorica*.'

Petra exchanged a few more pleasantries with him and then hung up, noticing as she did so that she'd missed a call from Doug York while she'd been speaking to Horvat. He'd immediately followed up with a text, in what she'd learned was his customary style, and she opened it as Koren bustled back over to the table and presented her with a perfectly golden *zavitek*.

> Just saw in the news that you caught the killer! Congratulations.
> Could I treat you to dinner one night this week? A token of
> my gratitude, for keeping the streets of Koper safe. Best, DY

She responded that she was free that evening and had a hankering for pizza and a glass of white wine, then immediately texted her mother to let her know. When she'd told her parents that she was staying on the coast, her mother had begun to fret that she would be lonely, that maybe she could persuade some of her friends to come down and visit. She got an immediate response asking for a photo of poor Doug, and locked her phone screen with a laugh. Doing one final check through her report, she spun the laptop around to face Koren.

'Ready to be the final set of eyes before I send this in?'

Koren choked on his coffee, taking a sip from his small glass of water while Petra watched in amusement.

'Final? That's a big responsibility, *Inšpektorica*.'

'I know,' she replied. She pulled her chair around so that they were sitting next to each other and cleared the frankly obscene number of pastries to the other side of the table. 'But I'll help you. We can go through it together, I'll show you what I do. Then, next time, you'll know what to do.'

Koren nodded at her slowly, placing his water back on the table and leaning forward, face inches from the laptop as a small smile formed on his face.

'Let's get started.'

# Acknowledgements

With thanks to the whole team at Constable, for taking a chance on this manuscript, and for putting so much work into getting this book onto the shelves. Thanks also to my agent, Kiran Kataria, for being so patient and thorough in leading me through this process.

I am eternally grateful for the encouragement and guidance of my wonderful parents, Janet and Ian. You are the best supporters, and most helpful proofreaders, that anyone could ask for.

Finally, thanks to my boyfriend and his family, for their kindness and willingness to share their country with me. I appreciate every second you have spent telling me about Slovenia, showing me around, and putting up with my appalling pronunciation. I hope I have done it justice.

# Author Note

The modern-day Republic of Slovenia (*Republika Slovenija*) has only existed since 1991, after they won their independence from the Socialist Federal Republic of Yugoslavia. Following the victory of the coalition party DEMOS in Slovenia's first democratic elections in April 1990, a referendum was held in December 1990 that saw 88% of the electorate vote in favour of Slovenian independence. Compared to some of the other Yugoslavian republics, Slovenia's separation from the federation was reasonably simple. The war of independence that broke out on 27th June 1991 following the formal declaration of independence two days earlier is now known as the Ten-Day War (*desetdnevna vojna*), finishing on 7th July 1991 with the Brioni Agreement, in which the Yugoslavian government agreed to both Slovenian and Croatian independence, although this had to be postponed for three months to allow more thorough negotiations. By the end of October 1991, all Yugoslavian military units had left Slovenia, the final few by sea from the port of Koper.

This book is set on the Slovenian coast, known as '*Obala*' in Slovene. Geographically and culturally, this area is part of Istria, the largest peninsula on the Adriatic, which is now divided between Italy, Slovenia and Croatia. The towns in this region were once part of the Republic of Venice, and so boast Venetian architecture. The most notable examples of this in Slovenia are Koper, Izola and Piran, whose buildings immediately mark them out as very different to the rest of the country. Many people in Istria, including the parts now in Slovenia and Croatia, speak Italian, and there is a significant Italian minority community on the Slovenian coast, as well as a significant Slovene minority community in the Friuli-Venezia Giulia region of Italy, on the border. The Slovene language is Slavic and is distinct from the languages of its neighbours. It also has a vast number of distinct dialects despite there only being just over two million speakers. Italian and Hungarian are also recognised as minority languages in south-western and north-eastern Slovenia, respectively. The majority religion in Slovenia is Catholicism, with over 70% of Slovenes identifying as Catholic.

Before Yugoslavia, Slovenia had a patchy and varied history, and was often geographically divided. After the dissolution of the Republic of Venice in 1797, coastal Slovenia became the property of the Austrian Empire, joining the majority of the rest of modern Slovenia, which was already under Habsburg rule. The First World War saw the twelve Battles of the Isonzo fought along the modern Slovene-Italian border, relics and structures from which can still be seen today if you walk along the mountain paths. During the Second World War, Slovenia was divided into three, with Nazi

Germany controlling the lion's share of the country, while Hungary annexed the north-eastern tip and Fascist Italy took control of the area along the border, including the coastal region. The Fascist regime undertook a wide-scale campaign of forced Italianisation, which saw thousands of Slovenes sent to concentration camps on the basis of their race alone. The establishment of Yugoslavia after the war saw Slovenia turned into one of the socialist republics under the federal leadership of Josip Broz Tito, and his name remains etched on mountains along the Italian border in white stone to this day.

Since 1991, Slovenia has thrived as an independent nation. It joined NATO in 1992, and the European Union in 2004, the first of the former Yugoslavian republics to do either. It is a popular holiday destination for hikers, with their highest mountain, Triglav, acting as their national symbol. The capital, Ljubljana, and the nearby picturesque Lake Bled, are also tourist hotspots, while the mountains in northern Slovenia offer multiple ski resorts. It is an amazing country to drive through, as the variety of influences and historical events are obvious in everything from the food to the architecture, making even a short journey interesting and varied. If you can visit, I thoroughly recommend it. With Slovenia's incredibly low crime rate, I can say with reasonable confidence that you won't be murdered.

# Pronunciation guide

## Slovene

Slovene has 25 letters. Compared to English, Slovene lacks the letters q, w, x and y, and instead has the letters č, š and ž. They also pronounce some mutually occurring letters differently. It is a phonetic language, and so very easy to read and spell once you are comfortable with the general pronunciation rules.

The letter 'c' is pronounced like 'ts' in English, as in the last syllable of 'cats'. The Slovene 'center' (centre), is pronounced TSEN-ter.

The letter 'j' is pronounced like 'y' in English, making the Slovene 'jogurt' and English 'yoghurt' sound the same.

The letter 'č' is pronounced like 'ch' in English, making the Slovene 'čips' and English 'chips' sound the same.

The letter 'š' is pronounced like 'sh' in English, making the Slovene 'šampon' and English 'shampoo' almost identical.

The letter 'ž' is pronounced like the 's' in the English word 'vision'. The Slovene 'živjo' (hi), is pronounced JIW-yoh.

Slovene also uses a rolled 'r', like in Spanish.

The most difficult part of Slovene for a native English speaker is the variety of vowel sounds. Slovene has eight fixed vowel sounds.

## Italian

Italian and Slovene sound very different, and are very easily distinguishable from one another, both when spoken and when written, although in the coastal region many Italian loan-words have crept into conversational Slovene. Like Slovene, Italian is phonetic. When these words are adopted, they are spelled phonetically in Slovene, creating 'čao' as opposed to *'ciao'*. There are a few main pronunciation rules to be aware of when reading this story.

The letter 'h' is crucial to Italian pronunciation. It changes the letter combinations 'ge', 'gi', 'ci' and 'ce') from a 'soft' sound, to a 'hard' sound. The best way to remember this is perhaps to think about 'spaghetti'. The 'h' after the 'g' makes it hard, 'spag-etti (without the H it would be 'spa-jetti'). An illustration of the opposite is 'gelato', a soft 'jeh', as it lacks an 'h'. This rule continues with other vowels following the 'g' or 'gh'. 'Gi', as in 'giallo' (yellow), is a 'j' sound, so –'jallo'. By contrast, 'ghi', as in 'ghianda' (acorn) is a hard 'gee' sound , 'gee-anda' (NOT 'jee-anda').

The impact of 'h' on the letter 'c' is harder for native English speakers, as it is counterintuitive – it is the exact opposite of English pronunciation. 'Ci', as in 'ciao' (hello) is a 'ch' sound, 'chow'. By contrast, 'chi', as in 'chiusa' (church), is a 'kee' sound, 'kee-usa'. The same is true of 'ce' and 'che'. 'Ce', as in 'cento' (hundred) is a 'ch' sound, 'chento'. 'Che', as in 'barche' (boat), is a 'kay' sound, 'bar-kay'. Thus the name 'Giulia' in the story is more or less pronounced the same as the English spelling 'Julia'; *spiaggia* (beach) is 'spee-AJ-ah', and '(la) Fenice' (the name of the famous opera house in Venice, which Giulia was meant to visit) is 'fen-EECH-ay'.

Two other smaller points are also worth mentioning. Firstly, the Italian 'z' sounds like the Slovene 'c', a 'ts' sound in English. This creates the Slovene loanword *pica* from the Italian *pizza*. This also raises the question of double letters in Italian. If you come across one, just make the sound longer.

## Character names

Petra – PAY-trrah

Aleš – Ahl-ESH

Ivan – EE-van

Marjan – MARR-yan

Giulia – JEW-liah

Eva – EH-vah

Franc – FRAN-ts

Jože – JO-zhay

Jakob – YA-kob

Božič –BO-zhich (a common Slovene surname, and also the word for Christmas)

Other names are said as in, or very similarly to, English.

## Place names

Ljubljana – loo-bee-AA-nah (for non-locals, locals say it 'loo-BLAH-nah')

Koper – KO-perr

Izola – EE-zolah

Portorož – porto-ROZH

Sečovlje – se-CHO-lee-eh

Strunjan – strun-JAN (for locals, people from Ljubljana say 'STRUN-jan')

Piran – pirr-AN

# Glossary (Slovenian)

*Burek* (BOO-rek) – Balkan street-food pastry with various fillings, cottage cheese being the most common in Slovenia.

*Cesta* (TSES-tah) – road

*Debel* (deh-BE-oh) – thick, large

*Dober dan* (DO-berr DAN) – good day, hello

*Dober tek* (DO-berr TECK) – bon appétit, enjoy your meal

*Grad* (grrad) – castle

*Girica* (GIR-its-ah) – small fish, deep-fried whole and served at fast food restaurants (pl. *girice*)

*Gospa* (gos-PAH) – Mrs, polite form of address for a woman

*Gospod* (gos-POD) – Mr, polite form of address for a man

*Gostilna* (gost-IL-nah) – inn, generally serving dishes traditional to the region

*Inšpektor/ica* (insh-PEK-tor/insh-PEK-tor-ITSAH) – inspector

*Jagoda* (YA-godah) – strawberry (pl. *jagode*)

*Jota* (YOH-tah) – bean and sauerkraut stew also featuring large chunks of meat

*Ljubica* (LYOO-bits-ah) – sweetheart (female), *ljubček* (LYUB-chek) (male)

*Malica* (MAHL-its-ah) – mid-morning snack common in Slovenia, similar to elevenses. Lunch is the most substantial meal of the day but is eaten in the mid-afternoon, necessitating an established snack break for a light meal.

*Malvazija* (mal-vaz-EE-ah) – popular white wine variety grown in coastal Slovenia

*Meduza* (med-OO-zah) – jellyfish (pl. *meduze*)

*Napolitanka* (napoli-TANK-ah) – Neapolitan wafer (pl. *Napolitanke*)

*Obala* (oh-BAH-lah) – coast, shore

*Olivno olje* (ol-EW-noh ohl-YEH) – olive oil

*Pelinkovec* (peh-LINK-ohvets) – Balkan answer to Jägermeister, bitter herbal liqueur

*Policist/ka* (polit-CYST, polit-CYST-kah) – police officer

*Potica* (pot-ITS-ah) – nut roll

*Prasica* (prahs-ITS-ah) – colloquially used as an insult or derogatory term, literally a pig

*Pršut* (prr-SHOOT) – cured meat very similar to prosciutto

*Rakija* (RAH-keeyah) – Balkan fruit-based spirit

*Rogljiček* (RROG-ljee-check) – croissant

*Rtič* (urruh-TICH) – cove, spit

*Slaščičarna* (slash-chich-ARN-ah) – patisserie

*Spaček* (sp-AH-chek) – Slovene nickname for a Citroën 2CV

*Špargelj* (shpar-GHEL) – asparagus (pl. šparglji)

*Svetnik* (sv-EHT-nick) – superintendent, strictly '*policijski svetnik*' or 'police superintendent'

Ten-Day War – also known as the Slovenian War of Independence, 27th June – 7th July 1991. Slovene victory led to their independence from Yugoslavia. In Slovene, it is known as *desetdnevna vojna* or *slovenska osamosvojitvena vojna*, literally 'Ten-Day War' and 'Slovenian War of Independence'.

*Trg* (trrg) – square

*Trst je naš* (Trrst ye nash) – Slovene for 'Trieste is ours', referring to the significant Slovenian minority living in the city and surrounding areas.

*Ulica* (OO-lits-ah) – street

*Vino* (VEE-noh) – wine

*Vstopite* (ooh-STOP-itay) – come in

*Zavitek* (zav-EE-tek) – strudel. In Slovenia, this largely comes in two varieties – *jabolčni zavitek*, or apple strudel, and *skutni zavitek*, which is filled with sweetened cottage cheese. Štrudelj, a Slovenisation of the original German, is also used.